EXPERIENCED

A *Beautiful* AMERICANS NOVEL

by the same author
Beautiful Americans
Wanderlust

EXPERIENCED

A *Beautiful* NOVEL
AMERICANS

by lucy silag

razOr
bill

AN IMPRINT OF PENGUIN GROUP (USA) Inc.

GIFT

To my dad

Experienced

RAZORBILL

Published by the Penguin Group
Penguin Young Readers Group
345 Hudson Street, New York, New York 10014, U.S.A.
Penguin Group (USA) Inc., 375 Hudson Street, New York, New York 10014, U.S.A.
Penguin Group (Canada), 90 Eglinton Avenue East, Suite 700, Toronto, Ontario, Canada M4P 2Y3 (a division of Pearson Penguin Canada Inc.)
Penguin Books Ltd, 80 Strand, London WC2R 0RL, England
Penguin Ireland, 25 St Stephen's Green, Dublin 2, Ireland (a division of Penguin Books Ltd)
Penguin Group (Australia), 250 Camberwell Road, Camberwell, Victoria 3124, Australia (a division of Pearson Australia Group Pty Ltd)
Penguin Books India Pvt Ltd, 11 Community Centre, Panchsheel Park, New Delhi – 110 017, India
Penguin Group (NZ), 67 Apollo Drive, Mairangi Bay, Auckland 1311, New Zealand (a division of Pearson New Zealand Ltd)
Penguin Books (South Africa) (Pty) Ltd, 24 Sturdee Avenue, Rosebank, Johannesburg 2196, South Africa

Penguin Books Ltd, Registered Offices: 80 Strand, London WC2R 0RL, England

10 9 8 7 6 5 4 3 2 1

Library of Congress Cataloging-in-Publication Data is available
ISBN: 9781595142931

Printed in the United States of America

JANUARY

1. PJ

Wish You Were Here

"*L*ook at this jacket! It's just like Catherine Deneuve's," my sister Annabel squeals from the corner of the thrift store she's just pulled me into.

I peer over a rack of vintage button-down shirts to see her twirling in front of an old cracked mirror, admiring her reflection. She's wearing a knee-length trench coat with a wide collar and big, flat brown buttons. It's less bohemian than the clothes Annabel usually wears, less feminine.

I shrug at the jacket, then turn around to see if anyone else has come into the shop since I last glanced at the door. "Cool. You almost ready? I think we should get back to the hostel." I'm thinking, in fact, that we never should have come into this store at all. If someone followed us, we'd never be able to escape!

"I'm going to get it. You should pick out something for yourself here, too, Penny Lane. Something," she sings out, "for our *new life*."

I wish Annabel would keep her voice down, even if the only other person in here is an elderly French lady wrapped up in a three-day-old newspaper.

"Go on, PJ, get something," Annabel urges me. "What about this?"

She holds up a gold strapless dress. It reminds me of something I wore once, just for a few strange, foreign minutes. My Parisian host mother, Mme Marquet, told me to try it on, but once she saw how well it fit me, she forced me to take it off.

"No, Annabel," I say, walking back to the front of the store. Outside the glass shop windows, a light snow dusts the tops of awnings and the roofs of cars parked on the narrow muddy street. Cherbourg. If this town isn't living up to Annabel's expectations, you'd never know it. She says it's just perfect. Perfect for our *new life*. To me, it looks as bland and unappealing as Rouen did, as everywhere does when compared with the beauty of Paris.

"We don't have the money for any new stuff, anyway. We spent so much of our savings on those backpacks, remember? Let's go," I say, marching back over to Annabel. She doesn't hear me. She hands precious euros to the older woman behind the desk, and then trails after me, delighted with her new coat.

★ ★ ★

Our "home" in Cherbourg is an old rain-soaked hostel not far from the harbor. The place is empty and unfortunately desolate in the off-season. We'd rather try to blend in with other people around us, but so far that amounts to only the girl who works behind the reception desk.

Annabel chose Cherbourg, not me.

* * *

As we dumped the backpacks near a bridge connecting L'Île Lacroix to the outer edges of the city of Rouen, Annabel looked shell-shocked.

"I can't take *anything* with me?"

"Nope." My voice was firm, calm. "Come on."

We hustled to the train station. I wanted to get out of town before those backpacks got found. Before anyone put up any fliers. Before anyone called the police.

"On the train, don't tell anyone *anything* about us. Just avoid questions," I said to Annabel as she scanned the train timetable, choosing the next place we would be calling home.

"The last time I told someone on a train something about my life, he ended up unconscious on the kitchen floor," I whispered, to make my point perfectly clear. Just saying those words gave me a chill. All I could think of was how Dennis's face changed as he registered what I'd done, just before he fell to the floor. His eyes went from menacing to afraid, and I realized then that he was younger than I thought. The hat pulled over his eyes concealed an innocent, youthful face. Just some young relative of the man who'd made my life in Paris impossible. M. Marquet.

Annabel rolled her eyes. "We'd better hope he was just unconscious," she said, meanly. "It's not like we stopped to make sure that guy was okay."

I didn't say anything. I felt itchy, desperate to get out of Rouen.

"Cherbourg," Annabel said finally. "There's a train in five minutes."

"Cherbourg?" I asked.

"Doesn't it sound romantic? Like that old movie? With the umbrellas?"

I didn't know what she was talking about. I didn't care. "Fine. How soon is the train?"

* ★ *

Cherbourg is a small city on the very tip of a peninsula that stretches away from France and deep into the sea toward English shores. The whole city is slick with water from the sea and from the canals and harbors carving into the old streets. Everything in Cherbourg is chilly and damp, from the clothes in the thrift store to the floorboards at the hostel where we've stowed ourselves for the past two days.

There are nicer rooms in the hostel, but we chose to stay in the basement women's dorm to save money. The cement floor is frigid beneath our feet, and sometimes when we wake up, we can see our breath in the air. There are twelve beds in here, but Annabel always sleeps with me in my narrow one. The hostel provided linens and pillows, but they won't turn on the heat for just the two of us. We have to use our coats for extra warmth.

I can't sleep tonight. Annabel's body is warm—too warm. She's making me hot and sticky under the sheets. She's too close; we're packed together too tightly. I try to scoot so there will be a few inches between our touching sides. The sinking mattress curves so much that I fall right back into her.

My plan only extended so far as to faking our own suicides. The note I scrawled out and tucked into the top pocket of the "PJ" backpack on the bridge in Rouen made it clear that I was through with this life, but it didn't explain why. I wrote the words carefully, wondering what my parents, in jail, would think if they were allowed to read it once it was found. Jay. I can't believe I've taken things so far. But I can't risk being found out. Not if I'm responsible for . . . The word *murder* clings to the back of my mind. I shiver.

Annabel rolls over, pulling my coat off of me. Its absence lets in a cold snap of air. I tug the coat back over me, biting my lip until the sting of the cold goes away. Annabel snores, catches her breath, and then shudders. She may be blithe during the day, but at night, she's in turmoil.

She's the only one I have left, and we *need* each other. I remind myself that *here*, wherever she is, is where I belong.

But Cherbourg isn't far enough away from Paris. We have to get somewhere the Marquets can never find us.

Wherever that is, I hope it is warmer there than it is here. Cherbourg in the winter must be the most frigid place in the world.

After having cold cereal and tea for breakfast, I walk with Annabel down to Cherbourg's massive harbor. I'm not eager to be in public, but I feel strangely very strongly compelled to go look at the channel today— enough so that I will risk going to a part of town where there would be no crowd to blend into if someone was following us. For some reason, today, I *have* to see the boats.

There's a big park before you reach the water's edge, with an enormous statue of Napoleon overlooking the ramparts he built hundreds of years ago. Beyond that, a big, empty skate park whistles in the bracing wind. We walk quietly, but Annabel is restless. Her new trench coat isn't very thick. She rubs each gloved hand over her shoulders and upper arms to try and keep warm.

"Pen, what are we doing down here?" Annabel whines when we reach the docks and the slips for thousands and thousands of boats. "It's freezing cold."

"I just wanted to look at the boats," I say, pulling her past a sign that marks the area ACCÈS INTERDIT. "Let's go check out that big cruise ship over there." Off in the distance, a giant ship hulks in the water. It almost looks fake—like a mirage. "Have you thought about what we're going to do next, Annabel? What we're going to do for money? How we're going to avoid the cops? The Marquets?"

"Who would think to look for us in Cherbourg? It's at the edge of nowhere," Annabel snorts, gesturing at the flat, vacant water of the channel beyond the harbor.

She's drowning in that coat. Annabel is almost bony now, without the soft lines that usually fill out her naturally thin frame. If I were looking for her now, I might not even recognize her, except for that dark hair, whipping around her face in the wind. That I'd recognize anywhere.

"We need to hide, Annabel. We need to *disappear*. Do you understand that? As long as we're in France, they could get to us." I'm gritting my teeth as I am saying it. "The Marquets."

"So, what? You want to stowaway on a cruise boat? Set sail for the South Seas?" Annabel asks me. I don't answer her. When she says it, it does sound ridiculous. But what then? Why doesn't Annabel ever worry about what will become of us?

We run into a dead end at the end of this side of the pier. To get to the cruise boats, you have to make a big U-turn around the canal, all the way back to the center of town. "Come on," I say. "Let's double back and check out the boats on that side."

"Why? What do you want with that cruise boat?"

Again, I don't answer her. "*Hermoso Atlántico Línea*," I read off the side of the boat as we get closer to it. The script flows along the white paint of the starboard side, big and red and jubilant despite the gray water the boat sits in. At the top of its mast are two enormous flags—one blue with gold stars for the European Union and the other blue and white striped with a gold sun in the middle. There must be a million windows on each side of the cruise boat. I've never seen a boat like this one before, except maybe in a magazine. It's big. Scary-looking. Tough. Impenetrable.

"We *could* just stowaway in that boat," I say to my sister. "Maybe it's not a bad idea. People falsify documents all the time. My friend Jay, for example, he's got relatives in the U.S. that got in using fake passports. It can't be that hard to do."

Annabel wrinkles her nose. "I don't like boats."

"As if your comfort is what matters at this point," I say. "Annabel, don't you see that we have to get out of here, out of France, away from where anyone can find us?"

Annabel takes my hand into hers. "We'll be okay, Penny Lane. Things will work out, you'll see." She smiles over at me, her eyes bright.

"How can you be so casual about this? This is serious, Annabel, and *you're* the one who got me into this mess," I say.

"I didn't make you knock that guy onto the ground," she says, lowering her voice and looking away. "That's the only really bad thing that's happened. And that wasn't my fault."

"Be quiet, Annabel," I whisper, tears threatening in the corners of my eyes. "Don't start."

Annabel turns away from me. "I'm going back to the hostel." I don't follow her for once. I stare at the Spanish words on the side of the cruise boat and think about the one person who still might be able to help me: Jay.

★ ★ ★

I go back to the hostel at sunset, my cheeks red and raw. I expect to find Annabel curled up and pouting on the bed in the girls' dorm, angry because I didn't follow her back to the hostel.

I hear Annabel before I see her, as soon as I pass the hostel reception desk.

She's singing, something she's well-known for doing, but I haven't heard her do it in a long time. "From the Ken-tucky coal mines . . ."

Her voice is as clear as a French church bell in a pious parish *à la campagne*.

But where did she get a guitar?

I bound up the stairs, my fists clenched. If she spent the rest of our money on a stupid secondhand guitar to get back at me when we could use that money to somehow buy our safety—

I throw the door to our dorm open. Before I can say anything, I see that it's not Annabel playing the guitar. Instead it is a woman, who is almost as old as my mom. The woman is big and soft, the guitar resting on her belly, and when it gets to the chorus, she and some of the other women sitting next to Annabel on the floor of our room chime in to harmonize with my sister. "Me and Bobby McGee . . ."

They notice me, smile, but don't stop singing till the song is finished. Then they all clap and rub Annabel encouragingly on the shoulders.

"Good job, honey! Your voice is as pretty as a bluebird's, ain't it, girls?" the guitar player praises her. "Is this your sister?" The women look up at me, still hovering in the doorway.

"It certainly is," Annabel answers, jumping up and giving me a hug. She keeps her arms around me as she presents me to the group. "This is my sister, uhhhhh . . ."

"Cathy," I finish. "I'm Cathy." Cathy was the name I used when I checked into the hostel.

"And *this*," Annabel goes on, "is the Goddess and Light Band, straight out of Austin, Texas. They're here in France, getting in touch with the spirit."

"The spirit?" I echo.

"That's right, miss," the guitar player says. "I'm Sunny and this here's my band—" Sunny points at each woman. There are five of them in all. Sunny tells me what instruments they play. The drummer, who looks old enough to be my grandma, wears a flowing tie-dyed dress with cowboy boots and long thermal underwear that poke out from under the skirt. She taps out a quick rhythm on a leather drum and nods at me. "We're doin' a little soul-searching over here on this side of the pond."

I smile weakly around at the group, and then curl up next to my sister on my bed. I fall asleep to the song "Blowin' in the Wind," Annabel and Sunny each taking a turn on the verses.

★ ★ ★

I wake up and all the lights are out in the dorm. The Goddess and Light Band has fallen asleep. The sound of their heavy breathing is comforting. "Having people in here makes it a lot warmer, huh?" Annabel says as she slips out of my bed and into her own for once. She looks at me for a long time, as if she is about to say something, but even she isn't sure what.

We both know this whole thing is a disaster.

"I want to go home," Annabel whispers in the dark.

"We can't," I say, hiccupping a sob.

"I do love you, Penny Lane," Annabel whispers. "I mean, Cathy."

"I know you do."

14

"I want to give up."

I sit straight up in bed, grabbing her hand into mine. "*Don't*, Annabel. Don't."

Annabel and I accept Sunny's offer of dinner with the band the next afternoon. There's a kitchen at the hostel, and Sunny tells us she's going to use it to cook us a big meal of fresh catch from the *poissonnerie*—we look too thin. Annabel is obviously charmed by the women and how easily they've accepted us, mothered us, even. I'm grateful for the free, filling food, but I'm distracted from the conversation as we eat gathered around a linoleum table in the hostel kitchen on the second floor. There was something in the way Annabel said that she wanted to give up last night that made me feel like I was in freefall. As if she were about to pull me off a bridge and into a cold, icy river.

I swallow a small bite of fish. The backs of my ears and my neck are chilly from fear. I put my fork down and force myself to smile at Annabel. She's gleefully tearing bread from a loaf and dipping it into the fishy olive oil pooled on her plate. She's making up for all those meals we've missed, but I'm not hungry at all.

I'm brewing a new plan, a risky one. We'll go to Paris, find Jay, and beg him to help us. It's not that I think Jay is in the business of making fake IDs. But of anyone I know, Jay understands the most about what it means to suffer, to chase freedom. He can help us. I know he can.

The reception girl walks into the kitchen and stands behind Annabel. "There's someone here to see you," she tells us in French. Annabel looks at me, waiting for a translation.

I gulp. "There's someone here?" My hands go numb in my lap.

"*Il attend dans la loge*," she says. We stare at her.

I take a deep breath and try to stand up from the table on buckling legs. "M. Marquet," I choke out. It's my first thought. My second is that maybe Jay found me, inexplicably, and he's here, and we can leave tonight for Central America.

"No, Penny, not him," Annabel says, and I almost can't figure out if she means Jay or M. Marquet, because her face appears so delighted that it's impossible to tell if she knows how terrible it would be if it was M. Marquet. She jumps up and pulls me down the stairs to the lobby, tripping with excitement. We come into the lobby in one mass of hair and long limbs and old wool sweaters tied around us against the everlasting cold of Cherbourg. We're falling over each other to see who it is, me because I just want my fate to be swift and direct, and Annabel because—

"Dave!" she shrieks.

I gasp, never having expected her to say that old familiar name again.

It *is* Dave. Dark-haired, slender, with rough skin and bitten-off fingernails. Dave, whose eyes and smile were the primary focus of all my romantic tweenage fantasies. He sits on the couch, wearing beat up paint-stained pants and a flannel shirt, right here in our little hostel in Cherbourg, as if we'd arranged to meet him here all along.

It's like a silent movie playing, the reels clacking around the projector. All this running. And now we're caught.

He smiles at us, as delighted as Annabel and not even slightly surprised to see me.

She jumps into his arms and snakes her long legs around his waist. They kiss for a full five minutes. I stand next to them, confused. And terrified. I have to look away.

Annabel and Dave claw and grasp at each other, unable to stop themselves from touching. Each of them traces each other's jaw line and collarbones with their fingertips, run their hands through the other's hair passionately.

"Dave!" I interrupt them, finally coming to. Forming my mouth into the sounds of the letters that make up his simple, casual name feels like wrapping my tongue around a knife. "*What* are you doing here? Who came with you?"

Dave tears his face from its connection to my sister's. He nods at me. "Hey, Penny Lane. *Great* to see you, too." Annabel hops off of him so he can hug me hello. "I came by myself. As soon as Annabel called."

I pat him awkwardly. Now that I am not thirteen, I don't actually see what Annabel sees—saw—in him. His smile *is* nice, and his eyes still sparkle with a private, personal joke, but his jagged teeth betray his backwoods Vermont roots. His beard makes him look aged and tired.

"I got my own room," Dave says to Annabel under his breath. "A single."

"Let's go," Annabel whoops. They dash back upstairs, past the second floor kitchen, and up one more flight to the single rooms. My mouth hangs open, but I'm too horrified to call after her. *But I had a plan*, I think. I was going to fix this. For good.

I search the face of the receptionist, wondering if she has any more surprise guests. "*She* called *him*?" I ask her, just because there is no one else there to explain to me what's going on. The girl stares at me, silently, then turns back to the television and turns up the volume.

★ ★ ★

I wake up to Annabel's lips on my cheek.

"Bye-bye, Cathy," she says softly, carefully trying not to wake up any of the Goddess and Light Band. "I'm going back to Vermont."

"Without me?" I sit straight up in bed. I can see Dave's shadow in the hostel hallway beyond the doorway, waiting for her. "What time is it? What's going on?"

Annabel looks at the old pocket watch she wears on a chain around her neck. One of the many things she took from the apartment in Rouen and managed to keep somewhere on her body. "It's almost six," she tells me. "Dave got us a flight that leaves from Paris at noon. We've got to go if we are going to make it."

"What about . . . the *cops*?" I mouth silently. "You can't go back."

"I've got to," my sister says. "Dave says I do. I can't let them just rot in jail, PJ! And Dave says he knows a lawyer who'll do a plea bargain for me."

"*Dave* says?" I pull Annabel down onto the bed so I can speak directly into her ear without him hearing. "What about me?" I ask. "*I* need you. What about Dennis Marquet? We just—we just left him there!"

Annabel clamps a cold hand over my mouth. "Shut up, PJ. No one knows about that—and no one has to if you're smart. Besides, that was *you* who left him there. Not *us*."

She looks behind her toward the door, and then over at Sunny, who's shifting in her bed. We've disturbed her. She's about to wake up.

Annabel, with her hand still tightly wrapped around my face so I won't make any noise, kisses the top of my head. "Gotta go, Pen," she says. "I mean, Cathy."

She runs out. I open my mouth, as if to scream for her to stop, but my throat is dry and the words do not come. It's as though this hostel basement is the bottom of an icy well, and Annabel is pulling the ladder up behind her as she climbs herself out to freedom. I clasp my hands together, feeling that same sensation of watching a silent movie, but this time with the scenes out of order. *How did I end up here?* I ask myself, wishing tears would come. How is it that she's the one who ran away, and I'm the one who's been banished from my own life? My real life, with its long walks, its hours spent painting, studying French, thinking about almost nothing at all besides light and color and how best to capture something beautiful on a canvas that I am working on. My real life, the one that included friends, and possible romance, and finally—*finally*—security after those horrible last few months I spent in Vermont last summer. In the dark, I hear Sunny sigh like a wise old woman. "Don't worry, kid," she says, her voice very much awake. "We all got secrets."

I don't say anything.

"The band here is headin' down toward Caen this morning. We's gonna write us some songs about my daddy, who got himself shot coming onto those D-day beaches. Freein' the Frogs from the Krauts.

"Traveling around, you sometimes give a young girl a ride, and she just gets up to her own thing. No one ever cares where she runs off to. No one says anything at all. What do you say? Want to come along?"

2. ALEX

Survival

I sit in the richly scented, steamy-windowed bakery in the square below the Cambronne métro stop on Monday morning, waiting for Zack. This is where we always meet to grab a quick café au lait before getting on the métro to go to the Lycée together.

I've pulled my hair back into a sleek, sober updo this morning. I smooth it under my hand idly and recall the absolutely horrid conversation I had with my mom over the weekend. I've been replaying it in my head, wondering at its wicked trajectory ever since it happened.

★ ★ ★

When I answered the phone, her voice was like honey, sweet and nourishing. I felt instantly calmer, my jaw unclenching and my body unwrenching itself between the brushed-cotton sheets I bought at Yves

Delorme when I first got to Paris.

"I spoke with Mme Cuchon," she told me. "Were you friends with that troubled girl? Are you okay? How are your other friends? Olivia? Zack? God, Alex, when Mme Cuchon called, I was terrified it was going to be about *you*. Isn't that what every mother would think, but about *you*, darling, it's usually true."

My mom went on. "My darling, darling Alex. I just got your heartbreaking voice mail. To think I hadn't heard from you since before Christmas! Of course, I assumed you were just being snotty . . . ."

Suddenly she unleashed a torrent of accusations, minor insults, slips into French, and of course, exultant affection—classic Caroline Ann Braun, my one and only mother. My body weakened with sadness, and relief.

She's here, I thought. *Well not here, not in Paris, like she was supposed to be, but here enough. She'll make everything better.*

I didn't cry, but there was a lump in my throat. "Mommy, it's all so *terrible*."

"It's a nightmare. Madame Cuchon called right after you did. Poor miserable woman."

"What did she tell you?"

"Everything she *didn't* say is right here on the *New York Times* Website—the front page! CNN, too. Everyone is talking about the American girls who committed suicide in the Seine. Though your school isn't quite ready to say that girl is dead . . . they still haven't found a body. Was she your friend, Alex? Are you just in agony, worrying about that beautiful girl? Penelope. Such a lovely name."

Through my latticed bedroom window I could see a few black crows making circles in the dismal afternoon sky. I flipped over onto my side and looked the other direction at my closet. It was overflowing with clothes, some dirty, some still tossed around from when I was trying to figure out what to pack for Montauban. Back when I thought it was going to be a fun adventure. "It's all so weird," I said. "Her story is in the *Times*?" The little secret mission my friends and I were on ended up being just one farcical chapter in a sad, terrible mystery story.

"Oh, my darling," my mom said, her voice buttery, "the whole thing is beastly. Did you love her very much?"

Did I *love* PJ?

I didn't know how to answer. All I knew was that she's dead and I wished with all my might that she wasn't. The truth about how I *feel* about PJ is a little more nebulous than I want to say aloud. I swirl another sugar cube into my coffee, Zack still not here yet, thinking about how I would ever define my feelings for PJ.

I thought I could save PJ. I thought she was just pulling a prank like spoiled girls in New York do all the time. They disappear, everyone misses them, amd then they come back to school with a new haircut, a better handbag, or some other improvement that made them feel better about life. I've seen it before, so I convinced all my friends that I could and would find her, even though I had no idea where she was. I never took her disappearance seriously, not even for a minute. And when we eventually gave up the song and dance of being on her trail, of being this close to bringing her back to Paris, I found out she's *dead*.

Sadness doesn't really cover it. In a lot of ways, it's a dreadful failure as well. If I had succeeded at finding PJ, everyone would be happy right now. Because I failed, not only am *I* miserable, but so is everyone I go to school with. And if we had found her before she got to that bridge in Rouen ... "Everything is so messed up right now," I sighed on the phone to my mom.

She cleared her throat. "I'm horrified—really devastated, darling—about your friend, but I have many other items to discuss with you. Shall I begin?"

I closed my eyes to the mess of my room, the shadowy mass of blanket and pillows I am buried under.

I knew my mom would want to discuss the letter the Lycée had sent to me about my grades last semester, and I was not quite ready to move on. I wanted my mom to ask me to tell her more about what happened over break. She didn't know that I went to my dad's pied-à-terre in the Pyrenees. She didn't know that I saw him in Cannes, at the hotel she used to stay in with him. She didn't know that when he saw me, he turned his back on me and tried to buy me off ... again.

"Go ahead," I sighed.

"Mme Cuchon is very reluctant to send you home, shockingly." My mom laughed. "You got the worst grade on the final comp. Did you know that?"

"No!" I gasped. I didn't believe that for a minute. I've been speaking French since I was a baby! There's no way I did the worst on the cumulative test. There is just no *way*.

"*Yes*, Alex. Mme Cuchon told me this, and very bluntly, I might add. And it's a very special situation, one from which you could really *learn* something in the long run. The entire faculty at the Lycée has been really shaken up by the—*events* surrounding your friend's passing. And frankly, if their program becomes known for being so rigid and strict, the media will make the claim the girl cracked under pressure. That's my personal opinion, anyway."

"No," I said. "PJ was really good at school. That's not what happened—"

"It doesn't matter, darling. Just use Mme Cuchon's leniency to stay in the program. We've struck a deal. You will return to the Lycée on academic probation. As long as you agree to take on extra assignments, you can stay. She doesn't want to lose another one."

"Really? I don't have to come home?"

"No, Alex, you don't have to come home," my mom echoed. She didn't sound too disappointed, I noticed. "However, there will be some *stipulations* on my part." Now I started to get nervous.

"Remember Mme Sanxay?"

I pretended not to recall who she was talking about. "Who?"

"Don't be ridiculous, Alex," my mom said. "You owe Mme Sanxay over a *thousand* euros. Alex, my daughter, this is just beneath you. Stealing? Leaving town with no explanation? What's gotten into you? Imagine how terrifying that it is for a mother."

"I can explain," I said.

"Oh, I'm sure you can." My mom laughed. "Go right ahead. I'm in the mood to be entertained."

As I realized that I didn't have anything to tell my mom that was at all respectable, I stopped being nervous and became truly terrified.

I was stuck. She would get only *more* mad if I tried to explain that I spent the money on a luxurious hotel room so I could do it (or, at least, try to) with a guy who wasn't even my boyfriend. I wished I had a better excuse!

And with a glob of guilt blocking my throat, I couldn't bring myself to tell her why I hadn't returned her phone calls. I just didn't want to. Again, I thought of PJ. PJ has a mom on some horrible ranch or in a forest or something in Vermont. That woman will never hear from her beautiful, bizarre daughter again. I sniffled, ashamed.

"I didn't think so. You'll go to Mme Sanxay's apartment tomorrow afternoon directly after school. You'll pay her back what you owe, and then you'll keep working for her so that you can pay me back, too."

I gasped. "No!" That was when I started to feel the world shaking beneath my feet. It sounds dramatic, but I could tell my whole life—the very fabric of my existence, I mean—was about to change.

"*Yes*. I haven't forgotten your shopping escapades this fall. Likely, the salesgirls living off your commissions still very fondly remember you, too."

"How long is this going to take?" I asked, pulling the comforter over my head. I wished I had stayed asleep and hadn't heard Marîthe calling my name. I wished I'd stayed in Cannes.

"The entire semester, darling," she told me. I could tell she was getting bored with the conversation, and her eyes were likely drifting back toward her computer screen, to the e-mails waiting in her inbox. I sucked my breath in and took a plunge.

"What if I say no?" I was gambling, snapping at my mom, but I was *certain* I couldn't do this. It was too much.

"*No*? What do you mean, no?"

"Seriously," I tried to protest one last desperate time. "There are *three* of those kids. Three! And the Sanxays live in a horrible apartment! It might be in the Sixth but you *so* can't tell once you are inside of it!"

"Alex, it's this, or you come home," my mom snapped back to attention, pissed. "You'll be right back at Brooklyn Prep, your little Thakoon tail between your legs. Is that what you want? If so, I can cancel the whole semester right now. I can put you on an evening flight back to New York. You can be right back at your old school first thing tomorrow morning."

I imagined myself at Brooklyn Prep, back in my old French class. Jeremy is a senior, but he'd be there, along with everyone else that I'd bragged to about how great things in Paris were going to be.

"There's *no* other way?" I thought wildly, scrambling for alternatives. "You really can't make this work?"

"No, Alex! Don't you see? You've got one last chance—one. Some people should be so lucky as you. You've completely ruined other people's trust in you. Especially mine." She sighed deeply. "It's not that I can't bail you out this time, it's that I *won't*."

I could imagine Zack in the back of my mind, nodding in silent agreement, looking around at the mess I've made of my room, the mess I've made of my life. I swallowed a wail of despair.

My mom started to say something but stopped. "I've got to go." She clicked off.

★ ★ ★

Over the din of the cappuccino maker it suddenly occurs to me that Zack still hasn't shown up. This is the first time he's ever missed this daily coffee date. I realize, unhappily, as I look around at the people bustling in and out with their hot drinks: He'll never forgive me for what happened over winter break.

He's not alone. I doubt anyone will be very happy to see me this morning. I didn't bring PJ back, and I didn't go for help. I am a dreadful failure indeed, and as of today, everyone knows it.

The e-mail Mme Cuchon sent out to all the students and parents said the authorities had found two backpacks, one of which they identified as belonging to Penelope Jane Fletcher, and they assumed the other belonged to her sister Annabel, since the suicide note was signed by both of them. PJ's passport with her Programme Americain student visa taped inside it was in the backpack. I'd convinced my friends to look for PJ in the south of France, but those backpacks were almost as far north as you can get without ending up in Belgium.

That backpack of hers was one of the first things I noticed when I met PJ. It was so big, green, and old and *ugly*. I would have died if that were all the luggage I'd taken for a year in France. But that day at JFK airport in New York, PJ didn't seem to be worried about luggage. She only seemed worried about making it to France. And when PJ put the green backpack on her shoulders, she was so beautiful that you didn't even notice it.

Why would she be in such a rush to get to Paris if she was so sad that she just ended up killing herself? I muse, deciding to grab us some to-go coffees and bring them to Zack at the Cambronne métro stop, just in case.

I sip a thick café crème, watching the commuters rush toward their trains, letting the hot milk burn my tongue. I brought Zack the same thing, cupped in the mitten on my other hand. It will make him more receptive to making up, I'm hoping, if he's adequately caffeinated.

Finally, after Zack's coffee has gone cold, after I drink it just so it wouldn't go to waste, after I watch a morning parade of Parisian commuters rush up to the train platform past me for twenty minutes, I admit to myself that I really need to get on the train if I am going to get to school on time.

Normally, being late doesn't bother me, but today has a funereal feeling about it. It's so overcast that the sky is charcoal gray, and the snow has melted and refrozen along the nasty, dirty streets curving around the Place Cambronne. Even the guys at the fruit market where I buy my morning banana had looked frigid and weary today. And in my black high-waisted skirt and tucked-in, loose gray top, I feel like I'm about to watch someone be buried. There's something about such a morose day that makes it feel wildly inappropriate to be late.

I chuck the empty plastic coffee cup and dash up the escalator to the approaching train, just sliding into the station.

When we pull into the next stop, I swear we pass Zack, waiting on the end of the platform. Did he walk all the way over here, several blocks out of his way, to catch the train one stop after I did? Did he do that just to avoid bumping into me on the platform?

I search for Zack in the crowd again when I switch trains at Charles de Gaulle-Étoile, and then again when I get off the métro at Ternes. I don't see him again. Maybe it wasn't him after all. It wouldn't be like him to go to school so late—then again, it wasn't like him to take our rental car all the way from Cannes to Paris in the middle of the night, either, and he seemed to be able to pull that one off.

As I get closer to the Lycée, I see a few video cameras and flashbulbs on tripods set up on the steps of the school. Reporters buzz around the entrance, harassing students into making statements on camera as they try to duck into the building. As I always do when a camera is pointed at me, I smooth my hair and stand up straighter, just in case I end up in a background shot. But even I know better than to talk to these ambulance-chasing reporters. How totally *tacky*.

A young woman in a cheap blue suit jumps in front of me, asking questions in rapid French. "Penelope Jane Fletcher . . . Penelope Jane

Fletcher . . ." is all that I can understand.

"*Laissez-moi tranquille!*" I say, trying to sound biting and in control, but the sudden appearance of the woman, her microphone, and all those questions I can't understand sets my heart racing. I pull the door out, not caring that I knock into the woman's camera guy. "Get out of the way!" I snap in English. "I have to go to school!"

I see that the funereal vibe is affecting our entire program as soon as I walk into the classroom. Everyone is wearing dark colors and a very sober, washed-out expression. I go to Jay first, wrapping him up in a long hug. I'm still mortified at what he must think of me now, but his heartache is so evident I can't not at least try to be a tiny comfort to him.

"Jay," I say, wiping at the muddy black corners of my eyes as I pull away from him. Normally a guy of considerable bulk, Jay looks smaller now. His face looks drawn, too, under the fuzz of his unkempt facial hair. "Oh, Jay."

"It's not like she was my girlfriend," he mutters, and I remember what it felt like to fall asleep on his chest. Safe and happy in a hurricane of confusion.

Jay shrugs and sits down at an empty desk, staring at the wood, etched with carvings made by bored students with the tips of their pens over the course of many years. I look down at it, too, and wonder if I should try to say something else.

I'm sorry I couldn't find her, I almost cry out. *I'm sorry I'm such a failure.*

I soothe myself with the fact that at least Jay is here at school. At least, the money my dad gave me went to some good purpose: paying for Jay's tuition since he spent his scholarship money on the search for PJ.

Zack walks into the classroom, registers me standing next to Jay's desk, makes a face, and grabs a seat next to Olivia. Olivia, dressed in dwarfing black warm-ups, looks at me with anguish, not sure if she should call me over or let Zack stake his claim on that side of the classroom. Her openly pitying look is almost as unbearable as the way Zack so pointedly ignores me. I want to go over and demand from Zack why he wasn't at the coffee shop this morning, or at the métro. But I don't.

"It's okay," I mouth and sit with Mary and Sara-Louise instead. They are tan from going on vacation over Christmas break to the Caribbean or Mexico; I can't remember which. Sara-Louise also cut her curly hair so that it falls in sophisticated layers rather than the childlike bob she had before. I open my mouth to tell her how cute it looks.

"Alex, is it true?" Sara-Louise blurts before I say anything. "Did you guys really know she was missing since Christmas and not tell *anyone*? That's what everyone is saying, but I couldn't believe you'd *do* that. . . ."

"Sara-Louise!" Mary cuts in. "It's not Alex's fault PJ killed herself." Mary looks over at me, her eyes searching my face for reassurance. "You guys tried to help her, right? We heard she reached out to you, asked you for help, and you couldn't tell anyone. . . ."

"You should have told someone, anyway," Sara-Louise says. "You should have called Mme Cuchon. What's wrong with you, Alex?"

I take two long breaths and try to answer her. It comes out like pitiful excuses. "She never *asked* for our help. She just wanted to say good-bye, and we thought we could find her and help her work things out."

Mary nods and rubs my arm but doesn't look at all convinced. "It's okay, Alex," she says. "We know you had good intentions." I look over at Olivia and Zack, wishing they could help me defend what happened.

Good intentions?

We didn't *do* anything!

But maybe that's what we did wrong.

Mme Cuchon sweeps into the classroom then, her face tight. Her red hair seems less bright than usual, her clothes much more subdued. Following her are all of the Programme Americain teachers, including her right-hand woman, Mlle Vailland.

Mlle Vailland has a voice that will make your hair fall out—she is *that* annoying. The boys like her because of her hot body and pretty, youthful face. Today, you can tell she's been crying. She won't even say anything to anyone.

"*Bonjour, tout le monde,*" Mme Cuchon greets us. "As you know, there has been a terrible tragedy. As I outlined in the e-mail I sent out to you, it appears that Penelope Fletcher has been in accident of some sort. The French police department, as well as the international agencies working on her case, believe that she has attempted to commit suicide. Several news services are reporting the story." Mme Cuchon gestures at Mlle Vailland, who has a stack of newspapers in her arms. "We encourage you to read the stories, as we know you will want to know what happened, and we think, of course, that you have a right and a need for this information."

Sitting in one of the desks in the front row, Mlle Vailland hands Jay a paper, but he refuses it. He won't even look at it. Mary grabs it from him and spreads it over her desk.

La une, the front page, is covered by a long story tracing the same details we all know, Mme Cuchon is saying, as other students open different newspapers, including the *International Herald Tribune* in English. Not all the stories are as big as the one in *Aujourd'hui en France*, the one on Mary's desk, but it seems as if all the major outlets have taken an interest in what happened to PJ in Rouen.

Above the article is a photo of a bridge in Rouen, roped off with CAUTION tape. There's nothing bloody or gory about the pictures—again, the bodies still haven't been found—but those two backpacks at the scene of *l'incident* look as morbid as a chalk outline on pavement. My stomach cramps just looking at them.

"No one—I repeat, no one—has found any *real* evidence about what took place," says Mme Cuchon. "There was a suicide note, but there is a real possibility that the suicide attempt was unsuccessful." I hear hope in her voice. She really doesn't want to believe one of her students would be so unhappy in Paris. "We just won't know until the investigation finds more concrete answers."

Aujourd'hui en France is one of those papers printed on smaller paper, so that we can read without having to unfold it, kind of like the *New York Post*, a paper my mom reads every day but would never admit. Like the *Post*, it also prints the front page in color. The backpacks on the bridge stick out, bright blue and red on the snowy bridge. They look new. In fact, they look *brand* new.

That's not PJ's backpack, I realize, looking at the photo. The thought sends a razor-sharp cold spell down my back. Her backpack is green. And it is about a hundred years old. I'll never forget that thing. It was an *antique*.

"Steel yourselves for the worst, *tout le monde*," Mme Cuchon says. "But pray for the best. We at the Lycée have contacted Penelope's family at home," Mme Cuchon's eyes drift toward the other teachers, "and we've also spoken with her host family, the Marquets. As you may know, Monsieur Marquet is a political official in the Dordogne region south of Paris, and so the media is even more interested in the story than they would perhaps otherwise be. For that reason, the Marquets are conducting their investigations about PJ from their home there rather than in Paris, for privacy's sake. I know both of PJ's families appreciate your condolences, but let's all agree not to bother them at this very sensitive time."

Olivia's eyes widen, her head and neck very still.

"We are all just waiting for more news. Until then, I'm afraid we will have to continue with our program as usual. Please do not talk to the press about this. Send any inquiries you may have to the staff here. We don't want to react publicly until we have some answers from the authorities. I don't want to give you—" Mme Cuchon's voice breaks. "False hope. But this case is still not closed for the police. And it is not closed for the Lycée, either. *Comprenez-vous?*

★ ★ ★

"Alex!" Mme Sanxay greets me after buzzing me up to her fourth-floor walkup apartment on the rue de Fleurus. She answers the door already wearing her wool coat and a matching black cloche. She has what my mom would call a Gallic nose, prominent but handsome, and expensively cut but unkempt dark hair. Same as the last time I was here, she seems as if she's just barely holding it together. "You're late! Your mother told me you'd be here at two thirty. *Il est trois heures maintenant.*"

"*Desolée,*" I mumble. "It was a nightmare trying to leave school. The reporters . . ." I shake my head. I can't stop wondering if Sara-Louise is right to be angry with us. Is that what the reporters want to know, too? How could you not help a friend in need? How could you think you could handle it yourself?

"Ah, the girl who is missing," Mme Sanxay says, taking my coat from me and hanging it on a rack with several smaller ones. "Who killed herself.

Was she getting a divorce, too?"

I twitch and do a double take. Mme Sanxay leads me in, oblivious to the inappropriateness of this joke. "Divorce is hell," she says. "Your mother had a bad one, *n'est-ce pas*? So you know how it is. Try to help my children through it. I'm afraid there's just so much I can't give them—emotionally—right now. I have to take care of myself. That's why I'm desperate for your help, even though I don't have the best impression of your work ethic so far. Simply put: I need you, Alex. I've got to give myself some, as you Americans call it, me time."

Bounding up the stairs as I follow Mme Sanxay into the foyer are two children, a girl and a boy, wearing tailored school uniforms. They are shrieking incomprehensibly until they see me, a stranger in their apartment, and stop short.

They stare at me, their eyes bugging out like cartoons.

I wish they *were* cartoons! Drawn in pencil and erased from existence when it pleases you to do so.

"Ah, Alex, *c'est mon fils* Albert, *et ma fille* Emeline. *Mes poupées, dites bonjour à votre au pair,* Alex."

Slow down, I want to tell her. I understand she is introducing me to them. But not their names or anything else she said.

"I have to run, *mes petits*," Mme Sanxay clucks at the kids, then smoothes her hair in front of the mirror. "Charles is in his crib, napping. Be quiet so he'll sleep for you, okay?" With that, she softly closes the door behind her, leaving me with the two children, each staring at me in wonder.

"*Où va Maman?*" the boy asks me.

"Away." I motion with my hand to the outdoors. "Away. Little while." I assume he does not speak English so I make it as easy as possible.

But he still doesn't understand me. Nor does his sister. They both stare at me with big brown eyes quickly filling with tears. I watch as the little girl opens her mouth very slowly, getting as wide as possible before she lets out what I know will be a very loud, very penetrating scream.

"No!" I try to stop her, but it is too late. It only takes one or two seconds of the high decibel screech to set her older brother off and then, from the nursery, the baby as well.

At least, I can remember that one's name.

"Charles!" I call as I dash into the darkened room with the crib in it. "Shhhhh!"

I lean over the side of the little white crib and look down at a wriggling mass of anger with its face all screwed up like it's releasing all the disappointments of the world. *I'm like that when someone wakes me up from a nap, too,* I think.

He just needs to know that it is totally okay for him to go back to sleep.

I reach down and pat his little belly. "Good boy," I encourage him. "Just go back to sleep. No need to wake up now."

He doesn't listen to me. Charles keeps screaming, and, horrifyingly, the others are still doing the same in the front hallway, as if their mother were never coming back.

Don't think like that, I shudder. *She* has *to come back.*

I snatch my hand back from Charles's tummy, wondering if that is the wrong thing to do to a baby.

Babies are very sensitive. I've read about this in magazine articles about celebrity moms. Maybe you aren't supposed to touch them until they get older? They might think you are trying to hurt them.

Someone once told me babies get aggressive because they are intimidated by you and how much bigger you are than them. You have to get down on their level, and *then* talk to them so that they won't feel attacked.

I squat down on the stained carpet, careful not to let my knees make contact with what looks like baby poo residue, and let out a sunny laugh that I hope sounds relaxed and calm. I don't look directly into the baby's eyes through the slats of the crib.

"It's okay, Charles, don't cry. Good boy!" I keep my voice very cheerful and nonthreatening. "Come on, baby, you can do it. Stop crying. Okay?"

Then I remember that whoever told me this piece of advice was actually talking about aggressive *dogs*, not babies.

I stand back up.

What am I going to *do*? Isn't this how soldiers torture POWs? They play recordings of screaming babies until the criminals surrender and tell them where they hid the bombs?

I surrender! Just please, please, please stop crying!

The little boy comes into the room, having stopped his own baying for a few minutes, though you'd never be able to tell because his baby brother screams like a champ. Apparently, this child is so surprised at my ineffectiveness with his little brother that he's been shocked silent.

The boy, who is still wearing his coat, motions for me to push down one of the sides of the crib. He's strong enough to pick up the baby. He takes Charles over to a rocker in the corner of the room and leans the little body against his right shoulder.

The little girl, also distracted from her crying by curiosity, comes in and tries to take my hand, but hers is filthy with some gooey substance so I won't let her.

Seeing how his brother has Charles all taken care of, I decide I should just watch all of them and make sure none of them does anything weird. I pull out a small child's chair from a tea party set in the corner and squat down on it. The little girl folds herself up on the floor next to me and lays her head in my lap.

I stay perfectly still for what feels like an *eon*, just perched like a frozen statue on that undersized play chair, until at last I hear Mme Sanxay's keys in the front door and let out my breath in one long moan of relief.

All three kids have fallen asleep. Without waking the little girl, I wipe the tears of fear and loathing from my face and carefully pry her cheek from my jeans.

I gather my bag and coat and barely say good-bye to Mme Sanxay, who looks considerably more refreshed after spending the afternoon by herself, having that "me" time.

I walk from the Sixth all the way down to Cambronne. When I pass Le Bon Marché on my way, its spring scarves fluttering in the windows and a thick breeze of perfume following customers out the door and down the street, I gag, remembering how it was in stores like this one that I screwed up my life in this royal, nonsensical way. Le Bon Marché, once such a haven of good taste and lovely fabrics, seems perfectly evil to me in light of my new after-school job. The memory of this afternoon is one I won't soon forget.

When those kids were screaming, all at once like that, all I wanted to do was scream with them. All I wanted was someone to comfort *me*.

3. OLIVIA

Not for Children

"*Bonjour, ma petite Olivia,*" Mme Rouille calls to me gaily from the kitchen as I enter with her miniature poodles on leashes. Somehow walking those dogs is more exhausting than a dance rehearsal.

The apartment smells nauseatingly of mint. "Would you like to join me for a cup of tea?" she says as I enter the room.

"No," I say, unleashing the poodles. They run straight to their real mother and nuzzle her shoes. "I can't. I'm already running late." I go into my room to change out of the sweats I was wearing to walk the dogs. Wrenching my armoire doors open violently, I consider briefly what to wear, and then decide it's just not worth it to care.

It's just *so* draining right now, trying to look pretty, trying to look excited about the day. All I want is to feel warm. Why do Parisians keep their buildings so frigid? Why are the people themselves so insufferably cold?

I think of one in particular and wonder how my whole life has become this one person, this one comfort. Thomas.

It was never like this with Vince.

I decide to stay in my old sweats. I pull on a parka that I found stuffed in the closet and leave the apartment without calling good-bye to Mme Rouille.

It's weird how people have such different reactions to tragedy. Some of the girls at school are weepy all the time, sniffling and excusing themselves from class. A lot of the boys, like Zack, are simply taciturn. Alex has become timid, not plopping down wherever she wants to sit, but carefully choosing a place where she will attract the least attention. Mme Cuchon is a chatterbox, though that's nothing new. But she's taken to coming into our classes unannounced to give us pep talks and remind us not to talk to the press camped outside the Lycée.

And me? I don't find myself overcome with tears. I hate myself, but since PJ was proclaimed as good as dead, I've been in a terrible mood, like an old witch in a cave. I'm not sad; I'm annoyed. When pushed, I don't cry, I scream. A very peculiar reaction.

I must be numb, I tell myself. The tears will come eventually. I wish they would. My whole body feels like a dam, holding back a wild river of emotion. But for some reason, I can't let it go yet. I guess I'm afraid of what will happen if I do.

I realize during a very boring math lesson with M. Paton later in the morning that I've called Thomas precisely *six* times since the news broke about PJ. I can remember where I was, what I was doing, each time that I called him. I know it has been six times because every time I call and leave a message on his voice mail, I add up how many times I've called and decide I won't call again until he calls me. He's probably just busy with classes. At least, that's what I tell myself.

It feels like a game. Thomas, of all people, wouldn't be one I'd expect games from. Thomas, the guy I lost my virginity to, the guy who drove me to Cannes on the back of a Vespa. The guy who wrote my name in chalk, followed by those sweet words, "*Je t'aime,*" for all the world, or at least all of Montmartre, to see.

My next classes are even more painful to get through. While Mlle Vailland tries to draw out a very detailed map of the 1848 Paris Commune on the chalkboard during history class, I finally break down. Texting isn't the same as leaving a voice mail, right?

I sneak out my new cell phone and text Thomas.

WANT ME 2 COME OVER 2NITE? I MISS U.

I really, *really* miss him. Ever since I woke up this morning, I've been trying to lift myself out of the dark thoughts that have crowded around me since I found out about PJ.

I watch the clock above Mlle Vailland's head for a full ten minutes, but the screen on my phone stays blank. That's not like Thomas at all. His head might always be in the clouds, but his hand is always firmly gripped around his cell phone.

The lunch bell rings, and Mlle Vailland waves us out, still working on her map. "We'll go into greater detail tomorrow," she calls to us in that sticky sweet accent of hers. I stuff my notebook into my backpack and make a beeline for Zack.

If Thomas isn't around to give this day some levity, maybe a good heart-to-heart with Zack will do the trick.

"Zack?" I reach forward as we're filing out the door and pat Zack's shoulder. As he turns around, he sees me and smiles. It turns into a scowl when he looks beyond me and sees Alex. I hadn't noticed her. She fixes us both with a big, studied grin. Zack rolls his eyes at her and turns back around, heading out to the lobby.

"Hey, Alex," I say. "I didn't see you there. Want to go grab some lunch? I don't feel like going home today."

"Ach, I wish I could, but I have to study," she says. There's a wrinkle of worry I've never seen before in her beautiful brow. "But there's some stuff I really want to talk to you about before I head up to the library. Do you have a minute?"

"Alex, you're being very formal! Of course, I have a minute. What's up?" I point and flex my toes nervously inside my shoes.

Alex shifts her eyes toward the staircase leading up toward the Lycée's library. "Not here. Will you come upstairs with me? There's just some things going on with my mom, and I've been thinking about this PJ thing. . . ."

My phone beeps, and I dig furiously around in my pockets to find it again. I'm so glad that Thomas finally got back to me that I don't answer Alex.

"Hey, you know what?" she says as I mess with my phone, trying to read the text. "It can wait till we both have time. I've got to go run through a bunch of flash cards, anyway. I'll see you later."

C'EST IMPOSSIBLE, the text reads. *JE DOIS ÉTUDIER. EXAM DEMAIN.*

My heart drops. Since when does studying come before me? Doesn't he know I need him right now?

"Wait, Alex," I say, tearing my eyes off the screen. But Alex isn't standing there anymore, and I feel wicked for the millionth time since this morning.

Like Alex, I should be studying. I should go up to the library, apologize for being such a bad listener, hear her out, and spend the rest of lunch period kicking this semester off to a good academic start if nothing else. I don't feel like it, though; I turn the opposite direction and go out the big front doors of the Lycée. I don't want to listen to Alex's problems, and I feel so mean thinking that. But today I just can't do it.

I hate that I feel like Thomas is the only one I want to be with right now; not only that, but, the only person who might make me feel better. I thought Paris was supposed to be making me *more* self-reliant, not less.

On the front steps, I decide to call André, my dance partner from the Underground Ballet Theatre, a Paris dance collective I joined in December. For some reason, it seems like a great idea to see what he might be doing for lunch, even though I've never once asked him to do something before. He's the only person besides Thomas and his Sorbonne crew that I know outside of the Lycée.

"Olivia, love, I'd be *honored* to take you to lunch!" he shrieks when I ask him very tentatively if he'd possibly have time to maybe have lunch today, like right now.

"No, I can pay for myself—" I say.

"Now, don't be dense," André interrupts. "You'd be proving all those rumors about Californians right. Now come down to the Square du Temple at this *instant,* and we'll have some jerk chicken and beans and rice! I can think of nothing I'd rather do than hang out with you, *ma belle!*"

Extraordinarily relieved, I run to the métro.

André swoops down and kisses me on the cheek when he sees me walking up the steps from the Temple métro station. I feel flooded with warmth and relief. André has deep brown skin, stretched smoothly over his gorgeous cheekbones and long neck; his elongated limbs seem to float out from his tightly compacted, muscular torso like wings. He purrs a little, then laughs, full and loud. At street level, the rue Bretagne is thick with a lunchtime crowd. André slips me under his arm and navigates me through all the people.

"Great to see you," I greet him as we hurry along. "Where are we eating?"

"You'll love it, I promise," André says. "It's not the best Caribbean food in Paris, but the ambiance is tops. I love eating outside—even in winter. This place has been in Paris for something like eight hundred years!"

"There have been Caribbean people cooking in Paris for eight hundred years?" I may not have been paying that much attention to Mlle Vailland in history class today, but that doesn't sound right.

"The *building's* been there for eight hundred years. Clever girl." André sticks one of his white iPhone earbuds into my ear for a quick moment, letting me listen to hard, pulsing chords harmonized with a wailing falsetto male voice. "Pretty fantastic, isn't it?" he asks with a grin. "I love this band. They're playing Bercy next week. I've got a friend who's a promoter who's letting me into the show for free. Bloody amazing."

"Wow, that's really awesome," I say, a little overwhelmed. I usually see André in the company of a pack of ballet dancers at a rehearsal where he is one of the most popular people in the room, never one-on-one, by ourselves. With just me as an audience, his attention feels condensed, concentrated, on me. I feel like I have to catch my breath, just keeping up with everything he has to say, even in just these last couple of minutes. He swirls around me, not unlike the tiny French cars zipping past on the rue Réamur. "What's the band called?"

André doesn't hear me; he's too distracted by how excited he is about lunch. "Here we are. Thank God, I was going to start eating my hand. I'm *famished*. After you, *ma petite*." André steps aside for me to go into a large covered market a little farther down the rue Bretagne. The market is called le Marché des Enfants Rouges. Its iron gates are pushed open, leading to four or five rows of market stalls. Some are selling cheese, produce or flowers, but more of them are selling their own type of cuisine à la carte—Italian, Moroccan, Lebanese, sandwiches, sushi. André steers me toward the back of the market to a leafy corner with bright pink covered tables and a thatched awning over the bar and kitchen.

"*Voulez-vous le* jerk chicken, *mademoiselle?*"

It smells delicious over here. André pulls a chair out for me, and we sit across from one another. He calls out to the waitress who is also the cook and seems to be an acquaintance of his. After he orders chicken and rice for both of us, plus a Red Stripe for himself, he turns back to me and whispers, "She's from Martinique. She won't believe I'm not Creole. But I'm British, mon!"

I giggle. "Your French is amazing. How did you learn to make it sound so natural?"

"French boyfriend. Well, I used to have one. The best way to learn a language is to sleep with a native speaker," André says absently, spreading his napkin over his distressed leather jeans, as the waitress sets down his beer and a glass of water for me. He looks up and winks at me. "Well, hey, you should know that, right? You've got one of those yourself."

"Hmm," I say. "Yeah, I guess."

"And hasn't your French gotten better since you met Thomas?"

I think about that, taking a sip of my water. "I suppose. But Thomas speaks English. So he mostly just speaks to me in my own language."

"There's the French for you," André says. "Show-offs. They always want to prove their superiority by speaking your own language better than you. I bet Thomas runs circles around you, reading Shakespeare and the lot. Is that right?"

I laugh and shake my head. "Not exactly. Thomas's English is about as good as my French. But for some reason, I don't try that hard to practice with him. And the last few days . . . I haven't even seen him. We've barely talked at all, let alone in French." I meant for that to come out playful, but I sound kind of bitter. I give André an apologetic look. I shouldn't waste André's lunch invitation, airing my festering doubts about Thomas and me.

"Anyway," I say just as André says, "You want to talk about it?"

We both laugh and look toward the kitchen for our food.

"Ugh, no," I say. "Let's talk about you. Or the Underground. *Anything* besides me."

"I'd be delighted. I'm so glad you pulled me out of the apartment today. I was at home, writing my own bio for my Website. I was starting to feel quite egotistical, crafting my life story for hours on end, wondering whether or not to falsify a little drama about my childhood on the tough streets of Kingston. It can't hurt—though I'd hate to be caught when anyone who knows my parents will find out that I grew up in dreary London, where everything is far too safe, far too boring."

"You have a Website?" I ask.

André smirks. "I do. A friend made it for me. One of the many reasons it's very lovely to date a computer geek. They help you do your online marketing every once in a while. I can have him make one for you, too.

As an artist you have to learn to sell yourself, girl!" André reaches over the table and pinches my cheeks.

"Sounds like you have a lot of friends," I say. I hate myself when I hear how it sounds—envious and resentful.

"I do, I do. Lucky is he who finds himself among friends with concert promoters and Web designers. I've just got to find a wine distributor, maybe a Jamaican chef, next!

"Anyway, it's lovely to be with you, socially, as I always assumed you were too busy off being a beautiful and popular American in Paris to give me or any of our fellow dancers the pleasure. I'm absolutely *elated* to find that's not the case." He leans over and rubs my cheek like I'm the cutest thing he's ever seen.

"Busy? Me?" I say. "Not really."

The waitress brings our food, roast chicken rubbed in unfamiliar rich spices with a mélange of rice and beans. I take one bite and start to cough, the chili peppers in the sauce inflaming my tongue instantly on contact. Hacking, I clutch around the table for my water glass, the entire time André popping around me, trying to make sure I'm not choking.

"Olivia! Good God! What happened? Shall I call a doctor?"

I shake my head, tears of embarrassment burning my cheeks. It's just chicken, but I feel like I have "suburbia" written all over my face, my body, my clothes. My whole personality. "It's just . . . really spicy. I'm not used to it."

"Olivia, wow," André says. "How terribly traumatic! I feel like an absolute *nightmare*, bringing you here. Why didn't you tell me you don't eat spicy food? Don't cry . . . we can get you something else. I don't want you to starve! You're a speck of thing as it is!"

"No, that's not why I'm crying," I say, wishing I could teleport myself back in time. Nothing about this place, this time, feels at all normal. "Why would you even want to hang out with me, André? Do you feel sorry for me or something? I mean, look at me." I throw my hands up at myself, tears running down my cheeks, my unkempt hair hanging in heavy untamed layers around my shoulders. "I'm a mess!"

"Let's get this wrapped up as takeaway," André says. "I think I better take you to my friend Marni before you really lose it."

Le Marché des Enfants Rouges is a stone's throw from École Nationale Supérieure d'Arts et Métiers—a big art-and-design school in a very hipstery corner of the Right Bank. As I walk with André up the wide rue Réamur toward the campus complex, I start to feel more and more self-conscious. Seeing the girls that go to school and hang out around here, with their fringe bangs and their swinging miniskirts and high boots and tights, I feel like more of a bumpkin than ever. I mean, I'm wearing *Ugg* boots.

"*On y va?*" André suggests, and we turn left down the pedestrianized rue Montgoreuil. All the stores and cafés over here are buzzing with youthful, creative energy. I smell a waft of something old and familiar and see that it's a vintage clothing store, its crammed racks being pillaged by girls with pink, purple, and blue hair. Another familiar smell is the bread baking from a Subway—one of the only fast food chains my brother Brian truly loves. He likes the tuna there, and only there. When my mom tries to fix him tuna salad at home, he won't touch it. But for some reason if it's from Subway, it's okay. I'd recognize the smell of a Subway anywhere. It makes me homesick, and then just annoyed at myself. As usual lately.

Finally, with our bag of still-steaming jerk chicken in André's hand, we head into a little boutique selling crystals and potions. The walls in here are painted black and purple, and a rotating disco ball illuminates shelves filled with books, incense, old LPs, and other assorted stuff for sale.

"*Bonjour,* Sylvie!" André calls out to a girl behind the cash desk. "*Est-ce que Marni est là?*"

Who's Marni? What *is* this store? It looks like a goth church bookstore.

"*Ouais,*" Sylvie grunts. "*As-tu un rendez-vous?*"

"*Non,*" André tells her as we rush through the store to the back room. "*C'est une circonstance critique!*"

We find Marni standing at a tall reception desk, eating a takeout salad with one hand and flipping pages of the magazine *Jalouse* with another.

"André! *C'est magnifique!*" Her waist-length orange hair swishes over her shoulders as she immediately tosses aside the salad and the magazine to kiss André happily on each cheek. "*Ça va, mon ange?*" She peers into the paper bag from the Caribbean restaurant. "*Tu as faim?*" She laughs and clears out a space at the reception counter for André to dig into his food.

"Hello, hello!" André greets her, setting his things down. "This is one of my dancing partners from the Underground—Olivia. Olivia, meet Marni. She owns this place. She's a genius."

"*Bonjour.*" I lift my hand up in a meek wave. The back room here is some kind of makeshift salon, with one industrial-size sink and a few chairs and mirrors. There are tables surrounding us, each covered with mixing bowls that smell like chemicals. Hair dye developer. Blech. I wrinkle my nose, even though by now I should be used to it.

"Olivia, do you have any cash on you? Marni only takes cash."

I actually went to the ATM just before I got on the métro over here. "Yeah, I have some. Why?"

"Good," André says. "You're in a terrible rut, and so I've brought you *here*, where *I* always come when *I'm* in a rut! You, my darling girl, are in a palace for people in ruts. A cathedral, if you will. Marni has *celestial* powers. Just wait!"

Marni beams, wielding a gleaming pair of silver scissors.

"Oh, no," I laugh, taking a step back. "I don't have time to get my hair cut." I take out my cell phone and see that it's even later than I thought it was. "I have to get back to school. Like, *right* now."

"No, Olivia," André says. "What you *have* to do is sit in this chair and let Marni do her special brand of magic on you."

"André, really, no, I never skip class," I say. "It's part of my agreement with the Lycée about getting to dance with the Underground. I have to keep up with my schoolwork or the director of the program will be really pissed. I have to go now. Thanks for the recommendation, and maybe I can come back over the weekend?" I'm squeaking out the question I am so nervous.

"Olivia, listen to me," André says, his large hands covering my shoulders and guiding me over and into the styling chair. "School can wait. Your fragile psyche cannot. I promise it's worth a truancy."

I gulp, watching myself in the mirror, but I don't try to get back up and leave again. André's lyrical voice is soothing, hypnotic.

I haven't had a hair appointment since September, back in California. My hair is three inches of dark brown, followed by ten of bleachy, dried-out honey blonde.

Seeing it under these lights and being watched by these two people who look more put together for a random Wednesday afternoon than I looked on prom night last year, I know I don't really belong in Paris. I belong back at Scripps Ranch, hanging out with my jock ex-boyfriend, my mom, and my baby brother. Even the girls in our little hamlet north of San Diego take better care of themselves than this. They make sure to blonde themselves every six to eight weeks, and they don't leave their houses in black sweatshirts with bleach stains on the sleeves, like I seem to have done this morning.

"*Un changement total,*" he instructs Marni. "*D'accord?*"

"*D'accord,*" Marni agrees, and in two minutes, my head is under a scalding faucet, my hair being shampooed for the first time in a week.

André breaks into applause. "This is just what I meant when I said genius," he gushes. Marni has finally finished tousling my hair just so. "Look, Olivia darling, look!"

Just like in every great makeover movie I've ever watched on TBS, Marni twirls my chair around and shows me what she's done with a great flair for the dramatic. The person staring back at me in the mirror is pale, with bright skin set off by dark mahogany hair expertly coiffed into a sweet pixie cut, ironed close to my head and smooth as silk. My whole white neck is exposed, which makes it look long and elegant. Like the cover of a French magazine. Like the cover of *Jalouse.*

"Oh my God," I say, reaching behind me at the empty spot to see if this is real. Is my hair really gone?

"You look beautiful!" Marni says, her accent rich and genuinely excited. "Look at yourself! *Regarde!*"

"My mom's gonna flip!" I squeal and throw my arms gratefully around André. I've never felt so perfectly Parisian in my life. And for the first time in weeks, all that pent up nervous energy inside me doesn't feel like anger. It feels like excitement.

"It's a whole new you," André chuckles. "It's tops!"

"*La coupe est parfaite pour toi, mademoiselle,*" Marni tells me. "So flattering on your little heart-shaped face!"

I hand all my cash over to Marni, and I finally take a bite of the spicy jerk chicken from the Styrofoam takeout container. This time it doesn't burn, or not quite as much, anyway. It's sweet and tart and unbelievably savory.

"This *is* a whole new me!" I say to André, reaching as casually as I can for his bottle of water to calm my raging tongue.

4. ZACK

Proof

Pierson calls late. I'm sitting up on my narrow, hard-as-Tennessee-mountain-bedrock bed, unable to make heads or tails of an assignment we were given in our new creative-writing class. While last semester we all took art classes, this semester, we are supposed to use our newfound prowess with the French language to write, not just coherently but creatively, and get graded on it. How *bogus* can this school get?

"Oh, Pierson, I'd do anything to be back in Amsterdam. I miss you!"

"Oh, hey, Zack?" an unfamiliar voice responds. "It's actually Bobby."

Oh. My. Gawd. As in Bobby, the boy who *almost* kissed me over winter break?

Holy pork smokers, was I not expecting this.

I nervously shift the phone to my other ear. My hands are slippery, and I almost drop the phone on the hardwood floor.

"Pierson said I could use his phone," Bobby says, sounding less confident as he continues. "I'm all out of minutes on mine."

I haven't said anything back to him yet. I make sure the door to my bedroom is all the way closed before responding. Just, you know, because.

"Hi, Bobby," I say, as if I've been expecting his call. "How's it going, hoss?" I try to make my voice sound subtly deeper.

"Great, dude, great," Bobby says. "Hey, listen, Pierson's right here and I'm sure he wants to talk to you, too, since he's paying for it, but really quickly, I thought I'd run my spring break dates by you. Would it be cool for your host family—and you, of course—if I come to Paris for a few days the first week in March? If it doesn't work out, that's cool—"

"Those dates are great!" I say, smiling wide. "Can't wait! You gotta e-mail your train info to me—you'll probably come into the Gare du Nord, since you're coming from up north. I'll come meet you at the station, and I'll plan some awesome stuff for us. Do you like museums? Oh, that's right, of course you do. Well, awesome. It will be a riot to have you come visit!"

"Oh, cool, I'm so glad you are still into it. Pierson says you got some bad news about that friend you were looking for. I thought you might be too down to have visitors."

I consider this for a second. As soon as Bobby offered to come, all thoughts of PJ jumped straight out of my bedroom window and onto the Square Saint-Lambert beneath my balcony. I feel guilty. "It's just really complicated. Have you seen any of the news about it?" I ask.

"Just that *International Herald Tribune* article you e-mailed to Pierson. Crazy stuff, dude."

"Yeah, it's insane. There are reporters lurking around our school, waiting for news to break so they can jump on us for a quote. But there's no new news." The reporters, from not only France, but from England and America, too, chill my bones whenever I walk by. They always ask us if we knew Penelope, if she has contacted us. All of us Lycée students pretend to ignore them.

"How do you feel about it?"

"Pretty crappy," I say. I'm afraid to go into it. "But whatcha gonna do? There's nothing *to* do. Just sit and wait."

"But how do you really feel?"

I stop short. Does Bobby really want to know? I mean, Bobby doesn't even know PJ. "Well . . . I feel . . . bad. I feel confused. I'm . . . scared."

Bobby stays quiet.

"I also keep having this weird hopeful feeling. Don't tell anyone this, okay? Not even Pierson."

"Okay, dude," Bobby agrees.

"I think she's alive," I whisper into my cell.

"What?" Bobby asks. "You're serious."

"Dead serious." I clear my throat. My eyes fixed to the back of my bedroom door, I decide to tell Bobby what I haven't told anyone yet. I stare at a tiny crack in the white paint, almost not seeing it, not seeing anything. "On the way back from Amsterdam, I had to make some weird connection in Rouen because of the train strike. I swear to God, I saw a girl looking just like PJ walk right by my train."

"You did?" Bobby gasps and takes a moment to think. "Was that after they found her suicide note?"

"Well, no," I admit. "It was before. But also . . . there's this picture of the backpacks they found with the suicide note on the bridge in Rouen. It's the photo they keep using over and over in the news. And I remember, when I met PJ, she was wearing a backpack. And it didn't look like the one in the picture I keep seeing."

"Hold on," Bobby says and covers the mouthpiece with his hand. Then he gets back on the line, his voice even quieter than before. "Sorry, I had to tell Pierson that I had to go into the hall for a sec. So, what are you saying?"

"I'm not sure," I say, rubbing my eyes and dropping my head back down. I'm so tired. Nothing makes sense anymore. Blinking as I go over it in my head for the millionth time, I strain my eyes as the words on the creative-writing handout lying on my lap start to blur. "But that's too weird, right?"

"You go to church, right, Zack?" Bobby asks me.

"Ha, bound and gagged. I wouldn't if my parents didn't make my room and board at home totally dependent on it. Why?"

"Well, I just mean, you believe in Jesus and God, right?"

"I guess so," I say. "Why?"

"Well, sometimes I think people really want to believe something, so then anything weird that happens seems like a miracle, or a sign, even totally normal everyday things. Other people don't know what to believe, but then God keeps knocking them over the head with proof one way or another."

"Which do you think this is?"

"Which do *you* think it is?"

"I think she's out there, and I think she's closer than anybody knows." It feels good to say it out loud, even if Bobby might think I'm crazy as a bat for saying so.

"You're not crazy, Zack," Bobby says, as though he's just read my mind. "I'd say you have pretty good instincts." He pauses for a beat. "Well, most of the time."

We laugh in spite of ourselves, clearly both recalling that awkward day by the canal. Then he quickly says *ciao* and hands the phone to Pierson. For a minute there, it was just how I always imagined talking to a boyfriend would be.

★ ★ ★

On the métro to school, I can't stop thinking about what Bobby was saying about faith last night. Some people are blinded by their faith. But for some people, faith is all they have to go on. My mind whirls, trying to decide which I am.

I wish desperately that Bobby would get here soon. The first week of March seems like ages from now. I want to see what that will be like so badly—to be with a guy you like, who likes you. A real boyfriend!

I think Bobby could be the one. It's like, he *gets* me.

A reporter glowers at me on the front steps of school, sizing me up. I want to scream at them, "Just go away!" What *they* want, with their TV cameras and their microphones and their flashbulbs, is so diametrically opposed to what *I* want.

Those reporters want PJ's waterlogged, half-frozen remains to drift ashore. They want to find out why a beautiful American teen would kill herself and what it means for her friends, her school, and her family. She was the visiting student to the magistrate of one of the most popular tourist destinations in France. Those reporters are out for blood.

What I want, what I keep hoping for, is PJ to just appear, with her ethereal smile and feathery voice, and for everything to go back to the way it was. Jay will have his beloved, Alex will be humbled, and maybe—*maybe*—we could put this all in the past.

"Mr. Chandler, I understand that you were good friends with *la Penelope perdue*. Were you aware that her parents, *les Fletchers de Vermont*, are linked to a large drug-trafficking network that might be the reason your friend killed herself?"

I stop short. "What?" I breathe at them. "What are you talking about?"

"Zack, don't say anything," says a low, purposeful voice from behind me. "Just go on into school."

I turn around to see who's talking to me, and I almost knock my glasses off trying to get a better look. I'm so surprised when I finally realize who the short little girl pushing me through the front door is. She's got short dark hair and is dressed to the nines in flowing black pants tucked into tall boots with a slinky long-sleeve top and big dangly earrings. I forget all about drug trafficking. Olivia's stopping traffic right here in the Lycée.

"Well, hot damn! Girl! You lookin' *good*. Cute as a piglet suckling its mama."

"You look at me, and the first thing you think of is a *pig*?" Olivia giggles, putting her hands on her tiny little hips and spinning around so that I can see the sexy cropped hairdo from the back.

"Piglets are just the cutest little things, I swear," I promise and give Olivia a hug once we're in the safety of the Lycée lobby. "California girls like you just don't know. Seriously, Olivia, I mean it. You're a whole new *femme. Quelle transformation!*"

"I know," she says, her round gray-blue eyes looking even bigger without all that dried-out blonde hair falling in front of them. Her face just pops, revealing her nice round cheekbones, the dash of light freckles across her little button nose, and her smile, flashing with rare enthusiasm. "That's what I wanted. Without even knowing it."

"So what's this about drug-running? What the heck were those hacks saying out there?" I ask, not sure if I want to know the truth.

"All those reporters dug up some stuff about PJ's life in Vermont, I guess," Livvy says, her face darkening as much as it had brightened when I first saw her. "Did she ever tell you anything about her parents? Do you think that could be true?"

I shake my head. If it is, then there might be a whole hell of a lot more reason for PJ to have jumped off a bridge. It's a realization that almost shatters the faith I had that she was out there somewhere, that feeling I was so sure about last night.

"Let's not even talk about it," Livvy says. "Madame Cuchon will tell us if we need to know."

How stupid were we not to tell her what we knew in the first place? And isn't that just what Olivia and I wanted to do? But Jay and Alex talked us out of it.

Just then, Alex walks into first period, clacking along in her black booties and wearing that preposterous fur hat she found at the condo in Montauban. It's not even that cold today. She waves at us, making huge, excited gestures at Livvy's hair, and Olivia waves back.

I know Alex wants to sit through the class with us, and I also know that Olivia wants me to let her. There are plenty of empty wooden desks all around us. But I can't just smile and invite her over. Not now. Not after everything that's happened—how she tried to hit on Jay instead of helping him rescue PJ. Not after I'm realizing more and more that all of this tragedy could have been avoided . . . if I'd only stood up to Alex on Christmas Day, when she and Jay were insisting on their harebrained plan to go to Montauban and then Cannes.

Did she know that PJ's parents were in trouble? I wonder as I watch Alex pout her glossy lower lip and go over to sit with Sara-Louise and Mary on the other side of the room. The rumors about PJ's mysterious life back in Vermont get more and more wild every day. Alex never said anything at the time, but that doesn't mean anything at all, I've learned. She flounces into a desk, spreading out her belongings as if we're all sitting in her boudoir—makeup, pens, stationery, even a book, something I've never seen her pull out of her huge camel-colored leather tote bag before.

I bet she did know, I think. That would make perfect sense in hindsight. Nothing gets by Alex. Nothing.

Alex always was just a little bit odd when it came to the subject of Penelope Jane Fletcher and why she didn't like the girl. I'd always figured it was because Alex, with her expensive clothes, luxurious, complicated beauty regimen, and wildly overzealous plans to become the most desirable girl at the Lycée, envied PJ. PJ had natural, easy beauty that she herself barely seemed to realize she had. But now, as I remember last semester, I realize that it might have been more than that. The two girls flew over on the same flight from New York, clearly having met on the airplane, yet barely speaking as they disembarked the plane. And then all of a sudden, Alex perked up with suggestions for where we might find PJ over winter break, making suggestions to travel south, to Montauban, then Toulouse, then Cannes. Each time we went somewhere new, we drifted farther and farther from where the police ultimately found PJ's belongings in Rouen.

I shudder in my metal desk, horrible thoughts and accusations running through my head. *What if Alex purposely led us south, because she knew PJ was in the north?*

I remember her, sitting on Olivia's living room floor, her eyes bright, her puckered lips shining in the candlelight, exclaiming how lovely Montauban was, and Jay encouraging her, desperate for her expertise. If anyone knew anything about France, it was Alex. Alex would be the first to tell you that. And Jay, sick in love with PJ, would have believed anything.

It makes me hate Alex even more than I ever thought possible. I want to punish her, run away from her, scream at the pain she's caused with her own selfishness. And yet I can't take my eyes off of her or her long, manicured hands pulling more and more stuff out of that stupid big bag. There's just something about Alex that demands attention, even when it's also feeding my total annoyance with her!

Alex opens a paper bag from Eric Kayser and spreads out a few *viennoiseries*—a chocolate croissant, a *pain aux raisins*, and some puffy pieces of brioche sprinkled with hard sugar crystals. "I brought breakfast, ladies!" Alex announces cheerfully. "You want some?"

"You brought that for us?" Mary asks her, looking hesitantly at the treats. "Really?"

"Sure," Alex says and steals a look at me before I can look away. "I guess I just felt like treating you. Or whoever else wants some."

"Anyway, Olivia," I say, turning back to my newly pixified friend. I make my voice super-friendly so it will hurt Alex all the more to be excluded. "I feel like I haven't really had a chance to talk to you—or anyone—in a while. A long while."

"What's going on, Zack?" Olivia leans in, immediately worried.

"So much has happened . . . in the south of France, and then in Amsterdam . . ." I can't help but grin at the word *Amsterdam*. I don't have to fake that, at least. And Alex looks just as wounded as I expected her to.

"Zack! What?" Olivia's frown turns over. "Did you meet a guy in Amsterdam? Oh, my gosh! That's amazing!" She jumps up and down at her desk. "Why didn't you say anything earlier?"

"Well, it's kind of weird, with all this PJ stuff going on. . . ."

"But, Zack, wow. I'm so happy for you!" Olivia bites her lip. "Isn't it incredible how love hits right when you're not expecting it?" She looks away, wisftful.

"Yeah," I laugh. "His name's Bobby, but I call him Canal Boy." Olivia's freckled face looks puzzled. "Long story—I'll tell you later."

"Hey, guys, want some brioche? I know how you like this bakery, Zack, and I also still have another chocolate croissant in here." Alex is now standing behind us, digging around in the Eric Kayser bag. "They're so yummy—don't even *try* to resist!" In her pale hand she holds out a buttery croissant filled with dark-chocolate paste, and she's right, I am hungry and I do want to eat it. "You know you want some of this!" She sounds like a used-car salesman.

"No, thank you, Alex," I say. Alex has been wearing all black for a few days now, but her outfits would make you think she is mourning the head designer at a Paris atelier. Today, she's got on opaque black tights, wool shorts with suspenders, her booties, and a black cashmere turtleneck. There was a time when I would have been petting that cashmere as if I were a crazy cat lady and Alex my baby Siamese. Not anymore.

Livvy smiles up at her, shaking her head. "Too much sugar for me, *chica*. Thanks, anyway."

"Are you sure, Zack?" Alex is looking only at me. "You're usually such a chocoholic!"

"Alex!" I snap. "I'm *so* not in the mood for you right now!"

I meant to say that I wasn't in the mood for chocolate right now, but *you* slipped out. Alex's already pale face looks like she's been slapped. "Sorry." I feel miserable. But she *does* deserve it. She's done *so* much worse to me over the last five months.

Sara-Louise and Mary are watching, too, their eyes buggy and ears perked. While Alex slouches back over to them, M. Paton walks into class and tells us to get our math books out. As usual, he's in a wicked mood and doesn't even say hello.

"I talked to Canal Boy on the phone last night," I whisper to Olivia as we find the page we're on. Alex watches us, out of earshot. "He's coming to visit for spring break!"

"Bobby is? So great, Zack!" Olivia squeals almost silently.

"I know! How am I *ever* gonna last until then? Things have been so . . . yucky lately in Paris. PJ, and those creepy reporters, and—"

"Alex?" Olivia whispers. "Can't you guys make up soon? I hate seeing you on the outs. It's, like, not natural."

"No way, Livvy," I say. "Alex is bad news. She and I are done." I feel a chill saying it—it sounds so final. I've never been good at cutting people out of my life—even the toxic ones.

"Zack! You don't mean that."

"It's the truth, girl," I say. "But you're right. Without her to run around with, things are a little slow in these parts. If you weren't always at ballet or studying or with Thomas, we could get up to some *business* together." I give her a look to show her exactly what I think of her impossible schedule. "Get our minds off all this!" I try to chuckle in a lighthearted way, shake off the icky thoughts about Alex, PJ, everything.

"Hey, actually, I wanted to introduce you to my friend André. He and I are going to a concert this weekend at Bercy. Will you come? I'm not sure if I'm cool enough to be there without backup," Olivia says. "He's so wild; he'll take your mind off Alex, and everything else, for *sure*."

For the first time since Alex walked in, I feel a true grin spread across my face.

★ ★ ★

The concert is at the Bercy sports arena on Saturday night. Olivia and I take the métro out to the Parc de Bercy in a train car packed with other people going to the show. We're shoved in between two tough-looking guys opening beers in tallboy cans. The concert is some Brit pop group that supposedly this guy André just *loves*. When Olivia told me who it was going to be, I recognized the name from the posters for the concerts covering the walls in the métro. All the times I've seen this show advertised, I never thought I'd be cool enough to actually *go*. And to go backstage with the passes Olivia's friend got for us?

That's cooler than anything Alex Nguyen ever cooked up for us in Paris. Maybe hanging out with people besides her will turn out to be even more wild and exciting!

"I've always wanted to see a concert here!" I shout to Olivia as we get escorted through security and led over to the side of the stage, where all the other VIPs and backstage people are hanging out. From the wings, we can look out over the stadium. It's absolutely enormous and packed with people as wild as soccer fans during the World Cup. All the biggest concerts in Paris happen here, and like stadium shows in the U.S., it's not just about the band or the music—it's about that crazy feeling of being a part of a huge crowd, everyone focused on the same thing. The opening band has already started—they are playing fast, short songs with great harmonies over the guitar parts. I bob my head to the music. I love music that rocks but you can also dance to—that *guys* can dance to, that is. Girls will dance to anything.

"I know, me, too! Look, there's André, my friend!" Olivia points and waves at a tall, dark-skinned guy bouncing up and down closer to the stage, convulsing in a controlled way—a cool way—to the thumping intensity of the music.

"Hi there!" Olivia calls to him and pulls me over. As we get nearer to him, I see that André is well dressed, wearing skinny jeans, a white V-neck T-shirt, and a shiny vinyl vest with orange and red flames painted on it. There are some cool woven necklaces hanging inside the V of his shirt.

"Cheers, man!" he greets me. "Nice to meet you. Love that scarf, by the way."

"You, too! I mean, it's nice to meet you, too," I nearly screech, because instantly, fantastically, I know this guy is gay. I can just *feel* it. Not like with Jay. Really, truly gay this time, or at least bi.

I mean, that vest?

And he's *hot*. Great body, shaved head, dark eyes and smokin' style. What's not to like?

"You're Zack then, right?" André asks me. I can't stop touching the scarf around my neck now.

"Oh, yeah, sorry, forgot to introduce myself," I say, blushing. I stick out my hand to shake his, but he leans in to kiss my cheeks. "This is insane! The concert, I mean."

"Bloody insane is right," André laughs. "Let me go get us some beers. Olivia?"

Olivia smiles nervously. "Well, okay. Why not?"

"Cut loose, girl!" André claps me on the back and pushes out of our row to go to the concession stand. As soon as he is out of sight, I whirl on Olivia with a little more force than I intended.

"Livvy! André is a babe!" I take her shoulders to steady my swoon. "How come you didn't tell me? And don't try and tell me he's not gay. I know. He's gay. There is no way. That he is not gay."

Olivia smiles, but it's a nervous, uncomfortable smile. She's wearing jeans, boots, and a cute top, but this show (especially backstage) is full of people in such crazy, hot getups that she might as well have worn overalls and ballet slippers. At least half of them are smoking, and I can distinctly smell a mixture of tobacco and something else that I remember from Amsterdam. Olivia, obviously, feels totally out of her element, and unlike Alex, who sees situations like these as chances to prove herself, Olivia shrugs back like a wallflower. I'm not sure, after all, if I'm really going to find the kind of fun with other people that I used to have going out with Alex.

It's a starkly disquieting realization, making the loud, insistent bass of the music feel farther and farther away. I feel so distant from this scene for a second that I could be watching myself in a movie. I wish I could forgive Alex. If only for moments like this one,

"You wish Alex were here, don't you?" Olivia asks me.

"Eh," I say. "Only for the entertainment value."

"Yeah," Olivia sighs. "I'm boring."

"Olivia," I say, turning her little body to face mine. "That is not true.

You are just as fun as Alex. I promise you. And no more of this self-pity! We can do this without her. We don't need her. We'll make our own fun in Paris! *Laissez les bon temps rouler!*"

Olivia rolls her eyes and slips her hand into mine. "Sure, Zack. We can try."

André comes back with the beers. He's bought six, so we can each chug the first one and then sip the second and dance around to the music. "You've got to drink the first one quick!" André instructs. Olivia looks at him doubtfully. "Ok, then it's not my fault if the second one is all nasty and warm when you finally get to it!" André swallows the contents of his bottle in a straight shot. I watch his large Adam's apple adjust as the liquid goes down his throat. He shakes his head out. "That'll set me right!"

I take my beer and do the same, but when the beer reaches my stomach, it gurgles and flips over, leaving me with a *terrible* case of the hiccups.

"I—hic—have the hic—hic—cups!" I manage to get out, clutching my full stomach. "Oh, no!"

It's enough to make Olivia finally relax. She's giggling hysterically, and I can't help but start giggling, too, while still hiccupping. The crowd around us is bumping along, and André takes charge.

"All right, here's what you gotta do," André says. "Bend down." He leans over so his neck and torso are parallel to the floor. "Take your beer like this." He puts the bottle in his mouth and takes a long drink upside down. "That'll untwist your insides! I swear it!"

Olivia cannot stop laughing. Despite feeling too ladylike to chug her own beer as I did, she apparently had no problem finishing it in a few drinks once she started laughing. I scowl at her when my hiccups crack her up again.

"Seriously, Zack, try it!" André insists. "It works!"

I love the attention, the concern for my hiccups. I bend over and try it, spilling my beer and getting a good amount of it up my nose. When I stand back up, I definitely still have the hiccups.

"Ah, I just wanted to get you to bend over!" André giggles, and Olivia has to clutch his arm to keep herself standing upright.

Beer is now running down the sides of my mouth and making nice stains on my T-shirt, and I'm practically choking I'm laughing so hard. André puts an arm around me, and I realize I no longer have the hiccups. "Worked, didn't it?" he says and squeezes me before letting go.

There's a quick break between the bands, during which André wants to know all about Memphis. "What you want to know all about M-town for?" I flirt with him. Or try. "Plannin' on comin' to visit one day?"

"Am I invited?" André asks, looking at me for a long moment, and Olivia cheerfully rolls her eyes. I can tell she's getting a tad drunk. She's still dancing a little bit, even though there's no music.

"Well, yes, sir, of course! We like to show you Brits a thing or two about Southern hospitality, don't you know?"

"Oh, yes, mate, they're starting!" André exclaims. He throws his arm back around me excitedly. It only lasts a second, but the warmth of his skin around my neck makes the concert feel like the whole, beautiful world is right here in this room, about to have the best night in history. In another moment, André pumps his fist in the air, screaming his appreciation for the band. The lights go down, and some pyrotechnics pop at the front of the stage. Within minutes, the whole stadium crowds in, moving as a giant, pulsating mass, singing along to every word and pounding fists in time with the beat. I smile like an idiot as Olivia dances on one side of me and André goes absolutely *crazy* on the other. The band is so close to us that I can smell how sour and sweaty they are under the lights.

Suddenly, I realize that this concert is more fun than a Sunday afternoon church baptism with free pie afterward! This is actually the most fun I've had in *ages*. More fun, even, than hanging out with Alex.

After a while, I look to my left and notice that Olivia isn't really dancing anymore. She's kind of lamely moving around, as though she wants the fun to keep going but she can't get there.

"Hey," I stop dancing and turn her to face me. The black eyeliner she put on for the show is running in rivers from her big, beautiful eyes. Very quietly, Olivia is sobbing. The first time I've seen her break down, well, *ever*.

"Livvy! What's the matter? Aren't you having fun? What happened?"

I have to yell over the music. This is definitely the loudest concert I've ever been to. It's louder than a revival hall. It's louder than my dad yelling at me not to "act gay" anymore.

"I feel so guilty. PJ's dead. And before that, she was suffering without us even knowing it. What if her parents really were drug dealers, like those reporters are saying? And here I am *dancing*." Olivia wipes her face on her bare arm, her chest heaving. "I'm here at a concert, backstage, *dancing*!"

"Oh, Olivia," I say, pulling her rocking body into my arms and kissing her forehead. "You don't have to feel guilty."

"How can I not, Zack?" Olivia moans into my chest.

"Because," I tell her even though I can't be sure anymore, either. It's like Bobby was saying about faith, maybe I *am* blinded by it. "PJ's not dead. I know she's not. I . . ." I'm not sure if I should really tell her this. "I *saw* her. At the Rouen train station."

"What? You were in Rouen? When?" Olivia stops heaving for a moment.

"I had to switch trains there coming back from Amsterdam during the rail strike. I saw her from my train!"

Olivia shakes her head. "No. I don't think you did."

"I did!" I insist. "Olivia, I know PJ. I swear on my life it was her! And that backpack in the photos in the paper—that's not her backpack! I know it."

"It's really nice that you're so hopeful, Zack," Olivia says, sniffling. "But what about her parents? It sounds like there were a lot of reasons PJ had to be sad that we didn't even know about."

"Even if her parents are in trouble, why does that automatically mean she's dead?" I ask. "Maybe she put that backpack out there on purpose. She wants us to think she's dead. You should have hope, too, Livvy!"

"You can't just *choose* to have hope," Olivia says, a hard edge in her voice. She sounds mad more than anything else. I think back to all the times I've seen Livvy walking into school, wearing something it looks like she slept in, slamming her locker door shut, and cursing under her breath. Her eyes are dry again, and her face is rigid. "It doesn't work like that." She's staring at the band, not really watching them tear up the stage but instead focusing on some point beyond the bright lights and the amps and the exploding special effects.

"Livvy, come on, you're usually so much more optimistic than this. What's gotten into you?"

"Hey, Zack!" André says to me, still dancing. He's charmingly oblivious to what's happening next to him.

I look back at him.

Before I can even say, "What?" his lips are planted on mine, and we're kissing, right in the middle of a packed sports arena. The song ends, and the crowd erupts into riotous applause. I imagine it is for me, celebrating my very first kiss.

This is exactly what I was just talking about. How's *that* for optimism?

FEBRUARY

5.PJ

Broken but Worth the Price

hen the train doors open in Caen, I almost grab my things and get off. There are no more stops between here and Paris. I'm not sure that I can go back there. In just two hours, if I don't get off now, I'll be rolling into the Gare Saint-Lazare, just steps from the Lycée in the Eighth.

The train whistle blows. People finding seats lean over to peek through the windows for a last look at their well-wishers. "*Au revoir,*" they mouth. "Good-bye."

I hold my breath all the way from the platform at the Gare Saint-Lazare until I'm on the métro, crawling under the Grands Boulevards toward the far reaches of the city. Each time the doors open, I smell that familiar, gritty underground Paris scent. There's an older man asleep next to me, his breath hoarse and audible. I listen to its rhythm, the way he wheezes slowly, completely out. He's rank with several days of booze and sweat on him, but I don't want to change seats. I don't want anyone to see me do anything at all.

At long last, I get off the train and let all the people around me stride ahead. I'm not in a hurry. Again, I don't want to look rushed. I don't want to look like anything. When I reach the street, I look up for a moment, and think strangely of how familiar this gray, frothy light is. I've been here before, at the Porte de Montreuil, in the early hours of the day. I've seen the light shine just this way. The last thing I did in Paris was go to Jay's apartment and slip a silly postcard on his door, before I went back to the Gare du Nord and got on the first train to Rouen.

"*Cigarettes, mademoiselle? Tabac?* La presse?" Out of nowhere a portly man is by my side, speaking thickly, as if there's silt in his mouth. I shake my head. He follows me for a few steps.

"*Non!*" I say, but still I feel trapped by how vulnerable I am out in Paris's open air. At any moment, someone could see me. Someone could recognize me. I don't have a lot of time. I need to find Jay. Today.

The Marché aux Puces de la Porte de Montreuil is a weekend flea market near where Jay lives. The market runs along the side of the boulevard Périphérique, just across the overpass from the métro station at the edge of the 20th Arrondissement, or the *Vingtième*, as the Parisians would say. Modern glass hotels rise above all the little tents and booths crammed into the small outdoor market space. Beyond the *marché* is the little suburb of Montreuil, no different from any of the other outer arrondissements. It's early, but the flea market is bustling, uncomfortably so. People crowd every table, studying the wares, fingering the objects for sale. The entire market and its surroundings reek of cigarette smoke. Everyone—vendors, shoppers, waiters tending to drinkers in cafés—seems to be smoking.

I walk the whole market, from the farthest edge, where poor women lay down tiny cloths to try to sell only a couple pairs of old shoes, to stalls unloading truck beds full of starched new merchandise, yelling "*Aux choix! Aux choix!*" as loud and as fast as they can to attract the attention of the throngs pushing by.

He'll come. I know he'll be here. Every Sunday, that's what he does.

Or that's what he did. Before I ran away. His habits could have changed. It's been so long since we saw each other. I wonder if I will even recognize him. Betting on him shopping the Sunday market as he always does, I hadn't let myself consider alternate possibilities on the train, because I'd been so terrified to even board it. But now, in this mess of people and market stalls and that nauseating smoke, I feel more alone than ever. It seems impossible that it would be easy to find him here.

It's grimy, not very beautiful, but Montreuil isn't a rough neighborhood or anything. It's just one of the more working-class areas of Paris, with modern, graying buildings with elevators to reach the upper floors and discount grocery stores—Leader Price, Carrefour—on the first floors of the buildings closer to the street. Big plazas with groups of kids playing soccer on the concrete. Chinese nail salons. Heavy cast-iron gates around the apartment complexes.

It's funny Mme Cuchon didn't select any girls from our program to live out here, just Jay, Cory, Sammy, and Lucas. It's as though she didn't think the girls could handle it. Like we wouldn't be safe.

She didn't think about how unsafe we'd be right in our own homestays. The nicest homestay in the program even, just a few blocks from the precious Lycée de Monceau.

Like many of the women working their way through the snarl of the market lanes, I wear my scarf over my face. Only my eyes show through.

After several hours, I leave the market center and go sit on a bench near the entrance to one of the hotels. Maybe this was a foolish idea. I can't trust my own reasoning lately.

Jay and I don't know each other, not like I sometimes fool myself that we do. Rattled and running from the Marquets, I've reached out to him but never revealed anything. I've trusted him implicitly. Been tempted to confide in him. Always assumed that he would be patient and helpful. But this time, what I want to ask him, I'm not sure if it's crazy. I think it might be.

I watch cars speed around a turnabout, entering the freeway and crossing the overpass. Since I got to Paris, I often find myself staring at strangers, wondering about their lives, what's happening in their heads. Do they, like me, have secrets that make them feel trapped? Or do they feel free, waking up every morning, leaving their apartments, and wondering at all the possibility that each day holds?

Then, I spot him.

I almost don't believe myself. He's with his friend Cory, and they look thin and tired, especially Jay. I croak from the back of my throat, pushing forward off my bench, anxious not to lose him in the crowd.

I cross the street, letting my scarf fall away from my face, my hair come out of my hood. Running headlong into the traffic, I never take my eyes from Jay.

A few degrees outside of his line of sight, I'm hiding behind a rack of old shoes while I stalk Jay and Cory looking through electronics parts.

Cory builds computers for fun. Bikes, too, I think. The two of them rifle through wires, cords, plastic black boxes. Jay finally picks up a small object off a folding table and shows it to Cory. Cory nods and grabs it out of his hand.

"*Combien ça coûte?*" Cory asks and then hands a North African guy some change. They move on to the next table.

Jay sighs and looks around, his dark eyes shaded. His skin looks sallow, not magically sun-kissed as it did even the last week of first semester. His hair is grown out a bit. Despite this, or maybe because of it, I find myself regarding him with more shyness. Has he been going to soccer practice, or has it been too cold? Or has he been too sad to go?

It's hard, it's so hard, not to run to him. The slope of his jaw, the little cave under his chin down to his shoulders and chest both look so safe. Jay's known for being jocular and easygoing, but he looks capable and smart, too. Right now, his feet planted solidly on the pavement in front of me, he looks like he could handle anything in the world.

But I can't do it. I can't run into those broad arms, bury my face in that rough, scratchy almost beard on the side of his face. Part of my body, my hands, my hips, even the tip of my tongue, seem to want me to do it, to just go to him, but my feet won't move. Until I almost lose them again, and then I follow them, ducking behind stall after stall.

Cory, especially, is deft at moving through this market. He seems to be very familiar with which booths to stop at and which to avoid, though from my perspective, they all seem full of junk. From where I am standing, all I see are computer keyboards, browned with years of use, cheap costume jewelry, wires, secondhand pots and pans, huge packages of toothpaste, and hair gel. Cory approaches certain tables with hopeful reverence. He doesn't seem to think he is surrounded by castoffs. He acts like he's on a treasure hunt.

Some sellers take drags off their cigarettes and watch me carefully. Maybe they think I look like the type of person who will grab something—a bracelet, a bootleg DVD—and run. I wrinkle my nose at the ones who leer at me, wondering what I am doing in this gritty market, obviously not checking out any of the stuff that is for sale.

"Sst, sst, sst," one guy hisses as I pass. I ignore him. I just follow the back of Jay's dark head as he makes his way through the market. He's hard to keep track of. He's dressed somberly today. Usually, I notice with a grimace, Jay is a good dresser. He takes good care of himself and always looks very put together. Today, though, it doesn't look like he has shaved in a while. With his stubble, his beanie, and his black sweatshirt, Jay looks like all the other young guys roaming the market. I catch a glimpse of his sneakers, which are dirty. That's not like him at all. The first time I met him, I remember we were both wearing white Converse All Stars. His were bright white. Mine were the dirty ones, the ones to be embarrassed about.

They still are, I notice, looking down. They are the only shoes I had with me when I ran away from the Marquets. They're all I ever wear now.

I let myself get a little closer to Jay. I know those dimples, those serious, knowing dark eyes. He looks so morose, much more sad than I was expecting. And beautiful. He's slumping next to Cory as he fastidiously inspects another table piled high with computer parts. Jay's doleful eyes don't seem to open more than halfway. Are they swollen from crying? How much heartsickness have I caused him?

And yet, through his sorrow—if that's what it is—my attraction to him after all these weeks away from him is magnetic. I don't remember feeling this strongly about him. I don't remember my palms sweating like this when I saw him from afar.

I want to touch him. I want to cup his face in my hands, stroke the dark hair on his forearms. I just want to feel the warmth of his skin against mine.

The last person who touched me, even just to squeeze my arm, was Sunny from the Cherbourg hostel. Her band poured out of the van at Omaha Beach, where the warships landed to liberate France back in World War II. She turned to me and smiled sympathetically. "Good luck," she said. I knew she wanted to help me, but only so much. She was letting me leave before she had to ask me to.

Looking at him with eyes that haven't seen him in so long, I have a moment of doubt. Jay is not just handsome. Jay is sexy. Will he even still want me?

I wonder if he ever did, or if I just imagined it.

But I wrote to Jay, I remember. I wrote to him, after I ran away, and he always wrote back, asking me to tell him where I was. How he could help me. He never forgot about me.

I move out of the way of a bickering French family who wants to get a closer look at a table full of hand mixers and other kitchen equipment. They're taking up the whole row as they lean together to fight over a purchase they can't decide on. The weather is strangely warm today, muggy. The vendors have to roll back the tarps over their booths to get some fresh air. The whole place feels slow and lazy like the inside of a balloon whose air is slowly being let out, as its rubber walls come closer and closer together. People shopping the market take off their jackets, plumping the aisles with even more bulk to maneuver around.

Jay and Cory leave the main part of the market. I follow them to an area where dealers are selling used cars and parts along the fence overlooking the Périphérique. There's also furniture over here—broken chairs and tables, some dressers that I can hide behind.

"What do you want with car parts, man?" I hear Jay ask Cory.

"It's just fun to look, you know?"

"I guess," Jay says.

"What, you got somewhere better to be?" Cory asks.

"Sure don't," Jay tells him. His eyes, creased around their dark edges, look forlorn. "I most definitely do not have anywhere better to be."

"Come on." Cory pulls Jay over to a guy selling Volkswagen parts—the little logos you stick on your trunk, stuff like that. Jay raises his eyebrows. He looks bored. Bored and miserable.

Now that there aren't as many people around, I am much more afraid of being exposed. But I also get a much clearer view of Jay.

Seeing him almost makes me feel tired. Exhausted. Like I should just walk up to him and end this struggle. He'd take my hand wordlessly and we'd go somewhere quiet.

Jay wouldn't make me explain anything about the past couple of months. He'd just make sure I had something to eat and somewhere nice to sleep. Then later, we could figure out what to do. I could ask him to take me somewhere warm, where shady pasts and big mistakes don't matter as much.

I shiver. I'm the only one around that has my coat on, even with this unseasonable heat. My dad's old sweater is buttoned all the way up underneath. I still feel cold. It's a deep chill that reaches inside me, where

I can't seem to warm up.

My body's still cold from the apartment in Rouen with Annabel, where we only had heat for two or three hours a day. It's cold from the empty hostel in Cherbourg. It's cold from the train rides, from riding in the Goddess and Light Band's clanking old yellow van with one of it's windows broken, letting the frosty air in.

I think, *Maybe, I'm still cold from my walk across Paris on Christmas Eve. I'm still cold from where M. Marquet touched me and wouldn't let me go without a fight.*

Jay turns slightly in my direction. I pull a leather fedora from a splintering hat rack and onto my head as if I am trying it on in the mirror. I fluff my blonde hair around my shoulders under the moldy hat, pretending to consider whether or not to buy it. In the corner of my eye, I see Jay and Cory walk away. I put the fedora back on the hat rack.

For some people, I realize as I let Jay move farther ahead of me, this whole thing might be the worst thing that's ever happened to them. Me. Me and my suicide is the saddest, freakiest thing they've ever experienced. And not only isn't it real and they shouldn't have to feel that kind of pain, it's all my fault that they feel it at all.

"Oh, look, Jay," Cory says as he stops short next to a couple old bikes for sale. "Check out these bikes. *Quel est votre meilleur prix?*" he asks the guy selling the bikes.

"Fifty euro," the man tells Cory in English. "For each."

"Fifty euro?" Jay scoffs. "No way, man. They're broken!"

"Broken, yes," the man tells Jay and Cory. "But still worth a good price. You know how to fix?"

Cory nods. You can tell he really wants to get one of the bikes.

Jay exhales. "No, man. Broken means it's not worth a good price. It's broken."

"Yeah, maybe." Cory still looks torn. "The parts are good, though. How about forty?" he asks the seller.

"Forty-five," the seller says.

"*D'accord*," Cory agrees and hands him the money. Jay rolls his eyes.

"Because you need another bike so bad, man," Jay says. "A broken one."

"I'll fix it," Cory says and hoists the broken bike into his arms. It's too bulky to carry around the market, so the boys decide to take the bike home.

"All right, guy, I'll call you later?" Cory says to Jay. I'm following them back to a big block of residential buildings where they both live. They are only twenty paces ahead of me; if they turned around, they would see me. There's nothing in between us. "You gonna be okay for the rest of the afternoon? Your host family is still out of town, right?"

"Yeah, they don't get back till later this week."

"You want some company?"

"No, man, I'm cool," Jay says. "I feel like chillin' alone for a bit."

"How about the arcade later? Sammy's down; I texted him earlier. Or we could go for Chinese. A little bro date. It's Valentine's Day today, you know."

"Is it?" Jay sighs. "I don't know. Maybe." Jay starts to walk toward his building, letting Cory go toward another. "I'll call you if I want to go out."

"Or we could watch a movie," Cory suggests. "I've got a Blu-ray of *Jaws* that will blow your mind."

"Ha," Jay grunts. "Maybe. See you later, man." Jay shuffles away. Cory rounds the corner and unlocks his front door. I wait for a few minutes and then continue to follow Jay down the path that leads to his high-rise. He's so oblivious. He has no idea anyone is following him. He's so innocent in that way. And so distracted by sadness. That much is obvious.

After Jay goes inside, I hang around his building for a while, not sure of what to do. It's quiet enough, this far from the market, that all I can hear are far-off cars honking and a few birds. When some sort of ventilation system hanging out of someone's window turns on, it sends a horrible shudder through me. Each bang of the rudder feels like a footstep coming closer.

I want to go in there and knock on his door. I also want to run away, not get him caught up in this—in me.

I sit down on a bench not far from the building's entrance. The sky seems to shift suddenly, and after a few minutes, it's raining lightly. As the sun goes down, the drops get bigger and heavier. It's not long before the grass under my feet is flooded with rain. My shoes will soon be full of water and mud.

I bend over and put my face in my wet lap. What am I going to do?

I came back to Paris because I need help. I can't do this alone. But now that I'm here, literally on Jay's doorstep, I'm not sure I can do this.

I'm not sure if I can need someone this much.

A light flickers on in the window next to me. I look up.

Jay.

I see him in the bedroom, a tiny little room he must share with his host brother. There are two narrow twin beds in there. They have *Tintin* sheets on them. Jay sits at a desk and pulls out a notebook.

I watch him write furiously for a few minutes, then turn and stare out the window at the rain. I stand up, feeling myself being drawn in closer, wanting only to get to the other side of the glass. I take one step, then another. My sneakers are full of rainwater, squishing so that it's like I'm walking across a trampoline. It feels unearthly.

I don't think to move, to hide. I just keep getting closer, wondering if he is going to see me. I want him to.

Very slowly, Jay lifts the windowpane. He doesn't look happy, or sad, or angry. He looks terrified.

"Are you . . . a ghost?" he whispers.

I shake my head.

"PJ?" he asks, afraid, maybe, to believe what he is seeing.

I burst into tears.

"*Que milagro*," he breathes. "Come here."

I pace toward him. After what seems like a long, long time, my wet hand reaches his. Once our fingers touch, we're grasping one another's hands so tight that I can feel my fingernails poking into his skin.

Jay pulls me into his room through the window, my elbows and knees knocking against the frame. Inside, I stand soaking on his carpet, just staring at him under the overhead light of his bedroom. He really does look like he's seen a ghost.

My teeth start to chatter—the only sound in the silent room—and it wakes Jay out of his reverie. He grabs the corner of a blanket on one of the beds and pulls off the whole thing, wrapping me up in it and hugging me.

"It's okay," he says, his own low voice cracking. "I've got you. You're safe."

I stare deep into Jay's eyes and feel like I'm seeing some sort of ghost, too. A ghost of what was meant to be.

Jay hooks his forefinger under my chin and lifts it so that he can put his lips on mine.

"You don't have to run anymore," Jay whispers. "Never again. *Nunca otra vez.*"

Then he kisses me, warm and soft—and I almost believe him.

6. ALEX

A Breath of Fresh Air

"Here is the—*comment on dit? La poussette*, Alex," Mme Sanxay says, raking her dark hair back from her red face as she pulls a stroller out of a corner of her dining room, which is loaded with other junk. The stroller itself has a bunch of toys and dirty plastic bottles in it. "Charles especially loves the puppet show at the Jardin du Luxembourg! You will have an excellent time."

I bet he does. Charles can't even form coherent words yet. How the heck would he know what's happening in a puppet show?

"Let *les enfants* play in *le jardin* for a little bit, okay? They are very excitable today," Mme Sanxay goes on. "They need to use up some of that energy."

That's an understatement. As we speak, Albert and Emeline (and, yes, I *did* finally learn their names) are playing an extremely violent game of leapfrog in front of a screeching Disney movie dubbed into French. Each of them has sticky purple juice running down the fronts of their white school-uniform shirts, and I can tell they've been eating paprika-flavored Lays potato chips because that's what the whole room smells like. Since I walked in, the two kids have paid me absolutely no mind at all. Every once in a while, one of them grabs a fistful of the other one's hair and attempts to pull it from its roots. Other than that, they seem to be having a marvelous time.

I close my eyes, trying to convince myself that this can only get better. It's already been a couple weeks, and things are already improving a little, right?

The first few days I just sat stiffly and let the older children scream and run around. I didn't attempt to change their behavior or interact with them at all. I definitely couldn't touch them. *Ew!* The only way I didn't run screaming out of the apartment was by reminding myself, over and over again, that it was this or back to Brooklyn. This or back to Jeremy's rejection. Failure in Paris. That would be something I could never forgive myself for.

A real French person, even a half-French person, can't fail in Paris. It is just not possible.

After that nightmare scream session the first day I babysat them, I have brought earplugs with me when I've returned. Good ones. The kind they give to people who work in the subway and on construction sites. I had to go to Mr. Bricolage, this horrible gardening/hardware place, just to find them. After putting the earplugs in the first time, I figured out where Mme Sanxay keeps the cereal and other stuff to toss at them if they looked hungry. The whole sordid situation is terrifying, even with the sound turned off, but it seems to work out okay. I mean, no one got hurt, right?

The next week, however, Mme Sanxay came home and was calling me from the door—where she was loaded down with groceries from Franprix—for five whole minutes without me hearing her. I was sitting in the playroom, with Charles in a playpen and Albert and Emeline building castles out of Legos in front of me. They weren't actually being noisy, but I wore the earplugs just in case they started to be. While I watched them make their castle, I was having this really involved daydream about Zack texting me that he forgives me and to make up for lost time he wants to take me out to drinks at the Hôtel du Nord, right on the Canal Saint-Martin. Then I came to and realized the older kids had left the playroom. When I turned around, Albert, Emeline, and Mme Sanxay were standing behind me, staring at me. Mme Sanxay's arms were folded across her chest. I took out the earplugs and shoved them into the pocket of my tulip-shaped brown skirt. She asked me, very quietly, to please help her carry in and unpack the groceries she'd left in the front hall.

Bored senseless of the Legos, I figured out how to use the Sanxays' Freebox cable and found an English-speaking channel playing *South Park*.

"Look, cartoons!" I told the kids, and now we watch those every afternoon until right before six, when Mme Sanxay gets home. I am very careful to turn the channel before turning the TV off so that she wouldn't see I'd been watching English programs instead of paying attention to her kids. Albert loves *South Park*, especially when anything bloody happens. For a brief moment one afternoon, we bonded when Kenny got killed by decapitation. But then Emeline started screaming and crying, and Charles woke up, and I had to find some cereal and a bottle, and I wanted to die all over again.

Later, Mme Sanxay lit into me about watching pay-per-view channels. And told me that I needed to start taking the kids outside while I am babysitting them. Like, doing *activities*.

"*Oui*, go to the puppet show, play in the park . . . anything else?" Mme Sanxay is now saying as she hunts around for her keys.

Mme Sanxay is not unattractive, but clearly, she's let herself go. For example, her features are quite cute, and her glasses are stylish. But her skin is practically dusty she needs an exfoliation so bad, and she doesn't ever seem to comb that limp mess of hair that sits on top of her head. She looks like someone in a mugshot every day of her life. It's *depressing*.

Even more depressing are the afternoons Mme Sanxay asks me to stay, even after she's come home, because she wants to talk to her Alsatian half sister on the phone. She doesn't even bother to go into another room because the two of them rattle on in *German*, of all languages, which the kids don't understand. I can't understand what's she's saying either. It's the only time I see her laugh, when she's cackling away with her sister.

I called my mom to complain about the situation after the pay-per-view incident. I mean, okay, I get it. Lesson learned. Can we please move on?

"Mom," I launched in. "Mme Sanxay doesn't even *need* a nanny. She doesn't have a *job*. She just doesn't want to be around her own hateful children!"

"She still has things she needs to *do*, Alex," my mom said to me disapprovingly. "How is she supposed to go to the bank? The grocery store? With three kids, one still in a stroller. Think about *that*, Alex— think about how chained down you would feel if that happened to you!" My mom's voice was suddenly shaking with anger. "You would just *crumble*!"

"She needs three hours a day to run errands?"

"Oh, Alex, get over yourself. You take three hours to go to Sephora."

I ignore her. Sephora isn't an *errand*. "Seriously, what on earth could she be doing all that time?" Why was my mom being so righteous when she herself hasn't been inside a grocery store in *years*?

"Maybe she's seeing her lawyer. Maybe she's seeing her therapist!"

"Five days a week?"

"It happens, trust me."

"Besides, what about when she comes home and just has me sit with the kids while she talks on the phone with that German sister of hers?"

"Oh, Ulrike!" my mom recalls pleasantly. "I know that sister. I met her years ago at a bachelorette party in Baden-Baden. Ulrike is the general manager of a hundred-year-old spa right in the heart of town. Lovely woman! She'll make you glow if you ever go see her, darling!"

"Fat chance of that," I say. "Even if I was invited to this spa, I'd have to skip it, because of this job. If I am ever invited *anywhere*, I won't be able to go!"

"It's only until you pay your debts, darling. And besides, I think you've done quite enough traveling for a long while, don't you?"

"Well, what happened to Mme Sanxay's other nanny? The one from Venezuela?"

"She was an illegal," my mom said. "Monsieur Sanxay didn't like the expense, so he reported the nanny to Immigration and she was deported within three days—*three* days. That's not enough time to fill a nanny position! That *bastard*."

"And the nanny can't come back to France?" I asked, hopeful that maybe this Venezuelan woman (who was obviously a saint if she could deal with these three day in and day out) was just working out a visa issue.

"No, Alex, she was kicked out of France for *good*," my mom said. "That's what an *asshole* Madame Sanxay's ex is. He got someone *deported* because he knew it would inconvenience his wife."

"And so I'm the new nanny?"

"Yes, Alex!" My mom was exasperated, sighing into the phone. "What part of this arrangement don't you understand?"

"The part where I'm doing a job for no money, a job that someone else used to do as, like, a career, for a real salary!" I shouted at her, finally losing my cool.

Why does my mom insist on being like this? So hot under the collar and so quick to get offended? It's bizarre. It makes me *so* livid.

"You aren't doing this for *nothing*, Alex! You are doing this because you stole someone else's money!"

"For the last time, I didn't *steal* it, Mom—"

"Yes. You. Did." I could just see my mom's strong New England waspy features tightening, barely able to get the words out through her rage.

I felt myself becoming increasingly angry, so I hung up. How can I convince her that all of the stuff I bought was necessary? It was just so complicated.

Our telephone conversation did not have results anywhere near what I wanted them to be, thus I was forced to return to the Sanxays. If I don't go to the Sanxays, an "option" I've spent long hours contemplating, I think it might just be the thing that gets me booted out of France—and cut out of the Braun family for good. My mom is simply not bending this time. I'm resigned to my fate. She wants to punish me. She thinks I have no good excuse for taking that money.

Still, I try never to rule out the possibility of something extraordinary happening, such as that Venezuelan woman coming back and agreeing to work for free just because she loves these mongrels so much.

Mme Sanxay waves good-bye to us and stealthily sneaks out before her children realize what is going on. A familiar tactic.

This time, though, neither Albert nor Emeline screams when they figure out their mom has just bailed. They heard the words *Jardin du Luxembourg* and *spectacle de marionettes* and are on their best behavior to see if those concepts are going to actualize. They stand still in the living room, the grape juice drying into a stain on Albert's chest.

I stare at them, waiting. After several moments, Albert and Emeline still have their mouths clamped shut.

"Good! *Bien!*" I congratulate them. "Great job!" I walk over to their coats, which they toss at the front door of their apartment. "Now put these on," I instruct. "And I will go wake up Charles."

Very much enjoying this new feeling of being in control of the situation, I wheel the stroller into the nursery. I usually let Charles wake up by himself, but Mme Sanxay told me to wake him up myself so that we can get to the puppet show in the park by three thirty. In the darkened nursery, I tap Charles's shoulder until his eyes open.

Don't cry, I will the baby.

He starts to cry.

Brat.

I take a deep breath. "Shhh," I try.

He continues crying. I sigh. Then I stick my tongue out at him, because I think I saw someone do that to a crying baby in the line at Duane Reade in front of me once, and their baby stopped. Charles does not stop.

I hear a noise like a sputtering sound, a little wet engine that won't start. Then I smell it. Charles needs to be changed. He *always* needs to be changed. As soon as I get the diaper off of him, what do you know? He's as happy as a clam. I might even be starting to get good at this baby-mind-reading stuff.

After he's all fresh and clean again, I go wash my hands thoroughly, fumbling around in the bathroom for some of Mme Sanxay's hand cream. When I finally find the bottle, it is empty. Then I wriggle Charles gently into a little winter parka suit, next his little shoes and a hat with a light blue knit bobble on top. He's kinda cute, all bundled up like that.

I lift him up by his miniature armpits and buckle him into his stroller. I wheel him out to the foyer, where Albert and Emeline have totally ignored my orders and do *not* have their coats on!

"Albert!" I yell at him. "Put on your coat! *Ton manteau!*" I remember the word for *coat* because I used it a lot when I was looking for a new winter coat this fall. "*S'il te plaît,*" I say more gently. "You, too, Emeline. *Aussi.* Go! *Vite!*"

It takes fifteen more minutes of cajoling to get them into their coats. By the time they finally have them on, and their scarves and hats and their mittens stuffed into their pockets in case it gets really cold, Charles is crying again and Emeline says she has to go to the bathroom.

"Ugh!" I stomp her into the bathroom. "But you have to wipe *yourself.* I've already wiped one of you today, and that horrid soap you guys have is making my hands all dry and chapped." I hold them up to show her. God, look at them. "*You* wipe. *D'accord*?"

Fifteen *more* minutes later, we roll through the east gate of the Jardin du Luxembourg about five minutes after the puppet show has started. I see a foot of empty space on one of the benches near the front and point to it. "Go! *Allez*!" I command Albert and Emeline. "Go sit down."

I don't mean for my voice to sound so, well, *bellowing*. All the children and some of the parents and nannies sitting on the little benches set up in front of the puppet theater turn around and look at me in horror. I've interrupted the show, and I've talked angrily to a child. It's a scandal, I guess. When everyone turns back around, I make a monster face at them. Charles sees it, too, and starts to cry. *Again*.

"Oh, shush, for Pete's sake," I grumble.

Emeline and Albert *won't* go to the empty spot, so we all stand in the back like idiots where we can't see anything, and to tell you the truth, I'm painfully *not* entertained. But at least, the older ones shut up for a bit. I take Charles out of his stroller and bob him on my hip, the way I see a mom nearby doing. *Her* baby is quiet. Mine should be, too.

"Come on, Charles, be a good boy," I whisper. "All the other babies are being so much better than you right now."

Charles takes some quick breaths. Usually, that means he is about to blow.

"*Non*, Charles, *non*!" I say under my breath. "Make your mama proud. Come on! Just be quiet, okay?"

To the left of me, I hear someone guffawing. I look up at the puppet show, which I can't understand, and it looks totally ridiculous. They think kids today, what with Nintendo DS and Wii and all that, are going to get a kick out of this puppet show? Not even. *I* don't even think it's cool, and

I'm as old as the hills compared to these rug rats!

But the kids are actually enraptured. They sit there, breathless, waiting to see what will happen next in the story. All I've gleaned so far is something about a fox and what looks like it could either be an angel or a sheep. How bizarre. I'm just not familiar with this particular fairy tale, I guess.

It's not someone laughing at the puppet show that I'm hearing. When it happens again, I snap my head to the left and catch a guy openly staring at *me* and cracking up.

I make a face at him. He covers his mouth, caught, but doesn't look away. He seems to think we are a sharing a *joke*. But I don't understand what that joke could *be*. I give him a quick once-over. He's not bad looking, not in any truly offending way, but he's awkwardly dressed in such a manner that only the French can be, as counterintuitive as it might seem.

This fellow laughing at me wears chinos of the variety that my dad might have worn in the early '90s, courting my mom as they played eighteen holes on his expense account somewhere. I can tell they were probably a nice brand a long time ago, but they are pleated in front and too short. He also seems to be fond of American-style sports gear, as he's wearing very un-Parisian sneakers and a hideous blue baseball cap. *Baseball caps.* Ugh. I shudder.

After another ten minutes, just as the nonsensical puppet show seems to be reaching its dramatic climax, the guy moves away from the crowd and motions for me to come talk to him. I shake my head at him, totally irritated. Why is he at this puppet show, anyway? He doesn't have any kids with him. What a perv.

I can still feel him standing there, though, even though I won't look at him. What does he want? And why is he laughing at me? I steal another look at him.

Despite the pants and the hat, the guy is kinda cute. He's not that tall, but not short, either. He looks like he can handle himself, something I definitely like in a guy. I'm not into super-skinny guys, ones that you feel like you could just fold up like a scarf. I like a guy to look strong. This guy has blond hair and blue eyes and wears a baseball cap. It makes me wonder if he's an American, like me. Maybe all he's laughing at is that he can tell I'm American and these kids aren't. I'm intrigued.

I slowly walk over to him, still balancing Charles in my arms.

"*Comment puis-je vous aider?*" I ask him dryly. I know how to say this phrase perfectly because that's what shop girls ask you in Paris after you've been browsing for a while.

"It is funny to see a pretty girl struggle to make her children behave," the guy says to me. He's not American, then—his voice has a heavy French accent, and not a Parisian one, either. He sounds, actually, like all the people we talked to in Toulouse and Montauban. "I'm sorry to laugh, but it is very adorable. You are very adorable. And so are your children."

"You think so?" I say, pleased to be called adorable but immediately losing interest in the guy after I hear that accent. French guys are trouble. They flirt for sport, date for sport, break hearts for sport. I haven't dated one (I would never!), but I just know. I mean, look at me. I'm only wearing jeans, my suede riding boots, and a plaid-print jacket from an old Helmut Lang collection. He's just being fresh, complimenting me. "Well, thanks. I mean, *merci.*"

"*Je vous en pris,*" he says.

I'm charmed, I think. *But I am not fooled.* He's French. Not going to happen. It's a promise I made to myself a long time ago—one that I will never break.

The audience applauds the puppets, and then the puppet master comes out from the little theater and takes a bow. I remember to keep an eye on Emeline and Albert, who've taken up with some other hooligan children running around the crowd while their mothers chat.

"So, do you come here often?" I ask. "I mean, hanging out a puppet show might be a great way to pick up girls, but it doesn't speak well of young guys who make a habit of it."

"Oh, no," the guy says. "You can call me Denny. I was having lunch at Bread and Roses and walked back here to take the métro from Cluny station. When I passed the puppet show, I had to stop. When I was a kid in Périgueux, I used to visit my uncle. He'd drop me off here, and I'd watch the puppet show. It was my favorite part of coming to Paris."

"Bread and Roses?" I ask. We passed the bakery on the way into the park. It's on the same street as the Sanxays' apartment.

"Yes, that's my *new* favorite part of coming to Paris," Denny says. "It's fantastic. Have you been?"

"No," I say. I hate it when someone knows about something really stellar in Paris and I don't have a clue about what it is. I make a mental note to drag Olivia or one of the other girls from school to brunch there the next time I have any money to spend on those types of things.

"Would you like to have lunch with me there sometime? I see that you are not wearing a wedding ring, so I hope you don't mind the assumption that you are single. How about tomorrow? Maybe someone could watch your children?"

"I am . . . *single*," I say, looking at my fingers for some reason, which are indeed bare. Why wouldn't they be? "My children?"

Denny nods at the baby in my arms, then looks beyond me to where Emeline is throwing rocks at the empty puppet theater. "Yes. Perhaps we could go alone, without your kids, so that we could get to know each other?"

"No!" I screech. "I'm only seventeen!"

Denny looks at Albert, who is seven, though small for his age. He looks confused.

"Well, I'm twenty-two," he says slowly. "Is that too big an age difference?"

"Denny!" I say forcefully. "You misunderstand me. These children do not *belong* to me. I mean, for right now they do, but . . ." I notice Albert about to take a big chunk out of another kid's sandwich with his bared front buckteeth. "Albert, *non!*" I yell at him. "Don't eat other kids' food!" He takes a bite anyway. "Goddamnit." Nearly dropping Charles, I run over to Albert and pull him away from the sandwich.

"*Desolée*," I say to the kid's middle-aged mom. She looks appalled—at Albert, at Charles dangling from my arms, at me.

"Are you going to give them up for adoption?" Denny asks me in all seriousness.

"No!" I say. "No!"

"So what do you mean, for right now they belong to you?"

"Just let me talk for one freaking second!" I say. "I am seventeen years old. These are not my children. Isn't that obvious? I'm their babysitter!"

I gesture at Albert and Emeline, who are now standing on either side of me, looking up in wonder at Denny. Charles stares at him, too.

"Ah," Denny says. He laughs impishly, not even embarrassed about his mistake. Typical French. "But you are so good with them. They cleave to you, I think. They always look for you. I was noticing it. They did not want to leave your side for the puppet show. It is very sweet. I thought for certain you must be their mother. Their young, beautiful mother."

They're brats and we all know it.

"Nope, just my charges," I say, ignoring how he called me beautiful. He might flatter my ego, but anyone who thinks I gave birth *three* times before the age of *seventeen* is messed up in the head. This is no ordinary French Romeo—he's got mental problems, too. I've got to get out of here.

Denny's smile sits on his face, steady and satisfied. Distressed, I turn away from him.

I shift uncomfortably as I stand there, just watching the brats run around. I wonder if maybe I overreacted. This Denny character, I realize, was probably joking around. Good God, one more day with these children and I'll have lost my sense of humor altogether. I put on my gloves, wishing I'd never been forced to go to this stupid puppet show in the first place.

Mercifully, my BlackBerry rings inside my camel-colored leather tote bag. I find it deep at the bottom, under extra diapers, a bottle of milk, and a plastic container of cheerios.

"Oh, look!" I say in a chipper way, turning back slightly to him, just enough so that Denny will see Jay's handsome picture pop up on the screen as my BlackBerry keeps ringing in my hand. "It's *Jay*. My very special male friend Jay." I fill my voice with meaning when I say Jay's name. "I better go. Nice to meet you."

I turn away from the skeever and start walking the kids toward the jungle gym as I answer the phone. "Hey, Jay, what's going on?"

"Alex, where are you?"

"The Jardin du Luxembourg, wanting to kill myself." The words slip out before I can stop them, and in the silence that follows my insensitive blunder, I really *do* want to die. I can't believe I just said that.

"Oh, Jay, wow, I'm sorry—I didn't mean to say that—"

"Alex, how fast can you get to your house? I'm right near where you live in Cambronne," Jay interrupts me.

"Really? Why?" Jay doesn't have any reason to be in Cambronne, unless he's been hanging out with Zack or something. Zack's pretty much the only other kid in our program who lives in the Fifteenth besides me. And I don't think Zack's spoken to Jay since he left our hotel suite in Cannes in a huff over Christmas break.

"I'll explain. Just come home, okay? We'll meet you at your house," Jay says. "It's urgent. Please hurry!"

Jay hangs up. I stare at my phone. Who is *we*?

"Come on, kids," I say, putting Charles back in the stroller and trying to herd the other two with my arms. "We gotta go back to *chez vous*. No more of *le parc*, okay?"

The kids protest the whole way home, but I get them back into the building and up the stairs without letting too much time go by. When we get inside, I am very relieved to see that Mme Sanxay is back already, reading a copy of that cheesy magazine *Femme Actuelle* on the couch with her shoes off.

"Oh, *c'est bien*! You're here," I say to her as I rush inside, pushing the stroller and the kids in her direction. "I've got to go. I'm needed somewhere really important!" I fling the door closed behind me and run all the way back to my own homestay in Cambronne. As I quickly climb the stairs up to my apartment, I text Jay to say that I'm back.

U CAN COME OVER NOW!!!!

OK ON OUR WAY, my phone spits back at me only two seconds later.

What is with this *our*? What is going on around here?

I hang up my coat and grunt a greeting at my host mother, who is drinking a glass of red wine and watching the evening news.

Not two minutes after I get Jay's text does the intercom in the living room buzz. "That's for me!" I exclaim, rushing to the door. "I'm having a friend or two over, okay?"

"Okay, Alex," Marîthe says. "I will go get some juice for you guys? Crackers?"

I want her to go into the kitchen so that I can sneak Jay into my room and talk in private. "Sure, sure," I say and fling the door open at the sound of footsteps in the hallway.

Jay bursts in and behind him, dressed in all black sweats that are too big for her, but looking as beautiful as a model in any of the Fashion Week shows at the Carrousel du Louvre, is, I can barely believe it . . .

Miss Penelope.

Jane.

Fletcher.

Risen from the grave.

"*The backpack*," I whisper, my voice catching in my throat. For one wild second, I wonder if I'm going to cry. "I knew that wasn't your backpack," I finally say.

PJ trembles. "No, it wasn't," she whispers back. "My backpack is still at the Marquets. I wonder if I will ever see it again . . . it belonged to my dad."

Jay pounds a finger against his lips and makes his eyes as round as plates to show he's serious. "Alex, let's go in your room." Jay hustles us both down the hall and into my room before Marîthe can come back out into the living room. "Are your host parents home?"

"Yes," I say, still staring at PJ as she gingerly takes a seat on my unmade bed. Her blonde hair is glowing like an angel's halo. "Is this a secret? They're right down the hall! Oh my God!"

"Okay, we need you to promise you won't tell them PJ is here."

"PJ is here?" I repeat, not really quite sure what's happening anymore. "Am I in a dream right now?"

PJ gives me a pained smile. "Hi, Alex. Long time no see."

I can't make my mouth produce any words. I open it, then close it. Then I open it again. I have to hang on to my open closet door to keep from falling over.

"This is so weird," I finally say. "Jay? What's going on?"

Jay sits down next to PJ, and at once, I thump right back into reality and feel coldly jealous of his protective hand on her knee. "PJ came back to Paris," he says.

I shake my head, try to get it together. "I can . . . see that." Suddenly, my manners turn back on, a minute later than my powers of reason or deduction, and I'm flooded with relief and a good deal of *true* happiness, too.

I rush over to PJ and hug her tightly, noticing, as before, her scarily thin body and the silkiness of her hair. "Oh, God, what happened? Are you all right?"

I'm so close to PJ that I can hear how hard it is for her to swallow and get the words out. "I'm okay, Alex," she says.

I stand back up, let her go.

"Alex, no one besides me knows that PJ is back," Jay tells me, looking me straight in the eye. "And now you."

"How long have you been back?" I ask. "Where have you been staying?"

"She's been staying with me since Saturday night," Jay says, not letting PJ answer. "I've been taking care of her."

"Do your host parents know?"

"No," Jay says. "You can't tell anyone this, either, but my host parents and my host siblings all went back to Casablanca for a while. My host dad's father is sick. They thought he was gonna die, so they had to go to Morocco. But it's kind of good because when PJ came back, no one was at the apartment with me."

"So you're staying there? In Jay's apartment?" I ask PJ. The elation I was feeling that PJ is alive subsides as I imagine them shacking up in their own little love nest on the edge of Paris.

"Yeah," PJ says, clearing her throat. "I was, um, staying in Jay's host sister's room."

I feel a *tiny* bit better, but not much.

"But my host parents are getting back tomorrow, and I can't take PJ back to the apartment once they get home."

I nod.

"We came here because we need your help," Jay tells me.

PJ looks away. I wonder if PJ wanted to come here at all. She looks acutely uncomfortable, picking unconsciously at the purple fabric of my comforter with her fingernail.

As much as I've accepted that I can never have Jay, I can't say it doesn't burn to watch Jay overflow with love and desire for PJ, right here in my own bedroom. At the same time, when I look at PJ, and remember how long and far we traveled to find her, and then came home to find out she was dead, it feels like falling off a building all over again.

"It was awful," I tell her suddenly. "I have dreams about you all the time. We all do. Where have you been?" I feel, somewhere deep in my chest, a powerful anger like a change in tide.

Yes, I scoffed at PJ for running away. But when I thought she'd jumped in a frozen river, I woke up screaming with night terrors for a week. Marîthe came in and rocked me back to sleep, without ever saying a word to me about it in daylight. I still don't look down at the water when I cross one of the bridges over the Seine. I didn't know if I would ever be able to stomach it again. Our whole program has been in agony, worried about her, wondering when they'll find her dead body. If she hadn't just come back to life, I'd want to kill her for the pain she's caused.

"I've been . . . dealing with some stuff," PJ answers me.

"Some stuff with your sister?" I ask her, not pulling my gaze from her big blue eyes.

"How do you know about my sister?"

"Everyone knows, PJ," I say. "Haven't you seen any of the newspapers? The cops found two backpacks, a double suicide note, and a marked up copy of *Madame Bovary* with the name Annabel Fletcher in it. All of Paris thinks you're dead. There's a troupe of reporters who come to the Lycée every day. How could you not know that? You're all anyone talks about."

"Really?" PJ chokes. She turns to Jay and grasps his hand. "Is that true?"

Jay nods.

"You haven't seen any of the press about you, PJ?" I ask her. "They've been asking us about you, your sister Annabel, your parents. . . . "

Jay gives me a warning look. I decide not to go any farther though I'm dying to know what's going on. The French papers say PJ is the daughter of drug dealers who ran a route from Canada to New York! With all the trouble I've been in lately, I can't afford to get involved with them in something shady.

"Listen, PJ," I say, shaking and standing back up. I put my hand on the doorknob, about to tell them both to leave. "I'm super-glad you aren't dead, but truly, if you're up to something, you guys gotta go. I'm in major trouble for a bunch of other stuff, and I can't risk going out on any more limbs." I accidentally glance at Jay when I say this. The limbs I've gone out on most recently have been for him, not PJ exactly.

Jay looks at PJ, then back at me. I notice he's clean-shaven, for the first time in a while. He must be so happy she came back; and she came back to *him*. My heart hurts at how good that must have felt for him. "There's no trouble, Alex," Jay finally says. "PJ just needs a safe place to stay for a little while. Somewhere no one else knows about."

I sit back down on the hardwood floor of my bedroom, crossing my legs and leaning back against the wall, thinking very, very hard for a minute.

"Please, Alex," Jay whispers. I can't resist that deep timber in his voice.

"I do know a guy who owns these model apartments—this hotshot club owner. He used to trade real estate around. My mom lived in one of his apartments for, like, nothing when she worked with all those models back in the day. I bet he'd buy that *you're* a model."

PJ and Jay wait for me to go on.

"We'll say you are a friend of Livvy's—some ballerina girl who's out of work," I instruct PJ. "Trying to make it as a model. That's perfect. Very Parisian."

"Okay," PJ says. "I can do that."

"But PJ, I need something, too." I say, thinking of that harrowing conversation with my mom from the other day. She hasn't called since. I know she's furious with me.

"What?"

"I have this problem," I say, an idea beginning to form. "My mom thinks I stole a bunch of money from this woman we know."

"What? Alex, really?" Jay asks. He scrunches that perfectly smooth, olive forehead of his, immediately worried. "Did you?"

"Of course, I didn't!" I say, twirling a strand of my black hair around my finger, not sure for a second how to frame my answer. "I just borrowed it. And I can't pay it back yet."

"Oh," PJ says. She looks down at the floor, a curtain of hair falling over her face. "Well, Alex, I don't have any money. Far from it."

"Don't worry, PJ, we'll figure something out," Jay cuts in.

"I don't want your money," I say. "What I want is to make a deal. I need to convince my mom that I stole it *for* you. You have to let me lie and say that you asked me for it, so that you could run away, and I helped you because you are my friend. And if anyone finds you, if you two get caught with this whole hiding in Paris scheme, you have to say that's what happened, no matter *what*. I took the money from this woman, and I gave it to you because you're my friend and I care about you. Got it?"

"That's it?" PJ seems befuddled. "That's nothing. That's totally fine."

"It might not seem like a big deal to you, Penelope Jane, but let me assure you. To my mother, Caroline Anne Braun, this is a *very* big deal."

"Well, then, of course. If you'll find me a place to hide, you can say whatever you want about me and the things I might have done last semester. None of that matters to me now."

Jay bites his lip. "PJ, are you sure?"

I snort and roll my eyes. "She's homeless! Of course, she's sure. Jay, I'll bring you that guy's number tomorrow to give to PJ. Now, both of you, *get out of here* before Marîthe bursts in with juice and cookies!"

That night, I stay up late in the blue light of my laptop screen, crafting an elaborate e-mail tale to my mom, explaining the real reason I couldn't tell her what I did with Mme Sanxay's money.

That beautiful friend with the lovely name, I remind her. She needed money, and I've been too ashamed to tell anyone because it's all my fault she was able to run away.

"Ah, PJ, you wily thing," I say aloud to myself. "We sure do make great things happen together." It sounds crass, even to me, alone in my room. "I'm so glad you're back," I whisper, and I genuinely mean it. Those photos in the newspapers were terrifying.

By this time tomorrow, my mother will have forgiven me. Alex Nguyen, au pair, will be history, and Alex Nguyen, life of the party, will be back in residence. And PJ, safe but just as disturbed as ever, has once again offered me the perfect excuse to get what I want. Looks like everything is getting back to normal around here.

7. OLIVIA

The Old Me

---

burrow under Thomas's covers Tuesday afternoon after school, not quite ready to leave for Underground rehearsal yet. I had a quick break between my last class at the Lycée and our evening rehearsal, so I came over to Thomas's dorm near the Sorbonne for a couple hours. It's almost dark outside, and Thomas has lit a candle. It feels like we are in our own little cave, shadows in the flickering gold light.

His hands are in my hair, down the back of my neck, tickling my spine all the way to its base.

"I miss your long hair," Thomas breathes. It's startling to see the bright glint of his green eyes without his glasses on against his milk-colored skin. It's one of the many things I notice when I am with him like this. "It used to hang in my face. I loved that."

I keep kissing him, even though my eyebrows are bunched together in confusion. In between kisses I ask him, "You don't like my new haircut?" I realize that Thomas has not really complimented me on the new hairstyle since I got it a couple weeks ago. We've been together a couple times since then, and besides the first surprised reaction, he hasn't said that he likes it at all.

"It is different," he says, massaging my scalp. "You do not look like yourself anymore."

I finally stop kissing him and raise my head off his chest. Cocking my head to one side, I say, "You really know how to flatter a girl, Thomas."

"What is flatter?" Thomas asks me. He doesn't know all the words I use in English.

"Make me feel good. That's what flattering means," I tell him. "That wasn't very nice."

Thomas bites his lip as if he knows he's made a mistake, but I detect impatience, too. "I'm sorry, Olivia."

It's sweet that he's so quick to apologize. You can tell he means it, too, the way his eyes immediately get crinkly at the corners, worrying that he's hurt my feelings. I melt immediately.

"It's too cold out there," I complain, tossing off the misunderstanding. "I like it better in here. I don't want to leave you." My lips go to his before I even finish my sentence.

Thomas pats his chest, and I lay it back down, loving the way my bare ears feel against his bare skin. "You should go later," he says. "Or do not go to dancing rehearsal at all."

I giggle. "Naughty! Putting those kind of ideas into my head. I could never!"

I can feel Thomas smile. "I know you would not miss it."

I raise my face to his and look at him with what I hope are bedroom eyes, trying to appear sultry. "You could *try* to talk me out of going," I say, wriggling my arms into the space between the back of Thomas's neck and his pillow.

"Well, I do need to study tonight," Thomas tells me. "Even if you did miss the rehearsal, I don't think I could be hanging out."

"Oh, really?" I tease him. "You'd actually rather study than lie around with me?"

"Yes, Olivia, I really need to study!" he says, not getting that I'm teasing at all. That happens sometimes with Thomas, too. I can't tell if it is a cultural thing, or if Thomas really doesn't like to be joked around with. Right now, his lips are lined with a deep frown, as if he really feels misunderstood. Thomas closes his eyes and his long, almost girlish lashes, as if he is totally fed up.

Right away I hold him a little tighter, trying to will away this freaky vibe between us. "I'm sorry, I know you have to study. It's just that we haven't hung out that much lately . . . and I've missed you."

Thomas is a medical student at the Sorbonne, which is a very distinguished place for any student to be. They call it the Harvard of France. He has to study all the time to keep on top of his schoolwork. However, I sense that a lot of Thomas's struggle stems from the fact that he is a medical student and he doesn't want to be. At all. He doesn't have any passion for it. The things he is interested in—philosophy, literature, poetry, art—do not play any part in his coursework. Over Christmas break, I found out that Thomas is studying medicine because his dad was a doctor and because Thomas believes that is what his mother wants most for him to accomplish.

"Well, this term is an important one," he says. "I don't want to fall behind."

"More important than *me*?" I ask, feeling that slip of a whine come out and regretting it. Ever since those few calls that Thomas never returned to me once he went back to school this semester, my time with him has been like doing a triple pirouette without having a good spot—I feel dizzy and out of control. I snort a forced laugh, to try to pretend like I am just joking again.

"Olivia," Thomas sighs. "Don't do these things."

My toes feel prickled with cold suddenly, poking out of the blanket. Thomas's body next to me doesn't feel inviting and warm anymore. I feel that same discomfort you have in the middle of the night when your covers aren't warm enough but you don't want to get up to put a sweatshirt on.

"What things?" I ask, back to where I was a few minutes ago—very, very peeved.

"These demands on me. It is getting very difficult to try to balance school and you," Thomas says.

"*Balance* me?" I cry, not even trying to hold it in anymore. He jolts upright at the unexpected indignation in my tone and twitches uncomfortably, as if he wants to shake me off of him. "Sorry I'm just another thing you have to *take care of*!" I feel close to tears, moving as far away from him as I can without showing any extra skin. "You know what?" I say. "I'm just going to go to rehearsal, okay?" I reach for my plaid oversize blouse and slip it on over my dance bra and leggings.

"You are unreasonable," Thomas says, and that slight bluntness that comes from not speaking the same language just *stings*.

"Whatever," I say. "Do you just want to text me when you've caught up on your work and all those other things you have to *balance*?" I wait for Thomas to answer with more than a shrug.

"I will text," Thomas finally says, but it's not convincing. He kisses me before I leave his dorm. For the first time, I notice how rough and chapped his lips are.

I make my way very slowly to rehearsal, my eyes cast downward. I don't want the other strangers on the street to see me crying. I must look like a total weirdo, shuffling through the Fifth Arrondissement weeping.

The thought of losing Thomas is so terrifying, not just because I love him, but because he's the only one in Paris that feels *good* to be with right now. Well, it feels good when I am not having a spaz attack. In my calmer, less ragey moments, he feels like the only place I have to land these days. And if I lose that, I'll be like one of those fishing boats in the Seine that has come unmoored from the docks in the middle of the night—just floating, with no purpose and no one to pull me back in.

André kisses me hello at the rehearsal space and helps me really pull out my splits by pushing down on my back while I stretch. "Damn, girl, you are tense today," he says. "You better loosen up or you're going to injure yourself."

I nod, knowing it's a real possibility that I should be careful about, but I also feel scolded. I just keep doing everything wrong. I stand back up and take a few deep breaths before again lowering myself into the splits. This time, my body melds with the floor a little easier.

Our choreographer, Henri, says he wants to work on a sequence that was inspired by watching World War II footage of soldier parades. He puts on heavy, hard rock music to listen to for a few minutes so that we'll get what the mood of the piece will be. During the crescendo, André whoops and jumps around, really feeling it. This is *totally* his kind of dancing. Henri cuts the music and starts arranging us dancers.

Setting the corps of the sixteen Underground members in a square formation, each of us facing the mirror, we go through sharp, robotic movements that channel old-fashioned military pomp. Like an army, we go through the dance over and over again, until we want to collapse. Only when we are practically broken from such forceful arm choreography and heavy impact jumps, all in perfect unison, does Henri show us a more languid section of the piece he wants us to emote as "the combat scene."

"*Il faut se battre ou vous allez mourir!*" Henri screams over the music, making us work through the heavy fatigue. *You have to fight or you will die!*

The whole rehearsal is so intense that when Henri finally lets us quit, I feel like I really have gone to battle.

"That was better than sex," André says, clapping an arm around my sweaty shoulders. "Don't you think?"

I smile weakly, too tired to blush. Whatever it was, it definitely took my mind off my real life for a while, and right now that's better than anything.

As the Underground dancers put their warm-ups back on and start to file of out the massive warehouse-cum-rehearsal space, Thomas texts me he wants to meet in the morning before school.

Y SO EARLY? I text back. Y NOT AFTER SCHOOL?

I HAVE CLASS, Thomas replies. AND I DON'T WANT TO WAIT TILL TOMORROW NIGHT.

OK, I say, raising my eyebrows. WHERE?

PONT DES ARTS, Thomas texts. C U THEN.

XOXOXOX, I text back, but I don't get a response.

I'm flooded with relief. Why was I being so crazy earlier? Thomas and I are *fine*.

★ ★ ★

The Pont des Arts is a wooden pedestrian bridge over the Seine, connecting the Left Bank and the Right Bank right in front of the Louvre. I take an early morning métro ride from Charles de Gaulle-Étoile to Louvre-Rivoli and pop out of the stairs into the bright sunshine over one of Paris's most chic streets. Even though I was up late studying French verb conjugations (as usual), I feel wide awake and excited to see Thomas again so soon.

Crossing the Quai du Louvre and jumping up the stairs of the wooden bridge, I can see Thomas across the river, just a small miniature of himself, climbing up the stairs on his side of the bridge. He has his worn-out corduroy pants on and a heavy army-green wool coat, bracing him against the cold. His sweet curly hair is all disheveled, from the wind off the Seine or from being up so early I am not sure. I giggle, wondering if he has even looked in a mirror yet this morning. He is such a space cadet sometimes.

Thomas sees me and waves. It's not an excited wave but a tired one. He doesn't even smile at me. A flash of annoyance spikes inside my chest. *It was his idea to meet so early,* I think. *Why did he arrange this if he was just going to act like it was such a chore?*

I fix a wide, friendly grin on him as he walks toward me. When he meets me halfway across the bridge, he points at an empty bench, and we sit on it. There's not too many people around right now, but there are a few—some who look like they've been up all night drinking espressos in the cafés near the Sorbonne, other, older folks on an early morning jog before work. There are also birds perched everywhere, on the little cases displaying local artwork set up by the city, on the railings and the light fixtures, and even pecking at the leftover wine bottles left by long-gone revelers from last night. The Pont des Arts, I've heard, is a meeting spot for bohemian party types, people who just want to sit and spend the whole night drinking and talking about art and life. People, in fact, a lot like Thomas and his friends.

I lean in and kiss Thomas on the cheek, not so much because I want to, but because I *want to* want to. I want things to go back to normal between him and me. Why has everything taken on this sour tone?

"How come you wanted to meet so early in the morning?" I ask him. "You look tired today."

Thomas nods. "I couldn't wait to tell you—that I want to break up."

I'm looking out at the morning rush-hour cars speeding west along the Quai de Conti, and I feel like I haven't heard him right. "What's that?"

"I don't want to go out with you anymore," Thomas says, his voice and his eyes flat and gray. His glasses fog up a little bit, and I wonder if he is going to cry. I ponder what he said in a state of mild shock—like I know what's going on and I know that I am sad about it, but the whole situation is so *completely* unexpected that I can't help but also gawk at it, in a way, too.

"When I met you, you were different, Olivia," Thomas says. "So sweet and caring and always smiling. Now . . . now you are so sad sometimes."

"Thomas," I say. "My friend *is missing*. She might be *dead*. I'm sad about it."

"It's not that," Thomas says. He shakes his head, as though he expected that I wouldn't understand right away. "It is like you do not like who you were. You have tension. Moods. You change the hair, you change the clothes. You used to wear color, flowers on your shirt. Now it is dark clothes, all the times."

I look down. I have my coat on, under which I'm wearing a Lycra dance top layered with a ballet sweater. Since I wasn't going straight to school, I put on some loose twill pants instead of just sweats. I know I haven't been as girlie, as tidy, as I was last semester, but that's because my old clothes don't really go with my new haircut. I used to get up every morning and put on, at the very least, clean jeans and a bright fitted T-shirt, often accessorizing it with jewelry, like the "O" necklace from Tiffany's that my mom gave me. But lately, I've been dressing more like the other dancers in the Underground: dark colors, not so much attention to wrinkles, or even matching. I've been trying not to try. It would be really hard to mentally prepare for such crazy, avant-garde choreography of the kind we had last night in rehearsal if I was in my old Cali-girl mindset. It just wouldn't work.

"Well," I say, not sure how best to defend myself. I mean, Thomas barely combs his hair. And now he wants to know why I look so unkempt? "I'm really busy. I go to rehearsal right after school almost every single day. It's not that fun to be running home constantly to change my clothes."

"And you wear makeup now, too," Thomas says. He gestures at my face with his mitten. It's a sharp contrast to the way he would normally lift his hand to touch me, to brush my hair out of my eyes. "Every day you wear this."

My hand immediately goes to my cheeks. "Makeup?" He's right, I have been applying makeup every morning. I usually take it off before rehearsal, so that it won't run all over the place while I sweat along to our intense routines, but during the day I like to wear eyeliner. It started in the days after I found out PJ had died. I couldn't sleep, and when I looked in the mirror, I would wince at how sallow I appeared, my eyes hidden behind puffy lids. Wearing eyeliner seemed to awaken my face.

"So dark, dark all the time," Thomas says. "I fell in love with a girl who was light, light as air. . . ."

I flinch, not sure if it is because I am offended or because this is such an inaccurate description of who I know myself to be.

I think back to our first moments together. Me hobbling down the street on crutches while he tried to carry my books for me. Twirling in tights and pointed shoes in front of him without realizing it because Mme Rouille had sent him to pick me up from dance class without me realizing it. Then I had blonde hair. I was always trying to make everyone feel better. Always trying to *be* better—a better dancer, a better student, a better guest in the Rouilles' house.

"I'm just more comfortable now," I say. "I'm actually . . . I think I've learned a lot so far this year. I think I'm starting to really find myself."

"Really?" Thomas says. "That's not what I think."

"Thomas, *qu'est-ce que tu dis*?" I ask him, aware that I could cry if he pushed me too hard but desperate not to after this barrage of insults.

"I think you just don't know who you are anymore. You are piss— *pissed*. Shifting, always. You have a new look, new friends, maybe a new boyfriend on the horizons—"

"A new boyfriend?" I ask, almost laughing in shock. "Thomas, what on earth are you talking about?"

"This guy, this ballet guy, André," Thomas spits out. For the first time,

I see how much actual anger he's been containing until now. "He takes you to get your hair done, to concerts at Bercy. He always wants to spend time with you. And you are always saying that we do not have enough time for each other! Maybe if you weren't always with André, we could be together more."

My mouth hangs open. "*André?*"

"*Oui*, André," Thomas says. He must know he's being really absurd because he won't look me in the eye.

"André is *gay*, Thomas," I say, cracking up for real. I can't help it; I wheeze with laughter for a few minutes. It's outrageously inappropriate, but this is the strangest turn yet in an already absolutely wacky conversation. André would be hysterical if he knew that Thomas was jealous of him. And jealous over how he took me to see Marni in a back room hair salon behind a musty vintage shop in the Third of all things! "André wants to hook up with *Zack*, Thomas. Not me!"

My laughter makes Thomas even more perturbed. "You think I am funny, but I am very serious, Olivia! You have changed. I am through with this. Too many up and down, up and down. With you, there is so much . . . drama."

Drama, used in this sense, is a word I know Thomas must have picked up from me. And hearing him say this particular American colloquialism is both very humorous and very heartrending because I know where it came from and I know that it is true. With me, there *has* been a lot of drama. I had a boyfriend, and then I didn't. I was going back to California, and then I wasn't. Then my friend was missing. Then she was dead.

But what about you? I would say if I were brave enough to. For a moment, I make silent accusations at Thomas that I know I could never voice aloud. Together we watch a homeless man tuck himself into a sleeping bag in a sunny spot near us on the bridge. Before he falls asleep, next to his pallet, he sets out a paper cup and a little cardboard sign asking for change. *What about you and your family secrets that reared their ugly head over Christmas break?* I want to shout into his cowardly, pale face. *What about all* that *drama?*

But I already know the difference between my drama and his drama. He can't help what rivalries his parents may have had with the Marquets in the past. But my drama is right here, right now. In other words, I could help it. But I don't want to. And that's just too hard for him to deal with.

"I'm gonna go now, okay?" I say to Thomas, finally facing him again. I squint at him in the sunlight, which haloes around his curls. I didn't think it was going to be a bright day; I didn't bring my sunglasses with me. I wish I had. It's easier than I would have guessed to keep my voice even, to keep myself from crying. For a minute there, I thought I might break down, but now I know that I won't. Just like with PJ, the tears don't come to the surface. "I get it. I'm not angry, but I want to leave now. See you . . . another time, I guess."

That's a lie. I am angry, somewhere deep in me that I can't get to right now. Angry and disappointed and strangely embarrassed. My body, everything, feels like it is on display, almost like the art in these glass cases all along this bridge.

"Olivia." Thomas takes my hand. "I still love you . . . I just don't think I want this anymore. It does not work."

I drop his hand and walk away, evenly and slowly, back over the Pont des Arts toward the Louvre.

I wonder how *this* will work. The breakup, I mean. In my slightly numbed, carefully held together state, I think about the logistics of this, which helps me to keep myself from thinking about . . . the hard stuff. Like being alone. In Paris. The beautiful royal city where everything has gone so royally wrong.

From now on the Seine will have to be like a border between our two warring kingdoms. He has to stay on the Left Bank, and I will stay on the Right. Of course, that will never work, not with my rehearsals at the Place d'Italie and his mother living in the Seventeeth. But for this morning, at least, I'm going to pretend that the farther I walk away from the Seine, the safer I am from the pain of having to let him go.

Before I cross the Quai du Louvre, I turn around and lean against the stone embankment lining the Seine. Thomas isn't sitting on the bench anymore. He's gone. The Seine looks healthy, gleaming, its waters placid, and all of Paris springing to life along its banks.

Thomas is right, I think, touching the bare back of my neck, where all my bleached blonde hair used to be. *If someone took a picture of me and showed it to me, would I even recognize myself?*

I can't bring myself to go back down into the métro and go to school just yet. I wonder if I should call someone, confide in someone that Thomas has just dumped me. For some reason, telling Zack or Alex feels desolate. Both of them would just cluck their tongues and busy themselves getting all the gruesome details out of me.

Alex once said to me, even though Vince and I were fully broken up by that time, "How is it that I have zero boyfriends, and you have two gorgeous ones?" It made me not want to confide seriously in Alex about either of them, ever. Somehow I know she won't understand how a boyfriend—even one who loves you—can be the very person who disappoints you the most.

I walk around the massive Louvre museum complex and down the covered sidewalk that lines the rue de Rivoli. The tourist shops, selling I LOVE PARIS bumper stickers and shot glasses with "La Tour Eiffel" on them, are just starting to open for business.

In the Jardin des Tuileries, I sit and watch tourists start to come in and make the rounds of the royal gardens as part of their visit to all the main spots of Paris. The gardens are not, in my opinion, that exciting. The ground consists of mostly brown, gravelly dirt paths, with an old creepy stone statue here and there. I can't bring myself to leave, however, and walk back up toward school as I should.

It's after ten when I'm still sitting there, on the exact same green bench, staring at the exact same fountain, listening to the exact same snippets of conversation from all the people passing me. Even though I can't understand Japanese or Italian or Spanish all that well, I know they are remarking how beautiful it is here, because they use a tone of voice identical to the one my mom used when she joyfully walked through the Tuileries during her visit to Paris. Over and over, she exclaimed at every royally placed stone.

My phone rings, and I look at it as if at a foreign object, taking a long moment to decide if I want to answer it. If it is Thomas, I'm too raw, too unsure of how I really feel, to talk to him. If it is someone else, I don't want to have to explain that I'm sitting in the cold Jardin des Tuileries, doing nothing. But it could be Mme Rouille, having found out I'm cutting school, in which case I would need to answer it and tell her I am ill and on my way home.

It's Jay.

"Am I in trouble?" I ask without saying hello.

"What? Olivia? No," Jay answers. "I mean, I don't know . . . wait, what are you talking about?"

"Are you at school?" I ask.

"I'm late. I haven't gotten there yet," Jay says, missing a beat. "So, *you're* not at school right now?"

"No," I say. "I mean, I guess I'm late, too. I don't know. I'm having a weird morning. Where are you? What's up?"

"Listen, I'm on my way to school. Sorry to bug you, but I need to know where it is that you got your haircut. Was it in Ternes?"

"My haircut? No, not in Ternes. I went to this girl Marni near Arts et Métiers, on the rue Beaubourg. She works out of the back of this totally random goth store—they sell crystals or something. Why, you're getting a haircut?" I'm confused.

"That's perfect! All right, cool. Crystal shop. Okay, thanks, Livvy, see you at school," Jay says and hangs up.

I close my phone and look at it again. How totally weird.

The conversation with Jay jerks me back to the reality of my day. I decide to blow off the rest of school—even though I just did that a few weeks ago with André—and go see if Jay went to that salon. If nothing else, I can say hi to Marni and thank her for my haircut and the whole new me she created . . . even if it did, strangely, seem to cost me my relationship with Thomas.

I am a whole new me. A whole new me without Thomas.

★ ★ ★

"PJ?" I shriek, nearly knocking a display of crystals over. Some swing wildly from their hooks, sending rainbow splashes of light onto the walls of Marni's little shop.

There she is, sitting in the same chair I sat in just a week or two ago. Like a mannequin, she looks frozen and frightened, her bright blue eyes staring into the mirror back at herself, then at me. Her pale, full lips are parted slightly, as if she's about to suck all the air she can into her lungs, and then let out a bloodcurdling scream.

Marni turns to me and purses her brightly painted mouth. "Olivia, is this your friend?"

"Yes," I breathe, almost afraid to reach out and touch her. "She is." I venture a small movement forward, fingering the fabric of the sweatshirt she's wearing. It has a big purple V on it . . . I've seen it somewhere recently. "PJ, talk to me," I say, shaking my head and trying to focus. "What happened? How did you get here? Where have you been?"

"Tell her not to do it, Livvy," PJ whispers, her eyes an ocean of dismay. I have a hard time pulling away from her—I've been so convinced that she was gone forever. I want to keep touching her cold hands, the fabric of the sweatshirt she's wearing. I don't want her to disappear again. "Tell her I can't do it. He wants me to, but I can't."

"Can't do what, PJ?" I ask, talking to her like I would talk to Brian—not too condescendingly, but softly, carefully. I look down at her stone-stiff legs, clad in dirty jeans and absolutely still. PJ's always been a little bohemian, but I've never seen her in such soiled clothes. "Who are you talking about? Is Jay here, too?" I arch my neck and look around, but Jay's nowhere to be found.

Marni holds a sharp pair of gleaming silver scissors in one hand and points them at PJ's swath of white-blonde hair. "She came in wanting me to give her a *transformation* like yours. She gave me the money already. But now—she won't do it." Marni's red lips curl with bemused annoyance. "She won't let me near her."

"Livvy, your hair looks really nice," PJ says in a meek voice. There are tears running down her cheeks. "But it's too much. Too different. Jay said I should do it, but I can't."

I look from PJ to Marni and back to PJ. This has got to be the most surreal day I've ever had in my life.

"Marni," I say in my most deferential, stickily polite French. "*Mon amie* is upset. She needs to think some more about such an extreme change. Can we reschedule this appointment?"

Marni sighs. "*D'accord.*" She hands PJ a roll of bills. PJ quickly stuffs them into the pocket of those dirty jeans. "What a waste of time," I hear Marni say under her breath in French as she walks away.

"Come on, PJ, let's get out of here," I say, pulling PJ out of the chair by her icy hand. Back on the street outside the shop, she registers the crowds, the bright sunshine, and whirls around like she wants to go back inside.

I hold her still. "PJ, what? What is it?"

"Livvy, you can't tell anyone that you saw me, okay?" she tells me. "No one!"

I lead her away from Marni's shop window, still confused.

"Okay," I say. "I won't."

"I mean it, Livvy." She looks even more terrified than she did of Marni's sharp scissors.

"I promise."

PJ takes a deep breath and nods. She can't stop touching her hair, as if it's her security blanket. I hug her. "I'm glad you didn't cut it."

"It feels like it's the last thing I have," PJ says quietly. "The only remnant of who I am. I've given up so much already."

"Don't worry, PJ," I say, still confused, and lead my friend away from the rapidly filling pedestrian zone. It's like leading a very tall, beautiful child through the bustling streets of the Second Arrondissement, and as I lead her, I can't help but feel grateful not only for her return, but for the relief that comes with not having to be alone with what happened on the Pont des Arts this morning.

That hard irritation, that dissatisfaction, I'd been feeling for the last few weeks is melting away as I register how glorious it is that PJ is back in Paris, safe in my care.

I think that selfish, horrible thought again and again as we walk down the street, searching for a place to get PJ a coffee and relax. *Now I won't have to be alone anymore.*

8. ZACK

Ain't That the Way It Always Is

"It's called Nouveau. It's right beneath that pub on rue Oberkampf that always has a million people loafing around outside?" André waits for me to give a sign of recognition from the other end of the line. It's about nine o'clock on a Saturday night. I peek out my window at a heavy rain pounding down on the street where my host family lives in the eastern part of the Fifteenth Arrondissement. It won't be long before the little park near our building floods completely.

"I think I might know it," I lie, thinking I will just Google Map it on my laptop before I go out. I've never even been to Oberkampf, a trendy, slightly hard-edged neighborhood on the opposite side of Paris from my homestay. "But yeah, it sounds fantastic. What time?"

"Let's see . . . midnight sound all right?"

"Sure," I say, gulping. "Olivia's coming to the club, too, right?" I'm nervous to be out so late, just André and me.

"Yeah, just got off the phone with her." André laughs. "I promised her she wouldn't be the third wheel. We've got to include her this time." André chuckles. "Well, include her in *some* things. Conversation, jokes, and whatnot."

In the privacy of my room, I swallow a huge, happy laugh. My face flames up with excitement.

"See you at Nouveau," I say, and press END on my cell phone. Then I go tell my host parents, Jacques and Romy, that I'm spending the night at Jay's house in Montreuil. Romy smiles blithely.

"Have a good time," she says. "*Prends ton imperméable.*"

"Bonne nuit!" I can't keep the glee out of my voice as I leave, with my raincoat in hand, for Ternes to collect Olivia for a pre-André drink with me.

★ ★ ★

Nouveau is at the edge of the Eleventh—a long métro ride from Ternes. On the métro next to Olivia, I twiddle my foot excitedly. "Do you think we are going to get there too early?" I ask. "It's still only eleven."

"Well, I did bring *this*." She reaches into her bag and pulls out an aluminum Sigg bottle—the kind backpackers take on long hikes. It has a sticker silhouette of a ballet dancer on one side. When she unscrews the cap, I can smell she's put vodka in it. "You want some?"

"Oh, no, *you didn't* read my mind from all the way across the Seine," I say with appreciation and take the bottle from her. This is so unlike Olivia, not to mention a remarkable improvement. "I'd love a nip or two! Excellent thinking." I swig *several* nips worth and quickly put the cap back on before anyone notices the fumes.

"Not so fast," Olivia giggles and takes a swig herself. "Oh, that's gnarly," she says. She bobs up and down in her seat as our bodies soak up the liquor. "Can't wait to *dance* tonight!"

My hip starts vibrating, and I check my text messages. "Look!" I say to Olivia. "That guy I met in Amsterdam."

Olivia reads the text over my shoulder. It's from Bobby. CAN'T WAIT 2 C PARIS W U, ZACK.

For a second, I feel a pang of doubt; Bobby probably wouldn't be texting with so much excitement if he knew I was on my way to a club to meet another guy. But any feeling of guilt quickly turns into giddiness.

"Is that guy coming to visit?" Olivia asks. She looks a little scandalized. "But what about? . . ."

I nod casually, letting her question die, and then I change the subject. "Yup. So when's your next Underground performance?"

Olivia raises her eyebrows, but she's far too polite to remind me that I'm getting text messages from one guy when I am *practically* about to start dating another.

Who would have thought? I think proudly.

★ ★ ★

Nouveau is a rock club in the basement of a super-gritty bar overflowing with hip Parisians in black jeans and dramatically layered hair. For our little outing, I chose to wear my favorite indigo washes and a forest green colored short-sleeve shirt with a wide rockabilly-style collar and country-chic embroidery along the chest. Everyone we pass smoking cigarettes on the sidewalk outside is super-stylish and definitely doesn't go to any lycée. A lot of the girls are wearing slouchy berets and long cardigans, and the boys are all in jeans even tighter than mine. I keep my eyes directed forward, pouting a little to fit in.

I try to emote that I belong here. I walk the walk. I talk the talk. Or at least I'm a good faker.

"Wow!" Olivia takes my wrist and squeezes her palm around it. She looks nervous, immediately touching her shorn hair. "Seriously, *wow!* Look at this place!"

"Not to worry, doll, you're on the list, so to speak," I reassure her. But for certain, neither of us is in Kansas—or even our side of Paris— anymore.

A deejay on a raised platform at the back of the club is spinning hard-rock records mixed with thumping beats that form a dizzying new genre. Even though it's early for Paris standards, the club is pretty packed already. "Shots?" Olivia asks me, and before I can answer her, she starts heading for the bar.

Here's the thing about drinking in Paris—nobody seems to really get drunk. Except Americans or other tourists, that is. Parisians tend to stay out until the wee hours, so they really pace themselves when it comes to alcohol. No one is truly hammered until three or four. And taking shots is really not all that necessary to fit in. It's not like we're at a frat party. We could sip wine all night at a bar or a club in Paris and no one would think any less of us.

But Olivia seems to be on a mission—she wants to get loud. And, hey, I ain't gonna stop her. It's not like her—at least, it's not like the girl I met last September when we all got to Paris. But Paris changes you, makes you want to do things outside of your comfort zone, sometimes for a night, sometimes for your whole life.

We take a shot of Jack Daniels, and I have to admit that it feels great. *Better* than great. As it burns its way down, I feel a newfound confidence bubbling up in me. Accompanied by the pounding bass in the floor and the rhythm of dancers moving all around me, the heat and energy of the booze hits me in a powerful wave. I feel looser, more excited . . . and only *slightly* less freaked out about seeing André.

"There are so many guys here!' Olivia giggles. "Cute ones!"

"Yes, indeedy," I say, though I haven't really even noticed. "But why do you care about that? You practically live with your true love. I'm horribly jealous."

"Oh, Thomas?" Olivia says, scrunching her nose. "That's kind of . . . over."

"What?" I pitch forward in disbelief, nearly losing my balance. "How? When? *What?*"

"Oh, you know, no big deal." Olivia shrugs her teeny shoulders. "Just didn't work out so well."

"Olivia, you two were the real thing. Connected at the hip. Soul mates. What happened?" Not to mention, I figured it was his influence that was making Olivia so drink-happy on nights like tonight. Thomas, it should be noted, definitely likes to throw one or two back a little more liberally than most of his Parisian counterparts.

"Oh, Zack, come on." She plays with the empty shot glass on the surface of the bar. "We were *not* soul mates." Olivia looks off at an undefined spot across the room. "Not at all."

"But I've seen the way he looks at you!"

"Not lately," she sighs. Rolling her heavily made-up eyes, she finally gives in. "He dumped me. Out of nowhere. Or out of somewhere. I don't know! All of the sudden, everything just felt way different. It's like I loved him, but it didn't always feel right."

"Are you devastated?"

Olivia pauses, craning her neck back and forth as if she needs to work out a sore muscle. "The truth?"

"Of course!"

"I'm not really sure," she says, her chin quivering. I can't bear to see her look so sad—sweet, pure Olivia with her rosy disposition and soldiering faith in the goodness of others. I throw my arms around her and stroke her short dark hair. After a while, she sighs again, pulls away, and turns back to trying to get the bartender to come over.

"André's awesome, huh?" Olivia shouts over the music after a few minutes of silence pass between us. The bartender finally returns. I buy us each another shot, then order a couple of cocktails—vodka and soda for Olivia, a tequila sunrise for me—and sit at one end of the busy bar to wait for them to get mixed. "He's got an insane body," she assures me as if I hadn't noticed. "He works out *all* the time. Plus, he's just so unique, ya know? He has an opinion about everything. He's just so charming and . . . alive."

I just smile, trying not to get too caught up in my crush. Olivia's wry expression is replaced by a thrilled one, but she doesn't say anything further, just watches me. Then I smile again, and after a while, we start jumping up and down and clutching each other's hands in excitement.

"Oh, my gawd!" I shriek in her ear.

"You two would be perfect together!" she says excitedly. "It would be the cutest of the cutest things!" Her enthusiasm is about the cutest thing *I* have ever seen, but she looks sad, too.

I press my lips together, willing myself not to fall too hard, too fast. "I'm not gonna say anything. Just have to see what happens next." I move my head up and down to the beat of the music ever so casually, but I can't keep myself from beaming like a total jackass. "Just see what happens next," I repeat to myself.

"Oh, yeah, definitely a good idea to keep your cool," Olivia rushes to point out, pulling herself together. But her eyes are still dancing.

"You really think we'd be good together?" I finally ask her, so excited that I feel like I could burst.

"Well . . . let's find out!" Olivia says, tilting her head forward a notch. I turn and see André coming toward us.

"Cheers, everyone! *Bonsoir et bonjour!*" André greets us, kissing us each on the cheek. "You're both looking like heartbreakers tonight. Having fun, pussycats?"

"This place rocks!" we say at the same time, still a little giddy from giggling like little girls a few minutes ago.

"Shall I get us a round?" André offers. "Your drinks look a little low." I notice the bartender responds to André with an immediate smile, whereas we had to wait for several minutes just to get acknowledged. When we have fresh drinks in our hands, we try to think of a toast. That's something I've noticed in Europe, both here in Paris and in Amsterdam: The night becomes so much classier when you start it off with a nice toast.

"I've got nuthin'," Olivia says with uncharacteristic self-deprecation. "My life's in shambles. You guys go."

"Hey, girl, don't say that. You've got us." I put my arm around her. "To Paris, I guess. And whatever's next."

"Indeed," André says with a smirk. "Whatever comes next." We clank our glasses together, cheek kisses all around. When André's lips brush my cheek, I feel it at the base of my spine. *This is going to be even better than the concert at Bercy!*

"Americans would say this is bangin', right?" André teases me as we move out to the dance floor. "Is that the lingo you Yanks are using these days?"

"Don't call me no Yankee," I protest, feigning deep disgust. "But yeah, this club *is* bangin'. Without a doubt." My words get lost as we all shuffle in double time around the floor to the crazy music, throwing our limbs around and just *feeling* it.

When you dance this much, you lose your buzz fast, but it doesn't matter. You get a different kind of buzz. André and Olivia, with their lithe ballet-trained bodies, can't stop moving. I let all my inhibitions go and follow their lead. I don't know what I'm doing, but it feels amazing, like I'm part of a rising sea of arms and feet and bobbing heads. Girls dancing around me let their long hair swing around their necks, swatting the slick backs of the sweaty people dancing near them. I'm holding my drink, and then another, and another, and people jostle me and spill alcohol down my arm and onto my jeans, but I don't care.

The deejay is spinning a crazy mash-up of hip-hop and hard rock, the kind of stuff that really gets you moving. It doesn't take too long for Olivia and André to start busting out some of their better bar tricks—people who have been dancing as long as they have can do some wild stuff—high kicks, goofy hipster robot moves. I'm cracking up watching them, and some of the others in the club are looking at the three of us like we are crazy. This is definitely not a Parisian way to behave.

André is a kick-ass dancer—he can bend, jump, and slide in time with seriously fast music. His crowning achievement is when the crowd moves aside and he crouches down, then executes a double turn in the air all scrunched up into a ball.

Olivia shakes her head, amazed that he even attempted to do that move in the middle of a club. I can't stop laughing at the Frenchies looking at André as if he's on speed or from another planet, or both. It's a scandal! The best part is how André brushes off his shoulders when he's finished and keeps on dancing

Then suddenly, a guy comes over and starts dancing right up next to him. He's Asian, with a tight, rock-hard body swathed in a loose mesh top and tight black shorts. He comes toward André like a bullet, fast and furious and way too close. His hair fanned out all around him in probably the chicest mullet to ever see the light of day, he flares his nostrils right into André's face, then hits the floor with quick, snakelike precision. He starts pulling himself up into a series of headstands, handstands, and wormlike undulations that have to be seen to be believed. When he's finished, he jumps up and bangs his chest with both palms, challenging our leapfrogging friend.

Is this a *dance off*?

André looks around the club, scowling comically, as if he's going to really show this guy who's boss. Some of the other people standing around us look scared, some look thrilled, and some are too drunk, stoned, or high to even notice. André walks forward very slowly toward his opponent and as close to the guy as he had gotten to André before. But just as my eyes have widened into saucers and my eyeballs feel like they're about to fall out of their sockets, André bursts into a huge grin and starts doing the running man and hugging the guy like they've just won the World Series. They both fall over laughing. Olivia and I are dying in the corner, having never—ever—seen anything like that.

"Break?" André suggests with a triumphant smile, and we find our way through to the restrooms. Miraculously, maybe because no one in this club wants to stop dancing for even a few minutes, there's no line.

I burst through the door and turn on the water faucet to take a long drink. When I stand up and wipe the excess water off my face, I see André standing behind me in the bathroom mirror. The door's still open.

André smiles at me in our reflection. I smile back, glad the music's so loud. I don't want to have to say anything right now. André comes up and puts his arms around my waist, closing the bathroom door behind him. Still making eye contact in the mirror, he puts his lips gently on that spot where my neck meets the back of my shoulder.

I don't move. I can't even breathe. "Is this okay?" André mumbles into my shoulder.

"Uh-huh," I say, and before I can stop myself, I whirl around and put my hands on his shoulders. Then I kiss André, not just for a few minutes, but for a long time. Until someone starts pounding on the bathroom door.

"Let's get out of here," André breathes. I nod and follow him back into the club, feeling like I'm about to have a heart attack. "I'll get Olivia a cab," André says. "You want to come back to my place? It's just around the corner."

I nod again. *Just see what happens next,* I remind myself, in hopes that it will make my heart stop racing so out of control.

★ ★ ★

Sunday morning, I wake up in my jeans in a strange bed with a headache like an eggbeater whipping up my brains. Someone—a *demon,* a horrible *devil* of a person—seems to be inexplicably playing an accordion from beyond the wooden door I see in front of me when I open one eye. I try to get a better look at where I am, but when I open both eyes, the painted green walls won't stop moving.

"Atta boy," someone says when I lift my head a few inches from the pillow. I freeze and put my head back down. He's awake, too!

A dark, smooth arm tucks under my armpit and slides across my bare chest. "How much of last night do you remember, sport?" The British accent, that intoxicating scent of some blend of soap and fruit and a little bit of sultry sweat. . . André.

"Mornin'," I grumble, trying not to open my mouth too much. I am horribly afraid I have the rankest breath known to man. There's about a gallon of tequila makin' its way through my system. I lick my lips and try to wet my cottony mouth. "I mean, good morning." I use all my strength to open both eyes and look over my shoulder at him.

Eye contact is too much. I look away very, very fast.

Oh, my God! I want to scream with exhilaration.

I am in bed . . . with a *boy*!

What the *heck* happened last night?!

And not just any boy. A boy with his own apartment, ostensibly. A wail of old-fashioned French café music snakes through the apartment at just that moment, making me shudder and want to dive under the covers.

"That would be my roommate, making that god-awful noise he calls music." André laughs. "Bloody lovely to wake up to, isn't it?"

"*Wow*," I say, not sure how long I can stand to lie here and act like I hook up with guys—in their beds—all the time. Not to mention, that accordion is just a bitch. "So, about last night . . ."

"How much do you remember, love?" André laughs, tossing my shirt at me from where it lies on the bedroom floor amid a pile of other clothes.

I squeeze my eyes shut and conjure some hazy and slightly—no, very—disturbing memories of myself singing my way up a long flight of stairs.

"When you got in here, you just about threw off your shirt," André says, still laughing. He points at a large roller rack of clothes, costumes really, in the corner. "Remember trying on my fringe vest? You said you thought it looked best with a bare chest underneath."

"I didn't," I say, though the telltale fringe vest is on the floor not far from the bed, proving me *so* wrong.

"And then you tried on the leather biker one, which I would have had to kill you if you'd done anything to, since it's my favorite, *then* you wanted to wear the flight suit but fell onto the bed as you were struggling to take your pants off. From there it was slumber land for you."

"That's not possible. I would never act like that. How childish." As I talk though, I feel a bit of disappointment—and also relief. "Besides, I already have a vest like that. It was my mom's from when she was Miss Tennessee and did an Appalachian clogging routine in the talent portion of the pageant," I say, finishing up the buttons on my shirt and giving him a sideways look.

"Your mother was a real live American beauty queen?"

"She was."

André cracks up.

"In fact, your story has a lot of holes in it. How did my glasses come off?" I challenge him prissily, pointing at my black frames folded neatly on a side table.

"Those I took off for you so you wouldn't roll over and break them in the night."

"Ah," I say. "Well that was very nice of you. *Merci beaucoup.*" I stand up, brush myself off, and put my glasses on. I don't want him to think I could get that far without them—though in truth I barely have a prescription.

"Killer time last night, Hiccups," André says, hopping up to kiss my cheek good-bye. I wait for a minute, seeing if he's going to ask me if I want to hang out again, but he just makes a hungover moaning noise and flops back down onto the bed.

★ ★ ★

All week at the Lycée, I walk through the halls in a daze. Olivia tells me Monday morning that she spent most of Sunday over the toilet, telling Mme Rouille she ate bad fish the night before.

"So you guys . . ." Olivia says. "How was the rest of your night?"

I blink and smile but won't divulge all that happened between the last time I saw her, getting into that cab, and now. Now I feel like a whole new person.

In class all week, I look at the other boys and wonder how I ended up so different from them. I look around at everyone, actually, and wonder if this is how it feels for everyone after they hook up for the first time. Entire class periods go by without me noticing anyone or anything. When I hear a British accent on the street, I immediately think of André. I mean, a month ago it was Bobby I was fixating on like this, but André is *here.* And more happened in two nights out with André than during my whole visit to Amsterdam!

And André brings out the fun side of me, the fun side of everyone. I ponder this as I eat lunch with Olivia on Friday afternoon, wondering if André will maybe call me this weekend and invite me somewhere, like last weekend. It's a rare rainless day but still very chilly, with clouds covering the sun every couple of minutes. I consider André's many admirable talents. The way he deflects discomfort and awkwardness is a true *art*. I found myself laughing at myself around him, telling him things about my childhood that I know he—as a Brit—will think are hilarious. Things like the Holy Roller BBQ Ribs Competition my dad enters at our church every year, and how one year he made me wear a pig mask while I was serving it up to our congregation. I like how it feels, from the vantage point of Paris, both getting to make fun of my dad and to feel like an exotic American bird that comes along only once in a lifetime.

And there are other talents, too. His kisses make my head spin.

Yes, Bobby is a great guy, but Amsterdam is six hours away. André could be *exactly* what I was looking for. Right in my proverbial Parisian backyard.

I push my glasses up the bridge of my nose and turn back to Olivia, who's sitting quietly next to me in the Parc Monceau, poking at a takeaway salad.

"Don't even say it," she says wryly. "You're in love, aren't you?"

I sling my arm around her and ruffle up that pixie cut of hers. "Just have to see what happens next."

MARCH

9. PJ

Shady Business

---

*a*lex and I are standing outside her homestay after she gets home from school on a rainy Monday afternoon. Alex keeps shifting from one black patent-leather high-heeled pump to another. It makes her look like she has to go to the bathroom or something. She holds out a purple umbrella as if she is about to pop it open. In place of the handle it has a carved alligator head made from wood, yellow beads for eyes. Alex really is just too much.

"I don't know his last name. He's just Freddie," Alex says impatiently, handing me a slip of hot pink paper with a Paris phone number on it. "If all you need is a place to stay, he's your man. I mean, it's just for a little while, right? Till you figure out what you are going to do next?"

"Do you need to be somewhere, Alex?" I ask her.

"Yes, as a matter of fact," she says, rolling her eyes. "I have to go, um, babysit. Don't tell anyone, but I had to get this heinous after-school job to stay at the Lycée. Can we walk and talk, so I won't be late? Or better yet, you go call Freddie and tell him you know me. Or my mom, actually." She opens the umbrella and starts hurrying down the street. She looks so quintessentially Parisian, I observe as I follow alongside her. Exactly the kind of scene I pictured when I applied for the Programme Americain last year. High heels, long black trench coat, broad umbrella—framed by the Eiffel Tower looming above Cambronne in the background. "Yeah, tell her Caroline Braun sent you. The famous Madame C.A.B., as Zack might say."

"So how come you're babysitting? And why don't you want anyone to know?"

"You might be surprised by this, Penelope dear, but I am more of a private person that anyone realizes. Not everyone needs to be up in my business all the time," Alex says, taking a long stride to avoid dipping her expensive shoes into a deep puddle.

"Oh," I say, immediately chagrined. "Sorry."

"Actually, it's nice to admit it to someone. It's so embarrassing, though. That woman I was telling you about, the one I owe the money to? I have to watch her kids to make it up to her. My mom is making me."

"And no one knows? Not Zack? Or Olivia?"

Alex shakes her head. "Not at the moment, no. I didn't think it was going to last this long. I mean, when I told her the story about giving the money to you, my starving model friend, I thought for sure my babysitting days were over. But my mom's not letting go of this one for some reason.

You know how sometimes your mom just gets an idea in her head about a lesson she is going to teach you, and she just won't let it go?"

I nod, but Alex stops talking. "Never mind," she says, and what she knows and doesn't know about *my* mom crosses my mind in a sad, anxious spell. "In any case, I've got to do this miserable job until further notice. It comes with all kinds of environmental hazards, too—one of the kids wears diapers, and *I* have to change them. And the other day, some creepy French guy hit on me in the Jardin du Luxembourg, thinking I was their *mother*. He, like, wanted to be their dad. How gross is that?"

Alex stops and motions toward the street she needs to turn down to get to her babysitting job, the swarming rue de Rennes that leads to the Sixth. "Are you sure you should be out in public like this?" she asks me sharply. "If you're pretending to still be dead? And how long do we have to pretend? When are you going to come back to school?"

"Yeah, you're right," I say. "I gotta get out of here. Thanks for the number."

"You are planning to come out of the closet, so to speak, sometime soon, aren't you? This whole hiding out in Paris thing is just temporary? I mean, PJ, I can't keep your secret *forever*." The tone of her voice is more whiny than worried, as if she's been extremely inconvenienced by not being able to tell anyone that she's seen me.

"Just keep my secret about being back in Paris, and I will keep your after-school job quiet. There's just so much I don't know yet."

All I know is that I might have killed a man, and my sister is back in the United States and could rat me out at any time, just like she did to my parents. All I know, I want to tell her, is that *I cannot be found*. Under any circumstances.

"You and me both, honey," Alex says. "But hey, you did me a big favor. My mom may not have let me off the hook yet, but she definitely feels more sorry for me than she did before. Your suicide earned me *tons* of pity points with her. It will just take a little more work; I just know it. And then I'll be off the hook and back to my old fabulous life, *tout de suite*! All right, for real, I gotta go, too. Stay safe. *Au revoir!*" She darts away and into the crowd.

★ ★ ★

Freddie answers the mobile number with a gruff, "*Ouais?*"

I introduce myself as a friend of a friend of Caroline Braun. I speak in perfect French, inflecting my accent with all the soft intricacies that separate native speakers from foreign ones. "Monsieur Freddie, I would be very grateful for your help in this difficult situation. I find myself suddenly without a place to live."

"*Vous êtes mannequin?*" he interrupts me. "You party too much?"

"*Excusez-moi?*" I ask.

"Are you a model? Did you get kicked out of one of the model apartments? Is that how you know Caroline? Fashion business?"

"Um, yes," I answer, still speaking my best French. "Not for partying. Because I . . . because I couldn't get any jobs. Not pretty enough, I suppose."

"Eh," Freddie answers. "Come down to my new spot. I don't do the model apartments anymore. I'm in clubs now. If you're half as pretty as the last girl, I'll give you a hostessing job. *Qu'est-ce que vous allez faire?*"

He gives me an address in Pigalle, a sleazy, wild neighborhood on the edge of the Ninth Arrondissement and Montmartre, on the north side of Paris and not actually that far from Ternes. I don't like the idea of being so close to the Marquets' town house, or the Lycée de Monceau.

But I have no choice. "Tomorrow night, ten o'clock. Wear something *suggestif*." Freddie hangs up.

Next, I call Alex on her BlackBerry to tell her I am going to meet Freddie tomorrow night. I don't tell her he doesn't have that model apartment anymore, remembering her comment about not being able to keep this secret forever. I figure from here on out, it might be better for her—and anyone else—to know as little as possible about what's going on. I hear some kind of animal baying noisily in the background. "What is that?" I ask.

"It's Emeline, one of the kids," Alex says. "She's got an eraser stuck up her nose. I gotta go."

★ ★ ★

Jay's host family has *five* kids in it—ranging from a baby to a fourteen-year-old student at a nearby Lycée. They all share rooms. Jay shares his with the thirteen-year-old host brother Hassan. Tonight, however, Hassan is sleeping over at a friend's birthday party in their same apartment complex. Jay has learned of the sleepover and is beaming when he comes to meet me at a bland shopping center in his neighborhood. I'm sitting on a bench outside of Carrefour, a discount place in the basement. Jay gave me an old brown beanie of his, made of rough acrylic to weather sporting events and hunting season, that I've been wearing over my hair.

"So just come to my window, like you did before. Don't come till, like, eleven, though. My host parents will be asleep by then. Knock on the window. I'll be waiting."

Far later than we had planned for me to come over, I hesitate for another minute, then tap lightly on the window. The curtain is pulled back, just enough so he can see out through a small panel of light. It takes Jay only a few seconds to unlatch the window and pull me into his room.

"Hey," I say, holding myself stiff in his embrace.

"Hey," Jay says, pressing his soft lips on mine. "*Hey.*"

Jay's kisses are slow and aching. I'm almost squirming. They don't match what I feel inside—the opposite of calm and quiet. I break away nervously.

"Are you okay, PJ?" he asks me. "Sorry if that was too forward. It's just that you look so beautiful. I've been dying to see you."

I try and relax. "Yeah, let's just . . . slow down."

"Sure, sure. You want to sit down?" Jay clears a spot on the bed for me. "You want some water or anything?"

"That would be great," I mumble. I'm not that thirsty, but I want to stall for time. I need a second to just *think.*

When Jay comes back, he latches and locks the door noiselessly and hands me a glass of tap water. I take a sip and thank him.

"You want to take off your coat?" he asks, almost timidly.

"Oh, yeah, sure," I say. "I guess I forgot." I slink out of it, immediately feeling a chill. I keep my scarf on.

"You love that scarf, huh?" Jay says with a smile. "You were wearing it that day we went to the Louvre. Remember? The day we first saw all the Ingres paintings?"

"Yeah, well, it's the only one I have," I say, tugging on the ends of it. "My mom made it for me."

"It looks great on you. The color is awesome with your eyes."

"Thanks," I say and take a deep breath.

"Tell me more about your mom," Jay says. "What's she like?"

145

Just keep breathing, I tell myself, but I have to concentrate really, really hard to do that.

"She's . . ." I don't know what to say. "Jay?"

"Yeah?" Jay moves toward the bed, gingerly sitting down on the edge of the mattress next to me.

"What were . . . reporters saying about me? About my family?"

Jay furrows his eyebrows and takes a second to respond. "Well, I'm not really sure. Some people think you might have—you know, tried to . . . whatever—because your parents are in some kind of legal trouble. Is that right? I mean, that they are in trouble?"

I nod because it is a matter of public record at this point. What's the use of hiding?

"Is that why? I mean, why you ran away?" Jay looks deep into my eyes.

I don't answer. I stare at my lap. My hands are wedged between my knees to keep them from trembling and betraying how much this conversation is affecting me.

"I'm sorry. Man, why do I keep doing that? You don't have to say anything."

I look back up at him. "Thanks."

Jay's worried expression softens. Those thick black eyebrows raised, he nods his head. "Trust me to push things too fast. I've just missed you so much. I've been dying to know where you were, why you were there. I just didn't *get* it. *¿Me explico?* Does that make sense?"

I take a shuddering breath. "Is it enough," I begin, "that I'm back? I mean, for now?"

Jay cups my face in his hands, my long hair getting caught in between his fingers.

"Yes," he breathes before he kisses me again. "It is absolutely enough."

Hearing those words awakens something in me, something more than just a longing to be safe. I adjust myself next to him so that I can put my arms around his neck and kiss him more deeply than I have before—more deeply than I have ever kissed *anyone* before.

"Penelope. Is that really you?" he asks me as our lips separate.

I laugh a little. "Yes, of course."

"You are so beautiful," he says, kissing my neck and my earlobes. The light touch of his lips on those sensitive parts makes me brace against him and catch my breath.

"I've been waiting so long to kiss you like this," Jay says, moving apart again. "But I can wait even longer. I will wait forever if that's what you want."

I keep still, not able to say anything but wanting him to continue. Finally, I find my voice. "Can we . . . can we turn the lights off?"

"Sure, of course." Jay walks over to the door and flips the switch. The room is immediately pitch black apart from a streetlamp's light creeping in behind his drapes. I sigh and feel him, rather than see him, come back over to me on the bed. Very carefully, he unwinds the scarf from around my neck and runs his fingertips along my collarbone. I feel his lips kiss me where his finger tips have just been, and in the dark, I find the back of his head, where his scalp meets his neck, and hold on to that place while I fight mightily to keep my bearings.

"It feels good," I choke out, because it really, really does. A weird part of me wants to cry. I don't deserve to feel like this. It's too nice.

Jay languidly slides his warm hands under my shirt. He strokes my stomach, exploring. When he touches me on these areas of my body that no one has ever touched, it's both thrilling and frightening. I feel him caress the skin underneath my belly button, right where my jeans start, and I wonder if that is still me he's touching, because I can feel it, but it feels so otherworldly and impossible.

Jay pulls up my shirt over my head slowly and carefully, placing it on the bed next to us. As my eyes adjust to the light, I can make him out, just barely. For a minute, his hands leave my skin and I realize he's taking his shirt off, too.

I gasp when I feel his skin next to mine, his chest brushing my chest, our stomachs touching as our kisses become hungrier. Jay reaches down and takes off my shoes, then pulls off my socks. I can't stop sucking in my breath from each sharp exposure to the air.

With painstaking slowness, I lean farther and farther back until my head is on the pillow, with my hair splayed out on either side in a fan.

Jay leans over me, and I see the glint of his white teeth in the moonlight. He's smiling.

"I'm glad you didn't cut your hair off," he says. "It makes you look like an angel."

His voice cracks a little.

"I love you, PJ. *Penelope*." The way he pronounces my name, with that slight hint of Spanish softness on all the vowels, floods me with an unfamiliar ache to be closer to him—as close as I can possibly be.

I don't answer him. Instead, I lean down and kiss his stomach, that little spot just above the drawstring on his sweatpants. He smells so good, everywhere. His body makes me feel like I'm on another plane of existence—a whole separate universe where feelings have color and shape.

"Everything's going to be okay," Jay tells me. It's a strange moment to be offering me comfort, but it fits. I slither down into his body, melding our shapes together. His mouth is like dried ice everywhere it touches me—hot on my elbows, my chin, along the straps of my bra. I can't stop shivering, that same deep chill refusing to let me go.

"Have you done this before?" Jay asks me, his fingers resting on the button of my jeans.

I shake my head, scared. "No," I say. "But I want to." As his hands move over me, it feels like I'm opening the door into another life, and that's the best feeling I've had since I can remember.

★ ★ ★

We arrange to meet at a fast food place the next day as I am climbing out his window at six in the morning. All day I walk around the Bois de Vincennes, alternating between a gut-wrenching fear that I'll be spotted out here in broad daylight by someone from the Lycée—or worse, the media—and a warm tingling feeling deep in my belly when I think about last night.

Jay orders us two *sandwiches grecs*, pitas stuffed with spicy chunks of chicken and salad. He gets french fries, but I don't want any. "I'm not that hungry," I tell him.

"Are you ever hungry?" he asks me.

"Yes," I lie. "What kind of question is that?"

"Tell me what things you like to eat," Jay says. "And then I can take you to get them. You never eat when I eat. It's been weeks of you picking at your food, hanging out while I stuff my face. You have to like *something*."

"I like this." I gesture at the mostly uneaten sandwich. "I'm just . . . I don't know. I feel nauseated lately."

"Well, what happened with Alex? She hook you up with a place to stay while you work things out?"

"Yeah," I say. "I'm actually going there tonight." I've already decided not to tell him or Alex that Freddie doesn't have the apartment for models anymore. Not until I find out more about the job he might have for me.

"You are? Why didn't you say anything?" Jay asks. "I'll go with you. I want to make sure it looks all right."

"Come on, Jay," I pretend to smirk. "Accommodation provided by Alex? I'm sure it will be top-notch and very discreet."

"Man, you don't even know," Jay says. "When we were looking for you, you know, in Montauban . . ." Jay looks embarrassed. "I mean, I don't even know why we thought you were there. But it seemed like a good place to start, and man, Alex's dad's place was incredible. The apartment, or condo or whatever, was in, like, a bell tower of an old church. And we just came in one night, and the guys handed us the keys and made us right at home. No flack, nothing. You get set up like that, you'll be golden." His voice is so positive, so chipper, that now I really can't tell him that's not how I think it is going to work out.

I take a miserable bite of greasy chicken. I figure that might make him feel better about me eating.

"I don't want you to come with me because I don't want this guy to think I'm just trying to find a place to hook up with my boyfriend," I say. A lame excuse. Then I can't help it—I start laughing. Not so much at the idea of that, but because I know I've just done something mortifying and we both know it.

"So I'm your boyfriend?" Jay says, abandoning the idea of coming with me tonight. Abandoning the idea of even finding out more about it.

He just wants me to say it again. "Yes, you're my boyfriend," I say. I pull my scarf tighter around my neck. The words are sort of chilling. He lays a hand on top of mine.

"That's awesome, man," is all he says because he's grinning too broadly to speak.

I giggle in spite of myself. When Jay leans over to kiss me, I feel the same heat in his mouth that I felt last night. It carries me away, even though we're surrounded by people in the middle of a fast-food place.

With Jay, I know I can do this. I can get through this, wait things out until I know more, until I turn eighteen. Until I'm really free.

★ ★ ★

The place at the address that Freddie gave me has a heavy metal door with a lot of locks on it. No windows. Inside, it's a dark club, just one strobe lazily pulsing in a corner. The music hasn't started playing yet. Instead, the bartender just has the radio on. It's not very loud.

"*Tu es la fille?*" the bartender asks me. He's one of those grimy guys whose age is difficult to gauge. "Freddie! The hostess girl is here!"

A short, rotund guy with long hair comes out from a back room. "*Ah, tu es très belle,*" he says, not in complimentary way. "You want to start tonight?"

"So it's like a job? I mean, *je vais travailler ici?*"

"*Ouais,*" Freddie confirms. "Is that what you are going to wear?"

I look down. Same old jeans, an undershirt of Jay's, same old wool sweater with the elbow patches. "Griselda!" Freddie shouts. "*Viens ici!*"

A woman comes out of the back. She's younger than Freddie, and her clothes aren't as nice. She's got a nice enough expression on her face.

"*Elle s'appelle Fiona. Aide-la, d'accord?*" Freddie stomps away. I've given him a fake name—Fiona—just in case anyone, anywhere starts putting things together.

Fussily, like a nurse preparing a patient for surgery, Griselda removes my sweater and ties the back of my T-shirt into a knot so that my belly is exposed. Then she rolls the white sleeves up to my shoulders. "*Alors,*" she says. "I will show you around."

Freddie's latest venture, I learn from Griselda, is a gentleman's club.

"*Vraiment?*" I ask. All signs up to now might have been pointing to this, but this is so incongruous to my notion of the friends Alex's mom has that I think she has to be joking.

"Yes, you did not know this?"

"No." I look around at the bare room, thinking that this would be an odd place to watch a stripper dance. There is just the wall of alcohol and a few places to sit alongside the bar. No tables or anything.

"But discreet," she insists. "Very nice place. The clients come in, they tell you what they want, you take them to a room. They might get a drink before. Most do not but some do. Mostly this is like a waiting room."

"We don't have a sign up out front because the men who come here are of a different sort than most that you find in Pigalle," Griselda continues, showing me out of the bar and into a hallway that looks like a shrunken hotel. There are four doors along either side of the hallway and one at the end. "The office is in back. That's where Freddie and I will be. We've got security back there and out front. The girls are in the rooms, and they have a call button if things get rough."

"Rough?" I choke out. "Rough how?"

"Well, we are a classy establishment. Dancing *only*. The clients cannot touch the girls . . . unless . . ."

I don't know what I thought she was about to say, but when she finally finishes her sentence, I feel the blood rush out of my head. " . . . unless the girl wants to make an exception. Then she has to take them upstairs. You won't have to worry about that. Security will accompany her and her client through the office. That is where the stairway is."

"This is a . . . brothel?" I ask. I instantly feel dirty.

"No! No," Griselda answers, taking a long look around at the establishment.

But the way she denies it sounds so odd that I'm still pondering her reaction as she shows me the podium near the door that will be my station at this job. Sex . . . such a different concept when you look at it in various contexts. What happened with Jay last night, his body falling over me and his gentle caressing that got steadily more urgent as I held onto him tighter and tighter . . . that was such a different thing than what this place is selling. There's a notebook on top of the podium. It has sheets of paper drawn into tables with eight squares, one for each of the rooms. My job will be to see which room is free at any given time and lead the clients to their dancer.

"If they want more than fifteen minutes, they need to pay up front," she tells me. "You can't let them decide they want more once they're in there. If they don't come out after fifteen minutes, tell the security guard."

I knock into the podium, banging my shin, when suddenly loud, provocatively pulsating music comes on from the speakers overheard.

"Don't worry," Griselda says. "I'll help you."

★ ★ ★

The last client is allowed in at 8:45 A.M. When he leaves after watching a dancer in one of the rooms for fifteen minutes, Freddie's club closes for the day. It reopens around eleven or ten every night, I leave with a green hundred-euro bill that Griselda gave me, as well as a pocketful of tips from the clients, just for showing them to their private dancer.

"Why do they do that?" I ask Griselda.

"*Parce que tu es très innocente.* Young. More beautiful than God. You are too good for this place, they think. You remind them of their daughters. Only they wish *you* would dance for them."

I balk, watching her walk back into the office. Are all French men like M. Marquet?

It's morning—early but late enough for people to be up and about. Pigalle at night is bad enough, but in the light of morning—with wheezy men coming out of the bars and clubs, looking around dazed as they try to remember where exactly they are, alongside teenagers and older people just going about their daily business—it is grotesque.

I remember, as I walk a maze of streets through the Ninth Arrondissement, its mess of markets and discount stores fading into quirky gift shops and haute bakeries, that the Petit Palais is free and usually pretty empty inside. I've been to the museum to see the art exhibits before. Today, I go to see if I can find a secret place to sleep until Jay gets out of soccer practice.

★ ★ ★

"So that apartment's working out okay?" Jay asks me, back at the Mediterranean fast-food place we met for lunch yesterday. Paris is full of little places like these, calling themselves Greek restaurants but actually serving fare that's more like Turkish or Middle Eastern. Heavy, cheap. Filling. Again, looking at Jay's sandwich makes my stomach turn over.

"You like it?"

"Yeah, it's great," I say sleepily. I sit next to him, rather than across from him, so that I can lean my head on his shoulder. I wonder if he can smell the sex, bought and sold, on me. If not actual sex, then the idea of it.

"How come you're so tired?" Jay asks me, kissing the top of my head before he takes another bite. "What did you do all day?"

"I went to the Petit Palais. There's this classical room that I just love," I say. It takes so much effort to appear normal. To make regular conversation. My eyes just want to slide shut.

"Oh, really? You like it there?"

I nod, feeling like I'm underwater. "Yeah, it's great."

"We should go together sometime. I don't know much about artists. I wish I knew more. I loved learning about Ingres with you last semester."

"Maybe," I say. "What time is it?"

"Almost seven," Jay answers after glancing at his cell phone. "Seriously, PJ, what's the matter? Do you not like the place where you are staying?"

"It's fine." I snuggle my face into the warmth where his scarf lies over his sweater. It's so cold again today.

Jay's quiet for the rest of the time we are in the restaurant.

I don't know why I just don't tell Jay what happened last night. What kind of place I've found refuge in. It just feels impossible. And Jay—he's out of options. We don't have any money; we don't have any safe places to hide. Alex, as much as Jay might think she makes things happen, won't have any more options than we do.

Pigalle is the least likely place anyone is going to look for me. And in the darkness of the club, I don't even feel like I could be recognized. It's the kind of place where everyone is wearing a veil. The dancers.

The bartender. The customers. *Especially* the customers. Even the ones that take my breath they remind me so much of M. Marquet. For some reason, I have to believe that he wouldn't risk the bad press coming into a place like this. If I want to get through this job, it's what I have to keep telling myself.

When Jay and I get outside, it's kind of wet but not raining. The pavement looks black all wet like that. "Can I walk you back to the apartment?" Jay asks. "You haven't even told me where it is. Where is it?"

"Oh, it's actually over in La Défense," I say, picking the first thing I can think of that is really far away from Montreuil. La Défense is a suburb to the northwest of the city. You have to take the RER to get there. "So I better get going."

"La Défense?" Jay asks. "Really?"

"Yup," I say. "I'll walk with you to Havre-Caumartin. You can get on the number three from there to Montreuil." I remember that you can get on the RER from a connecting station there, too, and take the train to La Défense. I've never been to La Défense, but I am glad I remember how to get there just from looking at my Paris métro map so much before I even came here.

"Yeah, let's walk," Jay says. He has an odd look on his face. He's not quite looking at me. He's apprehensive about something.

I tell Jay that I'm sorry for being so out of it today. "I just didn't get enough sleep last night," I explain.

"It's like you're back, but you're not," he bursts out at me, stopping right in the middle of the sidewalk. "*You* came to *me*. You sought *me* out, told me you needed *me*. But you haven't told me one thing about where you've been or what you've been doing. Why would you stage your own suicide? Where is this sister who was supposedly with you? Why won't you tell me anything about her? Why won't you tell me anything about *you*?"

"Jay!" I stop him, grabbing his hand. "Don't!"

"People are saying all kinds of crazy things. They say your parents sell drugs. They say your sister turned up back in the States as if nothing ever happened. Tabloid reporters know more than I do!" It is the same intensity as two nights ago but pointed in a very different direction.

"Please stop," I beg him, grasping his hand. I'm in turmoil with every question he lobs at me. Each one feels like a spear, and when the magnitude of what has happened hits me, I can't think. I whimper and cover my face with my forearm. "Please, Jay."

"You don't even tell me your favorite foods, or where you even live!" he spits out, very plainly hurt. "We shared all the things we shared the other night. And you still keep so many secrets from me. I tell you I love you, and you don't say anything at all!"

"Is that what this is about?" I ask, letting go of his hand. "Because you said that to me?"

"It's more than that! What were you doing in Rouen, PJ? Tell me!"

I move away from him, brushing sudden tears from my eyes.

"I wish you could just stay out of it! Just leave me alone!"

"Where are you going tonight, PJ? For real?" Jay says, shaking his head. There is so much turmoil in his face that I gasp and bite back a noise that's somewhere between being hit in the stomach and seeing the saddest thing in the world. I have to look away. I have to get away from this.

He can't just ask me all these questions, as though my life is an open book for him to read and discuss with me. Questions about my parents, my sister, those horrible days and nights in Rouen. I put a hand up as if that gesture could stop the torrent of inquiry.

"Please, PJ, don't run away from this. Please just tell me where you are going. Is it really La Défense? Why can't I come, too? We can do this, PJ," Jay pleads, his eyes glassy. Sweat runs out from under his beanie. It's taking him a horribly long time to catch his breath. He closes his eyes. His chest rises and falls under his black wool coat. When he reopens his eyes and looks at me, there is an open plea for an answer—any answer.

"No, Jay, I can't," I say, fighting tears. "I just—I ruin everything." It's so much worse because it's really true. Wiping my soggy face with my scarf, I tear down the street, making the nearest left turn toward Pigalle that's out of his line of vision.

★ ★ ★

In the bathroom of the club, I lock the stall door and lean back against it, feeling strangely safe in the semidarkness. Watching Jay go through that misery is torture, and knowing that it's me causing him such pain is intolerable. I wish I could stop hurting him, wish I could stop falling in love with him as much as he's fallen in love with me. The only difference, I realize gripping myself around the waist to stop myself from shaking, is that he lets himself fall, and I keep trying to fight my way back out of it.

10. ALEX

It Only Hurts for a Minute

---

*F*rench verbs are the very hardest thing about learning French. I mean, don't get me wrong, my French gets me around fine, but my French teacher has decided we all need to know the conditional tense for every single verb in the French language for our next test. I'm going over my flash cards for this exam in the library on my lunch break from the Lycée, wondering, once again, how my life went so wrong.

My PJ plan was perfect! I thought for sure my mother would relent after hearing the new version of events, but she only softened *slightly* when she got my e-mail about my friend in trouble. The next time I spoke to her, she just sighed and told me to buck up.

"Even if your intentions were pure gold, Alex, you have to learn to take responsibility for your mistakes," she said wearily.

"But, Mom!" I protested. "This is cruel and unusual punishment! I was only trying to help a friend!"

"Look, my darling little Robin Hood, I know you're sorry," my mom said. "But this is good for you, Alex. I mean, look at how much closer we've become because of all that's happened."

I swallowed the bile in my throat and resisted the impulse to hang up on her. What kind of ridiculous reasoning was this? My mom believes us to be strengthening our mother-daughter bond because I call her with more frequency now that I've been punished. Yes, of course, I call her more now! I call her to beg her to make it stop!

"I love you, my darling," my mom cooed at me over the phone. "But I've got to run. You'll thank me for this one day."

The hardest thing about these French verbs is figuring out when to use them.

Our French teacher told us that we should practice them by making up sentences about what we would do in extraordinary circumstances.

Si j'avais un million d'euros . . .

Si j'avais une vie parfaite . . .

If I had a million dollars, I would be able to pay back Mme Sanxay and say good-bye to her snot-nosed children forever.

If I had a perfect life, my best friend Zack wouldn't be so infuriated with me.

My BlackBerry rings. "Alex, dear," Mme Sanxay says, interrupting my train of thought. "I've got a horrible task for you."

"Excellent," I say. "How lovely."

"The children have to get vaccinated. Someone at their primary school went to Switzerland and brought home measles. Now the school says all of them have to be vaccinated or the whole of Paris will be infected," Mme Sanxay says bitterly. "They'll be quarantined if they don't get vaccinated today." She goes off on a trail of French swear words and insults. "A few years ago, no one was getting vaccinated, now they say you have to. . . ."

"I'm vaccinated," I say, as if this is helpful information. "In the States, everyone is."

"Good for you, Alex," Mme Sanxay says. "But if the children have to stay home until this outbreak clears up at school, I just don't know what I'll do."

"Does measles make you sleepy?" I ask, wondering if perhaps the kids will get sick for a few weeks and just take naps all day. I could then spend my afternoons, instead of my lunch breaks, studying for French. And maybe start to put some semblance of a social life back together for myself.

"Alex! Measles can be fatal. This is serious!"

"Okay, okay!" I say. I doodle a picture of a dress I saw in the window at Le Bon Marché in my notebook and wait for her to tell me what she wants me to do.

"There is a clinic in Clichy that gives walk-in vaccinations. I'm sure they will be flooded today with children from our school. If I bring the children to you, can you take them? Then I wouldn't have to cancel my appointment."

"Are you seeing the lawyer again today?" I ask.

"No, Alex. Not that it is any of your business, but I am seeing my therapist. I'm still working out a lot of my abandonment issues."

I make a scandalized face at no one, just for my own entertainment.

"*Je comprends,*" I say soothingly. "I know you're going through a lot."

She clears her throat in response. "I will bring Albert and Emeline to your school. You will walk with them to Clichy? And supervise that they get all the shots they need? I can take Charles with me to my appointment."

"*Oui*, that's fine," I say without thinking. When she rushes to hang up the phone, I realize what a horrible thing I've just committed to. Those children are coming to the Lycée. Everyone in our program is about to see why I've been MIA for all these weeks.

I kick a nearby bookshelf, stubbing my toe. C.A.B strikes again!

I take my BlackBerry out and write my mom another e-mail about how torn up I am over PJ's disappearance and my part in it. She responds with a scan of the Amex bill that got me on her bad side in the first place. I delete it and go back to my flash cards.

★ ★ ★

Livvy waits with me on the Lycée's front steps for Mme Sanxay. She told me she'd be coming with the kids in a taxi.

I haven't told Olivia much about what's been keeping me so busy these days. I had only said, actually, that I got a little internship to help me with my language skills.

"So Madame Sanxay is your boss?" Olivia asks me. She wrinkles her button nose, confused. "And she's dropping something off for you?"

"Kind of," I say. Olivia is the type of person who you don't exactly want to fill in on all the ways you've let other people down. I feel sort of ashamed about the way I spent my mom and Mme Sanxay's money last semester when I imagine trying to explain it to her. She's so good. She just wouldn't get it. That it was all for a stupid boy who didn't love me.

"She just needs me to run this little errand for her. In Clichy. Don't you have dance rehearsal?"

"Not till five," Olivia tells me. She slips her arms around my waist for a hug. "I feel like I haven't hung out with you in so long, Alex. I miss you. Tell me more about your job. It sounds really interesting. And it is so great that you are getting better at French. Actually, I had noticed in class that you were improving. That's awesome!"

"Eh." I shrug as I check each passing car for the Sanxays. "Not until five?"

"Nope. I mean it, Alex, I've really missed you. I'm so sorry I haven't been there for you." Her face is completely distraught under the hood of her purple sweatshirt. "I hope you haven't felt . . . left out. I feel really guilty."

I push my sunglasses onto my head and give her a puzzled look. "Why do you feel guilty, Livvy? You haven't done anything wrong . . . *have you*?" I jokingly lean forward, like I'm interrogating her on a cheesy cop show. "What's up?"

"Well, you know, when I wanted to give up on the Lycée, you didn't give *me* a hard time about it. You were such a good friend about it. You totally understood."

"I've seen pictures of Vince! I would have gone home to that piece of meat, too! I never would have left to begin with!" Vince was *so* hot. I couldn't believe Olivia just dumped him on Christmas the way she did. She told me later that she felt smothered by him, even though he lives in L.A. and totally has his own life at college. I told her I wouldn't mind smothering myself with him. She didn't really think that was as hilarious as I did.

My jokes are *so* underappreciated around here.

"And when *I* gave you a hard time about giving up on the Lycée, instead of celebrating with you or really giving you as much support as I meant to, I've been kind of doing my own thing. And I told you I would help you. I'm *really* sorry. I've been in a funk. Did you know Thomas broke up with me?"

"*Oh, mon Dieu!*" I say, truly shocked. "When? Why?"

"A while ago. I didn't see it coming at all. Things weren't really going that great with us. I still kind of miss him." Olivia fiddles with her big silver hoop earring. "Will you forgive me?"

"Sure, Liv." I give her a big wet kiss on the cheek. "You always feel so bad about everything. I barely even noticed. I figured everyone's just really busy." In fact, I'd figured that she'd been busy shacking up with Thomas in his dorm room! Now that I know differently, I do feel a little left out. I wonder if people have been doing fun things without me on the weekends that I don't even know about—people like Zack.

God*damn* this stupid babysitting and tutoring business! *When* is my mother going to call off this stupid thing? I want my old life back! No, I *need* it back.

I look at Olivia sitting there so wistful and vulnerable. I wish I could tell her something in exchange for her reaching out like this. For a second, I wonder how she'd react if I told her PJ was back. But I know I can't. At least not yet.

"I love your new hair," I tell Olivia finally, reining it all in. "It really is so cute dark like that."

"I just got it freshened up over the weekend," she beams. "I'm so into it!"

Mme Sanxay's cab finally pulls into the bike lane and spits out the two older children that consume so many of my waking hours. Before they can tear straight into the hallways of the Lycée and do something horrible that I don't even want to contemplate, I catch one under each arm and steer them back around. Mme Sanxay calls me over to the cab window and gives me directions. "*L'hôpital* is just across from the Square des Batignolles. Do you know it?"

I look at Olivia, who's openly curious about Mme Sanxay and has followed me over to the car.

"*Je le connais*," Olivia says. "I can tell Alex where to go."

"Good," Mme Sanxay says. "Who are you?"

"*Je m'appelle Olivia*," she tells her pleasantly. "*Et vous?*"

"*Je m'appelle Priscina Sanxay*," Mme Sanxay tells her. "*La mère d'Alex m'a parlé de vous, Olivia. Vous êtes danseuse, n'est-ce pas?*" Mme Sanxay seems to instantaneously pick up on the fact that Olivia's French is infinitely better than mine.

Olivia answers her, also in French.

"*Alors*, my appointment!" Mme Sanxay says, patting Olivia's hand through the rolled-down cab window and making a general sort of wave at her children. They pay no mind to her. They pull on my arms, having spotted an ice-cream cart en route to the Parc de Monceau.

"No, guys," I say, carefully watching the front door to the Lycée and trying to make my way down the block in case any stragglers come out the door and see me wrestling with two children. But Olivia is acting all clingy, trying to keep talking to me.

"So, your job is to watch these kids?" she asks, smiling down at them as if they're cute. Everyone knows they are monsters.

"That, and other things," I say.

"Like what?"

"Well. I just help Mme Sanxay with stuff. I don't know, just stuff."

"So you are their nanny," Olivia says, not accusingly, but like she just wants to understand better.

Albert pinches me to see if I'm paying attention. They still want ice cream.

"Albert! *Arrête!*"

Olivia kneels down and addresses Albert and Emeline on their own level. "So, what are you two up to today?" she asks them in French, her voice friendly but not condescending. "Fun things planned?"

"*Oui, nous allons chez le médecin,*" Albert tells her, letting go of the flap of my skin between his thumb and his forefinger.

"*Pour votre santé,*" Olivia nods very seriously. "*Très important.*"

"*Très important* indeed," I say. "Shall we, mongrels?" They don't know what "mongrels" means. Or I hope they don't. Regardless, they each start to follow me down the street. As they do when we go to the Jardin de Tuileries, Albert goes in front of me so I can make sure he doesn't get hit by one of those insane Paris drivers, and Emeline grabs one of my hands.

"They really trust you, Alex," Olivia says. She's looking at them with pure baby lust in her eyes. If I didn't think my mom would find out about it immediately, I would saddle her with this abhorrent task and spend the rest of the afternoon stocking up on free perfume samples at Marionnaud. "You must be a great nanny," she says with a wistful laugh. "It makes me miss Brian, watching you."

"I'm *not* a nanny," I say, rolling my eyes. "Bye, doll." We make off for the Square des Batignolles *sans* Olivia.

As we cross the Squares des Batignolles and head toward the facing hospital, I make a fatal, terrible mistake. It happens like this:

"When can we have ice cream?" Emeline asks me.

"Never," I say, even though Mme Sanxay slipped me a ten for just that very reason before she hurried off to her appointment. *"Jamais."* Sometimes, I just like to mess around with them.

Emiline starts to cry. *"Mais . . . Maman . . . a dit . . . que nous pouvons acheter une glace!"*

Albert joins in. Their racket is mortifying. "Hush!" I bark at them. "Of course, you can have an ice cream. I was only kidding around. You can have it *after* your shots." It came out before I could stop it, and then, I knew I was cursed for the rest of the day.

Mme Sanxay had repeated the words for vaccination shots—*piqures pour la vaccination*—for me several times so that I would be able to tell the doctor exactly what I needed for the kids. There's also a form, a stack of forms, actually, that the doctor needs to sign before the kids go back to school. The French *love* paperwork!

But she also told me that I must not say anything at all about shots in front of Emeline and Albert. Like all normal children (not that these children are normal—they are *terrors*, pure and simple), the idea of a shot sends them into psychosis. But there it is—I did it. I said the words. And now I am going to pay for it.

Emeline goes berserk. Crying, spitting, screaming.

Albert freezes. He won't go forward nor backward, to the right or to the left. He doesn't know what directions those shots are in, and he's not taking any chances. He won't move.

"*Pas de piqûres! Pas des piqûres!*" Emeline screeches. "*Non non non non non!*"

"Stop that!" I yell back at her. "You have to! And then I will buy you an ice cream after. I will, I will! I promise! Come on, you guys!"

Emeline throws herself on the paved path through the park. "*Non!*" She beats her little fists on the ground. A deep red spotting rises from under the collar of her school uniform up her neck and threatens to crawl up the bottom of her face. "*Non!*"

"Albert, tell your sister to please get up!" I say. Albert is still not doing anything but staring straight ahead. "*S'il vous plaît!*" I beg.

Across the park, I see a group of mothers conferring. *Assistance!* I think with relief. But when I squint at their facial expressions, I see that it's more like contempt. Another woman who does not know how to control her children.

"*Bonjour!*" sings a voice from behind me, "*Bonjour, mes petit amis!*"

Someone, a guy, is leaning down and speaking animatedly to Albert. "Are you stuck, *monsieur*? Do you need help getting your feet to work? Perhaps we've had a little breakdown here." He speaks English, and when he looks from Albert to me, I gasp.

It's that crazy guy Denny, from the Jardin du Luxembourg! I'd know those pleated chinos and that baseball cap anywhere. After all, they're the stuff nightmares are made of. The world would be such a better place if people didn't dress like that.

Jeez! I look around, hoping no one from the Lycée is watching me and thinks I have some kind of *date* with this guy.

"What are you doing here? I thought you lived in the Sixth," I say, putting my hands on my hips. "Did you *know* that we were going to be here?"

"Ah, I just scan the place looking for broken-down vehicles." He switches over to slow, kidlike French. He says something about the motor, and perhaps being out of gas. Then Denny lifts Albert's backpack up a few inches and lets it drop back down. "*Le moteur est pas mal*! Everything is working! Beep, beep! You're holding up traffic!"

He darts around Albert like they are two cars on a crowded Paris thoroughfare. Albert finally cracks up. Distracted from her tantrum, Emeline looks up from the pavement at Denny. Even in those chinos and his preppy jacket, he looks a bit like a clown. In fact, they make him look *more* like a clown.

"*Tu as un problème?*" he asks me mockingly. "The children will not go to the doctor?"

I look at him, still shaken by the fact that here he is, out of nowhere. "Denny?" I ask hesitantly, not totally sure I remember his name right.

"*Oui*," he says. "We met the other day at the Jardin du Luxembourg. It's great to see you again. I live near here, actually, not in the Sixth. I was just at the green market. Would you like some *myrtilles*? American girls, I have heard, eat nothing but McDonald's and Budweiser beer, but I think perhaps you are not like most American girls."

Denny holds out a brown paper sack of fresh blueberries.

"No," I say. "No, thank you, I mean. And I've never had a Budweiser beer in my life, if you must know."

"But McDo? You must love McDo! Even French women love McDo!"

I do, every once in a while, have a hankering for McDonald's french fries that just cannot be silenced. Before our fight in Cannes, I could always count on Zack to accompany me and pretend to eat his share of a large fries, even when we both knew I was the one eating most of them.

"You don't know anything about American girls," I mutter. "Especially not me."

This guy makes me nervous in a way that isn't just annoyance. I keep thinking I've met him before. There's this instinctive impulse in me not to let him know anything about me. It's probably just my well-ingrained repulsion at the idea of dating a Frenchman after my mom and I were so brutally betrayed by my dad . . . he's probably—I try to relax myself—perfectly normal.

Though it is definitely *not* normal for a guy, however cute he may be, to walk up to you and small children and offer you berries. This is just the kind of thing other girls' mothers warn them about. My mother, on the other hand, warns me about things like ruching (it's deceptively unflattering when placed wrong on the body) and that flea market in the East Village that seems like it would have great deals on vintage clothes but in reality is a total rip-off. My mom would probably think this guy is harmless, or even kind of fun. She wouldn't want me to date him, but she'd appreciate his kind as a cultural presence in Paris. A bon vivant in *la grande tradition parisienne*. It's very French to talk to random people in parks. But the berries—no one has ever offered me berries.

"Measles outbreak," I say, though I know I don't need to elaborate on our plans for the afternoon. "We're on our way to the doctor."

I notice Emeline and Albert are now happily gorging on the blueberries in Denny's bag, getting sticky purple remnants all over their chins and their palms. "Don't eat those!" I gasp, a beat too late, pulling them away from the paper bag, now getting soggy at the bottom with blueberry juice.

"Why not?" Denny asks, popping one into his mouth. "They're organic. And I don't mind."

"Because we don't even know you," I tell him. I take the silk handkerchief tied to the handle of my tote bag and wipe the kids' mouths.

"I'd like to know you," Denny says, twisting his mouth into a wry smile. "I'd like to take you to lunch, like I said the last time we met."

"I don't go out with bizzaros like you who follow American girls from park to park."

Denny laughs. "That's why I like you. You're so . . . what's that Americanism . . . *spunky*."

"Spunky?" How rude! I grab two purple hands and pull them away from Denny and his blueberries. "We're in a hurry. Sorry, I can't stay." I use all the disdain I have in me to let him know that I am *not* sorry I can't stay. I don't like the way this conversation is going. This time as the last time I saw Denny in a park, no matter what I do, I cannot get the upper hand. He acts like he knows me, and it's just plain unsettling, to the point where I can't even appreciate his cuteness. What's most annoying is that he obviously thinks I'm this quaint little well-behaved American. Hah! I am the *least* like that of anyone in our entire program!

Denny impishly waves at us in between popping blueberries into his mouth. "*Au revoir, mon Americaine!*" he calls as we walk away.

I tug the kids across the park and down the sidewalk beyond it. They protest, knowing we are en route to needles and pain.

"Oh, get over yourselves," I huff at them, pushing us all through the glass entrance doors. "This will take five minutes. We'll get an ice cream, take the métro back home, and hope never to see that blueberry freak again." I say that, of course, before I see the massive line of parents and children waiting to be seen by the one doctor administering the MMR vaccine. Apparently, it's not just Saint-Ignace kids who might have been exposed to the kid who went to Switzerland—it's also every child who ever played on the same playground with him, as well as all kids who live in his building.

About forty children in front of us, each panicked senseless about the shot.

"Oh. My. God." I look around, wondering if there's a nurse I can talk to. I have to be able to bargain my way to the front of this line. I look in my wallet. As I suspected, there's still only that ten-euro bill for ice cream in there. If I had more, maybe I could slip an orderly a twenty and skip this madhouse. But slipping someone a ten—they'd probably poke me with a needle, they'd be so insulted.

It takes an eternity to get to the front of the line. We get held up further because the idiot nurse asks me how old Albert and Emeline are.

"Oh, you know," I say. "School age. They go to school."

The nurse stops filling out the intake form and asks me in a very unnecessarily withering voice if I really do not know how old my charges are.

"Ask them if it's such a big deal to you," I say and push them forward. When they hold up the fingers for how old they are, I learn that Albert is seven and Emeline is five.

Good to know.

Luckily, the doctor is a pro and sticks Emeline and Albert so fast that they don't even know it's already over.

I hustle the kids out of that place with one aim—métro, apartment, collapse on the couch in front of the TV.

"Alexandra?" whines little Emeline as I'm pulling her and her brother along. "Didn't you say we could have a sweet after the shots?"

"Um, yeah," I say. "But we have to get it back in the Sixth. I don't like this neighborhood, okay?"

"But, Alexandra . . ." she starts to cry.

"Oh, give me a break, kid," I huff. "It will take ten minutes to get back to your apartment. Just chill out."

I'm within sight of the station when, out of the blue, I'm again waylaid by a face that is becoming obnoxiously familiar. I cross my arms over my chest and raise my chin up so that I will look older.

"Alexandra," Denny says to me, falling into step with us as if we were expecting each other. "Why wouldn't you want me to know your beautiful name?"

"How do you know my name?"

"Because your 'daughter,'" Denny laughs, "just called you Alexandra."

"Good work, investigator." I roll my eyes and look past him as if I've got more pressing things to think about than all my admirers. This guy cannot take a hint. "Can we go home now?"

"Alexandra—"

"Alex," I interject. "No one calls me Alexandra." I don't know *why* I felt the need to come out with that bit of personal information, but it was true. Only Emeline can't seem to get my name right.

"Alex," Denny says. "You must let me get to know you better. You might be my dream woman . . . gorgeous, sassy, great with children . . ."

"I am not great with children," I growl. I put my Gucci sunglasses on even though it is not sunny out, so that I'll look more sophisticated. "Which shows what a great start we're off to—you already have a

173

completely misguided impression of who I am. Who says 'sassy'? Besides, I'm not sure why a grown-ass man such as yourself is hanging around in parks, flirting with babysitters and saving the day for brats like Emeline and Albert. Don't you work? Go to school? Anything?"

"I work for my uncle," Denny tells me. "He's out of town at the moment. So I am taking care of his affairs in Paris. He lives in Ternes. Remember, I told you."

He did tell me. So that at least gives some credibility for why we've run into each other again. Sort of.

"Well, that's fascinating, but we have to be going home," I say. "The three of us are all due for a nap."

"I thought you promised *les enfants* they could have ice cream if they got their shots," Denny says. I glare at him. "Didn't she say that in the park?" he asks the kids, who nod shyly.

"Ugh," I say. "Yes, I did say that. But they got candy in the hospital from the doctor who gave them the shots, plus blueberries. Isn't that, like, a lot of sugar?" Then again, I'm no reasonable judge of how much sugar kids are supposed to eat. I just know not to give them cigarettes or booze or hot dogs. Something about nitrates, whatever those are. "Besides, that was before I realized I was being stalked in this neighborhood. We really must be going."

"In France, we don't have this word 'stalked,' I don't think. Here, I believe we would just say that a beautiful woman is being pursued," Denny says. "Before you depart for the Left Bank, how about I show you the best sweets shop in Paris?"

The kids immediately start wailing that they have to go to the best sweets shop in Paris, and I give up. I follow Denny along, shaking my head in defeat.

Denny takes us to a candy store that could have been on the set of Willy Wonka. The walls are covered in pink-and-white gingham paper, and all the shelves are painted in rainbow colors and overflowing with concoctions of every possible mixture of caramel, chocolate, marzipan, and hardened sugar. It's a fairy-tale land for cavities. I half expect that if the kids shut up for one second, we'd hear the gently running stream of a chocolate river somewhere nearby. But there is too much to look at for them to be quiet. They squeal over the lollipops, the stacks of fudge, and *patés de fruits*, the glossy hand-pressed fruit jellies dusted with crystallized sugar. When Albert sees a miniature castle carved from white chocolate, I think he might truly lose his mind—it's not every day that dreams come true.

The shopkeeper, who must see this exact scene about eight hundred times a day, finally shoots me a look to rein the children in. I hold out my hand to the two of them, flashing the ten-euro bill.

"This is all I have!" I shout. "So don't go crazy, midgets!"

Emeline and Albert have no idea what I am saying. They see the money, and all the chocolate and pastels and fruit jellies, and their brains practically explode.

We finally settle on lollipops, lemon fondants, suckers with clown faces painted on them, some cherry-flavored salted caramels, and a peppermint patty for good measure. I pay, short by thirty-three centimes, which Denny graciously gives to me to cover the cost of the candy. Then, as Emeline and Albert hurriedly unwrap their enormous rainbow lollipops and start licking them furiously, as if they are in a contest, Denny asks me if *I* want anything.

"No, that's okay." I shake my head. I hadn't even thought of getting myself anything here. It strikes me as odd, when I've always had such a sweet tooth for Parisian treats before. I guess I just wanted to make sure to get enough for Albert and Emeline to keep them quiet for the rest of the day. "You've done enough, thanks." I look up at him, catching him winking at the shopkeeper as I shrug my shoulders at all the candy.

"You must have something," Denny protests. "You spent all the money on the children. You like dark chocolate?" Denny asks me, spotting what my eyes immediately go to in the glass case. "*Moi aussi. Deux petits sacs de boutons, s'il vous plaît?*" he asks the shopkeeper, a middle-aged woman who has definitely had plenty of samples over the years. She hands us each a baseball-size package of individually wrapped dark-chocolate buttons. The bag is tied with a pink bow.

"It's actually been a while since anyone got me a gift," I muse as the four of us go back outside and eat our candy, standing on the sidewalk. George once bought me a pack of cigarettes, and I convinced myself they meant something, but they didn't.

"I would have thought you would want one of the rainbow lollipops," Denny says, pointing at the enormous tree of lollipops in the window.

"Really? Why? Seriously, you have very much misjudged me," I say. "I would never want anything as tacky as that lollipop."

"Never?" Denny asks. "I have a hard time believing that."

"Why do you keep acting like you know me so well?" I ask him. "You don't know a thing about me. And if you did, you'd be *very* shocked." I'm surprised at how dour I sound.

Denny just laughs.

Behind the lollipops, the shopkeeper turns the lock on the candy shop door and pushes the sign around so that it says FERMÉ. The sun is starting to go down, even though daylight savings time is already in effect. It must be really late already.

"Oh, crap," I say, and check my BlackBerry, which is completely out of battery power and has died. "I bet Madame Sanxay's called me four hundred times! Where's the métro from here?"

I expect Denny to make more jokes to try to get me to stay, but he doesn't. "I can't wait to see you again, Alex," he says and watches us go down into the métro before walking away.

So it's official, I think, surprisingly calmly. *I've got myself a stalker.*

★ ★ ★

I've never really liked my French teacher, Mlle Hebard, but today I feel about as sympathetic toward her as I would toward someone who stole my cab on upper Broadway at midnight in the pouring rain. She's chosen today of all days to really rip me a new one about having not completed a stupid "*que* vs. *qui*" worksheet, and I am just not having it.

"Is it really that big a deal?" I ask her, pushing my bangs out of my eyes. "It's one worksheet, one time."

I've never not had my homework completed because last semester I copied off of Zack's every day, and this semester I've been too terrified of further punishment (more time with *les enfants*!) that I've been doing it religiously.

I'm usually not so mouthy to teachers, but maybe those kids are having an effect on me. I am feeling *decidedly* immature. I stick my tongue out at Mlle Hebard's back, and she catches me.

"Aleecks! Do not argue wis me," Mlle Hebard says, shocked. When I look around the room, I see twelve other shocked faces staring back at me, including Zack's and Olivia's. George and Drew are not even trying to suppress their laughter, and the Texan twins look disgusted, as though they just came across a dead rat.

Okay, so that was a tad psycho, I say to myself after I've been dismissed by Mlle Hebard to go talk to Mme Cuchon about my attitude. Well, what do you expect? I ate seventeen chocolate buttons for dinner last night, since my host family had finished their meal long before I got home from the Sanxays. And the only conversations I have with anyone these days are about diaper rash and SpongeBob. Think about how much better my French would be if I ever had time to practice it with people who weren't in grammar school!

I tell Mme Cuchon what happened with my homework. I leave out the part about sticking out my tongue.

"I'll have to give you two work hours for this afternoon," Mme Cuchon tells me, taking her glasses off and rubbing the bridge of her nose.

"Work hours? Today?" I say. "I have to go . . . " I stop myself before actually saying aloud that I can't go to *detention* because I have to *babysit*. It's all really too mortifying to put into words. When did I become a high school cliché?

"Alex, you and I both know you were doing well for a good while, and you've been letting your schoolwork slide again in the last few weeks. I'm not sure about this job of yours. I understand you're trying to make up a debt incurred by Penelope, but I need to see that you can be expected to handle a program this rigorous with that kind of extracurricular time commitment. Report to the office at three this afternoon. We have some filing you can do for your work hours."

★ ★ ★

One of the ways the Lycée saves on payroll costs, evidently, is by farming out unpaid tasks to their troublemaking students. After school, I report to the office with about eight other students, no other Americans but me. We are each given a job to do for the next two hours. Some of the younger girls have to go peel potatoes in the dining hall for tomorrow's lunch; the boys mostly have to haul winter gym equipment into a storage unit. Another older girl and I are assigned to stuff invitation envelopes for a board of directors fund-raising auction happening in April. We get to do this in the headmaster's office since he is in a meeting.

We sit cross-legged on the floor and silently put an invitation, two raffle tickets, an RSVP card, and RSVP envelope into each of the larger envelopes. There are hundreds of envelopes to fill. This will definitely take the entire two work hours. It's better than potatoes or the gym, though.

The other girl working with me cracks her neck joint and moves over so that she can lean against the wall. I decide that looks way more comfy, so I do it, too. The only bad part is that we can't see if anyone is coming in or out of the office. I check my BlackBerry stealthily (I'm in the middle of a long e-mail conversation with my cousin Emily about what she should wear to her first sorority formal at Georgetown, where she is a freshman this year), but I don't want to get caught unawares.

All of a sudden, the door to the office next to the headmaster's—Mme Cuchon's office— slams viciously. The other girl and I exchange amused looks. We wait to see if Mme Cuchon will swear or say something funny. Through the wall, we can hear her pick up a phone and then ask for someone. The next part is too fast for me. I can't figure out what she is saying.

"*Qu'est-ce qu'elle dit?*" I whisper to my envelope-stuffing partner.

I didn't realize this before, but the girl totally speaks English. Score! She translates for me.

"She is saying something about *Le Monde* calling her today," the girl says. "She says they want answers—what is she supposed to tell them?"

"I don't know." I shrug.

"No, that is what she asked." The girl shakes her head at me and goes back to the invitations.

I listen for a while longer. I know they must be talking about PJ. I want to ask the girl to keep translating, but she obviously doesn't care what Mme Cuchon is saying. The French students at the Lycée don't know Mme Cuchon. They don't really pay her any mind. She's not, like, this central force in their lives like she is in ours.

"*Je vais aux toilettes,*" I tell her and duck outside the headmaster's office so I can hang around Mme Cuchon's door. She really doesn't realize how loud she's speaking. I can also tell she's not talking to a colleague or a school parent. She's too familiar, too emotional. This could be good!

I concentrate very carefully on what Mme Cuchon is saying, the same way I do when the kids are talking to me and I know I'm never going to get them to tell me in English. My French really is better than people think; I *have* been speaking it since I was a baby.

"Those horrible Marquets," I hear Mme Cuchon telling the person on the phone. "Every year, I wonder about them. This year the man was literally salivating when he saw Penelope's picture. But I never imagined *this*!"

I'm so surprised I nearly place my hand on the door and push it open to ask, "What is that supposed to mean?" But I stop myself just in time.

I keep listening.

"She was a good girl, a strong girl. Very tall. But so thin. So fragile. And too beautiful. I should have given them an ugly one. What if he . . . oh, God, he couldn't have," Mme Cuchon continues. Her voice breaks and I can hear her start to weep. The pure shock of it brings a moan to my throat in empathy, as if I might start weeping, too.

"The board won't let me talk to the press and will barely let me talk to the police. No one seems to be finding anything! I don't think they want to. I think they just want it to go away. But it's been two months . . . no body . . . we haven't been able to reach her family to confirm any of these rumors flying around.

"Every year, he leers at all the girls' pictures and tells me which one he wants," Mme Cuchon sobs. "And every year, I send one to him like a lamb to a slaughter. And I watch them, I watch them so carefully. But this one, I didn't realize . . . I thought she was a troublemaker . . . it's all my fault. They're such big donors, I was too afraid to stop him. . . ."

A phone rings in the reception part of the office, piercing the air. I jump away from the door, but I can still hear her faintly.

"I have to get off," Mme Cuchon says quickly, sniffling. "*À bientôt*." I run back into the headmaster's office and sit back down on the floor. I stuff envelopes, listening to Mme Cuchon gather her things, open her office door, and then leave. It's clear she thinks the office is empty.

Interesting.

Very interesting, actually, I muse as I stuff some more of those envelopes on the floor.

This is *quite* a dilemma.

My thoughts are running a mile a minute. The oh-so-perfect Lycée de

Monceau is actually corrupt and immoral, apparently.

Pervy rich men getting whatever they want is nothing new. I've been around New York society long enough not to be surprised by that. But a school knowingly sending a beautiful girl into the private apartment of a childless couple, crossing their fingers she'll finish up her year in Paris unscathed?

That's absolutely tawdry.

I wonder what PJ would do if she knew what I know.

I remember those backpacks on the cover of *Aujourd'hui en France*, and suddenly, it feels as though someone turned off all the radiators in the office. It's suddenly cold and clammy, like there isn't enough circulation in the air. PJ's on the edge already. This information could ruin her already fragile sanity.

And yet this might be the very information she needs to save herself.

I tuck a strand of hair behind my ear, and for once in my life, have no *clue* what I am going to do next.

11. ZACK

Something in Between

On Wednesday afternoon, Olivia and I pop into the computer lab before she goes to dance class and I go to PE. Alex is in there, too, eating cold udon noodles and getting the sauce all over the computer she's Gchatting on. I hear her snort at something on the screen, and when I look at her, she's rolling her eyes and chewing at the same time. She looks up as though she's expecting me to ask what's so funny. I ignore her. The noodles look good, though. Last semester, I would have just stuck my fingers in there and grabbed some for myself.

I just can't let myself fall back under the spell of her friendship again. I mean, what kind of friends go behind your back to get your crush to fall in love with them? She only ever thinks of herself. In fact, I'm glad she showed her true colors over Christmas break. To think what other damage she could have caused if given the chance!

"Hey, Alex," Olivia says. "What are you up to this weekend?"

"Hey, Livvy," Alex says. "I've got to meet with my private tutor on Saturday. But other than that, I'm free. What are you guys doing?" She assumes Livvy and I will be hanging out together, which we often are now.

"I don't know. Wouldn't it be fun if we all did something together?" Olivia says. She looks hopefully at me. Her puppy-dog eyes suggest that I should organize something. "What are you up to this weekend, Zack? Have you heard from—"

I turn my head a notch to keep her from mentioning André. I don't want Alex to know about him. I remember the pact we made, that we'd help each other get boyfriends. I'd never help her now. She'd just find a way to ruin things somehow.

I turn my attention to my Gmail. There's a forwarded e-mail from the Netherlands railroad Website—an e-ticket itinerary for a train from Amsterdam to Paris, with Bobby's name on it. Arriving this Friday at four PM.

"*À bientôt*, dude!" Bobby typed along the top of the e-mail.

I release a long breath, having completely forgotten that this was the weekend Bobby was coming. My stomach flutters. Bobby and I had such a nice time together in Amsterdam—that is, until I accidentally pushed him into a canal. But all that is forgotten now. Maybe this weekend, we'll get to know each other the way we are supposed to.

I tap Olivia's arm, about to tell her that actually I do have plans this weekend, exciting plans, but then my screen refreshes, and I have a new e-mail. When I see the name in bold at the top of my in-box, I gasp in alarm. "Oh, Livvy!" I squeal, not even caring if Alex is still listening in. "Look!"

"What?" she says, leaning over to see. "Is it him?"

Anybody free this weekend? I have got an extra ticket to a great show happening at Qualité du Sound. Text me if you want to go.

Bisous!

André

I break into a wide grin, Bobby's visit whisked clear out of my mind. "That's so amazing. I was just thinking about him."

Olivia smiles generously. "Really?" she says, though she knows I think about André constantly. "Oh, wait," she says, looking back at her screen. "I just got the same e-mail."

I prickle a little, hearing the note of pity in her voice. "Still. It's nice that he's inviting me. I'd kind of like to take him up on it."

"Yeah," Olivia says. "Definitely. You should, Zack."

At my homestay tonight, I pluck through all my clothes, trying to decide if I have anything cool enough for Qualité du Sound. I'm working up the nerve to e-mail André back and tell him I'd love his extra ticket. I'm thinking I might wear this shredded T-shirt I got in Amsterdam. It's a little over the top, but it might be *perfect* for a hard rock show!

For the second time today, I realize I've forgotten Bobby's visit this weekend!

I run into the kitchen and check with my host parents that it's okay I have a guest stay with us.

"Sorry about the short notice," I tell them. "It'll be okay, right?"

"Sure, no problem," Romy, my host mother, says. Jacques, her husband, shrugs from behind his laptop. He doesn't care what I do, even less than Romy. He's the reason they signed up to be host parents—he's a Lycée de Monceau alum and speaks great English because he works for an international security firm and does a lot of business abroad. He works a lot, and Romy also has a job, but they seem to be pleased enough with their family and like being host parents okay. I mean, what's not to like about me, right?

"He does not mind sleeping on the couch, your friend?" Romy asks. "Or maybe you will?"

"You're right," I say. "I hadn't thought of that. I'll sleep in the living room; Bobby can have my bed."

"We have a—what is it called?—mattress of air, too," she offers. "If you want to sleep in the same room."

I purse my lips and try not to blush.

★ ★ ★

Friday I go to meet Bobby at the Gare du Nord. I'm wearing a new cobalt blue toggle coat, and the snow has melted enough so that I can wear my leather wing-tip shoes instead of my snow boots. I hang out sipping a takeaway coffee in front of La Brioche Dorée like I told him I would be when he got in. I have to say, no Hollywood stylist could have set a more perfect scene. I even came straight from school, so I was over an hour early for him and didn't have to hurry through the métro or risk messing up my hair or wrinkling my clothes.

Bobby nonchalantly wanders up to me before I even notice him. "You look awfully familiar," he says. I nearly dump my coffee over in surprise. How did he manage to sneak up on me like that?

"Give me a hug, you big klutz," Bobby says with a grin. When we hug,

I feel that same sense of ease that I felt when Bobby showed me around Amsterdam over Christmas break. "Well, hello," he says, taking a step back and looking me up and down. "You look great, dude."

"Oh, yeah, well," I stammer.

I forgot how attractive Bobby is. He's the kind of guy you really have to know to appreciate how handsome he is. His smile is his best feature. It lights up his whole face, dimpling his cheeks and crinkling his broad forehead. His face is so open, confident without being cocky, like André. He's taller than I remember, too, and I notice he's let his blond hair grow out a bit, so it's shaggy and kind of hipsterish. It works. All of him absolutely works. I feel weak.

"Actually, you seem kind of ill or something," Bobby says, giving me a closer inspection. "Are you feeling all right?"

"*Oui, bien sûr!*" I say, super-loud. "I'm fine!" I give him another hug, keeping my coffee held high so I won't spill any more of it on myself or him. "Great to see you, buddy!"

"Yeah, buddy," Bobby says. "Well, shall we get out of here? Where to next?"

When Bobby and I get home from the train station, Romy tells us she's going to make *pavé de boeuf* on the grill. "I'm making dinner for us, yes? You do not have plans to go out?"

"That sounds wonderful," Bobby says before I can decline. "We can't get any decent beef in Holland. I wouldn't know how to cook it if we did, either."

"*Merveilleux!*" Romy seems very pleased. "Would you boys like a glass of wine?"

"Sounds great," Bobby says, again too quickly for me to answer first.

I want to tell him that Romy is so boring that we can't possibly stay out here in the kitchen, drinking wine with her while she makes dinner. We'll use up all the conversation topics before we even eat! But Bobby drags one of the kitchen table stools over to the counter and watches Romy chop carrots. "So, you like to cook?"

Bobby finds this out and more during the course of his glass of red wine. When he finishes, Romy immediately pours him another glass. "Help me with the salad, okay?" she asks him, looking girlish. "This sauce is just about to boil over."

It's odd that Romy is suddenly acting like she's a total homebody. Most nights, she bakes a casserole from Picard and throws some lettuce in a bowl. Mireille, Romy's ten-year-old daughter, cooks more than Romy does!

"*Oui*, I wish I got to cook more," Romy says. "You know, cook real food. But after work, I am very tired, you know."

"Totally," Bobby says. "This looks delicious. Can't wait to try it."

Jacques and the kids come in. Romy is obviously very taken with Bobby.

"Why don't we all go to Mass at Chartres on Sunday morning?" Romy says after a few moments of steak chewing. "It is supposed to be a gorgeous day. We can have brunch after."

"What a great idea!" Bobby says and beams around the table.

If he's trying to impress my host mother, it's working. She stops me as I'm helping clear the table after dinner and tells me that my friend is "*très gentil*" and that she's very glad I had him come to stay.

Bobby's brought a bunch of American DVDs with him, stuff that his parents send via the Foreign Service mail. He asks if I want to watch one tonight as he's getting settled in my room.

"Yeah, sure," I say. "But they probably won't work with Jacques and Romy's DVD player."

"We could watch it on your computer in here," Bobby suggests.

I shove my hands into my jeans pockets, rocking on my heels. "Oh, yeah," I say. "That would be good." We pick a romantic comedy I never saw in the theater, something with a bunch of boys and girls in New York, all falling over each other to date the others. I don't think it ever came to the theaters in Germantown, Tennessee. I try to set up my twin bed like a makeshift couch, with the pillows along the wall so we can lean against them without having to lie down on the bed. We prop up my Mac between us and slide the disc in.

"Your *parents* sent you this?" I ask in disbelief after a few minutes. So far, boys have kissed boys, girls have kissed girls, and someone has suggested a threesome. "My parents wouldn't just throw this across the room, they'd build a bonfire and burn it."

Bobby laughs. "They would not."

"You laugh," I say, "but it's true. You're from the South, you know what I'm talking about."

"But here's the question: Would they hold the condemnation service and prayer meeting before they threw the DVD in the bonfire, or after?"

"Oh, definitely after," I say. "As Pierson would say, there ain't no question. And before they took to the pulpit, they'd have called all the local news stations to come out and the Christian Coalition so that someone would bring the frankfurters for supper after the event."

"Sounds like the Southland," Bobby says. "Old fears do die hard."

"How is Pierson, anyway?" I say. "Still wild about Hannes?"

"*Ja, natuurlijk,*" Bobby says in Dutch. "They're as in love as ever. Haven't you talked to him recently?"

"No," I say. "Not since you guys called that one time. I've been . . . kind of busy." Busy waiting for *André* to call.

Bobby doesn't say anything. We watch the rest of the movie, which is campy but not very funny. Awkwardly, we say good night, and I go out to the couch for the night.

The next morning, I lead Bobby from my apartment building to the Eiffel Tower. It's only about a twenty-minute walk from my homestay. He's seen it before, on a trip to Paris with his parents, but he's got a new camera, and he wants to take photos of it. Afterward, we hang out on the plaza underneath it for a while and people–watch. I take him over to the Princess Diana memorial near the avenue de New York. People still decorate it with pictures and photos.

"I'm so glad I'm not touring Paris with *that* guy," Bobby says in a low voice as we cross the street to the banks of the river. He nods his head at an older, obviously American middle-aged guy in shorts (in March!) with a camcorder and a wide-angle lens camera around his neck. He keeps barking at his wife and kids to hurry up because they have more to see. An enormous road map of Paris is tucked in his hand, which they're all gathered around, trying to figure out how to get from here to the Louvre. "You could be French for how well you know Paris! Thank God, I'd hate to have to compromise my reputation by walking around with you if you didn't."

"You think?" I say, flattered. It's something I secretly pride myself on, but I didn't think anyone else would notice. Even among the Lycée kids, I think I've got a better sense of direction around this place. Even better than Alex's, and as she'll tell you, she's been coming here since she was a baby.

I remember the day everything started to click. It was last November, right before Thanksgiving. I went to get a haircut, and I realized after a few moments of chatting with the stylist that I was getting everything she said. When I came out of the salon, I had the exact haircut I'd imagined. I'd explained what I wanted perfectly!

I kept noticing things like that. It wasn't just the language, but I could also eat a croissant as I walked down the street without getting any crumbs on my jacket or my scarf. I knew exactly which car to get in on the métro so that my transfer would be easiest when I got to the right stop. Paris was just working. I had finally made it feel routine.

"Definitely," Bobby says. "You've assimilated among the natives quite convincingly, I'd say. But then, I didn't know you before. It might have been an even more impressive transformation than I'm giving you credit for. You can tell me, Zack." He puts an arm around my shoulders and looks me straight in the eye. "Did you come out here in a mullet and a muscle tee? Were you missing teeth? Was your neck as red as a *langoustine*?"

I shake him off and roll my eyes. "If you don't know by now that I take very good care of my teeth and always wear an SPF of at least fifty, especially on my neck, then I might as well send you right back to Amsterdam."

"So sorry to have offended, my lord," Bobby says in a mock-deferential tone, bowing at the waist. It reminds me of the way I used to tease Alex about her super-fashionable mom, C.A.B.

"Oh, stop it." I laugh, lifting him back upright. "Do you feel like going to the Musée d'Orsay? It's right near here." I point down the Seine to the stately art building that looks more like a train station than a museum. "Or we could walk around Île Saint-Louis."

"Sure, anything," Bobby says. "It's just good to be here with you. We had some loose ends to tie up, I felt like. You know?"

"Did we?" I laugh.

Bobby glares at me. "You know we did. We do. You never told me why you pushed me in that canal!"

"Bobby, we've been through this." I can't help laughing because I have spent so much time e-mailing and Facebooking Bobby apologies for that business. "I did not 'push' you in! It was a frickin' accident!"

In my sappier moments, I would imagine the canal incident as the most hilarious story we could tell together—as a couple. But it's been twenty-four hours and Bobby's company is far from couple-y. I can't help feeling a bit awkward. I am still haunted by memories of music and dancing and falling onto André's bed in Oberkampf.

"Ah, well, you *were* pushing me away. If you hadn't pushed, I wouldn't have fallen," Bobby says. "Not to be too bold or anything, but you've never come out and said if you were scared or freaked out or disgusted or what. And you haven't given me much else to go on since I got here." He looks at me expectantly, his eyes wide and waiting for an explanation.

"Well . . ." I say, remembering how I awkwardly set him up in my bed, alone, last night. Was he expecting something more to happen after the movie?

"So anyway," Bobby says. "What's been happening in Paris? Anything new? Pierson was saying that while I was here I just have to meet some friend of yours—he kept calling her Medusa."

"Oh, Alex," I say, biting my lip. I hate the way missing her sneaks up on me when the thought of all the fun we used to have together catches me off guard. Things have changed so much. "Alex and I aren't really friends anymore."

"Oh, what happened? She turn someone to stone or something?"

I look out over the river at some boat tours going by, full of tourists waving at the shore and snapping photos. When they see people along the sides of the river, they all wave in one giant movement. "She just turned out to be . . . disappointing." I wonder if I should tell Bobby about one of the rumors I heard at school. Sara-Louise told me that PJ ran away with money Alex gave her. It only makes me more convinced that Alex was being duplicitous over Christmas break. If she *knew* PJ was leaving town, and played along as if she didn't, what's to say she didn't *purposely* take advantage of it so that she could get Jay all to herself in the South of France? Sounds, actually, like a classic Alex plan.

"Kind of . . . cosmically disappointing," I say. "Like the most disappointing a person could be."

"That's too bad," Bobby says mildly.

"Yeah, it happens." We stop to look at antique postcards being sold from fold up booths along the river. They're overpriced here, but it's fun to browse.

"Did you tell her you were upset at her?" Bobby asks.

"Yeah, she knows," I say.

"I mean, did you explain why you felt the way you felt? Or did you push her into a canal?"

"Very funny." I pull out a silhouette of Oscar Wilde and wonder if I should buy it, as a show of GLBT solidarity, since I'm pretty sure he's known for being a really witty homosexual. Not having actually read any of his work, I decide against it. "But since you're so interested, I will say that, no, Alex and I haven't had a heart-to-heart about all the ways she's destroyed countless lives on her ruthless quest for world domination." I want to make it sound silly, because how true it might be really scares me. "I have not made any attempts to thwart her evil plans."

"You should," Bobby says. He's picked out an old pictorial card of Notre Dame. "Talk to her, I mean."

I snort. "Aren't you bossy? Fine, I will one day." It's a lie. I'm dying to change the subject. If you don't know Alex, you'll never understand. And of all the people in Paris, I know her the best of anyone. I know what disasters she is truly capable of.

"Let's not go to the d'Orsay today. It's too nice out to be inside. Is that cool?" It's a gorgeous day. Spring in Paris is bipolar—just this week I've worn three different types of jackets. Today, I am just wearing a cardigan and a scarf.

"No problem," Bobby says. "Like I said, I want to do whatever you feel like doing." We walk east along the Seine, whistling at the long line leading out the door of the Musée d'Orsay, all the people waiting just to get in. I'm glad we chose to stay outside.

"So do Romy and Jacques know that you're gay?" Bobby asks me after a while.

"I'm not sure," I tell him. "I don't think they really care, either way. It's kind of nice. At home it is such an issue. Or would be if they knew. My family's so dramatic. I wish I could trade them in for a less Evangelical model!"

"What do you mean by dramatic?"

"Where to begin." I think of my dad and how he gets into these really long rants about good versus evil. He definitely doesn't condone homosexuality. My mom doesn't either, but she's the type of super-Christian that likes to hang around with sinners on a volunteer basis. I could see her thinking of my gayness as a mission for her—she wouldn't reject me, but she'd be convinced that with the help of Jesus, she could talk me out of it. "If I came out to my real parents, they'd freak. My parents would cry, and there would be prayers and our pastor would probably have to come to our house and go through all my stuff to see if there was anything too gay in it. The whole church would find out. They'd all be called on to pray for me! It's kind of like I hide being gay from them not because I'm afraid of what they think, but because I don't have the energy for all the *activity* it would require to deal with."

"That's understandable," Bobby says.

"But I also *want* to tell them, in a way, because I am so fricking sick of hiding who I am. That takes a lot of work, too. And on some level, I *know* they know. They have to. I mean, I wear jewelry." I shake my wrist with my heavy ID bracelet on it. The tag has a rose on it and says PAZ. I bought it online.

"You ought to tell them." Bobby looks at me laughing and shrugs. "Why not tell them while you're over here? You could write them a letter. Then, at least, they can deal with the initial shock while you're away. They might be more calm by the time you get home."

That's not a bad idea, actually. I imagine myself writing the letter, putting a stamp on it, and pushing the envelope through the slot of the mailbox that says "*Étranger*" on it. Then there would be nothing I could do to change it, short of committing mail fraud. And though I might be somewhat, oh, you know, *countercultural* in many ways, I ain't no good for nothing law breaker.

"Maybe I will," I say, grinning at Bobby. "You know, I'm glad you came to visit. First with Alex, now with coming out to my parents. What would I do without your guidance?"

"Be miserable and lonely," Bobby says. It's really nice, having him to shoot the breeze with. It sounds obvious, but the things he says just make sense. It is pretty sweet to have another guy like me to talk to after a semester of drama queens and overprivileged jock guys at school.

"You like ice cream?" I ask him.

"Who doesn't?"

We walk east, commingling with tourists from absolutely every corner of the globe. At the Pont de la Marie, past the picturesque medieval stone landmarks of Notre Dame and Saint Michel, I take a left and cross the bridge over to Île Saint-Louis, the smaller of the two little islands in the middle of the river. I weave Bobby in and out through the tiny streets, first constructed during the Middle Ages. Back in the day, these little islands were the whole of Paris. Mlle Vailland told us all about it in history class. For some reason, when you are on Île Saint-Louis, you always feel like whispering. It's so quiet, even though it's practically in the dead center of the city and loaded with tourists.

Alex introduced me to the sorbet shop Berthillon when we first got to Paris—back when it was still warm out and Alex still had plenty of money. Alex never deprives herself, so she bought us each two scoops of the famous ice cream. I laugh a little, thinking about her making love to her little wooden spoon. Alex *loves* sweets!

Bobby loves the ice cream, too. "You're so smooth when you order, too," he says. "My Dutch isn't even as good as your French."

"Not true," I say. "Aren't your parents Dutch?"

"Yeah," Bobby says. "But in Amsterdam everyone speaks English. I never have to use it at all."

I feel proud of myself for making sure I speak French as much as possible and also for trying not to wander around looking like a tourist. Even if a waiter or a clerk tries to speak to me in English, I always just go on in French as if that's the only language I will deign to speak in. Covering for Alex all last semester really gave me a lot of good practice.

I've noticed Alex's French is getting a lot better, though. Livvy told me back at the beginning of the semester that Mme Cuchon made her get a tutor to stay at the Lycée. She's been so MIA lately; I guess she's still hitting the books. 'Bout time.

"This just feels kind of perfect, huh, dude?" Bobby asks me after we finish our ice cream, sitting on a bench in the sun at the very eastern tip of Île Saint-Louis

"Uh, yeah," I agree, snapping my thoughts from Alex back to Bobby. It feels so difficult to keep my thoughts on Bobby, even though he is sitting right next to me with that sweet smile of his. "Perfect."

And it would be, too, if I were here with my real boyfriend, eating ice cream, enjoying one of the first real spring days in Paris. That night at the beginning of the semester, when Bobby called me from Pierson's cell phone about PJ, I was giddy thinking about this exact type of scene taking place. But now, I feel melancholy, lost a little. If things had worked out, I'd have everything I want: a boyfriend *and* Paris. Instead, I got ambiguity. Like always.

★ ★ ★

Sunday morning, Jacques pulls the car around and we all hop inside. Mireille sits on her mother's lap in the front seat so there is room for all the boys in the back.

"Chartres is very beautiful," she turns around to say to us.

"So I've heard!" Bobby says. "Mass is at eleven?"

"Yes," Romy says. "But you are not Catholic, right? Everyone in Holland is Protestant, I am thinking."

"No, not Catholic. Not Protestant either, I don't think," Bobby says. "I don't know what my family is. My parents are pretty secular."

"Zack is not Catholic." She hands us each an orange and a paper towel from her purse. "So you two can eat something. The rest of us have to wait to have communion."

I sneak Paul a couple slices of my orange since he's looking ravenously at it. Now I know my church is weird and all, but not getting to eat anything for another two hours? That's just not right.

The cathedral at Chartres is, as André would say, bloody enormous. Its two mismatched spires won't even fit within the viewfinder of my camera, even when I stand all the way across the plaza from the entrance. Bobby and I ooh and aah at the Gothic structure with a lot of holy-cow-we're-from-America-and-don't-know-nothin'-about-nothin'enthusiasm for Romy's benefit. When we walk into the church, all four members of my host family dip their fingers into a stone bowl of holy water, then cross themselves and kneel at the end of a row of wooden chairs before we take our seats.

I start to laugh when the priest walks in, preceded by two altar boys in white robes. "What are you thinking about?" Bobby whispers.

"My parents already think I'm going to hell for acting gay or whatever," I say. "But if they saw me in this church, they'd just go ahead and exile me from the family."

"But Catholics are Christians," Bobby says, confused. "Aren't they?" He seems to have a moment of doubt but looks to the soaring cross hanging from the vaulted ceiling for confirmation that we are, indeed, in a Christian house of worship.

"Not the right kind."

Romy shoots me a questioning look. I smile to show her that there is no problem. I should shut up, but I can't resist speculating how weird it is that my parents find any kind of religion except their own holy-fire-and-brimstone brand of Southern Baptism incredibly unacceptable. "They wouldn't even think this was beautiful," I say. "And it's like the most insanely beautiful building I've ever seen. You know?"

"Yeah," Bobby says. Even though I know his parents probably don't burn romance novels or Communist newspapers at weekend revivals like mine do, I know he knows what I mean just because he's from the South.

"Until our church got built, we had our services in the high school gym," I whisper. "How can you fully praise God in the presence of the stinky foot smell that He created?"

Bobby cracks up behind his hand.

The priest begins the Mass, and the kid in me who thinks church is boring feels like translating for Bobby, but messing up the translation to make him laugh. Romy would just keel over in shame if I did that; you can tell she thinks coming to Mass here is a rare treat. And besides, the Francophile in me—as well as the lover of beauty and culture and gorgeous old things put together in just the right way—thinks it's really pretty special, too.

The priest intones prayers that seem like the weekly rituals. The whole congregation knows just what to say and when. They know when to sit and to stand, and at some point, everyone puts their palms in the air, held just a tiny bit away from their body, all at the same time. There are no theatrics, no speaking in tongues.

The candles flicker in the darkness. I let my thoughts carry me away, up into the rafters, decorated with perfectly placed stone from French quarries from nine hundred years ago. The paintings, the organ, all of it arranged just the way it would have been back then. Feeling all that history around you is breathtaking if you stop to really analyze how long people have been sitting in this same room where you're sitting, doing the exact same thing that you're doing. When you think of life like that, it blurs what should be important and what probably shouldn't be.

I think of PJ, and my heart aches for her all over again.

★ ★ ★

After a brunch of *tartines* and wine for Bobby and me, the whole family drives back to Paris. I get a text message on the way back. I squeeze my hand between Bobby's hip and my hip to get my phone out of my pocket. I figure it's Pierson, teasing me about having Bobby coming to visit. He desperately wants his two best friends to be a couple.

It's not Pierson. It's André.

HEY U MISSED THE BEST SHOW LAST NITE. U WANT TO GO 4 A DRINK THIS EVE?

I look at Bobby and smile nervously.

"Who is it?"

"Just this British guy I met," I tell him. "He's a ballet dancer in the same company as Olivia. He wants to hang out. You up for it?"

"Sure," Bobby shrugs, completely oblivious to my suddenly racing heart. I can't believe I am about to text back that all three of us should get together. It might be the recipe for the most awkward evening of my life. But that's how much I want to see André again.

★ ★ ★

André's been at brunch, too—a Sunday afternoon affair that's lasted until almost five o'clock. We meet him and some of the other dancers at a place near his apartment. It being in André's neighborhood means he of course knows all the best places to go. Oberkampf teams with activity day and night—there are so many people hanging out at outdoor café tables and others browsing through bookstores and gift shops stuffed with Japanese imports and fair-trade goods. Its mix of people throws you for a bit when you get off the métro—old North African men selling newspapers, tall black women in brightly colored headdresses going to the post office, big groups of French kids sprawled out on benches, ripping chunks of bread off of a shared baguette. Now that I have been here a couple times, I roll with the varied crowd. I feel even more like an insider bringing Bobby here. I can tell he's just taking it all in.

André's dancer friends greet Bobby and me with friendly smiles when we walk into the crowded corner bistro where they are having post-brunch drinks, but then all immediately go right back to speaking in French among themselves. They are in a big, fashionable group, some smoking cigarettes right there in the bar even though technically it's illegal to do so in Paris. In the smoke, against the rough raw-wood walls and the blurry mirror behind the bar, they look hazy, as if we've stepped onto a movie set ten years ago, before we had digital photography. Everyone is colored the way pictures of my mom and dad were when they were first married look—old-fashioned, leisurely, faded.

"Which one is your friend?" Bobby asks me in a low voice.

"That one." I point at André, holding court across the room. He's standing at the end of the table even though everyone else is sitting down. His lips are stained purple from the glass of red wine that he is drinking. He gave me a *bisou* on each cheek when we arrived, but once we found chairs he went back to the conversation he was having.

"You know him through Olivia? Is she here?" Bobby asks me.

"No, she's not here. She's probably at home studying," I say. "Do you want to get something to drink?"

"Well, don't you have school tomorrow?" Bobby wonders. "I mean, I figured that I would be able to sleep in, but you probably have to get up pretty early, right?"

I look at the time on the screen of my cell phone. "Bobby, it's five thirty. I think I'll be okay with a drink, even on a school night. . . ." I roll my eyes. "You should have one, too."

"Okay," Bobby says easily, but I hear a note of sarcasm in it. We wait awkwardly for our drinks to come, not saying anything to each other, and no one really saying anything to us, either. We each get a beer, a 1664. I drink half of mine in one gulp, hoping it will take the edge off if I get kind of buzzed.

André looks *good*. Of course he does! André is hot. Dark brown skin, hair shaved close to his head, big brown eyes set far apart, making him really stand out. As a dancer, his talents supposedly lie in his strength. He's a great person to partner with, according to Olivia—not too showy and always very aware of other dancers. His body emotes confidence, a perfect sense of being just where he wants to be. In the thick of a crowd, in a large mass of people and music and conversation, he holds his own very, very well.

It occurs to me that this could be a great opportunity, what with Bobby being right here, and looking so sweet and cute and catalog-handsome in the railroad-worker hat over his shaggy blond hair and loose-fitting, comfortable jeans, to make André notice how desirable I am. I mean, why not make him a little jealous? Doesn't he deserve it, ignoring me like that after inviting me to come all the way to the Twentieth Arrondissement?

Scooting my chair closer to Bobby's, I inch my hand up to hold the top rung, right near the center of his shoulder blades.

"So Hannes and Pierson are still at it all the time?"

"Like rabbits," Bobby says, sticking his tongue out. "You'd think they would have chilled out by now."

I crack up as if Bobby is just the most hilarious person in the world, catching André's eye as I slap my knee. "Totally like rabbits!" I howl.

André immediately floats over from across the room and throws his arms around me. It worked!

"Hiccups! I've missed you!" he says as he claps my shoulder, beaming at me with those purple-brown, wine-stained teeth. So, *that* part of him doesn't look so hot. But the rest . . .

"Hiccups, hiccups," André repeats, then tugs on my cheek. "So cute!"

I grimace but try to hide it. At first, that joke was cute, but hearing it now makes me feel like his little cousin or something. Not desired like I want to be.

"How come you didn't wear one of your vests?" I ask, hoping to elevate the discourse. I take a swig of 1664.

"My vests?" André looks down at his slim white T-shirt. "What are you on about?"

"You know, one of those vests I saw at your apartment, the cowboy one and the black biker one?"

"Oh, yeah, my vest," André snorts. "Just not a vest day, I guess. That's a bit of a random question."

"Hmm, yeah, you've just got great vests," I say lamely, not able to come up with anything else. We swallow the dregs of our beers, and André makes a move toward another friend.

"Well, I guess we'll be going now," I say.

André grabs my shoulders and kisses me on both cheeks. "Lovely to see you! And give me a call soon—you know, I did have a splendid time with you the other night."

The mention is just what I'd been craving—proof that André didn't forget what had happened between us—but it's the wrong time. Bobby sucks in breath and closes his eyes.

Bobby is disappointed and embarrassed. I can tell. Back on the street, he won't say anything. He's pretty frigid for the rest of the day, going to sleep in my room early and leaving for the Gare du Nord early the next morning without even waking me up to say good-bye. He does, however, leave a sweet note for Romy and Jacques, thanking them for a nice weekend.

WHO WAS THAT GUY WHO CAME W/ U THE OTHER DAY? André texts me later in the week after PE one day.

NOBODY, I reply. JUST AN OLD B-FRIEND. JUST FRIENDS NOW.

An old boyfriend makes me sound *very mature*, I think, waiting for André to text me back, to keep the conversation going. It makes me sound like I've woken up in more strange beds than just André's.

Please let me not have made a giant mistake, I keep thinking after I don't hear back from André. Please let me have thrown all my eggs in the right gay basket.

12. OLIVIA

Black and White

"Remember Kiki? From New Year's?" André asks me as we walk out of rehearsal at the Place d'Italie.

"Yes, of course!" I stretch my arms up over my head, trying to loosen up a shoulder cramp. "How could I forget Kiki?" Kiki is the Moroccan singer who accompanied André and me while we did a dance duet at the Revue Bohème on New Year's Eve. Tall, totally intimidating, insanely gorgeous, and blessed with a voice that brings tears to your eyes, Kiki is someone I could *never* forget.

"She does cabaret in Belleville every Friday night. At Le Zèbre. Did you know that?" André goes to the Vélib' station, Paris's citywide bike-loan station, and inserts his membership card so he can take one of the few bikes left in the docks along the sidewalk. Almost all the dancers in the Underground Ballet Theatre use Vélib' except for me. I always take the métro. I'm terrified of getting hit by a car while riding a bike. Paris drivers are insane!

"Kiki does?" I say, wrapping my cotton scarf around my neck, then taking it back off. It's muggy tonight; the scarf will just make me more sweaty than I already am from rehearsal. "I bet it's incredible."

"Should I ask her for some tickets? Say three—for you, me, and Zack? Or is Zack's ex still in town? Perhaps four, then?"

"Zack's ex? You mean Bobby?" I ask.

André nods. "That's the one."

"Bobby actually decided to go back to Amsterdam," I say.

André purses his lips, bemused.

"So just . . . " I wonder if we should invite Alex. I don't think Zack is quite ready to start hanging out with Alex again. If he ever will be. He goes silent if I even say her name. ". . . three tickets. She's just going to give them to you? For free?" My experience with Kiki was not unlike that I've had with strict Catholic catechism or a master-dance-class teacher. You just do what they say; you don't ask them for anything.

"Yeah, she offered them to me when I saw her at the boulevard de Belleville market last Saturday," André says. "Should be fantastic. I'll text Zack about it now."

I smile to myself, kissing André au revoir as he rides away on his bike. I head toward the métro. *Zack's day just got a whole lot better,* I think. But somewhere deep down, I feel a pang of loneliness.

"How was Bobby's visit?" I ask Zack as we settle into a park bench at the Parc Monceau with hot quiches in hand for our lunch break. "Did you two have fun?"

"It was okay," he says. "Most of it, anyway. Did André tell you I brought Bobby out with some of his friends while he was here?"

"No," I say, surprised. "How was that?"

"Stupid," Zack says. "I barely got to talk to André, and Bobby got pissed. André said something about that night I went home with him."

My eyes bulge. "Really?" Zack looks wretched, remembering it.

"I guess it's not that big a deal," Zack says. "I wasn't really feeling Bobby, anyway." He brightens. "And it's great André got those tickets to the cabaret this weekend! I can't wait."

"I know, me neither." I unwrap my quiche and inhale deeply, savoring the decadent, buttery scent. Once a month or so, I'll have a fattening lunch like this. In Paris, it would be a sin not to, though I always feel a little guilty afterward, as if my body hates me for having to work off all those lipids. "Having visitors in Paris is strange, isn't it?" I muse as I take the first steaming bite of onions, egg, and spinach. "When Vince got here, I wasn't sure whether to laugh or to cry."

"Really?" Zack asks me, popping open a can of Coke and taking a fizzy sip. "How come?"

"I spent so much time missing Vince first semester that I didn't realize how much I was changing," I explain. I watch a park worker organize a bunch of toddlers onto the backs of elderly ponies for a ride around the park's circuitous path. Their parents follow closely behind the ponies, ready to catch them if they topple off. "I mean, I didn't even get a cell phone until Madame Rouille made me, after the whole drama going down to Cannes and Perigueux. I spent a ton of time in phone booths, trying to get a hold of Vince so we could keep up our connection! When I saw him in person, I, like, immediately realized I was *so* over it."

"Right when you saw him?" Zack asks. "Like, falling out-of-love at first sight?"

"Exactly," I nod. "Obviously, it took a little while for me to fully let go of him and what we had, but I knew something was up as soon as I had that weird first reaction to seeing him in person. It was the beginning of the end." I finish my food and search for a Kleenex in my backpack to wipe my hands. The quiche is so buttery I'm afraid I'll leave a stain if I touch anything now. I find one and wipe my fingers individually, then my mouth. Zack takes longer with his quiche, savoring each bite and making less of a mess of his hands than I did.

You aren't supposed to sit on the grass in Paris parks, so that the grass will grow green and bright, the way it is starting to right now in the first fledgling days of spring. Most Parisians ignore that rule, and sunny days like today bring families out in full force. I notice how Parisian children dress so much more elegantly than American children, donning mini-trench coats and V-neck sweater vests. They're so cute, rolling around in the green grass. When Brian was that age, he used to just sit in the sun for hours, watching the breeze move the blades of grass back and forth. Zack and I watch the scene in silence for a few minutes before he responds.

"But if you didn't have Thomas, maybe you wouldn't have felt that way," Zack says. It cuts into me to hear someone else put it in such a straightforward way, but he's right.

"Most likely, no, I wouldn't have felt that way," I say. "But Thomas was just a catalyst. Vince and I weren't right for each other. We grew apart."

"How do you know?" Zack asks. I detect a slight drop in his tone, a small clue that he might be looking for a little positive reinforcement.

"Alex would say that love is something you can read in black and white," I say.

Zack rolls his eyes and snoottily adjusts his glasses. "Alex would say love is a battlefield. Winner takes all."

"What I mean is that you know right away whether or not you still have that spark, or if you ever did. But I don't agree. You have to give it some time. Love grows, or blows up, or burns out. Don't you think?"

I wait for Zack to weigh in, but he doesn't. He brushes invisible crumbs off of his perfectly ironed jeans, and stands up to go back to school.

At the gates of the park, we see a big group of boys from the Lycée standing around eating sandwiches: George, Drew, Robbie from Orlando, and two other guys they hang out with, Kyle and Nathan. Kyle recently started hooking up with Anouk, Sara-Louise's host sister, and Nathan supposedly has a crush on Sara-Louise. "Hey, guys!" I call to them, smiling. "Beautiful day, *n'est-ce pas?*"

Drew shrugs. The first time I met tall and lanky Drew, I was convinced he was from California, like me. Just as right now, he always wears shirts and jackets slathered in surfer logos, and if he's not wearing flip-flops, he's got some worn-out Uggs on. He's actually from Connecticut and is one of the spaciest kids in the program. Anytime you get stuck working with him on a class activity, he spends most of the time beating out some reggae rhythm on the desk. "It'll probably start raining," he says.

"It's not supposed to rain today," Zack tells him. "Don't you ever look at the weather report?" Zack can't hide his disdain for Drew, but I think he's harmless. If I hadn't been still going out with Vince at the beginning of the school year, I might have taken Alex's advice and been interested in getting to know Drew on another level, when she was interested in George.

Now George is with Patty, one of the twins from Texas, and Drew is rumored to have taken Patty's sister, Tina, on a couple disastrous dates. I realize with a start that we're both single now—at the same time. It's a thought that makes me long for Thomas and also blush with the possibility of finding out Drew's the one I should have pursued all along. Somehow, I doubt it. But then again, if there's one thing Paris has taught me, it's that love is not a predictable thing.

I giggle. "Drew doesn't need to look at the weather report," I say. "It's not like rain would change what shoes he was going to wear." I've seen Drew come into the Lycée with his Uggs soaking wet. He just doesn't care.

"That's the truth," Drew says. "All that's on the news these days is that PJ girl, anyway. That's a real buzz kill."

Zack's eyes widen, but I give him a look to let it go. "So, what are you guys doing tonight?" Drew asks us. "These douche bags are all going out with their *girlfriends*." George looks away. It's still a little awkward with George and me, because I'm Alex's friend, and we know he really stomped on Alex's heart. But Alex has a rubber soul—she bounced right back from that misstep. I haven't seen her look twice at George since we got back from Cannes.

"Since when do you have a girlfriend?" I tease Nathan, enjoying watching his face color.

"Ah, he tries," Kyle says. "Me and him are going to see a movie at the Odéon with Anouk, Mary, and Sara-Louise. Some French artsy movie. Feel like going in my place, Zack?"

Zack stiffens. I look between Zack and Kyle, feeling like I've missed something. Why would Zack want to go to the movie?

To avoid elongating the weird silence, I jump in and tell Drew that Zack and I are going to a cabaret at Le Zébre.

"Are drinks included?" he asks.

"Um, yeah," I say. "Did you . . . want to come with us?" I'd have to ask André for another ticket.

"Sounds awesome," Drew says. "See you tonight."

★ ★ ★

"How did this happen?" Zack says in my ear as he, André, Drew, and I are seated in a small dinner theatre and each brought a glass of cheap dark red wine. "Why is Drew here?"

As the waiter tops off Drew's wine glass, Drew drums out an idiosyncratic beat on the tabletop. There's no music playing. Drew just always kind of has some beat going on his head.

"So, all your friends went and got girlfriends, huh?" I ask Drew, leaning forward across the table, feeling brazen, powerful. "And now you have to come out with us just to have anything to do at all!" I smile to show him that I'm teasing. "I'm glad you came. I think it's going to be a lot of fun!"

"Just bring on the booze," Drew says with a smirk. "Anything's great if you drink enough." We watch a group of brass musicians set up in the corner of the dinner theater. When I look at all the tables around us, I notice that most of the diners are men. The ticket price includes unlimited free red wine, and the bottles keep on coming. I take a long sip and motion for the waiter to come refill my glass.

"I like the sound of that," André says, and downs his wine so he can get some more while the waiter is tending to me. Drew and Zack ultimately do the same.

All at once the lights dim, and a slow, long note bellows from a trumpet just to the right of the darkened stage. A spotlight flashes on, and the frayed purple velvet curtain jerks open, revealing Kiki. Unlike the times I've seen Kiki in the past, however, tonight she is wearing a long sheer skirt and a belly-dancing top, complete with a jangly belt and clinking bangles on either arm. The audience explodes into applause, hoots, and hollers. "Kiki!" shouts a man from the back. "*Je t'aime!*" The audience laughs and continues to go crazy.

André yells, "*Nous t'aimons aussi, Kiki!*"

Kiki squints out over the audience to find our table. When she sees who we are, she points at us with one long finger. "Ah!" she laughs, delighted. "*Mes amis, les danseurs. Bonsoir!*"

Silence washes over the crowd gradually as Kiki waits for her first note from the band. Suddenly, the same trumpeter launches into a jazzy solo, and then is accompanied by his fellow musicians in an intro that brings the crowd to its feet. Kiki bobs her head, sways around, and then begins to sing with that big, beautiful voice of hers. She sprinkles fresh pink and yellow flowers all over the stage, decorating the space and filling the small theater with their pungent, almost tropical scent.

Everyone is entranced by her, and as her song continues, the waiters circle the table, refilling glasses of wine and bringing out dinner that no one touches. It's some kind of fish that looks as if it's been sitting on a truck all day. The food doesn't seem to be the point of the cabaret. The point is to drink, but most of all, to watch and fall in love with Kiki.

Isolating her hips, her waist, her shoulders, and her neck, Kiki flits around the stage making over-the-top come-hither postures and singing *very* suggestive songs that she often acts out with hand movements. Everyone roars at her jokes. She's so much different in this context. I've admired her since the first time I heard her sing, but tonight some part of me wants to be her, too, to have all these guys look at me in that same desiring, breathless way. When she bends down or rolls through her hips, you can hear the guys in the room practically moan with how much they want her. It's like an art in its own right, and I wonder briefly if I'll ever be the kind of person who could be so seductive.

Everyone claps along to her salacious songs all the way through until intermission. I'm overcome with respect for her and inspired by her as a performer. She works a crowd better than anyone I have ever seen.

"Bloody fantastic!" André yells over the applause and grabs my hand to bring me backstage to say hi to Kiki. She's uncapping a large bottle of vodka as we walk in.

"André! Olivia!" she shouts when she sees us. "*Mon amour! Ma petite!*" She pours him a shot, then one for me, then takes one herself. "What a night!"

"Olivia," she then stops to ask me very sagely, "would you like to join me onstage tonight?"

"*Mais bien sûr!*" I laugh and nod, thinking she is joking. "I would love to!" The vodka is so warm going down my throat. André squelches a burp next to me, which makes me crack up.

"Please, Olivia, will you join me? I need another back-up dancer for the final number. One of the girls missed her train and hasn't shown up yet. I know you can dance. Will you do it?"

I immediately blush and shake my head. André makes an "O" with his mouth and puts his hands up in enchanted surprise.

"Oh, Kiki, I couldn't!" I say. She cannot be serious. "How could I? This whole . . . *thing* is way out of my league."

"Don't be silly," Kiki says, brushing my doubts aside like so many flower petals on the floor of the stage. "This is nothing. The other girl will teach you the routine. Please say you'll do it. They'll love you out there." Flattered and terrified, I'm at a loss for what to say to her.

"Have another shot, love," André says, handing me the bottle. "Then make your decision." He winks, and I realize he and Kiki have a lot in common—they can both convince you of just about anything.

★ ★ ★

And that's how I end up under the glaring lights of Le Zèbre, rotating my hips and shaking my *derrière* along to the punchy music of a jazz band in front of a sweaty crowd on a Friday night. The other dancer taught me the routine after André went back out for the second half of the show. The steps are easy, and with the help of the Absolut I'm plied with for courage, the attitude is not hard to affect at all.

In fact, it's pretty incredible, being up there, knowing I have the admiration of a room full of people. I feel so powerful and strong. I'm wearing black fishnets, a black bikini bottom, a black push-up bra top, and a long white men's shirt over it. Affixed to my high-heeled pumps are little golden bells that ting with every step. As the music gets going, my smile stretches wider and wider. My splits and my kicks are high and perfectly in sync with the other backup dancer's. I feel almost as if I'm in a dream, except for the look on Zack's face in the middle of the audience. He's smiling, but he's also shaking his head. He can't believe what he's seeing. I love shocking him! Everyone assumes I'm so innocent and incapable of being different.

The music stops and the song is over. The other backup dancer and I flank Kiki in a Vegas-showgirl style pose with our arms above our heads, our white shirts ripped open to expose our scanty bras beneath. Our last move is to let our shirts fall to the floor. As the applause thunders and the catcalls and whistles reach my ears, I don't know what comes over me. I turn around, unhook the back of my black bra, and throw it behind me into the audience. I run backstage laughing hysterically with my arms covering my chest. Kiki takes me in her arms and rocks me like a drunken baby. "You are the best! *La meillure!* You are a natural!"

I'm so proud of myself! The applause alone is totally worth it!

★ ★ ★

Feeling like I am floating on praise, I find my clothes and then the boys, waiting outside the stage door. They erupt in whoops when I come out!

As we walk over to a nearby bar, Zack keeps looking at me and shaking his head in disbelief. "That was not Olivia. That was your secret stripper twin," he says. "Am I right?"

I still feel a little drunk from Kiki's vodka, but when I get up to the bar to order drinks, I find myself craving something stronger than a glass of wine. I want to drink something that a cabaret star would drink after a show! I order a martini, just because it is the first thing I think of.

Zack puts his arms around me and squeezes tight. "This was really fun, Olivia. Sometimes I'm really surprised at how much fun we've been having, in spite of everything."

Zack's usually not such an emotional drunk, but I see that his brown eyes are misty. I wonder if guilt about PJ is still sneaking up on him, making him feel like he doesn't deserve to be having fun. I used to feel that way, sometimes, when I was with Thomas and I didn't know yet that PJ was in Paris, safe with Jay.

"You know, Zack," I whisper. "There's something I haven't told you about PJ yet—"

"Olivia, you were brilliant!" André sings, interrupting me. "Your timing was perfect! And that wink you gave the audience was genius!" I fall back into the shower of compliments. Everyone raises their glasses in the air.

"To you, *ma belle!*" André toasts me.

"Damn, Olivia," Drew says, appraising me thoughtfully. "You were smokin'."

Drew's looking so handsome tonight, in a lavender and white striped collared shirt. He dressed up for the cabaret! I didn't notice until now. I wonder why not? I tell him I think so.

Zack makes a face at Drew, but André laughs. "Olivia, I *still* can't believe you did that. You are truly my hero. Cheers!"

"No biggie," I giggle, tapping my toes on the floor of the bar. "Who knew Kiki was a burlesque dancer? Who knew she was such a porn star?" I can't stop laughing. "She's such a slut! A whore!"

Zack shushes me. "Olivia, you're wasted. Quit it with that dirty mouth!"

"Dirty mouth?" I shriek, pretending to be shocked. "Me? Never!" The boys laugh. "Okay, *sometimes.*" I crack up.

André takes a swig of the Stella Artois he's drinking and almost spits it out. "Olivia, the truth comes out!"

"I am very dirty," I announce again, a little more loudly than I intended. I just kind of wanted to see what it would be like to say that.

Drew puts his arm around me. "Very dirty," he says. "You ought to be ashamed."

I wrinkle my nose. "Don't try to bring me down, Drew!" I shout, pretending to be wounded. "You're just jealous! You *wish* you could dance like me." The thought of Drew dancing around on a stage in fishnets sends me into another uncontrollable fit of laughter.

Suddenly, I lose my balance and I pitch forward, the floor coming strangely close to my forehead until Drew lifts me back upright. "Oooh, you're strong," I say. I grab Drew's biceps. "Look at your big muscles!" I know I'm exaggerating a little—compared to the dancers in the Underground, Drew is not half as built. I also realize I must sound kind of silly, but the whole thing is just so funny. Me, Drew, hanging out, flirting. I took off my shirt! Could this night get any crazier?

André and Zack look at me, then each other. "I'm going to go look for a table for us, okay, Liv?" Zack asks me. "Don't go anywhere. I'll come back and get you when I've found one."

"Okay, Zackie," I say, never having called him that before, but suddenly thinking it's such a cute and clever nickname. "Love you, Zackie!"

While they go look for a table for all of us, I lean in close to Drew and tell him how much I like his muscles and also his smell. "You smell very sexy," I say matter-of-factly. "*Je t'aime!*"

"Hey, Livvy," Drew says, nuzzling my ear. "What do you say we get out of here? My host parents don't care if I bring people back to my apartment. You want to? I'll get a cab."

Going over to Drew's house sounds like a lot more fun than continuing to stand up in this crowded bar. I'm suddenly really tired. "Totes!" I say. "Drewie!" It doesn't really work, making Drew's name into a nickname like "Zackie."

I follow Drew outside and jump into a cab with him. As soon as I sit down, I feel like I could fall asleep. Paris's streetlights whiz by. I wake up briefly to him kissing my neck. "Heyyyyyy," I start laughing. It really tickles. "You're not supposed to do that." I'm so sleepy it's nothing more than a mumble. A little cross at being woken up, I push him away gently.

"Why not?" Drew says, placing his lips back on my clavicle. "You're so hot tonight. God, I can't wait to get you in bed."

"Hmmm, bed," I say. I become alert for a brief moment. "Hey, where did Zack and André go?"

"Hmm, probably went to do some gay stuff," Drew says, fiddling with the top button on my blouse. "Don't worry about them."

"Okay," I say. I follow his advice and settle back into the warmth of the backseat of the cab. I want to fall asleep, but I can't quite get there. There's so much movement around me. Drew won't stop *moving*.

"*Merci*," I hear Drew say, and I watch him give the cab driver some euros. "Come on, Livvy, we're home," he tells me. Sleepily, I follow him into his apartment building.

"This looks just like my neighborhood," I mumble.

"That's because it is your neighborhood, dummy," Drew teases me. As we get into the elevator, he presses me up against the wall and kisses me. "We live in the same neighborhood. Silly girl."

"Oh, yeah," I say, my mouth full of tongue. "Drew, I'm sleepy. I just want to go home."

"No way, Livvy," he says. "Let's go upstairs. Come on, we're almost there." The elevator door opens, and Drew unlocks the door to his homestay. "Come on, right through here."

I can't decide if this is a good idea or not, but at least it's warm inside, and Drew smells so clean and sexy, and . . . he has a rich-boy scent that's so unlike how Vince or Thomas ever smelled. It's all so different.

I lean on him, stumbling down a long hallway to a bedroom. Drew doesn't turn the light on; he just keeps kissing me and messing with my clothes. We lie down on the bed together, me falling onto it with the express hope that I might get to fall back asleep. At the same time as Drew is trying to undo the buttons on my shirt, he's tugging my skirt off. I still have my boots on, but he manages to rid my lower half of my skirt, and then he starts fiddling with my underwear. Coming in and out of consciousness, I notice that my clothes are falling away. When I realize what's happening, I pull away from his wet, hungry mouth and protest.

"No, Drew, I mean it," I say, the words thick. "I don't want to do this. Can we just take a nap?" Suddenly, I'm really unclear about what's going on and how we got this far this fast.

"Shhhh, Livvy, shhh," Drew says, pinning me down with one of his broad shoulders. He slips that hand between my legs and inside my underwear. "Oh, God," he breathes as he wriggles them down my legs and onto the floor. I start to panic—I can't move him off of me.

"No, Drew, stop!" I say, his shoulder pressing into my chest so hard that my vision is spotty. "No!"

"I thought you were a dirty girl, Livvy," Drew says hotly. "I thought you said I was sexy." My stomach lurches.

"I'm going to throw up," I say, not sure if I actually will but desperate to get him off me. "I'm really sick."

Drew puts his tongue back in my mouth. I bite down on his lower lip, hard, tasting a little blood in my mouth. "No!" I scream.

Suddenly, I hear Drew's doorbell chiming, the buzzer to his apartment shrieking that someone is trying to get in. "Shit," Drew says and struggles to right his clothes in the dark.

A minute later, the door bursts open. "Drew?" someone calls, fear in their voice.

Drew's host dad is in the doorway. He flicks the lights on. I roll my head to the side and see Zack and André beside him, their mouths agape in horror. I look down at where my skirt should be and only see bare flesh.

I turn back over and throw up all over Drew's comforter. After that, everything goes black.

★ ★ ★

Saturday and Sunday are strange, numb days. I spend them sleeping, mostly. Once when I wake up, I see Zack sitting at the end of my bed. Another time, Elise brings me some soup, but I leave it cold, untouched.

Monday morning, I wake before dawn in the middle of a dream in which I am walking along the Seine with Thomas when a group of men attack us, beating Thomas and carrying me away. My sheets are soaked. I'm dripping with sweat and crying, hard. I wish with all my might that Thomas were here to hold me.

I go to the bathroom and take a long, hot shower at full blast. I wash my underarms and my feet, but I can't touch the rest of my body with the washcloth. In painful, humiliating flashes, I remember myself saying, "I'm a dirty girl" and thinking I was being adorable. The words make my stomach clench in pain.

At school, somehow everyone knows. I can tell as soon as I walk into my first period class. George is sitting by himself, and the other guys they usually hang out with glare at Zack and me. Patty does, too. Tina, however, just looks at me strangely, like she's seen a ghost.

My heart sinks. I hadn't even thought about other people *knowing.*

Mme Cuchon comes in and calls me out of the class. We walk back to her office, and I imagine that I'll be sent home. I can't believe how crazy things got at Le Zèbre. Mme Cuchon must be horrified that one of her students would actually take their clothes off in front of a crowd.

Mme Cuchon closes the door to her office and stands to face me. Her expression is a terrible contortion of emotion.

"Madame Cuchon," I break the awful silence in the room. "I'm so sor—"

She raises her arm, and for a moment I sense she is going to slap me, and I close my eyes, knowing that I deserve it. I've never felt so horrible, so useless, so worthy of suffering. How could I have been so stupid?

She doesn't slap me. Instead, she's holding me tight in her arms and crying. "Oh, Olivia, my poor, poor thing," she says, and I find myself steadying her. "How did this happen? How could this have happened on my program?"

Big tears roll out the corners of my eyes. "I didn't know . . . I thought Zack and André were with me," I wail. "I'm so sorry . . ."

Mme Cuchon finally disentangles herself from me and sits me on the brown leather couch in her office with a box of tissues.

"How does everyone know?" I finally catch my breath and ask her.

"Zack called me Friday night when you left the bar without him," Mme Cuchon explains. "He was terrified. He thought I might be able to reach you before he did, that together, we could cover more ground. "

"PJ," I say softly. "He was scared I had disappeared like she did." This thought echoes despairingly in my head. To know that Zack was feeling that level of terror because I'd made such a stupid decision to go with Drew. I sob quietly for Zack, knowing fully what a good and true friend he is to me.

"Yes, PJ. Exactly. Zack went right to Drew's homestay, where Drew had indeed taken you," Mme Cuchon tells me. "Do you remember?"

"Sort of." I wipe my eyes with the back of my sleeve. I do remember realizing that I didn't have half my clothes on and being in a room full of men. "I was feeling really sick."

"Drew has been dismissed from the program," she says. "He flew home to Connecticut yesterday. He won't get any credit for the work he has done this semester."

"Oh, no," I say, feeling dreadfully guilty but relieved.

"He broke a very major tenant of this program," Mme Cuchon says. "I had to send him home."

"You told Madame Rouille?"

"Yes, Olivia, I had to. She came and took you home. You were no longer conscious at that point. I was there, too." Mme Cuchon again puts her arms around me. I wouldn't doubt for a minute how hard she is taking this. "You girls frighten me so much. I was so scared we had another . . ."

"PJ," I say again. I want to tell her that PJ is fine so badly. She's so distraught that I'm dying to do something to make this better. But I know I can't.

"I'm worried about you, Olivia. I agreed to let you continue at the Lycée and dance with the Underground Ballet Theater only so long as you kept up with your schoolwork and didn't break any rules. What happened to you on Friday night wasn't your fault. But you've fallen behind in school. Your peers are speculating about your alcohol use. Your teachers report that you are distracted in class. Our students' health and safety are our number one priorities. If you can't handle the demands of both the Lycée and the Underground, you'll have to choose between the two. *D'accord?*"

I sniffle. "*Je comprends.*"

"I have to call your parents in San Diego and tell them, too. Do you want to be here with me while I do that?"

I shake my head furiously. "No!" I say. "Don't call them. Please don't call them."

"Olivia, I must. You're under my supervision in Paris," she says.

"I'd—I'd rather do it alone," I say, lying. "Let me talk to them tonight from home. Please?"

"Can you promise me that you will do it?"

I nod. "Yes, of course I promise."

"And can you please promise me that you'll play it safe from now on? I know this is an exciting city, and you have a lot of new older friends from the Underground. But you have to be careful here, Olivia. Terrible things could happen to you."

I keep nodding. "Yes, I will."

There's a light knock on the door. Mme Cuchon goes to see who it is, and when she lets Zack into her office, I jump up and then collapse into his arms.

"Don't you ever walk out on me like that again!" Zack says, gripping me as tight as he can. "You scared the shit out of me."

"Let's get out of here," I say. "Madame Cuchon, is it okay if Zack and I go talk in the *bibliothèque* for a little while? Just until next period?"

Mme Cuchon nods. "Don't forget what we talked about."

Zack and I walk upstairs to the library. There's a set of reading chairs in there that have been worn from use so that the leather is cracking but soft. We collapse into them. Zack is looking at me intensely, never taking his brown eyes off of me. I can't bear to look back at him.

"Olivia," Zack finally says. "We need to talk."

"Please, Zack, no," I beg, closing my eyes. "Can't we just sit together and say nothing?"

I feel Zack put his hands on my knee. I open my eyes and find that he hasn't removed his plaintive gaze. "What, Zack?" I ask him, exhausted in my heart, my legs, my hands.

"Before Drew took you home the other night," Zack says. I wince. "You said something to me about how you haven't told me something about PJ . . . do you remember?"

I gasp. I don't have any memory of letting anything about PJ slip out. It's enough to make me choke up, the fact that so many pieces of that night seem to be outside the sphere of what I can remember. "I don't know, Zack."

"Tell me, Olivia! You have to tell me. She was my friend, too. If there is something you know, I have to know, too."

"She's alive," I whisper. I know she stood in front of me, demanding that I never tell anyone that I saw her at Marni's salon. But Zack's voice is breaking. When I see the tears welling up in his eyes, I start to remember. Just a sliver of a moment in a bar: Zack and me about to tell him the truth, and something stopping me before I went through with it.

Zack nods. "Who knows?"

"Just me," I say. "And Jay."

Zack leans forward and pulls me closer to him. We cry together in the empty library. "It's going to be okay," he keeps whispering as he rocks me back and forth, but I think he's really saying it to himself.

There's no way, I think, *that he could really expect me to believe that everything is going to be okay. Not after this.*

13. PJ

Guilty Parties

***T**rying to establish itself as a classy gentleman's club, Freddie's doesn't stay open during the day. It's strictly a place for men to come at night. That means that when the dancers go home for the day, their rooms are empty. I don't want Griselda to know that I'm homeless. But she must know that I usually sleep there during the day.

It's bad. Really bad.

But it could be worse.

I'm usually so tired by nine A.M. that I crash on the floor using my canvas shoulder bag as a pillow and my coat as a blanket. Jay e-mails me and asks me to meet him for dinner one night. In the e-mail, he asks if he can take me somewhere nice.

I can ask Alex for a good suggestion. I'd love to be able to take you on a real date, finally. And tell you how sorry I am for the fight we had. It was all my fault, and I'd do anything to make it up to you.

I'll meet you, I write back from an Internet café, changing my Gmail password for the millionth time. I'm paranoid someone has broken into my account and sees that I'm not only still alive, but I'm right here in Paris, an easy target. The Marquets could be reading my messages with the help of a good computer hack, waiting to make their move to silence me forever. The FBI might have access to my account, too. Or Annabel could be out there, working with the Vermont cops to guess a password for me and bring me home and punish me for what happened in her apartment in Rouen. Someone will have to pay for the dead Marquet nephew on Annabel's apartment floor.

I'll meet you, but only if we go to that sandwich grec *place we went to before. I can be there at seven. See you then.*

Jay doesn't realize how terrified I am of being spotted by kids—or worse, host parents—from the Lycée. The *sandwich grec* place is unlike anywhere the families from the Programme Americain would normally hang out.

Tonight I sit on a bench outside, my scarf pulled around my hair and my face, waiting for him. I spot him coming down the street, looking around the little restaurant expectantly before he sees that I'm not there yet.

He takes a seat facing the windows. I walk in, shivering from the chilly night, and rub my hands together as I sit down across from him.

We look at each other for a long time. I open my mouth, about to try to explain somehow, but Jay puts his hands up and then covers mine with his. "Don't," he whispers. "It was my fault. I pushed too hard. I just have to give you time. I know that. I'm sorry. Please forgive me."

"Jay, I—" I look away. His gaze is so intense.

"I love you. Just stay with me," he says. "I'll support you, no matter what."

I snatch my hands back under the table. "I'm not so sure about that." Jay's too good. I still haven't asked him for what I really need—a plan for the future. A way to be free again, out of hiding. If I tell him how serious this is, he will want to know why. And I can't let him become an accomplice.

Jay reaches out and gently lifts my chin up. "I am."

I shake my head.

"PJ, I mean it. Whatever you need, I am here for you. I will help you. No matter what. All you have to do is ask. I can't help you if I don't know what you need."

I bite back tears and almost laugh I am so relieved. I didn't want to have to say good-bye to Jay, not yet. Even though I know it can't last like this. These are feelings borne of a desperate situation.

Jay strokes my face and shushes me from saying anything else. Finally, I smile and kiss his hand. "Thank you."

★ ★ ★

Walking around Pigalle before the club opens, I find myself watching the tourists and the johns and the immigrants selling cell phone covers and bootleg CDs and DVDs and missing Annabel urgently, despite everything.

In between my sock and the insole of my shoe is several weeks' worth of pay. Money I have been saving, not knowing exactly how or when I could use it. When I have enough, I figure I'll know what to do. Until then, I'll just lie low and try not to get noticed.

At a covered bus stop, I crouch down and pull my shoe off. I peel a ten-euro bill off the wad of cash. I buy a phone card with it. I still remember the numbers to Dave's cell phone back in Vermont. I waste some of the minutes on the card listening to Dave's outgoing voice-mail message. "Hit me up later if I don't call you back . . . I probably forgot to return my messages," he says, laughing into the recording. He sounds just like the stoner he is. I wonder why my sister considered marrying him at all.

But I know why she fell in love with him. Dave is painfully good-looking. Even with messed up bicuspids and untended facial hair, his movements, his build, the way his eyes pierce into yours, he makes you want to pull him toward you. When I was younger and they first started going out, I always felt different when he was around. I wanted to shed clothing, lie around with the sun on my skin. He and Annabel would often come back from hikes or drives with her hair looking just like it did when she got out of bed in the morning. He just had that way of drawing women to him. Of course, he never wanted anything to do with *me*. He loved Annabel, ravenously.

I bang the back of my head against the wall of the phone booth. Pressing my finger down on the receiver hook, I think for old time's sake I'll call my dad's cell phone number. He's in jail; I know he'll never answer. But the way hearing Dave's voice mail message draws to life all kinds of memories of him makes me want to have that with my dad. I want to be reminded of his dry humor, the way a short conversation can turn into a three-hour discussion about war and peace and everything in between. I want to hear his voice.

I dial the familiar numbers and listen to the ring. All of a sudden, someone answers. I bang the phone down, panting with fright. All night I can't stop thinking about the phone being answered. Was it my parents' lawyer? And why is the phone still in service?

I can't help it; I find another pay phone after my shift and try the number with my calling card again. This time, it's only three in the morning there. But again, someone answers.

I don't hang up because the voice on the other end of the phone is unmistakably my dad's.

"Who is this?" he asks sleepily. He doesn't sound angry.

The lump in the back of my throat dissolves into tears that fall on the phone receiver.

My dad listens for a while. Then I can hear him swallow pretty hard. I'm not sure but I think he's crying, too.

"PJ?" he says finally. I can hear someone make a noise in the background, something like a nose blowing and someone sputtering out something unintelligible. I have vertigo. It's my mom. But it can't be my mom. They are in separate parts of the jail, each awaiting trial.

"PJ . . . people here are saying that in France everyone thinks you girls are . . . dead, for Christ's sake. Where are you? Are you safe?"

I think about Freddie's. Safe? "I'm okay, Dad."

"Can you tell me anything else about it?"

"No," I whisper.

"How do you have your cell phone?" I ask him. "Aren't you . . . in jail?"

"New evidence, sweetheart. We're not a flight risk. We got out for a little while on bail."

My mind races, hoping against hope. "What does that mean?"

"Dave bargained her, baby. When she called him, he was ready. She was court marshaled on the plane."

"What?" I see flashing lights down the boulevard de Clichy, blue and white and red coming toward me. I blink and realize that it's just the shock of what my dad is telling me. "What?" I ask again. This time it comes out as just a rasp. I hold the phone with both hands.

"Oh, PJ, it kills me to have to tell you this," he says. "Annabel and Dave had a little business going. We suspected it, but we were never sure. We asked her about it the day of the wedding. I couldn't sleep the night before—do you remember? You couldn't sleep, either."

"Yeah, we watched those old movies until late," I say, remembering the innocence of watching goofy Buster Keaton dance around the silent set in the dark living room, my dad nursing a tumbler of Scotch. I figured he was just sad to see one of his girls growing up.

"Yup, we did, sweetie." My dad is quiet for a minute. I know he's caught up remembering nicer times.

"Well, your mom and I sat Annabel down and told her we knew she'd been skimming some of the medicine and selling them in Boston to college kids. People who paid a lot for them. We told her we wanted her to stop. Not only because she was stealing but also because we didn't want Dave to get in trouble if she ended up getting caught. She laughed at us. You know Annie. And then, as you know, she ran away. We know now that Dave was in on it, too. We also know that Annabel took all the money they made and stole a lot of other money from Dave's bank account before she left town. Dave plea-bargained that if he could get her back to the United States, he wouldn't have to do any time. He did his end of the deal for the cops. So now he's walking free."

"No," I say. "No, Dad, that's a set up. Annabel explained it all when she was here. I saw her—I found her. She didn't want to go home because she didn't want to have to testify against you . . . she saw the police before she left."

"Sweetie, Dave's bank has the surveillance tape. She went in and took out ten thousand dollars with a forged signature on one of his withdrawal slips. She didn't go to the police. She went to Europe."

"No, Dad," I say, blood banging my eardrums. I can't be hearing this right.

"Yes, PJ," my dad says. "I wouldn't lie to you."

I can't breathe. So many people have lied to me. I clench the phone hard enough to stop the circulation in my fingers. When I can finally find words again, it seems as if I can't get them out fast enough.

"But she told me! I saw her, Dad, here in France!" I cry. "Tell me the truth! For once! Can someone please just tell me the real story? What is really going on?"

My dad sighs, deep and heavy. "I am telling you the truth. Annabel's got a lot of charges against her. Fraud, selling drugs. Some of the Boston campuses have civil lawsuits against her, too. Endangering minors. Some of the kids she sold drugs to weren't even eighteen."

"So she didn't go to the police?" I whisper.

"You think your *sister* would have gone to a *police* station?"

"So are you guys . . . still in trouble?" I ask. The rank smell of the phone booth is starting to go to my head. "What about that?" I don't know what to believe anymore. I have half a hope that he's going to tell me that I don't know the real story about that, either.

"Yeah, we've got some trafficking charges we're fighting. We're trying to prove that this is a human rights issue. We've got some lobbyists down in Washington that are getting us some great publicity, and to be sure, the liberal media is really standing by us. . . ."

The excitement in my dad's voice drains me in an instant. Defeated, all the anger, the hope, the worry seems to leave my body. He doesn't see how this hurts anybody—how his politics lost him his house, his freedom. He lost *me* for them. He sees himself as a crusader. He's saving the world. And leaving me to save myself.

"But we're definitely still going to have to serve some kind of time in the pen. You can't bring those kind of black-market drugs over the border and not expect to. The bank repossessed our house but otherwise we're still in this . . ."

"Dad, I have to go," I say before he finishes.

"Okay, sweetie. It's great to hear your voice. I'm so relieved you're safe, baby. Be careful out there. Please. I can't bear to think of . . . Anyway. You're all right now, and that's all that matters." I hear him sniff. "Call us anytime, okay?"

"Okay."

"I love you, Penny Lane."

"Me too, Daddy."

I quietly rest the phone back in its cradle and walk away. I have to hurry to get back into the club before Griselda locks the door and I won't have anywhere to sleep for the rest of the day.

I'm sitting in a darkened movie theater with Jay, and like a spinning top, my brain spits out the same few images at me, again and again and again. My mom would call it a whirling dervish. There's Annabel and me, running through the train station in Rouen. We don't know Zack is there somewhere, watching us. Then there's Dave, standing in the lobby at the hostel in Cherbourg. Annabel runs to him. She ran out of money and hopes he has more. Hopes they can go back into business together. She's sick of our plans. She doesn't know Dave's turned against her. She wraps her whole body around him, and he knows she trusts him completely. Then there's Annabel in a jumpsuit in a federal prison. Every time it pops into my head, I want to scream. *How can this have happened?*

Then, of course, there are the nagging thoughts under the surface. *I helped her run . . . I protected her . . . she won't be able to stand going down alone. She'll tell them about me. And then they'll find out about Dennis Marquet. The man we left dying on the floor. Annabel won't want to be the only one who goes down. They'll find out. It's only a matter of time. . . .*

Jay shifts in his seat in the movie. I'd suggested seeing a Spanish film. Jay had been thrilled. It's a comedy, with French subtitles. I don't even read them. Whenever someone swears in the dialogue, I think of Marco, the Spanish guy Annabel had brought home to our apartment in Rouen. He'd hated me, and I'd thought long and hard about what to do to get him to leave us sisters alone.

He was the least of our worries, I think, remembering a slack, lifeless Dennis Marquet on the floor of the apartment where we all lived for a brief time.

At a funny part in the movie, Jay leans into me and smiles. I take a deep breath and smile back.

You might be dating a killer, I think wildly as he kisses my hand held in his. *You don't know she works at a brothel, you don't know she sleeps where Russian girls dance on businessmen's laps, and you don't know she might have killed someone. Her blackmailer, as a matter of fact.*

When the insipid movie mercifully ends, Jay and I walk down from Bastille to the Promenade Plantée, a narrow park that skirts the edge of the port to the Seine. Jay gets us two espressos.

"I noticed you kind of falling asleep in the movie," he says. "You looked like you needed one of these."

"Thanks," I say. I drink it fast, hoping the hot liquid will warm me up. I have the chills again. Jay's lips look so inviting, so distracting. I kiss him. He tastes like coffee and salt from movie-theater popcorn. It's delicious. I keep kissing him, despite how I feel him resist. He's tense. But I don't want to stop. I just want to escape to that place that I know he can take me.

"Can I ask you something?" Jay asks me, turning his face from mine. His lips are raw from where I've been ravaging them with mine.

"Go for it," I say, wishing he wouldn't.

"Why do you always run away?" he wants to know. "Don't you know how crazy it makes me? Every time, I think you're not just going back to your place. I always think you are leaving Paris again, leaving France. You don't know what it was like over winter break, not knowing if we were ever going to find you. And then thinking you were dead! Don't do this to me!" He tosses the cardboard coffee cup into a trash can and shoves his hands into his jacket pockets.

"I know you were going crazy, Jay. You wrote me and told me. And I've told you I'm sorry."

"Oh, that's right," he says. "I wrote to you every day. I told you every single thing we were doing to find you. And you got those e-mails, I know you did, because you responded. But you never felt like letting me in. You never wanted me to help you!"

"No, Jay," I admit. "I didn't want your help then."

"And that time we were on the street, and you told me that you ruin everything, and then you just ran away when I tried to figure out what the hell was going on. No matter what it is that you have to say to me, I can take it. And you still haven't told me what's up now. Please just tell me. I know I can fix it. I *know* I can."

I stay quiet. Suddenly, I start to get angry. Very angry.

"Everyone always *wants* something from me," I say in a low voice. "You. Alex. Olivia. You guys want answers. My sister wanted me to go to Rouen. When I got there, she wanted to raise sheep! She wanted me to keep quiet. Then she wanted me to keep quiet when she abandoned me here in France. My parents want my support for their stupid ideas about what it really means to be free. You know? Everyone wants something— everyone!" I can't help it. I'm crying again. "You! Why can't you just be happy with things the way they are? Why can't anyone let anything just *be*? Not you. Not Annabel. Not Monsieur Marquet!"

I get up to leave, but Jay takes the sleeve of my coat and pulls on it. "*No me digas,* PJ. Please don't go again. I can't take it anymore, PJ!"

"I thought you just said you *could* take it," I accuse him coldly. "Which is it?"

"If you go, don't come back," he says. "It hurts too much for you to storm off every time things get deep."

"Fine, then," I say. "I won't."

14. ZACK

Misguided

O n a wet afternoon after PE class, I head home in the rain, looking down toward the pavement, hoping not to tramp my leather shoes into a puddle. Finally reaching my building, I punch in the key code and enter the courtyard. I stop for a moment, mopping my glasses, before crossing to get into my apartment.

I look up then and see a familiar shape leaning against the wall, under the short ledge to keep out of the rain. Long and lithe, her blonde head dipped low, there's a peek of periwinkle scarf coming out from under her hood.

PJ.

Even before I say anything, she lifts her head and meets my gaze. She looks almost sheepish, a little frightened, but her eyes are kind.

"Hey," she greets me.

The rain starts to come down in heavy sheets. I can't stop staring at her. Her long blonde hair darkens as it gets wet. I knew that was her periwinkle scarf that I saw out the train window. I *knew* it. I never forget my colorways.

"Howdy, stranger." I try to stay friendly. I don't want to scare her away like a lost kitten.

I'm a little afraid of her myself. She took off last Christmas Eve like a firefly confronted by a little kid with a jar in the middle of summer. I almost hold up my hands to show her there's no jar. "Want to come inside?"

"I'd love to," she says gratefully. I unlock the front door and let her inside.

Nobody's home and it's just as well. Romy and Jacques follow the happenings at the Lycée. They'd know that this is the girl who's gone missing. I can't promise that they'd take such a backseat approach if they saw her sitting in their living room.

"Can I get you anything?" Before she answers, I go to the kitchen and pour us two glasses of mineral water.

PJ gulps hers down. "I guess I'm kinda dehydrated."

"You're kinda somethin', but I ain't sure what yet. You wanna tell me what's goin' on or do we need to play twenty questions?"

PJ looks at me for a long moment, and then breaks into a smile that would sell a million magazines, even if her hair is dirty and she's been wearing that same sweatshirt of Jay's since the last time I saw her.

"Some crazy stuff has happened. I'm sorry I ran away the other night."

"Girl, sometimes shit gets way too real. I know how it is."

"Do I look as gross as I feel?" she asks me.

I nod. "I'm gonna run you a bath."

I fill the clawed tub in the bathroom I share with Mireille and Paul with hot water and add about half of Mireille's pink kiddie bubble bath. PJ goes in the bathroom, and I hear her sigh deeply once she lowers herself into the tub. After a few minutes, I'm checking my text messages for anything from André when I hear her calling me. I crack the door.

"Yes?"

"Will you come in here and talk to me?" she says. "Just don't look behind the shower curtain, okay?"

I open the door all the way and step into the steamy bathroom. "Whatcha wanna talk about?"

"Boys," she says. It's the girliest thing I've ever heard her say. "Jay in particular."

"Oh, what about him?" I say. I'm glad she can't see me behind the purple plastic shower curtain. It still stings a little to think about Jay, nonetheless talk about him with his statuesque supermodel *girlfriend*.

But, at least, I know what they have is the real thing. "I think he loves me too much," she says.

I swallow a half laugh, half groan. I really cannot do this. I'm glad she can't see my eyes bugging out of my head right now.

"Zack?"

"Too much, huh?" I prompt her.

"Well, I know that sounds bad. But I don't deserve someone like him. I've done too many bad things. He loves me too much for his own good. It's just going to hurt. . . ."

"PJ, are you plannin' on runnin' away again?" I ask her, staring at the purple barrier between me and the expression on her face. "Sorry if that's too bold a question to ask, but what the *hell*."

"I have nowhere to go," she says sadly. "But this all has to end sometime."

"I'm gonna throw your clothes in the wash, okay?" I say. "And bring you some other stuff to wear. Olivia and Alex leave stuff here all the time. Don't move."

She laughs. "Well, I can't run away if you take all my clothes. So, yeah, I'll be right here."

I come back with a pair of Olivia's dance leggings and a jersey dress Alex used to wear a lot but hasn't, of course, since she left it here and I stopped speaking to her. I hate it how girls always leave their stuff everywhere. Though today, it's quite useful.

"I don't have any underwear for you," I say. I bet she can feel me blushing. I ain't never talked to a girl about underwear before.

"I don't usually wear any," she says, and suddenly I feel nothing but honest-to-God pity for Jay. She doesn't make it easy for him to stop wanting her. PJ gets dressed in the bathroom and finds me in my room. The clothes I gave her fit okay. Her slim figure would fit into anything, and I've never seen her wearing anything so clingy. If I didn't know her, I would think she was just any other wannabe model wandering around Paris.

"I suggest we go for a walk before my host parents get home," I say. "Or else you're going to be on the cover of every paper in Paris tomorrow morning—with the word TROUVÉE over your picture."

"Where are we going to go?" she asks nervously.

"You want to do a best of Paris walk?" I ask her. "We really can't stay here."

"What's a 'best of Paris walk'?"

"Oh, it's just this goofy thing that Alex and I made up. Since we live kinda close to the Eiffel Tower," I explain. "It's like, before I came here, I was super-excited to see the sights of Paris, you know? But I also knew that those sights weren't going to be part of my everyday life. I'd only see them once in a while. But then, this miracle happens where I'm put in a homestay where I get to see the Eiffel Tower every day on the métro ride to school. And so does Alex. So we started doing this thing sometimes, when we didn't have anything to do, where we'd walk from Cambronne to the Eiffel Tower and then cross at the Pont d'Alma and walk up to the Champs Élysées and then down from there to Jardin des Tuileries and the Louvre and everything. You know, the walk all the tourists must make every day."

"Ah," PJ says. "Well, I guess we could. But I was kind of hoping to stay anonymous."

"Girl, this is the most anonymous route you can take in Paris. It's all Italians and Brits snapping photos. They'll never recognize you."

PJ puts her coat and sneakers back on, and we head out the door. We walk in silence together for a while.

We're rounding the corner to join the throngs on the Champs Élysées. Suddenly, some tourist's child darts in front of PJ's legs and trips, dropping her bag. We gather the kid's things and stand up. PJ's shaken. I slip my arm around her and guide her down the street. "It's okay," I assure her. "It was just some kid."

"I don't know, Zack. This feels weird."

"We don't have to keep walking," I say. "If you're not comfortable."

"No," PJ decides with a deep breath. "I've really missed this."

I smile in recognition. "I thought you might have."

It still gives me a thrill to look behind me and see all the cars whooshing around the traffic circle at the stately Arc de Triomphe. The Champs tries to be a classy shopping boulevard, and it is, but it's not so much a reflection of Parisian style as what tourists hope Paris is. I can't help but love strolling down it, though.

"PJ," I say. "Where have you been staying?"

"Oh," PJ replies. "Just this sort of random place. Actually, Alex set me up with it."

"Alex knows you are back in Paris?"

"Yeah. Jay thought she could help me find a place to stay, and he was right. She found something for me just like he said, but unfortunately it's not really turning out the way I thought it would."

I swallow the deep seed of hurt that Jay went to Alex for help before me. "Ah. Well, with Alex, the only thing you can predict with any accuracy is that she will, in fact, cause something totally unpredictable to happen. The world doesn't work the way Alex thinks it does."

"What do you mean?" PJ asks me.

"Well, like, at the beginning of the year, she had this idea that we would make a pact to get boyfriends. Like it was that simple. And then we'd have them, and we would be happy as clams in a bucket. But dating feels way different than that. It's not just like, somethin' you can *get*. Like a new coat. Does that make sense?"

"Well, of course it isn't," PJ says. "Being with someone you really, really like—"

"Or love—" I interject, noticing that she hasn't yet once told me that she loves Jay back.

"—it's the most amazing feeling. It's not the same as when you buy something or do something you always wanted to do. It's almost, like, a paradox. Because the more you kiss someone, the more you touch them, the more you want to do it again."

"It's insatiable," I say.

"Exactly!" We laugh. I can almost forget that what she's so accurately describing is how she feels about Jay. My Jay. Or my used-to-be Jay. Or my used-to-be-want-to-be Jay.

After I make some disparaging comments about the line of people waiting to get on the big Ferris wheel at Concorde, I lead PJ down the rue de Rivoli around packs of people snapping photos. She's so tense on that bustling street that I change my mind and suggest we go to the Jardin du Palais Royal. I'd heard they were doing a little festival of some sort in the park, and I thought it might be a good place to get something to eat. I'm starting to get hungry.

"Well," PJ says. "I've never been in there. That might be okay."

The sun has dipped behind the clouds before it sets, which is too bad because otherwise the day was a nice one for being outside. We enter in through the side of the garden. Usually, this park is relatively quiet, a place for people in the financial district just north of us to sit and eat lunch during the day. Whatever festival the city of Paris is sponsoring here this week hasn't really seemed to take off—there is only a small crowd gathered around a live acoustic band. There are a few carts selling some kind of flatbread with a bean paste on top. It looks like a dirty sponge, so I don't have any.

"So did you and Jay have a fight or something?" I ask finally, though of course it's what I've been wondering ever since she showed up at my door. We take a few of the chairs that are about fifty meters from the little stage. We can't see the performers, but we can hear the music. With the glowing red lights decorating the park, it does in fact feel quite festive. I'm glad we came here this evening. "How come you aren't with him right now?"

"We did. We—we might have broken up," PJ says, kicking the pebbles on the ground with her dirty sneaker. "I'm not sure."

"Are you okay?"

"No," she says miserably. "Everything changed—my whole life—when he kissed me for the first time."

"Yeah, I know what you mean," I say. Though André called me every day for a week after the night at Le Zèbre, he was just checking on Olivia and commiserating at what a terrible experience it had been, chasing Drew back to his apartment and having it revealed what a bad, bad guy he was. He hasn't called me to do anything. But I can't stop thinking about how ecstatic I felt when he first touched his lips to my neck in that bathroom at the club. It felt secretive, exhilarating. "PJ? What's wrong?"

PJ's staring straight ahead, looking at someone who's walking away from the small crowd listening to the band. They've finished their set and people are clapping, chatting with one another. "PJ?"

Suddenly, PJ turns to me with a panicked look on her face. "Um, Zack. Kiss me," she says. "Kiss me now!"

"Uh, PJ—uh, what—"

She wraps her slinky arms around me and scoots closer. In seconds, she's kissing me with so much passion and longing that I almost think she's transposed what we were talking about earlier with Jay and André onto me. That or she's got multiple personalities, and she is disassociating right here in front of me. Not sure which.

"Oh, God, Zack," she says, coming back to life and breaking her mouth away from mine. "I thought—I thought I saw a ghost just then."

"Of whom, might I ask?" I say, wiping my lips with my jacket sleeve. "What on earth was *that*?" I stare at her big blue eyes, thinking there's no way she can get away without at least filling me in on some aspect of that move. "PJ?" She won't answer.

"Zack?" someone says as they walk up to us. "What's happening?"

Sweating in front of us, surrounded by a bunch of other people in similar outfits (costumes, perhaps?) is the one person I've been thinking about all day: André.

"Well, hello!" I say, for some reason finding cheerfulness is the best emotion to feign right now. "Nice to see you! Love the outfit!"

I grab PJ's cold hand and jerk her off the bench. "PJ, darling, don't we have an, um, important meeting to get to? *Ciao!*" With that, we run to the Pont Neuf, both of us gasping for air but not stopping till we're back on the other side of the Seine. The next morning, I go to check my mailbox in the computer lounge at school. The only people who ever write letters or cards to me are my grandparents out in Knoxville—probably because they got nothing better to do.

There's something in the box, a flyer of some kind. I open up the folded pink paper and drop it to the floor in horror when I see what someone's written on it in black marker:

"DIE FAG."

I can't sleep that night. I toss and turn and get up and down to go to the bathroom several times, all along wondering if PJ's bizarre kiss in the park ruined my chances with André forever. I was so hopeful that he'd be the one. Then, conversely, I roll over and wonder who left that awful pink note in my mailbox. Who in the program is so openly homophobic?

That leads my thoughts back to André because André is the perfect antidote to hatred. He makes being gay look like a party that I can't bear not to be invited to.

The next day, during lunch, I decide to call him and apologize. It's my only chance to make things right.

"Hey, André, I'm so sorry about the other day. That was my friend PJ, the one Olivia and I sometimes talk about . . . she's really messed up in *la tête* right now. She just kissed me, I think because she saw someone she knew, and she kind of wanted to hide, you know?"

"Cheers, man, it's okay," André says. "I'm glad you called, Zack. I wanted to see if you'd come with me to find some new trainers. I liked the ones you were wearing the other day, and I think you told me you got them here?"

I meet André at the bottom of the escalator at Les Halles. Les Halles used to be this massive food market, but now it's just a mall and a park or something. Lots of French kids hang out here. I never thought I'd move all the way from Tennessee to be hanging out in malls, but what's a boy to do when his true love wants to do some indoor shopping?

André kisses me hello and shows me a new canvas tote he bought: a "murse" with a silkscreen of the view of the Eiffel Tower looking up from under it. "Cute, right?"

It's much more feminine than anything I would ever even consider picking up off a shelf, but it is kind of clever and fun. "Yeah, it's great,"

I say. The words from the pink note flash in my head. *This is exactly what fags do*, I think horribly. *They buy purses and show them to each other.* My stomach turns over, and I wish the memory of the note would leave me alone.

"BHV. Can you believe it?" André says. I attempt to show my lighthearted shock. Since when is André shopping at BHV? "I know, I know," he goes on. "I was in there to buy a fan, and then I had to go to the loo, and of course the only bathrooms are up at the top in the maternity ward—"

"You mean the maternity department."

"Right, right," he says. "Whilst I'm making my way through about a million prams and old broads with big bellies, I see all these bags and pillows with the Eiffel Tower on them, and I just had to have one of each. I put the pillow on my bed. Looks quite good, actually. You should come round to my flat and see it sometime."

I look from some gaudy pink dresses in the window of a trashy mall store to André and back again. Did he really just invite me over so quickly after seeing me make out with a girl in the middle of a park in Paris?

"André, it really doesn't bother you that you saw me kissing my friend? I mean, it's nice of you to be so cool about it, but I would honestly feel a whole lot better if you gave me a hard time about it."

"No, it doesn't bother me at all," he says. I notice again that delicious way he pronounces the same words I use that makes the sound totally different. *At all* sounds like *a tall*. "Aren't you a cheeky one?"

"Well, we've hooked up a couple times now. If I saw you in a park kissing a girl, I'd be pretty upset."

"What, you think we're boyfriends now or what? That would make a pretty picture, then, wouldn't it?" André looks at me, sticking out his tongue and laughing. His tone is still light, and he continues to browse the shop windows as we blaze a trail through the after-school crowd and over to the shop where I got the green and orange sneakers I'm wearing. I can see that his forehead, though, is tense, like he's not as relaxed as he wants to seem, just shopping for shoes with a friend.

"Okay, André, fine. I get it, you don't care." I struggle for some way to make it seem like this isn't such a big deal. "But, you know, it wouldn't kill you to be polite. No other guy I've ever been with has ever been as commitment-phobic as you are!"

"Well, you don't have to be so serious about it," he says, fake pouting. "Or is that an American thing?"

"What thing?"

"You know, thinking everything's going to end up like a fairy tale, complete with a dog and a picket fence? Paris isn't like that, you know," he says. "*I'm* not like that."

I don't know what to say. I know if I try to explain what I meant, it will come out all wrong. But I also just can't bear André looking at me like I'm this sappy, lovesick little boy who thinks he's practically engaged after a few kisses.

Didn't kissing me have that same effect on him, though? That the-more-you-do-it-the-more-you-want-it thing? How could he not have felt that?

My stomach sinks, my whole body pinching and crawling with self-loathing. *How did I let this happen? How has everything gone so horribly wrong?*

"I'm gonna go," I say, trying to keep my voice as steady and casual as possible. "The sneaker store is over there." I point toward a neon sign. The store is unmissable; I didn't really need to point to it. I just don't know how else to end this conversation. "Bye," I say abruptly.

"So now you're just going to pull a runner, are you?" André laughs. "Figures. See you later."

I have to dodge a big crowd of French teens holding court in the center of the mall. They're blocking the escalator up and paying no mind to anyone else. A few of them are even kicking around a soccer ball, hitting a cell phone display with a missed kick. I nearly trip over the outstretched leg of one of the boys horsing around with his friends. He looks at me as though it ruins his day just to cross paths with me, let alone to have to move out of my way.

I don't know why I ever thought I belonged in Paris, I despair as I walk through the sculpted park outside Les Halles entrance. Everything I thought I was so close to is just slipping away, and I can't do anything to stop it. I don't belong anywhere.

15. ALEX

Getaway

---

*T*hursday morning I can't take it anymore. If I have to put on another sad T-shirt, jeans, and sneakers combo I am going to go insane from lack of creative expression. I fling the door to my closet open and start pulling spring dresses off of hangers, desperate to go back to the old me—the me who used to take some pride in my appearance.

I finally settle on a white tank top under a baggy, flowery silk dress with a long draping cardigan, a big cotton scarf wrapped loosely around my neck, and short teal high-heeled booties with nude fishnet tights. Arranging my hair in tumbling waves around my face, I nod at today's look in satisfaction. It makes a big difference when you dress up. I can already tell that *today* is going to be a fabulous day.

It's all about attitude. And clothes.

At school, I grab a café crème from the machine in the hallway outside my first class of the day and find a seat next to Olivia. She seems distracted throughout class, not really taking any notes. That's very unlike her. When I offer her a piece of gum halfway through the lecture, she stares at the pack like she's never seen gum before.

Of course, I know about what happened with Drew. Everyone does. There are tons of wild stories flying around the Lycée. Katie and Elena, two Midwestern girls that have become really good friends with one another, sometimes go for runs with me during PE, and they told me that Drew threatened Olivia with a knife to have sex with her. Another story is that Olivia and Drew have been secretly sleeping together for a long time—all year, in fact. It was only when Livvy was found out that she tried to say it was rape. Some guys have commented that since we all got back from Christmas Break, Olivia has been dressing and acting much more forward than she used to. People know about her doing the deed with her host brother, and some people think she's a slut for dumping her boyfriend from home and hooking up with a French guy so quickly. There are even rumors about Livvy having a threesome with Zack and some dancer friend of hers!

I always, *always* defend Olivia with my teeth bared and my loyalty firmly expressed.

How *dare* they attack her! She is seriously the most good-hearted person I've ever known.

The only people who know the full truth, of course, are Livvy, Drew, and Zack. Drew's gone, sent to a military academy for the rest of the year last I heard, and Livvy and Zack haven't talked to anyone about what really happened that night. Normally, I would be fiending to know the whole story, but in this situation, I know that Livvy will tell me if she ever wants to. And if she doesn't, that's fine, too.

But I'm worried about her. I look over at Zack, bent over his notebook. His hair, normally coiffed ostentatiously with gel and hairspray, is laying flat, without any product in it. In just a black sweater and dark jeans, he looks devastatingly morose. Livvy's taken to wearing black again, too, the way she did right when we got back to school for second semester.

Suddenly, the bright colors of my flowered dress seem sort of *inappropriate*, considering the atmosphere at the Lycée. And it's a little too early in the spring for this outfit. I shiver from the cool breeze let in through a cracked window of the classroom. I should have worn jeans, like usual.

"Katie and I are thinking about leaving the program," Elena tells me as we change out of our PE clothes back into our regular clothes later that afternoon. "It's too sad here. Too much bad stuff keeps happening."

"Really?" I ask. "Did you tell Madame Cuchon?"

"Not yet," Katie says. "I'm a little afraid to. She seems so fragile lately. It's like this whole program is falling apart."

"Would you ever leave the program, Alex?" Elena asks me. A short, pretty girl from a wealthy suburb of Chicago, Elena has always kind of taken an interest in me. She loves celebrity gossip, so hearing about the cover photo shoots my mom arranges for *Luxe* totally make her day. I think about her question as I roll my stockings back up my legs and under my dress. I could tell her about all the things I've endured just to stay in this stupid program, but that would take all afternoon and I have somewhere to be.

"Never," I tell her, combing my bangs back into place in the mirror. "I would never give up on Paris."

★ ★ ★

That afternoon, I get to the Sanxays' a little early. Before I open their front door with my key, I stop cold and listen. Ugh. It sounds like all the kids are crying. Again.

I walk into the entryway, half expecting Mme Sanxay to be waiting behind it, hoping to make a getaway as soon as possible. To my surprise, I find her standing in the living room, holding a silk scarf in her hands. "Alex!" she screams. "Did you know anything about this?"

She holds out her hands, and the scarf separates into several pieces and flutters to the floor. I step forward, inspecting the pieces. "What happened? Wasn't that a Louis Vuitton?"

Mme Sanxay doesn't exactly answer, just wails. I realize that it must have been *she* who was crying as I arrived. "Hey. Hey! What happened?"

"Emeline. That terrible *enfant*. She cut up my scarf after I told her she couldn't play with it. . . . I just found it under the bathroom sink in pieces."

I clutch my neck in horror, imagining what finding that must have been like. "No!"

"Yes!"

"Why did she do that?"

"*Parce que je ne l'aime pas!*" Emeline screams from the hallway, where she's stretched out on the floor, weeping into the rug. I didn't see her there before, and she just about gives me a heart attack.

"Emeline!" I gasp. "Why would you ruin your mother's scarf?"

Emeline jumps up and runs to press her face into my waist. She cries and cries. Mme Sanxay shrieks again, another wordless, pained sound. "Keep her away from me!" she yells as she grabs her coat. "Keep her away from my things!"

The door rattles for a full minute after she slams it. I kneel down and pat Emeline's thin blonde hair softly. "You okay?" I ask.

Emeline shakes her head. "I hate Maman," she sniffles. "She won't make Daddy come back."

"What?" I ask. "What do you mean?"

Albert emerges from his bedroom, taking tiny, timid steps over to us in his dark brown school shoes. "Maman can't make him come back, Emeline. He doesn't want to." He speaks to his sister in French, but I understand him.

"Is that why you ruined your mom's scarf?" I ask Emeline. "Because you were mad about your dad not being here?"

Emeline clutches her arms around my neck and nods into my chest. "Oh, Emeline," I say, and all at once I feel so weary, sad, and unbelievably *needed*. "Well, there'll be more scarves," I say to Emeline. "Your mom will forgive you. Good moms always do." I chuckle in spite of myself. "She's mad, but she won't stay that way forever. You'll see."

Yes, I am sure there will be many more beautiful scarves in Mme Sanxay's life. *But*, I think as I untangle Emeline from my neck, *there won't likely be any more dads in Emeline's life.* I wish I didn't know that as well as I do.

I take the kids back to the Jardin du Luxembourg to play on the jungle gym. Setting up on a bench, I take Charles out of his stroller and hold him in my arms. He's just had a bath and smells fresh and powdery.

I do something I've never done before. I take his little torso in my hands, wondering at the tiny girth of his little baby body, and hold him up above my head in the air. Then I make silly faces at him, the way moms do to their babies in movies. Charles can't get enough. He opens his tiny, toothless mouth wide and lets out these big burbles of laughter that shake his whole body. I do it again and again till I am laughing as hard as he is.

"Are you positive that you aren't that child's mother?"

"Hello, Denny." I know it is going to be him before I even turn around. "How are you?"

What I didn't expect was to see Denny standing there with two dozen pink tulips, held out to me with a flourishing gesture. "When you do have children, you'll make a wonderful mother," he greets me. "How are you on this lovely day?"

I put Charles back on my lap and smile at the tulips in spite of myself. "Those are for me?"

"I knew you would be here!" Denny says. "So I took the chance and bought you some flowers. I had a feeling these might be your favorite. Am I right?"

"They're not my favorite." I say, my feathers ruffled that he would think he could guess my favorite flowers so easily. "But they are beautiful. Thank you." I clear my throat. "What are they for?"

"I wanted to ask you to dinner."

"Sorry, Denny, I'm just not interested. I thought I'd made that clear by now." Denny's sweet treats the other afternoon showed me that he wasn't actually creepy, just overly *amoureux*. It smacks a tad of desperation. And those pants! He's *still* wearing them!

"*Alex, regarde-moi!*" Emeline calls from the top of the slide she's about to come down. I look over and watch her make it halfway before her chubby behind gets stuck on one of the humps of the slide and she loses her momentum. Just the same, I give her a thumbs-up sign.

"Do French kids know about thumbs-up?" I ask Denny idly.

"The whole world knows about thumbs-up," he assures me.

"Emeline," I call out. "*Ou est ton frère?*" I don't see Albert anywhere.

"*Je ne sais pas,*" she tells me. She climbs the ladder to try the slide again.

"Albert?" I call, my eyes darting in every direction around the playground. "Albert!" I still can't seem to see him. Where has he gone?

"Hold this," I say to Denny, placing Charles in his arms. Luckily, he doesn't drop the baby. I jog around in my high-heeled booties, looking everywhere in the vicinity for Albert. Finally, I see him from the back, standing to the side of one of the park's long promenades next to a tree.

"Albert!" I shriek as I run up to grab him and haul him back to the playground. "I've been looking for you everywhere. Don't run away like that!"

At the sound of my voice, Albert whips around in surprise. Unfortunately, he's not quite done with what he came over here to do. Still aiming up and out, like he would at home or at school, a heavy stream of yellow liquid comes flying at me, soaking the entire front of my beautiful silk dress, from the careful white embroidery around the neckline to the flared, flowing skirt.

I've just been peed on in public. My humiliation knows no bounds.

"Why is this my life?" I shout at Denny, taking the baby back from him. I'm sopping wet and starting to smell. "Why?"

"He didn't," Denny breathes. "Is that? . . . "

"Yes," I hiss. "It is."

"You're dripping," he says, looking down at a droplet that falls from the hem of my dress onto the tip of my boot.

I grab Emeline and yell at Albert that we're leaving. I leave Denny's tulips on the park bench. Who the hell does he think he is, anyway? If he hadn't been distracting me, this would have never happened.

★ ★ ★

Friday night, I'm sitting on the floor, slouching against the side of my bed. Laid out in front of me are index cards with all the French verbs I need to know how to conjugate in the pluperfect tense before I meet with the tutor my mom hired for me. There are forty verbs, and the meeting is tomorrow at ten A.M.

"*I hate my life,*" I scrawl on a piece of binder paper. I think about PJ, hiding out in Paris, and Olivia, sinking into herself more and more every day since the incident with Drew. I insert a caret between "I" and "hate" and write "sort of."

"*I sort of hate my life.*"

A loud rap on the door forces me to get up and forget my self-pitying moment. It's Sebastien, the ten-year-old I live with at my homestay. He's a little brat. The very definition of *un morceau de merde.*

"What?" I ask him.

"Someone's at the door for you," he tells me in English, reminding me once again of how his English is years and years more advanced than my French.

"Who?" I ask, pushing past the runt and padding down the hallway to the front entrance.

"Your boyfriend," Sebastien cackles.

My heart lifts. "Zack?" When I turn into the foyer, I take a step back at the sight of that guy Denny, standing in the doorway with another bouquet of tulips, this one double the one from Wednesday.

I notice as I walk toward him that he's not wearing his hat today.

"You forgot your flowers the other day," he says by way of explanation, holding the tulips forward. Marîthe stands in the living room, watching us without knowing how to jump into the conversation.

"How did you know where I live?" I ask, truly alarmed. I keep my voice down because I don't want to worry Marîthe.

Denny grins. "I'm really good at finding people." There is something about the way he says it that I don't especially like, but I'm distracted by the brown package he hands to me. It's flat and wide, covered in the name of a German designer I've been reading about in all the magazines lately. *"Von Düsseldorf zu dir!"*

"Is that German? What is with all the German lately? You, Mme Sanxay . . ." I ask, barely paying attention. I'm too surprised. My hands are tembling as I turn the thin box wrapped in heavy paper over. "What is this?"

"Just open it!" Denny says. *"Öffnet sie!"*

I look at Marîthe, who's having big fun, watching this scene play out. "Open it!" she echoes. Even Sebastien looks incredibly curious to see what's inside.

I unwrap the box and open it to find a flat bundle of gold tissue paper. Careful not to rip it, still fully confused at how exactly this whole scene has come to transpire this evening, I separate the tissue paper and find a gorgeous silk dress inside it. It's shiny and green, with delicate cap sleeves and a round neckline. I let the box and the paper flutter to the floor, holding the dress up in surprise.

Marîthe gasps. "Guillaume! Come quickly!" she yells at her husband in French. She stumbles forward to gently touch the silk. *"Mon Dieu!"* She looks at me. "It's beautiful."

I nod. "It is beautiful." I look at Denny in wonder. "Why?"

"Your dress from the other afternoon is ruined, no?"

I grimace. "Yes." Guillaume steps into the foyer, too, which is now quite crowded with the five of us.

Marîthe points at the dress. "He loves Alex," she informs her husband to catch him up. "He gave her that dress."

Denny smiles briefly, overhearing Marîthe. "And did the *real* mother of those children offer to replace it, or have it cleaned?"

I shake my head. "Ha. As if."

"I figured you'd need a new dress, and when I gave it to you, you'd finally let me take you on a date."

I cluck in surprise and appraise the dress again. Taking the tulips under my arm, I close my eyes and give in.

"Fine," I say to Denny. "I'll go to dinner. But *just* as a friend."

Denny takes a small bow, as if he's won a competition. I realize he's not only without that terrible hat this evening, but he's wearing different pants today, too. They're jeans. Not pleated or tapered or any other terrible thing.

The cocky bow makes my temper flare, but then I look back down at the green silk, the beautiful tulips, and feel a high-pitched, excited giggle escape my throat.

"You really do show up in the oddest of places, you know that?" I laugh and toss off any worries about this one date. It'll be a story I can tell to my mom, my cousin Emily, Zack, if he ever speaks to me again. The night a love-struck Parisian came to my door, delivering flowers and couture.

Denny's smile is so huge Marîthe runs to get her camera. I shoo him out before she comes back, closing the door firmly behind him. I stare down my host family, with the green dress slung over one arm, the pink tulips crowded in the other.

"Show's over, people," I say, marching back to my room. "*Finit*."

I hang up the dress, so bright with shiny newness that it makes all my other clothes look haggard and totally forgettable.

* * *

Saturday night, I shave my legs and pull my hair back, letting a sleek black ponytail flare out from the back of my head and graze the back of the dress. The green silk is great with my hair. He picked the perfect color for me.

Denny arrives at seven forty-five on the dot, and as I pull a jacket on and step out into the courtyard of my building, it strikes me that this is what I'd been imagining when I had decided last spring to come to Paris for a year. *Exactly* this.

Le Boudoir is the kind of place where the menu changes every day. There are two seatings, one at eight in the evening and one at nine. Denny pulls my chair out for me and waits till I've arranged myself before he sits down.

"I thought this was a friend date," I say, narrowing my eyes at him skeptically.

"Just so long as it's a date," Denny says. In the candlelight, without that idiotic baseball cap, he looks mature and at ease. He's not like the guys at the Lycée when they bound into a restaurant in a big group, sitting down in the nearest chair and expecting fast service with a smile. He's patient, elegant almost. And tonight, in a dark suit, I start to wonder if I might have misjudged him. He looks *handsome* tonight.

He catches me looking at him and smiles. He could be an actor in a French black-and-white drama, with his distinctively deep-set blue eyes and large features. He has a memorable face. I wonder why he hides it under that hat. He's got the sort of powerful build that, despite the fact that he isn't tall, makes a statement. He seems to like being in control.

The waitress brings around a chalkboard with all the menu choices for tonight written out on it. My French skills are getting so good that I can recognize every single thing written on there. Denny starts to order something fishy for each of us.

"I'd like to order for myself, please," I cut in. "*Je voudrais*," I say in French to the waitress, "*la salade de betteraves, et après un steak avec lardons.*" I'd never let anyone order for me, contrary to how much he might think I want him to. And anyway, fish is revolting. I like my protein wrapped up in fat and doused in cognac, thank you very much.

Denny orders a bottle of wine. I only take a little. Despite it being Saturday night, I've got to be up early to study for an upcoming history test, and then I have to write a short story for our French creative writing class. Then I have to search the Internet to find an SAT-prep class in Paris, which should be fun—about as fun as the time my cousin Emily and I got stuck on a Westchester-bound Metro North train in a blizzard with about three hundred drunken Wall Street brokers during the Final Four tournament.

"What are you thinking about?" Denny asks me.

I almost tell him the truth; that I'm thinking about the stupid SAT class. Mme Cuchon's new thing is an obsessive interest in all the Programme Americain students scoring really high on their tests when we take them in Paris next month. That will convince parents of prospective students that the program in no way hinders kids from getting into college—indeed, it only helps us, is the theory. Of course, my mom (now regularly in contact with Mme Cuchon about the academic life at the Lycée via e-mail) thought me taking a weekend class to prepare for the test was just an *excellent* idea.

Then I realize talking about the test will make me sound like a Goody Two-shoes high school kid. I clam up.

"Oh, nothing." I look around the restaurant approvingly. "This reminds me of a place I go to a lot with my friends. I can't live without their fois gras terriné," I say, even though I hate fois gras, and the consistency of terrines makes me gag. I don't know what to say after that, because for the life of me I *still* can't think of a way to prove to Denny that I'm not who he thinks I am—a sweet babysitting type with a penchant for pink tulips.

I grab the bottle of wine and top my glass off.

Taking a long, restorative sip, I realize how long it's been since I had alcohol. *Too* long. I down the rest of my glass, loving the sour tang as it coats the back of my throat. As soon as my glass is empty, I find myself relaxing enormously. You could even say I'm having fun. I feel like myself again, *finally*. And I know Denny's green dress makes me look like myself again, too.

That's the funny thing—Denny's perception of me can't be *that* off base. I mean, he did choose a dress for me that I love. I give him a long look while eating our appetizers and wonder if I've been wrong all along. I bat my eyelashes invitingly.

"So tell me about yourself, Alex," Denny says as we wait for our first course to arrive.

"Not much to tell," I say in a way that makes it clear that's not really true at all. "I'm just Alex."

"Why don't you start with where you are from?"

I tell him that I'm from Brooklyn and my dad is French-Vietnamese. I ask him if he has ever heard of *Luxe*, and he seems impressed that my mom is on their masthead. Once I feel like I've given the requisite amount of information about myself, I turn it back over to him.

"So where are *you* from? Didn't you say you aren't native to Paris?"

"I grew up in the Dordogne," he says. "On an estate outside of Perigueux. It's my family's place."

"Really?" I ask, suddenly *very* much more curious about Denny. Rolling hills of sunflowers, dotted by estates complete with swimming pools and tennis courts pop into my mind. I picture myself in the front seat of an Italian sports car, an Hermes scarf tied around my hair, riding toward a château of my own. "What's it like?"

"It's a dream," he says with a faraway smile. "We have sheep and horses and lots of dogs and cats roaming the property. It's the biggest parcel of land for many kilometers around."

"And that's where you grew up?"

"Yes. The château has been in my family for centuries. However, it is very expensive to look after the main house, so my family used to rent it out. I grew up with my father and mother in the smaller house, the one built for the caretaker."

"Hmm," I say. *That* doesn't sound as glamorous as I'd been imagining.

"A couple years ago, my uncle from Paris got married, ran for office in Perigueux, and decided that he wanted to live in the main house again. He doesn't have as much money as he wants people to think he does. When company comes, he pretends my parents are his servants."

The gears in my head are turning. I'm listening very carefully but not quite sure what's sparked my sudden feeling of recognition about that château. I take another piece of bread from the basket and chew it thoughtfully.

"The Dordogne is beautiful. Have you ever been?" he asks.

"No," I hate to admit. "I've been wanting to go for a long time. My mom has been."

"Would you like to come for a weekend? Perhaps next weekend, we could take a trip. You can try some of the butter my mother churns. She salts it with *fleur de sel*. You can see the granules in the bar—it almost crunches when you bite into it. *Très delicieux*."

I look at Denny in wonder. "What is wrong with you? You barely know me, you bring me flowers *twice*, and now you ask me to come home with you and meet your mother? How conceited are you? You must think girls are just dying to meet your mother. Let me assure you, not all girls are dying to meet a guy's mother."

"You do not like the attention I give you, Alex?"

I laugh. "I'm not sure *what* I think. But—" I take a minute to enjoy looking as coy as possible. "You tempt me with the Dordogne. If I didn't have to babysit all next weekend, I'd go in a heartbeat."

"You can't find anyone to cover for you?"

"Ha! I wish," I say. "Not too many of my friends seem to be talking to me right now."

"They are angry at you?"

"Sorta." I wave away his question with a flick of my bangle-clad wrist. "But no. No one would ever cover for me."

"What if I hadn't told you that my family lives in the caretaker's house? Would you go with me if I'd said my family name was Peugeot? I was going to grow up to inherit a small dynasty of wealth?"

I laugh. "No, I can tell you have class without all those society trappings. My mom's a society outcast herself. We're used to being the redheaded stepchildren." I tell him a little bit about my mom, how my grandparents wrote her out of the will when she ran off with my dad. It was only when they divorced that my grandparents would talk to her again. Then they bought her and me the brownstone in Brooklyn Heights. And now we see them all the time.

"So no, your family name has no bearing on my decision not to go to the Dordogne with you."

"Yes, well Marquet is a particularly prominent one. I'm glad you are not 'using me' for my name."

I've just refilled my glass of wine and am about to bring it to my lips when I hear that awful familiar name. I drop the glass, splashing cherry-red merlot all over my plate, the table and the napkin in my lap.

"Oh *shit*," I whisper, on my feet before he can stop me. Marquet. Denny Marquet! He's related somehow to PJ's host parents! This is not okay. I can't be here. I need to make sense of this. Trailing my jacket and purse behind me, I make for the front door as fast as I can. Running all the way back to my homestay, I realize I'm in tears. Perigueux. Political office. It's the same thuggish family that drove PJ out of their house and into untold danger. Why? Why is *this* the kind of guy who always enters into my life! He was only stalking me to find out what I know about PJ. I'm sure of it. I feel disgusting.

I throw the dress, stained with red wine, right into the trash and cry myself to sleep. How do I always, *always* pick the wrong guys?

This one, I shiver, burying myself under my covers as if they could protect me from the mess I'm in until morning, *might be the worst one of all.*

APRIL

16. OLIVIA

Resurrecting the Past

When I have to, I look at the mirror and watch myself dance. But mostly I don't want to see what my body looks like in all the different positions of our new routine. I let Henri, the Underground's head choreographer, correct me.

"Relax your face, Olivia!" he shouts at me as we mark the steps to his clapping beat. "*Souris!*"

I lift my chin and try not to squint in concentration. When I do see my reflection dancing, my face and shoulders look so *naked*. I wish I still had all my hair so that I could hide behind it.

"Nice arch, Olivia!" Henri calls. "Keep it up!"

Henri is not your average choreographer. Certainly, he's nothing like my ballet instructors from home. Henri has a Mohawk and stretches his earlobes out with plugs. He's got tattoos all over his arms and chest. He's openly bisexual. And according to Katica, the Hungarian dancer I've become friendly with through the Underground, he's hooked up with both André *and* Kiki after rehearsals on various occasions. "*Très bien*, André! Perfect, perfect! *Et arretez.*" He stops clapping and goes to his bag to find the music he's arranged for us.

All the dancers drop their poses and wait for Henri to give small notes privately to individual dancers before going through the sequence again. "Olivia!" he calls, fiddling with the stereo system hidden in the studio's closet. "*Viens ici.*"

I jog over to him. "*Oui*, Henri?" I do my best to relax my face.

"I never have to give you notes on smiling, Olivia," he says in English. "Where's that all-American spirit I hired you for? I can usually count on you over everyone else!"

"*Desolée*," I mumble back. "I'll fix it."

"Good girl," he says. He looks down at me almost paternally. I wish he'd stop looking at me so intently. I wish I could disappear. "Let's take it from the top!"

For the rest of the rehearsal, all I can muster is a terrible clown grimace. When Henri watches me, I can see him shake his head almost imperceptibly. The worst part is, I don't even care.

★ ★ ★

Thomas is at home for Easter weekend before he, Remy, Inez, and Xavier drive to the Basque country for their spring break from the Sorbonne. That is to say that Thomas's duffle bag is in the living room, and there is a set of sheets folded up at one end of the couch. But I haven't seen him at all.

It is late Friday night, and I'm wide awake, staring at a picture of Vince I'd slid into the side pocket of my purse. I remember how many times we skirted the issue of sex the first year we dated. When I turned sixteen, he brought up that he thought he should wait till he went to college to start being sexually active. "Unless . . ."

"Unless what?" I'd asked, smirking. I thought it was so sweet that he wasn't ready, either. But I know we were both really, really curious.

"Unless you are ready before then," he'd told me. "I think it would be really special to lose my virginity to you."

I'd been flattered and scared. I told him I wanted to wait until I was seventeen, maybe junior year. I just wasn't ready. Then I went to France. And promptly lost my virginity to Thomas, without discussing it even once.

I hear Thomas come home late, ending a quiet conversation on the phone with someone as he unlocks the front door. I wonder if it's a new girlfriend he's talking to. Someone smarter, more passionate, with a more steadfast character.

When I wake up late the next morning, for some reason unable to respond to my alarm clock until it's gone off several times, he's gone for the day.

Mme Rouille gives Elise the week off, too, so she's in Brittany with her family. Mme Rouille is apparently going to cook Easter dinner tomorrow afternoon.

"Would you like to help me? I'm roasting a lamb," she asks when I get back from rehearsal. Waiting for the kettle to boil for some tea, Mme Rouille shows me the massive leg of bright pink meat she got from the *boucherie*. It looks slippery and wet, almost bloody.

"I don't eat lamb," I tell her, and then burst into tears.

"Olivia!" Mme Rouille's still holding the meat in the air as though it is a prize she has killed by herself. She puts it back in the fridge and washes her hands before she comes to put her arms around me. "It is okay. You don't have to help me. Or even eat the lamb. I can make something else. Or we could go out. . . ."

I shake my head. "Don't make something else. I'll eat the vegetables."

"Tell me what's the matter," she says, but I know she already knows. "That boy," she says.

"Ever since," I hiccup. "The thing happened with Drew . . . I feel so . . . *heavy*. Like . . . I . . . can't be myself anymore."

Mme Rouille's eyes turn glassy. She pulls me to her. I let myself cry into the thick shoulder pad of her vintage Chanel suit as if she were my own mom. Of course, my mom would be wearing an Ed Hardy hoodie. But that comforting, mom-like feeling is still there.

And with Mme Rouille, I know she knows what it's like. Over break she told me a story not unlike my own. "Will it always feel like this?" I ask her.

"No," she says firmly. "It will not."

* * *

Mme Rouille puts me to bed with extra-fluffy pillows from her own bed so that I can sit up and have my tea. When I met Mme Rouille in the fall, I thought she was cold and out of touch, with her formal day suits and her perfect silver hair. I never imagined feeling so close to someone who may as well come from the moon in terms of similarities to my family in Southern California. But she and I have been through a lot together. Not least, when she came to pick me up from Drew's house, that terrible night. I've blacked out most of the memories, but I do remember that she brought one of her furs with her in the Mercedes and carried it upstairs when she came up to collect me. I was sitting on the couch with Mme Cuchon and Zack, shaking and trying not to throw up again. When I saw her, I started to cry.

"Please don't tell Thomas," I said, overcome with guilt, even though everyone kept saying it wasn't my fault.

Even though Zack was still wiping the remnants of vomit off my face and out of my hair and my top, Mme Rouille threw her mink around me and took me home without asking a word. Once she'd parked and let the concierge take the keys from her, all she said was, *"Maintenant, tu es hors danger."*

"Shall I call one of your friends?" she asks me now. *"Peut-être* Alex?"

"No, thank you," I say, pulling my black duvet embroidered with tiny white flowers over me. "I'm okay. I just want to sleep."

Lately, that's all I want to do.

★ ★ ★

When I wake up, I am so thirsty that I think I'm sick or dying as I come into consciousness. I stalk out into the kitchen. I don't want just water or tea—I want something I can really taste, like orange juice or soda. I settle for raspberry flavored sparkling water that's on its way to being flat. On the way back to my room, I see that the TV's on. Thomas is asleep in front of a news magazine show.

I take the remote and click the television off. Thomas stirs on the couch. "Are you awake?" I whisper to him. "Thomas?"

"Olivia," he mutters in such a familiar and consoling way that I find myself sitting down next to his sleeping body and putting my hand on his chest over his T-shirt. Thomas is a thin guy. I can feel his heart beating faster and his deep breaths quicken as he wakes up.

His eyelids flutter open. The glow of the clock on the cable box is reflected in his eyes. In this strange bluish tint, he registers me and pulls me down into a hug. The couch is big enough for us both to lie down there together. I burrow into him and feel him bury his face in the crown of my hair, still a little dirty and salty from rehearsal this afternoon.

"*Tu me manques,*" he whispers.

"I miss you, too," I tell him, my lips pressed into the fabric of the shoulder of his T-shirt. "So much."

"You are ill?" he asks me. "You sleep all today, Maman has told me."

"I wasn't feeling well," I say. Thomas smells deliciously musky, like soap and bar smoke and the grit of Paris from riding around the city on his bicycle. "I'm feeling better now." I raise my face up to his, hoping to receive his kiss.

"Olivia," Thomas breathes. "We shouldn't do this . . ."

But his lips are too tender, too luscious, for me to thwart my desire to kiss them. I want Thomas and me to be the way we used to be—back in that innocent time I found love with him when I couldn't possibly have expected it. Nothing ever felt dark or frightening with Thomas. When I met him, I felt he understood some crucial part of me.

I kiss him hungrily, desperate to feel that deep-seeded mutual understanding that brought us together so wholly on Christmas Eve, the first time we slept together. I want to block out all the suspicious looks I've been getting at school, the pitying looks from my teachers, Mme Rouille, and Zack.

I'm still wearing a leotard from dance class. Without taking my eyes off of his, I pull each strap off my shoulders.

"Are you sure?" I ask him, knowing this might be the last chance we have to stop ourselves.

Thomas says nothing. Instead he slips his hands around me and carries me gently into my room. A feeling of warmth and safety washes over me, and I close my eyes against his chest.

17. PJ

Caught in the Act

_B_efore I collect my pay one Saturday morning, Griselda stops me.

"Penelope," she says. "You must try a little hard to look nice when you come to the club from now on. You are beautiful, yes, but you have to show us. Give the customers a taste of what's to come in the dancers' rooms. _D'accord?_"

I raise my eyebrows. "Okay." But I have no idea what to do next.

That afternoon I go to Zack's house. I don't really know what else to do, and I'm afraid if I ask Alex for help, she'll find out where I've _really_ been staying.

Zack's family is quite different from your standard French family in that not only do they have a washing machine, but they have a dryer as well. I take another bath while I wait for my clothes to get clean, wondering if he might be able to help me with what Griselda asked.

When I'm all done in the bathroom, I put on Zack's plush robe and consult him.

"I need . . . to try a little harder," I say, trying to sound casual.

Zack immediately bursts into uproarious laughter. "What on earth *for*, darlin'?"

"Um, you know," I say. My palms immediately begin to sweat. This is so not like me. "I just wanted to kind of . . . look nice for Jay."

Zack nearly chokes. "Jay doesn't think you look nice as you are? I have a hard time swallowin' that one, child."

"Can you help me?" I ask. "Please?"

"I do love a project," Zack agrees. He takes off his glasses and sits down at his desk for a moment, thinking.

"You stay here," he says finally. "I think I know what we can do." He gathers his wallet and keys and instructs me to stay in his room and dive under the bed if anyone comes home.

After Zack leaves, I tiptoe out to the kitchen and look around. There's a ripped half of a seeded baguette from the morning still on the counter. I pop a tiny bit into my mouth. It tastes really good. Before I can stop myself, I grab the rest and take it into Zack's room.

Zack is back in a flash, armed with what look like medieval torture devices. "All right, my dear," he says, leading me back into the bathroom.

Zack positions me in front of the mirror and starts combing out all the tangles in my hair. I wriggle away. He's not the most gentle hairdresser. "Be still, child," he scolds. "Let me style you!"

"You like it?" he asks me when he's done with my head. "Pretty sexy if I do say so myself. Southern gentlemen have a way with hair. It's part of our culture."

I take a look at the curls falling around my shoulders. "Yeah. Thanks."

"Let's just put a little makeup on you. When Jay sees these red lips he's going to be putty in your hands!" He dabs a deep color onto my mouth. In the mirror, I look different. Griselda will like it, I'm sure, even though Zack is much too sophisticated to fix me up the way the other girls at the club look.

"*Et voilà!*" he announces. I give him a rueful smile. I do look nice. I wish it really were for Jay.

We walk back into the bedroom so that I can gather my things and Zack can see me out.

"Hey," Zack says, reaching down and noticing something on the bedspread. "Were you eating in here?" Zack's meticulous in his hygiene. He starts furiously pawing at the bed. "There's *crumbs* on here."

I step out of the shoes and put them back into the plastic bag.

"Um, yeah, I hope you don't mind," I say, my face heating up.

"PJ, are you hungry? Have you been eating lately?" Zack stands up, holding his hands in front of him as if he'd like to go wash them, and looks at me pityingly. "You don't have to sneak around if you want something to eat. Let me make you something. Just give me one sec."

"No, Zack, that's okay. I'm not hungry at all," I say. It's true. The bread filled my shrunken stomach up uncomfortably fast. "I better get going. Thanks for the makeover." I give him a twenty-euro bill, even though it pains me to give away some of my escape money.

★ ★ ★

To kill time before I have to be at the club, I go to watch the sunset from the top of Montmartre hill. It's good for me to make the trek up to

Sacré Coeur before I start my night's work. The steep, winding staircases make for a vigorous, distracting walk. I'm still mortified about the crumbs. I don't know what came over me when I saw that bread. I wasn't even hungry, I don't think. I can't ever seem to tell when I should want food. I hardly ever think about it.

The light changes from clear to hazy pink from the setting sun, from la butte Monmartre over the skyline of Paris. It's heartbreakingly gorgeous— the exact opposite of the place where I spend my nights and much of my days. And yet they are of the same city. How can that even be possible?

When I finally pull myself away from the view of Paris and make my way down the hill to the club, no one is there yet. This isn't uncommon, since the dancers don't usually arrive until they absolutely have to, and Griselda and Freddie have their own apartments elsewhere. The bartender sometimes comes and opens the bar early to air the place out a bit (being a private club, the men can smoke in there, and they often do), so that it won't be so rank when the first costumers come in.

The inner workings of a gentlemen's club are, day to day, very much like any other small business. Freddie is the boss. He's a surly man with a very short temper. He has little interest in his employees as people. He manages the club as if he is running a dairy farm. Each cow is kept in her own little room for her day's work, and then released without any true concern for her well-being. If a girl is sick, Freddie might have Griselda send her to the doctor, but only because that means he'll lose one eighth of his revenues if she's absent for a night.

Griselda is like the floor manager. She makes sure the place is presentable, the girls don't complain too much, and the bar is well stocked. She collects the money and makes sure everyone gets paid at the end of the night.

The strobe light is on in the bar. I can see Griselda has left me a note:

"*Viens au bureau quand tu arrives, Fiona. Xx Griselda*"

Having never been in the office before, I approach the door with some trepidation. *Am I in trouble?* I think warily. And then, more fearfully: *am I about to lose this job? Where will I sleep if I can't sleep here?*

Griselda is sitting on the leather sofa when I come in, sorting through some utility bills. Freddie's at his desk, smoking a cigarette.

"Fiona!" she says warmly. "We have a change of plans for tonight. *Geneviève est malade ce soir. Elle reste chez elle.* I need you to dance in her place."

"*Quoi?*" I back against the door. I heard her correctly. But I don't comprehend what she is saying. "Geneviève?" Geneviève is one of the dancers. I saw her yesterday. She looked fine. Maybe a little exhausted from taking care of her little boy during the day and dancing all night. But she was definitely not ill.

"*Son bébé* has given her *la grippe*," Griselda explains in her strange mix of English and French. It comes from being from the south of Spain— she learned English before French and interchanges them when she's speaking aloud. "She should have called earlier to tell me, but she didn't. *Alors, maintenant* you must be the dancer."

"*Non!*" I protest. "I don't dance."

"You look like you do," Freddie cuts in, the first thing he's said since I've been standing here. I raise my hand to my lips, smearing the red lipstick in shame.

I swallow hard. "I don't know anything about dancing."

"You can shake *ton derrière* around," Griselda says. "Sometimes all the clients want is someone to talk to. I'll work the front. I'll only send you the ones I know aren't expecting too much. *Ca sera bien.*"

I shake my head, but from the way Freddie and Griselda are looking at me, I know I have to dance or I'll lose my job. And with it, the rolls of green bills I've been saving. I need more, much more, if I ever want to escape Paris or the Marquets.

"What if someone won't leave my room?" I ask miserably. "What do I do?"

"Some guys will try to bribe the security guards to let them stay longer," Freddie says. "But luckily for you, I give the security guards more money than the clients do. My girls are my most valuable assets. You'll be fine."

Before she leaves me for her post at the bar, Griselda squeezes out a generous dollop of fruity-smelling hair gel and slicks all my hair away from my face. It hangs in a long cascade down my back. "*Oui, c'est bien,*" Griselda says to me and kisses both my cheeks. "Good girl."

In Geneviève's room, there is a couch where I've sometimes slept. Men can sit there to make themselves comfortable while they watch her dance. Directly in front of it is a raised platform. There's a pole installed there, and a few feet from it is a wooden chair. Dancers must sit on the chair so that they look ready when a man comes in.

Griselda doesn't send me anyone until almost midnight.

When the man comes in, he greets me and takes off his jacket. "*Je suis nouveau,*" he says with a giggle. He's balding but has tufts of hair on either side and also in the back. Short and paunchy, he looks just like how you'd imagine a first-time strip-club client would look. Absolutely giddy. Very nervous, too.

Music gets piped into the rooms from the office. Remembering that I've slept where he sits makes me feel queasy.

I stand up, terrified, and feel myself sway forward.

Stumbling on the ledge of the platform, I heave forward, tripping over the high heel of one shoe with the elongated toe of the other. Dizzy, unable to see clearly, I curl up in a ball near the edge of the makeshift stage. My head feels damp and I think there's some blood on the stage.

"*Je suis desolée,*" I whisper. "I don't feel very well." The bread I scarfed down at Zack's house does a somersault in my stomach.

The man looks at me in surprise, and then his face becomes frightened. Without saying anything, he grabs his stuff and leaves.

★ ★ ★

Griselda comes in a few minutes later, her arms folded over her draping cleavage. "Fiona!" she scolds me. "What's the matter with you?"

Woozy, I stand up and push her away from me. "I can't do this!" I tell her, realizing too late that I'm screaming. I rush past her through the door and leave Freddie's forever.

Leaving the lights of Pigalle behind me, I walk as fast as I can toward Ternes, even though it terrifies me to go back to my old neighborhood. I'm dizzy just thinking about it. I haven't been there since the night M. Marquet tried to touch me and I ran in the opposite direction toward the Gare du Nord.

My hands holding my stomach, I trip along toward Olivia's house. I am as weak and nauseated as I was my first day in Paris, when I passed out in a phone booth and Olivia found me and took me to Mme Rouille.

They had been so kind to me, so discreet. Mme Rouille had never asked me where my host family was, or made any complaints about my having to stay for so long. In fact, she barely noticed me. In my terror, I wonder if she and Olivia would be as welcoming to me now. This time, it means much more.

The closer I get to Ternes, the more convinced I become that Mme Rouille still won't know who I am. She was a distant guardian last semester. Why would that have changed? And Olivia is a true friend. In the middle of the night, even with blood streaking in my hair from where I fell off the stage and hurt myself, there's no one who will be more of a silent comfort than she will.

At least, that's what I am hoping, because without Jay, there's no one else.

I dart past the men on the streets, holding my coat around me. I could be robbed; I could faint right here in the street if I don't hurry.

"*Olivia,*" I whisper to myself. "*Please be home.*"

★ ★ ★

Mme Rouille answers the door in pink pajamas, the three miniature poodles at her feet. They don't bark at me. For once, they are absolutely silent. The apartment is dark except for the front hall light.

Perhaps she's finally trained them, I think over the hammering pain coming from the side of my head where I hit the floor. Mme Rouille's face shows no sign of recognition of me at first. She stares at the blood coming from the gash on my forehead and soaking the collar of my shirt poking out of my coat.

Then she remembers me from when I had to stay here at the beginning of the school year.

"PJ?" she asks hesitantly. "*Vous êtes l'amie d'Olivia, n'est-ce pas?* Is that blood?"

"*Oui,*" I gulp.

"*Pardonnez-moi, cherie,*" Mme Rouille says. "But you have been missing, no? What's happened to you? Have you been hurt?" She looks behind me into the entry hall. "Who's with you? Are the Marquets following you?"

I gulp. "No, no. I'm alone. Is Olivia here?"

"She was not feeling well earlier," Mme Rouille tells me. "But I think she is fine to see you. Follow me."

The house is so quiet I tiptoe along after her, afraid to make noise. The dogs trot after us, still quiet but very curious.

"She is sleeping," Mme Rouille says as we pass the darkened living room and get to Olivia's bedroom door. "You go ahea—"

In the various glows of electronic clocks and streetlamps outside, a strange moving mass is writhing on top of Olivia's bed. We stare at it for a long time, trying to register what's happening. Then the dogs, waiting breathlessly around our ankles, lose it and the three begin to bark, not happy cries of recognition, but signals they know their master is deeply, deeply disturbed.

Mme Rouille's first reaction is not to say anything but to take a nearby book and throw it across the room at the window. I wince, waiting for the glass to break. It doesn't, but the drapes come crashing down. A flood of streetlight comes in. Only then does Mme Rouille let out a ferocious scream of disgust.

"Olivia!" she rages. "Get out! Get out of my house right now!"

Olivia and Thomas jump off the bed, neither of them dressed behind the blanket they're holding up to shield themselves. They share a look of complete dread.

"I'm sorry," Olivia says, her voice dead.

"Oh, how could you?" Mme Rouille's voice bubbles in a fresh round of sobs. "Olivia, have you lost all your dignity?"

Olivia's jaw drops. "How can you say that to me?"

"How could you bring more trouble into this house?" Mme Rouille gestures at me. "When you know so well how hard I've tried to protect Thomas! How dare you try to seduce him!" Mme Rouille whirls around and points one finger into my face. "You! That's right. They rode away that night to find you. Is that when this all began?"

She walks forward and takes Thomas by his bare shoulders. Olivia pulls the blanket around her, looking so ashamed. "How long has this been going on? What else have you been hiding?"

"Nothing!" Olivia answers for him, desperately. "He hasn't done anything wrong!"

"I told you to get out!" Mme Rouille says, low and guttural. "Both of you, Olivia and your cursed friend. I never want to see either of you again. Go!"

Thomas makes protesting noises as he hurries to find his pants. "Maman, please stop! Just calm yourself!"

"Don't you dare say anything to me right now, Thomas. I mean it, Olivia and your friend—GET OUT!"

Olivia is crying as she pulls the nearest sweatshirt on and steps into some Ugg boots. Thomas is still struggling into his clothes, protesting to his mom to calm down. In a daze, I follow Olivia, breathless, down the stairs.

In front of the building, Olivia stops in her tracks. "No, wait," she says and turns as if she's about to go back inside. Then we hear a shriek from an upper floor's cracked window, and she whirls back around, stopped short.

"Let's just go," I say and grab Olivia's hand. I pull her along the street, and she doesn't give me much resistance. It's chilly but not freezing. We can make it for a few more minutes, long enough to find somewhere else to go. It's just Olivia and me, alone in the Paris night.

Olivia keeps muttering, "I'm sorry," over and over again, and I just keep wondering who else's life I can ruin now. I've been here before, and it never turns out well.

We dial Alex's BlackBerry and wait for it to ring.

18. ZACK

Follow Me

_S_aturday evening after PJ runs off all primped and pampered for her date to make up with Jay, I'm sitting in the Place Cambronne, watching a few pigeons pick over a discarded container of pad thai. I'm tossing my cell phone back and forth, from one hand to the other, making my mind up whether or not to call Bobby.

"What should I do?" I ask the pigeons, who peck closer and closer to my feet but flutter away every time I stamp or shoo them. "To call him or not to call him?"

I decide that I'll let fate decide for me, and that I'll flip my cell phone in the air like a coin. If the numbers land face up, I'll dial Bobby.

Bobby it is. Oh, Jeez.

Bobby answers after several rings, almost when I'm thinking I'll be able to get to his voice mail and be home free. "Hey, Zack." Bobby doesn't sound the most thrilled to receive the call. "What's up?"

"Hey, dude!" I say, overly chipper and sounding unconvincing, probably even to my pigeon audience. "Just callin' to say hi . . . how's it going?"

"Fine," Bobby says. "How are you?"

"Oh, you know, busy, but good."

"How's André?"

I scratch the back of my head and try to come up with a way to brush this off quickly. My time runs out. I sigh.

"Oh, Bobby. Listen. I'm sorry," I say. "I know I wasn't the best host. Please don't hate me."

"Zack, I don't hate you." Bobby sounds tired. "It just seems like you've got a lot of unfinished business to deal with in Paris."

"Yeah." I cross my ankles in front of me. Talking to Bobby shouldn't be this tense. I feel awful.

"Well, maybe it was too much, too soon. Regardless, take care of yourself, okay?"

"Okay," I answer. I don't want to hang up yet. "You, too."

"See you later, Zack," Bobby says and clicks off. His number blinks back at me as the call disconnects.

It's too dark to sit in the Place Cambronne anymore, and besides, the winos and bums are starting to take over where moms with strollers and happy couples were hanging out on benches. I stare at my phone, willing someone to call me. But who would?

Olivia, God bless her, is too depressed to want to do anything. PJ and Jay are probably off mooning at each other somewhere, wherever it is that they go to hang out. André's moved on to someone else by now, I am sure.

And Alex, as perfect as Alex always is in moments like these, I still can't forgive her. For Alex, a Saturday night in Paris is a treasure hunt, a Choose Your Own Adventure book. She'd greet a night like this—no plans, no expectations—with the kind of joie de vivre they write operas about. I wish I could just give in and call her because hating her is a burden. I lug it around like it's an over-packed wheelie suitcase with a broken handle. It's clunky, obnoxious, and takes far too much energy. But every time I think of her, scheming her way around the south of France, clinging to Jay and casting me off whenever it pleased her, my chest gets tight as if I've swallowed too big of a piece of steak. But no. I won't do it. She can't break me that easily. When I told her in Cannes that I was through with her, I meant it.

Back at my homestay, things are just as desolate. Romy and Jacques went to a Saturday night mass at the Église Saint-Étienne de Cambronne with Mireille, and Paul is eating dinner at a friend's house. It's just Kevin, the family cat, and me.

It's never a good idea to spend a Saturday night trolling around on Facebook, but that is what I find myself doing for the next half hour or so. I look at people's profiles from home, seeing what they are up to in Memphis. I see that Pierson's page is as popular as ever, with comments in English and Dutch, continuing conversations, inside jokes, and offers to meet for a drink or to go to a hash bar in Amsterdam. The kids at home think it's endlessly cool that Pierson's in Amsterdam. My own page doesn't have nearly the amount of Tennessean well-wishers as his does.

I almost leave Pierson a comment, just so I won't feel so left out, but then I realize that he (and everyone else) will be able to see the date and time that I left the comment, and they'll know I was at home, alone, on a Saturday night.

My own page is lackluster. In the corner, where Facebook pops up pictures of random friends, Mary and Sara-Louise smile out at me. Each of them has the same profile picture: the two of them on a carousel in the Champs de Mars. Only Sara-Louise would be enough of a goober to ask the carousel attendant to take their picture as they came by.

I wonder what those two are up to. They are sometimes with Alex lately, but not always. Clicking on Mary's page, I see a comment from Sara-Louise from earlier today: "If you steal the gin from your host parents, I'll bring the tonic! C u tonight, *mon amie*! Xxx SL"

And then two other people from the program had clicked "like" underneath her comment.

Is Mary having a party tonight? I wonder. How did I miss that?

I ring up Mary before I can convince myself that this would be a pathetic move.

"Hey, Zackalicious," she says. "Where you been all *ma vie*?"

"Oh, you know, around," I say. "What are you ladies up to tonight?"

"Drinking. Next question," Mary answers. "Actually, you feel like braving the Fourteenth tonight? I'm having people over for a Michel Gondry retrospective."

"Fantastic!" I say, wondering if I sound as eager as I feel. "See you then!"

Relieved, I hang up and start thinking about what to wear. Almost immediately, the phone rings again. My heart lifts. I'm suddenly so popular!

It's André.

"Cheers, what are you up to?" he asks me, his voice echoing in the empty apartment. Kevin, lying on my bed, twitches. "Want to go get sauced somewhere? Have a little vest fashion show at my place later on?"

"Sorry," I tell him. "I'm seeing some friends."

"So I'm not invited, then?" he asks impertinently. "Don't punish me, Zack! Not when I've got such a hankering for my favorite American."

"Well," I answer. "It's just a small thing, watching movies. I'm not sure if I can invite anyone."

"Ah, an exclusive engagement," André says. "Is Olivia going?"

"I don't think so," I say. "She's been so different. I don't know what to do."

"How about this?" André asks. "You swing round Olivia's house to get her to come cheer herself with her dear friends, and I'll meet you there with a bottle of champagne and some chocolate cake. Lovely!"

I can't say no to André. I don't even try.

"Well, Mary's going to show the first movie at seven. Don't be late, okay?" I give him the address and click the phone off.

I get to Mary's homestay about six thirty, and realize as I'm punching the access code into her front entrance that I completely forgot to stop by to see if Olivia wanted to come. I take a few minutes to try to call her on her cell, but there's no answer. When I ring up Mme Rouille's home number, Elise tells me that Olivia's napping.

"Napping?" I ask. "Are you sure?" Olivia never naps. She doesn't have time.

"*Oui, monsieur,*" Elise tells me. "Mme Rouille told me not to disturb her."

"Okay," I say. "Well, tell her I called." It feels lame to say that. I should have gone over to her house like I told André I would.

Aside from Mary and Sara-Louise, the crowd gathered here to watch the movies isn't my typical crowd. I shift anxiously when I spot George, Robbie, Nathan, and Kyle on the couch in front of the massive television in Mary's living room. Drew's crew. They're lined up like a football team or a military advance: broad shoulders, take-no-prisoners posture. Their gaze shrivels. I can't stop thinking about that pink note in my mailbox at school.

Did one of them write it? Why would they want to scare me? What are they going to do?

What's worse is that the boys have reinforcements in the shape of the program girls.

Patty is sitting on George's lap. Tina's leafing through a magazine, sitting cross-legged on the floor at their feet. Anouk, Sara-Louise's host sister, is nuzzling Kyle heatedly, as if they were totally alone and not surrounded by people on all sides!

"Aren't they disgusting?" Sara-Louise drawls next to me, putting a wine glass in my hand. "They never quit. You like Bordeaux, right?"

"Anything with alcohol sounds good right about now," I say. "How's it going?"

"Shall we sit?" She gestures to two empty ottomans off to the side of the room, near a table of spreads and a loaf of bread.

I take one of the seats gingerly, careful not to spill my wine. Sara-Louise rolls her eyes at her host sister again, and then assumes the hostess role, something that Mary is apparently too busy in the kitchen to handle.

"You want some pâté?" Sara-Louise gestures at the food near us. "Anouk and I made them."

"Sure," I say, suddenly starving. The spread looks like bean dip, brownish gray, but tastes a little more earthy. It's not bad, kind of oily and very salty. I fill up several pieces of bread with it and chow down while Sara-Louise patters on.

"So, y'all excited for Easter break?" she asks cheerfully, looking around at everyone with widened eyes. "I'd say Paris isn't a bad place to spend a week with nothing to do. Sure beats college visits, which is what my mom wanted me to come home for this break," she laughs. One day, Sara-Louise will grow up to be a wonderful PTA reception hostess. She's blonde, has a cherubic face, and I bet she makes a mean pan of peanut butter bars.

No one answers Sara-Louise. Patty gets up to get George another glass of wine. People pretend to watch *La Science des Rêves*.

After a long scene wherein the star of the movie flies above what looks like a cardboard version of Paris, Tina snorts, "This movie is gay. Why are we watching it?"

Tina and her sister are identical, but one of them always wears her stripey highlighted hair up, and the other one wears it down. Tina's got the ponytail tonight, high and tight, pulling the skin of her forehead back so much she might be in pain. Short, compact little cheerleader types, in the wrong light, they look like little blonde rats. Tonight is one of those nights.

Patty walks back in and hands George his wine. A wineglass looks too delicate in his rough paws.

"Come on, Tina, you don't like the movie?" she asks her sister. "I think it's just amazing," she says sarcastically.

"Ugh, I'm just bored."

Sara-Louise stiffens. "Dude, give the movie a chance, guys!"

Mary, who is a total film nerd, doesn't even hear them. She is too enraptured by Gael García Bernal.

"Seriously, this movie is for homos," George says. "It's a Saturday and we're sitting around watching movies? Faggy movies? What's happening to this program?" There it is, that word again. Something I hadn't heard anybody use since I left Tennessee in September. It feels like a paper cut: just a scratch but it still stings so much you want to cry.

"What would you rather do, George?" Sara-Louise asks him. She looks prim and proper in a lavender short-sleeved Lucille Ball–style dress. All that's missing is the apron. "You're free to leave at your leisure if you have other plans."

"I want to watch the movie," I say, hoping to earn points with Sara-Louise. "I think it's good." My voice comes out too high and squeaky.

"Well, you would, wouldn't you," George says, his eyes turning dark. He's still looking at me. "Like I said, this movie is for homos."

I gulp. George's eyes are locked on mine, as if he is trying to stare me down. His brown hair flops into his eyes, but he doesn't brush it away. He doesn't move at all.

"Excuse me, I'm in the middle of watching a Michel Gondry retrospective," Mary cuts in, rolling over and sitting up to face George. "Can you pipe down?" Mary recently dyed a purple streak across her side-swept bangs. Seeing her and George go head-to-head is like a punk versus preppy contest.

Tina and Patty look away. Good Southern girls, they're not going to insult their hostess, but they can't tell George to shut up either because he is too popular for them to risk insulting, too.

"Michel Gondry is gay," George says, still staring right at me.

"How would you know?" Mary asks. "What, did you go read this on IMDb? Did you call him and ask him to come out to you?"

"Haven't you heard, Mary?" George says out of the corner of his smirk. "The gays don't have to officially 'come out' anymore. Like Zachariah here. He never came out, and we all know *he's* gay."

"George, stop it!" Sara-Louise says. "What is wrong with you? What do you have against Zack?"

George starts to laugh, hard enough that he finally drops his gaze on me. He laughs so hard that he holds his head in his hands. He might be going crazy, or it might just be a show. Whatever it is, it's frightening. We're all watching him, barely breathing.

Finally, George stands up. "What do I have against Zack? What do I have against Zack?"

Mary bounces up off the floor. "Yeah, George, what is it? Why are you being so heinous to Zack tonight? He never did anything to you!"

George takes a sip of wine, then puts down the glass on the coffee table and cracks the knuckles of each of his massive hands. I can't believe Alex ever looked at this guy with anything but complete revulsion.

George leans down to me. "I'll tell you what I have against you. You and your little slut friend. You ruined Drew's chances for college, for life. How's he going to get into an Ivy now? He's not even going to get into Humboldt State at this point. You ruined his life, fag."

Trembling, I look into my own glass of wine. George's voice is so hateful, so full of rage, that I know it's only a matter of seconds before he builds himself up enough to hit me.

"Drew ruined his own life," I whisper. I'm so terrified of him punching me that my stomach hurts. "He ruined Livvy's life. I didn't do anything to him."

"Bullshit!" George shouts. Tina and Patty spring up to hold George back.

"George, you gotta go," Mary says, pushing him toward the door. "No homophobic bullshit in my house. That's it, you're done."

"Zack and I are just working some things out," George says, his tone immediately relaxing.

"I think it's time for you to work out what an asshole you are," Mary says, still pushing him. "By yourself. Good-bye."

"Yeah, George." Sara-Louise laughs. "Go get to know yourself. Intimately."

"Come on, Mary. You're gonna kick me out?"

Patty puts her hands on her hips. "Mary, what's wrong with you? George has a right to stand up for our friend."

"It's not his business," Sara-Louise says. "It's none of any of our business. Where are your manners, Patty?"

George grabs his pack of cigarettes. "Fine, I'm going." But he doesn't go out the front door, as if he would if he were actually leaving. He goes to the balcony. Tina and Patty follow him.

I turn and ask Sara-Louise the most banal question I can think of. "So what's in the pâté?"

"Raw duck gizzards," she says quietly.

I shudder and run for the bathroom. While I'm washing my mouth out with soap, I hear the doorbell ring. "Oh, God," I say. André. I fling the door open and come back out into the hall to see a girl named Katie letting him in. Everyone's sitting in the living room, quietly talking among themselves. They see the unfamiliar guy in the foyer and shut up.

"Hey, everyone," André greets us with a big white-toothed smile. "Hey, Zack, great to see you." He's got a bottle of champagne and a cake box in his hand. "Where's Olivia?" He steps forward to give me a kiss on the cheek, still looking around for her.

George is back on the couch, in the middle of a comforting Tina-and-Patty sandwich.

"Get out, George," Mary says tightly from behind us. "I'm fucking serious. Go. *Now*."

"It's okay, Mary," I say, lifting my jacket off the back of a chair. "*I'm* leaving. See you guys later. Enjoy the movies."

"Hey, what was that about?" André asks me as he follows me down the street to the métro stop. Cambronne really isn't that far of a walk, but I really want to be at home already.

"Just some bros making a point," I say. "One of Drew's friends was trying to get me to come out of the closet."

André looks incredulous. "Cheeky bastard! Hasn't he got any class? I thought your program was for the *crème de la crème americaine*. The most upper-crust Americans there are."

"Guess not," I say. "Anyway, sorry to be a bore, but I'm just gonna head home. I'll give you a call later this week."

"Zack, you've got to be kidding me. You're going to let that wanker ruin your night? When you're already out? And dressed *fabulously*, I might add." He runs his hand down the front buttons of my shirt. "Let's go somewhere and eat this glorious chocolate cake I bought at Ladurée."

"Nope, I'm not really feeling social anymore," I say. I head down the stairs, too tired of defending myself to keep having this conversation.

There's a train pulling away from the platform. If I hadn't been stuck talking to André, I'd already be on my way home, watching all the stops on the number six line fly by.

André follows me through the turnstile and sits down next to me in one of the goofy plastic chairs in the station, the cake perched in his lap. The station smells dirty. I desperately wish I were someplace—anyplace—else.

"Zack, this is stupid. Why don't we ride up to the number two and just go back to my place? We could hang out, maybe watch a movie."

"No, thanks," I say. I feel spent from tonight, still shaken up by George in my face. "I really just want to go home."

Another train pulls in, and we step into a crowded car full of tourists just having boarded under the Arc de Triomphe. The people sitting in the fold-out seats near the doors grudgingly stand up to accommodate us.

"Zack," André says. "The night is young! Think of all we could do with it! We'll have cake and champagne and watch people through their windows from a park bench. Then we can go to a club, dance . . ." He rubs his body against mine and gives me a coy look. "And then, we could go back to my apartment and really catch up. . . . Doesn't that sound like fun?"

Despite all the people surrounding us, some standing so close I can feel when they sigh or shift their weight, André doesn't even lower his voice. The whole subway car can hear his plaintive requests for me to change my mind.

At the Grenelle stop, a bunch of people get off, and André pulls me over to one of the benches to take a seat. He puts his arm around me.

"André, come on, stop," I say. My skin prickles, remembering what it was like when he kissed my neck in the bathroom at Nouveau. "We're in the middle of the métro!"

"All right, mate, I am sorry. You just look bloody handsome tonight." André laughs. "I could eat you for dinner!" The way he says it, it doesn't sound funny or cute . . . it sounds *dirty*.

I suck in my breath. A couple of preteen girls laden with Mink shopping bags stare at us. I'm not sure if they are enthralled because they understand what we are saying or because they can't.

André giggles. "So, join me, okay?" He seems so sure of his ability to change my mind, so confident that I'll follow him back to his cake and his kisses and all the other things he wants me to do, that I'm overwhelmed by fear that I actually will, not because I want to, but because I know I can't say no to him.

But this—this plan of his is way out of my league. Kissing is one thing, but all that romance with the cake and the champagne can only lead one direction. A direction I am definitely not ready to go. Besides, when I wanted to be boyfriends, André didn't. I don't know how he expects me to trust him now.

I see that we're at my stop, but when I jump up to catch the closing doors, André grabs my arm and forcefully pulls me back down. "No you don't!" he laughs.

I take a deep breath of severe annoyance.

"What is this, André?"

"Don't go playing your games tonight!" André teases me. "You've got your Bobby games, pretending you've got a little Dutch boyfriend. Then you're snogging a girl in the Palais Royal, just as I walk up to you. What's that about?"

"Those weren't games," I protest. "I was definitely not the one playing games!"

"I know of some games we could play," André answers, leaning into my neck and giggling.

"André, quit," I mutter, pulling out my cell phone. I'm getting scared, and the queasy-frightened feeling, like I'm on some horror ride at a carnival, won't go away. Is André ever going to let up? I need backup. I pull out my phone and start texting. I've sent the text to Alex before even realizing I'm doing it.

A second after I send the text, Alex calls back, breathless. "Where are you?" she demands. I'm surprised at the level of concern in her voice. We've barely spoken in over a month.

"I'm just about to get off the métro at Sèvres-Lecourbe." I turn my head and speak softly into the phone. "This sounds weird, but can you meet me?"

"Of course!" she says, her voice authoritative and sincere. "I'll be right there."

I feel confidence and relief flood back into me.

When the doors open, I preempt André's Goliath dancer-strength and shake his hand off my arm. "André, no," I say. "Good night." I shake him off. Making a clear beeline for the doors, I jump out of the train car and take the stairs out of the station two by two.

When I come out, I see Alex, dashing down the dimly lit rue de Vaugirard in plain straight-legged jeans, a hoodie, and some very broken-in tennis shoes. I barely recognize her. She isn't wearing eyeliner. In fact, there's not even any lip gloss on her lips. I've never seen her so simplified.

"Hey, what's going on?" she asks. "I got here as fast as I could."

I'm touched to see Alex out of breath and sweating in front of me. "Do you have a cigarette?" I ask her, wanting suddenly to have all my stress erased by puffs of nicotine, the way she does.

"I don't have any," she says. "I quit."

"You did?" I ask, truly shocked. "When?"

"Oh, you know, recently," Alex says. "It's not that cool to smoke anymore. I figured it was time. So what's going on? Are you okay?"

"It's just this guy." I take a look around me on the street, not sure if André had the wherewithal to make it out of the train behind me fast enough. "He was kind of bugging me on the train."

"A stranger?" Alex makes a face. "How *sleazy*."

I can't stop looking around. It feels like even though I can't see him, he'll just pop up any minute.

"Zack!" Alex exclaims, looking at my hands. "You're shaking!"

I get that feeling I sometimes get when I stand up too fast. My doctor said it's because I have low blood pressure. I start to sense that the oxygen was not getting to my brain fast enough. I turn quickly enough to miss her, but just barely. More of Sara-Louise and Anouk's gizzard pâté goes flying onto the sidewalk.

"Zack!" Alex shrieks again. "Oh, my God! Are you okay?"

I wipe the corners of my mouth and shudder. "Uh, sorry. I ate something weird."

"No worries. Believe it or not, that's not the first time I've had to dodge projectile vomit this week."

Supporting me with one of her shoulders, she walks me into an *alimentation générale* she seems to be pretty familiar with. In a daze, I watch her gab a little with the guy behind the counter. I figure I must be hallucinating because there is no way Alex could carry on this long a conversation with a stranger in French. Putting a few euro coins on the counter, she turns to me with a bottle of orange juice and a package of biscuits. "For you," she says. "You want to hang out here for a while? Zamir says it's okay. You can sit on his stool if you want." She speaks to me so loudly, enunciating every word as if I am five years old. For some reason, it's soothing.

"No thanks," I say. I take a timid drink of orange juice. "That's okay. I feel better now."

"Sheesh, Zack, that really freaked me out," Alex says, collecting her change and shrugging at the guy as we leave the store. "*Bonsoir!*" she calls to him.

I tell her about George's nasty comments.

"He did not!" she says. "What did Patty say?"

"She just sat there. Everyone was kind of shocked."

"Yeah," she grunts. "What a total prick. If that is not grounds for dismissal from the program, then I will personally see to it that a bag of marijuana suddenly appears in his backpack just as he's forced to open it in front of a teacher. I'd do that, you know. He can't treat people like shit and get away with it."

I know she's not just mad on my behalf—she's also still pissed about how bad George treated *her* last semester. She thought he liked her back— turns out he was two-timing her the whole semester.

Alex is studying the ground as we walk.

"Hey, Zack," she says suddenly. "Who's Bobby?"

I flinch a little. "Bobby? How do you know about Bobby?"

"Olivia said something, I think by accident, that somebody named

Bobby was coming to visit you or whatever." Alex isn't looking at me when she says this, and her smooth honey-colored face looks wounded. "Did you get a boyfriend?" She laughs ruefully and finally meets my eyes. "Without me?"

"Bobby isn't my boyfriend, not really." I cock my head and frown. "I mean, especially not anymore."

"Oh," Alex says. She rubs one of her calves against the other, leaning to one side thoughtfully. "Eh. I'm not dating anyone either."

"Yeah, Alex, I didn't think you were," I say. Who would Alex be dating without my knowing about it? Who would Alex be dating without the whole *world* knowing about it? "Hey, I thought we were going to my house. Are we going the right way?" We're obviously not. We're all the way up rue de Vaugirard, almost at the entrance of the Jardin du Luxembourg.

"Uh, about that," she says. "I'm actually really glad you called me. I kind of desperately need your help with something."

"What is it?" I say warily.

"I mean," she hurries to say. "As long as there's nothing else you want to talk about. Because, if there is . . . I'm here for you."

"No, I feel better now," I say. "What's going on?"

"I don't know if I told you this, but I got a *job* this semester . . . babysitting for this woman my mom knows." She punches an entry code and pushes open a dark green door. The hinges squeal as she shows me inside.

"What? *You* are babysitting?" I look down the bridge of my glasses at her. "I'll believe *that* when I see it. Ha! Alex Nguyen babysitting. Elvis lives!"

"Shhh," Alex scolds. "Don't talk about it so loud. I *do* babysit. Quite a bit, as a matter of fact. And the woman I babysit for left this morning, saying she'd be back this afternoon. Afternoon has passed, right? It's not afternoon anymore." There's an edge lining her voices I notice Alex is getting a little panicked. "I think she might not be coming back at all."

"What?" I'm still not beyond Alex Nguyen babysitting. "How do you know she's not just late or something?"

She rolls her eyes and tosses her dark glossy hair over her shoulders. All at once, I see a glimmer of the old Alex again—the one I was such good friends with. I realize with a pang how much I've missed her sarcasm as she turns to me before shoving open the apartment door and announces wryly, "You haven't met her kids yet."

19. ALEX

Unattended Crowd

I lead Zack back upstairs to Mme Sanxay's apartment. When I got his text, I decided to leave a thirteen-year-old neighbor girl with the kids—she was the only one on the entire floor who was even home!

As soon as we unlock the front door, the pubescent girl jumps off the couch and bolts for the hallway. She mumbles something bitter at us in French that I don't bother to comprehend. You can't understand her, regardless, because of the decibel level in this apartment. The pictures are practically falling off the walls with all the vibrations.

"Welcome to my after-school job!" I yell over the noise as I show Zack inside. "Weekend edition."

Charles, the baby, is wailing adamantly in his playpen. He smells like a toilet, and I know I need to change him. He hasn't had a nap today. For some reason, he just won't go down. He needs to sleep to feel better, but he seems not to understand that.

As for the two older kids, Albert and Emeline, they were throwing tantrums after I'd had to punish them for sneaking around Mme Sanxay's room when now she's more freaked out than ever that Emeline will ruin all her best stuff. In their mom's closet, they'd found their hidden Easter baskets from La Mère de Famille, a sweets shop in the Sixth. When I saw the packaging, I imagined Mme Sanxay going into the store, thinking she'd make peace with her children by treating them to extraordinary chocolates and lollipops and everything they could want on *Pâques* Sunday. *I bet she couldn't wait to surprise them with it,* I thought, sad for her in a way that made me feel uncomfortable and shifty. I cleaned up the mess as fast as I could, stuffing it back into the closet. *I'll deal with that later,* I thought. *Whatever happens I have to make sure I don't have to witness another scene like the one with the destroyed scarf.*

The older kids had been pissy enough as it was all day. Apparently, Emeline had been up all night demanding Mme Sanxay make M. Sanxay come back, and no one had slept at all. Now, with the sugar high and subsequent crash, they are positively monsters. I point them out to Zack with a wary eye. "Watch out for those two!" I yell. "They have sugar poisoning. And they're going through a divorce. Deadly combination, I'm telling you." I had called Mme Sanxay several times so far. Every time I hear her voice mail I'm filled with foreboding. *Where* could she be? By the time Zack called, I was so anxious to be rescued that I picked up on the first ring.

Zack can't help me find the mother of these children, but he does have a couple of sniveling brothers and sisters back in that godforsaken place in the South where he comes from. I banged on every door till I found that thirteen-year-old so I could go get him and lure him into my lair of screaming children to help. I promised I'd be back in fifteen minutes—it was more like forty-five—and sprinted down the street to the métro stop where Zack said he was getting off.

In the time since I left, Albert has stopped puking up chocolate, but Emeline has decided that Albert is disgusting for having done so in the first place. In response, Albert has pulled out a fistful of his sister's hair, and they are brawling heatedly in the living room, their baby brother watching them with those big, soulful eyes full of tears and discomfort.

"Where is your crazy mother?" I ask the baby. I pick him up, all stinky in his blue sleeper, and hold him away from me as I head for the nursery to change him.

"This is Charles," I say to Zack. "He's the only one of them that I like. Those two are absolutely wicked." They look it, their matching sets of blue eyes both ablaze.

"Hey, *hey!*" Zack bellows. "Y'all better shut up right now!"

Zack stands over the kids with his palm opened in the air like he's going to hit them into next Tuesday.

"Zack!" I jump in. I can see the impulse, but he has to resist. I put the baby back in the playpen. "You can't hit them. It's not allowed."

"I ain't gonna hit them, Alex. But that doesn't mean I can't show 'em who's boss with the threat of a little violence," Zack explains in a low voice.

"Is that what you'd do to your own brother and sister?" I ask.

"Hell, yes, I would," Zack says.

"Okay, then," I say, deferring to his expertise. I cross my arms over my T-shirt, feeling powerful with Zack by my side. "Carry on."

Albert and Emeline look up at Zack, wide-eyed and fearful. "Grab one," Zack tells me. "Take it in the other room."

"Which one?" I ask breathlessly, bending my knees in preparation.

"Either!" he yells. "Whichever one you get a hold of!"

Since Albert's been vomiting, I lunge for Emeline and escort her into her pink princess bedroom. Like a beast in a bar fight, I practically have to pin her down to keep her from jumping right back onto her brother. When I get her inside her room, I slam the door closed and block her from it. She tries mightily to peel me off and get by me, but I'm tougher than I look. Finally, she gives up and throws herself facedown on her sparkly polyester bedspread in hysterical tears.

I can't figure out what she's saying, and I know Emeline doesn't speak English, but her sobs sound like, "Let me at him! Let me at him!"

Is this what growing up with a sibling is like? How categorically horrible! Thank God, I'm an only child. This is like an HBO boxing match! Except with *more* blood and tears.

Panting, I listen to Zack wrangle Albert with similar effort.

They bang around in the bathroom for a while, until Albert finally submits.

"*Lave-toi bien,*" I hear Zack instruct Albert. "And cool off for a while!" Then I hear the pipes turn over and the shower curtain rustle. There's a knock on the door after a minute. Zack comes into Emeline's room, holding Charles.

"Wow, Zack," I say, impressed. "That was a side of you I've never seen!"

"Between Pierson and me we've got five rug rats to look after every Sunday while our parents are at Perkins after church," he says. "You give just one of them an inch, they'll all take ten miles. It's all about domination from the first moment. They'll run you if you let them."

I've never really thought of myself as being the boss of these children so much as their hired help. This is very interesting. "You're like the Kid Whisperer," I say, watching as Emeline slides off her bed and goes over to her dollhouse. Zack hands me Charles to change and sits down next to her. Without saying a word, Emeline hands Zack a blonde doll and an outfit to change her into. He dresses her skillfully. He's done this before, too.

"Kids respond to boundaries," Zack says in the careful way of a motivational speaker. "They behave better when there is a clear difference between right and wrong." He gives me a meaningful look.

"Oh," I answer. I pat Charles on the back, bouncing him the way he seems to like. I think I'm being scolded, and I know I deserve it. I smile sadly at Zack.

"So how've you been?" I ask him, watching him get another doll ready for Emeline's game. "I mean, not just tonight, but in general?"

"Oh, you know," Zack says. "It's a circus as usual in my neck of the woods." I want to ask him more about who Bobby is and what happened tonight. He turns around and smiles at me holding a baby in my arms. "You're pretty good with that baby."

"You'll be shocked to hear this," I say, "but that's not the first time someone has said that to me." He laughs.

I furrow my brow, still confused about something he said earlier. "Zack?"

"Yes, Alex?"

"What's Perkins?"

Zack rolls his eyes. "A place you never want to go, Alex. Let's just leave it at that."

★ ★ ★

After Albert is done with his bath, we send Emeline in for one. When she gets out, I search her scalp for bald spots, what with all the hair Albert ripped out. She looks fine. I am enormously relieved, since I don't want to get in trouble for hair loss on top of everything Mme Sanxay is going to come home to.

That is, if she ever comes home. I keep thinking that maybe she's been in an accident of some kind, but if that were true, the hospital or a witness would call her home phone number. They'd contact her soon-to-be ex-husband. So that's not what I'm worried about.

What I'm worried about—every time I remember Mme Sanxay clutching at the shreds of her Louis Vuitton scarf and staring venomously at her five-year-old daughter—is that she bailed. She can't bear to come home. And that now it's up to me to raise these children.

Their baths make them sleepy. Albert and Emeline fall asleep on the couch watching a French-dubbed *Little Mermaid* DVD. Charles is in his crib with a fresh diaper, watching a night-light mobile spin around. Everything is *finally* back to normal. Except for the children's missing mother, I keep thinking.

It's nearly ten o'clock! With every passing moment, I'm more and more sure she's abandoned her children. And as that becomes more and more obvious, anger wells up inside of me. How could she do that to them over a freaking scarf? Over a few tantrums?

I mean, you don't see me abandoning them, do you? And I am not even *related* to them.

"What am I supposed to do?" I ask Zack as we huddle at the table in the dining room. "What if something happened to her?"

"We could call the hospitals," Zack says. "Or call Mme Cuchon."

I remember how Mme Cuchon had praised me last week for my changed lifestyle and how I'm so responsible now. "I don't want to call her just yet. I don't want her to think I can't handle it. She hates me enough as it is."

"Do you want to wait a few more hours, and then if Mme Sanxay *still* isn't back, we can call her?" Zack asks.

"Yeah," I say.

"What about Her Royal Highness la C.A.B.?" Zack says. "When do you want to call *your* mom?"

"*Never,*" I say. "CAB is on a need to know basis in this situation—in all situations having to do with me in a jam."

"Did y'all make up after the Christmas thing?" He says this casually, as if he doesn't care, but his ears are perked in such a way that I know it's troubled him.

"Preliminarily," I say. Of anyone in France, Zack knows the absolute most about my fraught relationship with my mom. "Things are still really dicey. I don't want to push it."

"What shall we do then?"

"Well," I say. "I saw two thirds of a bottle of shiraz in the fridge. I could use a drink. You?"

"*Absolument,*" Zack agrees. At that moment, his phone rings. "It's Sara-Louise," he says. I go to the fridge and come back with two glasses of wine. Well, not glasses—Mme Sanxay doesn't seem to have any wine glasses. In fact, the only clean dishes are sippy cups in the back of the cupboard above the fridge.

I tap my plastic cup against Zack's.

"So what did Sara-Louise say?"

"She and Mary were worried about me. I kind of stormed out of Mary's apartment tonight without saying good-bye. Would it be cool if Sara-Louise and Mary come over here?" Zack asks. "Seeing them tonight, it made me wish I hung out with them more. Before George ruined it."

"They better come over!" I say. "If you haven't seen them in forever, then I haven't seen them in forever and a day. Let me go see if I can dig up another bottle of wine."

Zack and I carry Albert and Emeline to their rooms and shut off the singing mermaid on the TV. Looking around the Sanxays' apartment, I feel a little embarrassed that anyone would be coming over and seeing it in such a slovenly state. However, this isn't *my* house; if Mme Sanxay wants to raise her kids in a pigsty, who am I to say anything?

I swing the door open to welcome Sara-Louise and Mary. I rush in to hug them both at the same time and find myself welcoming not just them but Anouk, Kyle, Nathan, Sammy, Cory, and a French girl who I vaguely remember tried to make out with Zack fall semester.

"Je m'appelle Tallis," she says, greeting me with a cool outstretched hand. When she sees Zack, she blushes and slips her arm into Cory's elbow.

"We brought beer," Nathan says. "Where's the fridge?"

I look at Zack in alarm. Mme Sanxay might forgive me if she came home late to find that I'd called a couple friends to keep me company, but this many would make her hit the roof!

Zacks's face contorts—he wasn't expecting all these people when he asked me about Sara-Louise and Mary. Our eyes meet, knowing what it's like with these kids, they'll take over the whole apartment with drinking, smoking, and generally carousing until the wee hours.

I take a deep breath and remember that Mme Sanxay owes me *big* for tacking on extra hours of work with zero notice. I make a sweeping gesture as I lead my guests into the messy living room. "*Faites comme chez vous,*" I say grandly.

"My host parents threw us all out when Patty and Tina started trying to take shots of some forty-year-old Port wine they have in a special case in the living room," Mary tells us, making herself comfortable on the couch with a travel mug full of a pungent boozy concoction she brought along. "You got any ice? My drink's getting kind of warm."

"Mary, this is France," Zack says. "Do you think there's ice just hangin' around?"

"Zack, go check," I say. He ignores me. "Go on, Mary. What happened? I hope you gave them a tongue lashing for that one. I mean, I know they are from Texas, but there is no excuse for not appreciating a good vintage."

I would relish a story of Patty and Tina being bitched out in front of everyone, but Mary's too magnanimous for that, apparently. "Eh. It's no skin off my back, as long as everyone got booted before any real damage could be done."

I exchange a glance with Zack, which Mary catches. "Let's have a do-over for this night, okay?" she offers. "New party, better people, more fun. No drama!"

We all say cheers to that. "Who feels like dancing?" I ask as Zack turns on an old Madonna record from the eighties. It's just like the old days!

Zack and I, we can always dance together. Clubs would hire us to get the party started if they knew what they were doing. We're shimmying around, putting on a good show for our friends. At one point someone asks if a baby is crying, but when we check on the kids, they're fast asleep.

I should have thought of this earlier! I think. The Sanxays is a *perfect* place to party. It's centrally located and not nice enough to have to worry about damage control.

In the middle of doing the lawnmower with Zack, the back pocket of my jeans starts buzzing. The caller ID display lights up with the last person I was expecting to call me at midnight.

I run into Mme Sanxay's room, leaving Zack to teach his best moves to Sara-Louise and Mary. "Olivia?" I ask, breathless and sweaty.

"Alex?" she asks, her voice tinny. "Are you at home?"

"Uh, no," I say. "Had to babysit—long story. Why? Where are you?"

"Oh, I'm at the Ternes métro stop. I was just—"

"Come over! I'm having a party at the Sanxays! It's on the rue de Fleurus."

"Oh." Olivia is quiet for a second, and then I hear her whisper to somebody.

"No," comes a forceful voice in the background. "We can't go there."

"Is that PJ?" I ask. I whirl around and check to make sure I closed the door behind me. "What's going on?"

Olivia starts to breathe fast, then melts into cries over the phone. "I don't know what to do, Alex. PJ said you would help us. She said you owe her. We don't have anywhere to go . . ."

I don't know if it is the wine I have been drinking or the return of my social confidence and prowess, but suddenly I feel invigorated, like I can solve any problem fate throws my way. Eventually, I'll find the right solution to this Mme Sanxay mess. For now, I'll have a party and help Olivia.

"You two will come here. Text me from the courtyard downstairs. And *don't* worry. I have everything under control."

I rejoin my party, pouring drinks, air-kissing my guests, feeling genuinely happy. But I don't forget about Olivia. When she texts, I fly down the stairs as if I have a superhero cape attached to my collar.

"What do you mean, I owe you?" I ask PJ right away.

"Freddie," she says simply. She pushes her blonde hair back to show me a deep gash in her forehead. "They wanted me to dance tonight. In one of his 'clubs.' That's where I was staying, Alex." She lets her hair drop and casts her eyes down to the pavement.

"Oh, God," I stutter. "Why didn't you tell me?"

She shakes her head, and I notice what looks like some crusty blood on her forehead. What the *hell* happened tonight? "I don't know. I thought that was my last option."

Olivia looks at me, her chin wobbling like she is going to cry again. "What are you guys talking about?"

I don't answer her. Instead, I say to PJ, "You should have told me. I promised I would help you. Why didn't you believe me? Do my promises mean nothing to people?" Even to my own ears, the words sound hollow and false. Especially considering the weight of what I heard in Mme Cuchon's office—which I still have not told anyone.

PJ shrugs. I can't tell if she is angry or just defeated. "You can help us now."

I clear my throat. "I will," I say, feeling resolute. "I definitely will. You just have to follow me upstairs and try not to get seen by anyone."

They nod. I text Zack before we go inside.

TAKE THE PARTY INTO THE KITCHEN, I tell him. PLAY A DRINKING GAME

UNTIL I COME IN. OKAY?

Zack's text back is quick. GOT IT. WHAT'S UP? SCHEMIN'?

WILL EXPLN L8R.

With the living room now clear, I whisk Olivia and PJ into the back of the apartment. PJ I put in the room with the baby. There is a cot near his crib for nights when he's sick or crying, but no one ever uses it. "He's a good sleeper," I choke out. I'm suddenly emotional, guilty. "You can sleep in here and no one will bother you. If he wakes up, he can't really talk yet, so he won't be able to tell on you or anything."

I put Olivia in Mme Sanxay's big king-size poster bed.

"You'll tell me?" I ask her as she falls asleep. "In the morning?" But she doesn't answer.

I go back into Charles's room to check on PJ. She's sitting on the edge of the cot, listening to Charles breathe in the glow of his nightlight. Her lips are shining blue, parted slightly.

"What happened to you guys tonight?" I ask.

PJ laughs ruefully. "I don't know where to begin."

"From the beginning," I say.

"Well, that would be the first day of the Programme Americain. The day the Marquets never showed to take me to my homestay."

"Ach, you'd have been better off if they'd never showed at all," I say, tossing my hand in the air.

PJ is silent for a long moment. I'm not sure why I thought she was about to tell me what had happened tonight. "Why do you say that, Alex?" she finally asks me.

I laugh. "Oh, I don't know."

"No, really," PJ's voice is very serious, even cold. "Why did you say that? What do you know about the Marquets?"

I realize then that PJ must not have told anyone about how shady the Marquets really are. After all, I only know from the small bits and pieces I've put together. It makes sense. She ran away without telling anyone why. Olivia and I would have never even suspected M. Marquet of being a creep if it hadn't been for the story her host mother told her. And that was in the past, between adults at a party, not between host father and international guest. What sealed my belief that M. Marquet was the real reason PJ ran away was what I heard in Mme Cuchon's office . . . nothing more.

"Oh, they just always seemed weird. Going out of town all the time, you know. No children. Stuff like that."

"Alex, is there something you aren't telling me?" Her eyes are narrowed and, to tell the truth, I'm horrified.

"She knew," I blurt. "Madame Cuchon knew Monsieur Marquet was a lech, and she gave you to him anyway. I found it all out when I overheard her talking on the phone to someone. The Marquets donate lots of money to the school, they want to be involved because it makes them look more international to voters. That's important in the Dordogne, you know?"

"Alex, you knew this?" PJ raises her eyes at me, disgusted. "Why didn't you tell me?"

"I only just found out," I beg her off. "And besides, you are away from them now. What does it matter now?"

PJ shudders. "They could still find me. They could still get me and make me live with them . . . or worse. You should have told me. Is there anything else you haven't told me?"

I shake my head, pushing Denny Marquet out of my thoughts as swiftly as I'd just pushed PJ past the living room and into Charles's room. It still doesn't make any sense. If he were using me to get to her, why haven't I heard from him since that night? And why hasn't he ever said anything about PJ to me? Is it possible that he doesn't even know that PJ and I know each other?

"Good," she says wearily. "Can I sleep now?"

"Yes, of course," I say. Just then, Zack bursts into the room. "PJ!" he gasps. "What are you doing here?"

"Get out, Zack!" I say. "I'll be right there."

"Hurry up, lady. There's someone at the door," he tells us. He wiggles his fingers good night at PJ and gives her a frown. "Makeup sesh with Jay didn't go too good?" he asks, hiding his envy well. Or maybe he's less envious now that he knows that I liked Jay, too.

PJ cracks a small, pathetic smile. "I'll tell you later." She won't look at me. And she doesn't even know about Denny Marquet.

We leave the room and head straight for the front door. "It's probably just Tallis's friends," I say to Zack. "Just keep them all out of the bedrooms. Livvy's in the master, too, so don't smother her when you go to sleep tonight."

"Wha? . . ." Zack asks, but before I can explain, we've opened the door, and who's standing in front of us but an incredibly sloshed George, a bottle of Jägermeister in his hand.

"Forgive me?" he asks Zack drunkenly.

Before Zack can answer, a stream of kids behind him pushes him forward, into the apartment and closer to his friends.

"I think we're about to have a rager on our hands," Zack says when he finally manages to get the door closed behind the crowd.

20. OLIVIA

Nowhere to Go

---

got an e-mail from my mom the other day. She wanted to make sure I was collecting copies of the programs and of any press clippings that the Underground Ballet Theatre was generating this spring. She said I'll need them when I'm putting together my UCLA application.

For some reason, her e-mail made me want to go home and take my folder of Underground keepsakes and rip them to shreds, just to spite her. I'm not sure why. I felt horrible having such a negative reaction to my mom's interest in my life. But I hated getting that e-mail, just the same.

My mom still doesn't know about Drew and that night. She doesn't know because I haven't told her, even though I promised Mme Cuchon that I would.

It makes me feel so far away from my family, this burden of having something I don't want to tell them. Sure, there have been times when I didn't want to go to a dance competition in another city or I wished I could blow off studying for a test, and I didn't complain to my mom about it. But this is different. If she knew *this* secret, she'd probably break down. She'd get on a plane. She'd try to press charges. She's so scared for Brian and me in the world. This would confirm it, for always.

Another e-mail from my mom, this one about a week ago, urged me to write to Vince, because his parents are such close friends of her's. I didn't do it. Instead, I logged onto Facebook and looked at his photo albums. He still hasn't taken any of the photos of me down from when we were going out.

I looked at them for a while, feeling nothing but anger that he still felt he had some kind of ownership over me. There was one of us at a Cinco de Mayo parade, and I'm up on his shoulders, riding around like a little kid. There's plenty from the beach, with me in a bikini and a dark tan with my arms around his waist. I untagged myself in all the photos and then deleted Vince from my list of friends.

Then I went through and found Drew's page in my friends list. His profile picture was one of him and George making a lewd pose with one of those street artists that paints themselves gold and stands perfectly still around the Trocadero steps for hours at a time. George and Drew had someone—Kyle, most likely—take a whole series of photos of them trying to make the statuesque woman flinch. I deleted him, too. Then I deleted George.

Mme Cuchon told me that Drew is at a corrective school in Maine. If he tries to contact me, I am not supposed to answer, even if it seems like his intentions are good. I can't imagine getting a letter from Drew, telling me he's sorry. The thought makes me laugh—it's one of the only things that makes me laugh lately. Like a psycho, I can laugh about that for hours.

Alex comes back into Mme Sanxay's room to check on me after a while. I've never seen her act so maternal, fussing over me and making sure I am comfortable.

"Those kids have really changed you, Alex," I say. "But seriously, you can go back to the party."

"Alex!" Zack yells from the foyer. "About half the Lycée is in the courtyard of this apartment building!"

"Ugh!" Alex shouts back. "Well, make sure they have booze!"

"Alex," I sniffle. "Isn't this your boss's house? Are you sure you should be having a party right now?"

She shrugs distractedly and grabs a beautiful Aran throw blanket from the footboard and tosses it around me. "I'm so glad to see you. And I have changed. Just wait. I'm going to fix whatever happened to you guys tonight, make up for not being totally there for you both before." She looks determined. Alex loves a challenge.

"Oh, I am not sure you're going to be able to fix this one," I say.

"Just tell me what happened," she says.

"Alex, get out here!" Zack calls down the hall. "Where are all the glasses?"

"Hang on!" she yells back. "Tell me, Livvy."

"I'm kind of in trouble."

Alex looks stricken. "Are you pregnant?" she whispers. "What are you gonna do?"

"No, I'm not pregnant!" I laugh. "It's—Mme Rouille got really mad at me—"

I can hear Nathan shouting over the noise of the stereo. "This game is called Landmines," he tells a group of French guys. I bet he's taking out a euro coin and showing them how to flick it so that it will spin across the table. Already drunk from another party, the guys won't be able to get it to spin, and they'll all have to drink more and get even more wasted. The living room erupts in cheers and whistles.

"I think some Frogs are going *down* tonight!" I can hear Sara-Louise holler. "We're gonna drink them under the table!"

Zack pops his head into the room. "There's a baby crying in the next room, Alex!" he says. I can tell he's drunk because one side of his shirt collar is popped and the other isn't. Sober Zack would never let this happen. "Do your magic!" He jogs back out to the party.

Alex jumps up. "The baby! I have to get him. I'll be right back." She closes the door behind her.

I lean back on the bed, kicking my Ugg boots off and staring at the dimmed light fixture above Mme Sanxay's luxurious bed. Rolling over, away from the door, I wonder where Alex's boss is. Part of me feels perturbed and angry, the same anxious feeling I've been carrying around all week. And another part of me feels somehow lulled and comforted, as if I am safe in a cocoon of friends who know how best to take care of me.

I close my eyes and wonder if Thomas has fallen asleep yet. Did he think about me as he drifted off? Is he glad that his mom interrupted us before it could go any farther?

I curl my knees up to my chest and take a deep breath. I want to text him, but I won't. I won't depend on him anymore. I can survive this on my own. I don't need him.

A few hours later, a very giggly Alex and Zack are in their underwear, pulling the blankets back on either side of me.

"Scoot over!" Zack says hoarsely.

"We're comin' in!" Alex adds.

"Wait . . ." I sit up, looking around drowsily. The lights are still on, but all the noise from the party has died. "Where did everyone go? PJ . . ."

"They left," Zack says, switching the light off nearest to his side of the bed. "Thank the good Lord! Go back to sleep."

"What time is it?" I ask. I hear a birdsong coming from the window that's ajar.

"It's nearly six," Alex says. "Happy Easter."

"Where's PJ?" I ask. "Is she okay?"

"She's in the baby's room," Alex mumbles.

I pad down the hall and into the room with the lamb painted on the door. It's warm inside, and a baby sleeps peacefully wrapped up in a yellow and white blanket. Curled up on the cot is PJ, shivering despite the warmth.

I find a blanket in the closet and drape it over her thin, long body. Her eyelids flutter and she twitches, like she's having a bad dream, but she doesn't wake up. There's still dried blood on her face. I take a baby wipe from the changing table and rub it, very gently, clean again.

"What are we going to do, Penelope Jane?" I whisper miserably. As if in response, PJ sighs heavily in her sleep.

I go back to Mme Sanxay's bed between Alex and Zack. Mercifully, I fall into a blank, dreamless sleep.

21. ALEX

It Takes a Village

"*J*oyeueses *Pâques!*" a high-pitched little voice says right into my ear about three hours after I've fallen asleep Sunday morning. "*Bonjour, Alex! Joyeueses Pâques!*"

I sit up and push my hair out of my face. "Emeline!" I say. "Where is your mother? Is she home? *Ta mère est ici?*"

Emeline shakes her head. "*Non, Alex. Où sont les chocolats? De la cloche? Alex! Où sont-ils?*"

"Chocolate?" I ask. "You want chocolate? You've had way too much chocolate. *Où sont tes frères?*"

Emeline doesn't answer. Olivia is asleep next to me, but Zack has gotten out of bed and tucked his side of the covers perfectly back into the mattress. I grab Olivia's long sweater and follow the little girl to the dining room.

The hardwood floors are cold on my bare feet. We left the windows open to air the place out after the party. It's freezing.

"Well, well, well," I yawn at the sight of PJ and Zack feeding Charles some pureed peaches out of a jar. Albert is eating cereal at the table with them. "Don't you make a happy family."

"Hey, Alex," Zack says. "Mme Sanxay called."

"Thank God! What did she say?"

"She's, uh, out of town." Zack pauses, then looks at Albert and clears his throat.

"What!"

Rage courses through me. One does *not* simply leave town and strap the babysitter with the kids without any warning.

"Yeah, she said she's with her sister," he says. "Call her. She says her *mobile* is on now. She had it shut off yesterday. Something about needing 'me' time." Zack rolls his eyes, then continues to feed peaches to Charles.

I grab the landline phone from its carriage and call Mme Sanxay's cell phone from Emeline's princess room. I've memorized the number after calling it so many times yesterday.

This time, she actually answers.

"Where are you?" I ask, forgetting that I just hosted an enormous party at her house and letting my anger take over. My hand trembles violently, trying to keep the phone to my ear. "You can't just leave me with your children for twenty-four hours without asking! Without even calling me to tell me there is an emergency."

Mme Sanxay clears her throat. "I wasn't in good shape yesterday, Alex. I'm sure you've noticed things haven't been very pleasant at home—"

"That sucks," I interrupt, switching the receiver to my other ear. That one is burning up. My whole face and neck feel so hot that I could be in Saint-Tropez on Bastille Day. "But your children are *here*. They are *your children*. You are not only biologically bound to them but legally, too. Come back here! Now!"

"You don't understand," Mme Sanxay tells me. "You don't understand. You are but a child yourself. Besides, you owe me the hours."

"No! No!" I shriek. I could take Emeline's dolls and knock them right off their shelves, I'm so furious. "Don't you tell me I don't understand! What's to understand? Your marriage was a wreck, now you're taking it out on your children. You're trying to abandon them and *that is not okay!*" I'm bellowing now. Zack pops into the doorway, his face a mixture of fear and curiosity behind his black glasses. He shuts the door so the kids won't be able to hear me yell at their horrible mother. "You are coming back to these children if I have to come get you myself!" I hiss at her through the phone. "Do you even know how screwed up these kids will be if they ever find out that you have so little regard for them as to leave them on Easter with their nanny? What if something had happened? What if no one could have found you?"

"Alex, I already told you," she cuts in. "I needed some time away."

"No!" I don't let her finish. I've heard this kind of appeal before, from my dad, even from my mom. "You don't just abandon your children when they need you. You just don't do it."

"Once I have some time to restore myself, I'll come back to Paris, but until then, I've got to do some work on my delicate psyche . . . things have been so awful. . . ."

"Awful? Do you know what's awful?" I demand. "Awful is when

your children have to pay for their father's mistakes. Don't punish them because he left you!"

"Ach, Alex," Mme Sanxay says. I can hear her frustrated sigh. "Since Christmas I have just been trying to get you to do the job you agreed to. Please just do it without any complaints. I have to go now." I hear her put her cell phone down, trying to muffle the noise. "*Na klar,*" she calls to someone. "*Mauvais moment—los geht, nicht wahr?*"

"Who is that?" I shout. "Who are you talking to?"

"*Au revoir,* Alex," Mme Sanxay says. "I'll see you when I am ready to come back to Paris. Kisses for my children."

I stare at myself in the mirror above Emeline's dresser. Oh, that did not just happen. She did not just fit that conversation in with me between plans that she has with other people who are not her children. Fuming, I pound Emeline's little bed with my fist. Who was she talking to? Now, my French might not be as great as PJ's, or Zack's, or even Olivia's, but whatever it was that she said was as unfamiliar to me as . . . wait a second. I've heard her talk that way before. To her sister!

I know now where Mme Sanxay is—that German spa town with the funny name. I rush into her room to find my jeans and my T-shirt. As I put them back on, I wrinkle my nose in distaste. I can't believe *this* is what I wore to the only party I've hosted this year. At least the T-shirt was a vintage Van Halen concert tee. With my hair messy and all the lipgloss I put on last night, maybe I looked like I'd been wearing that outfit on purpose. Maybe.

Sweeping my hair into a high ponytail, I walk back out to the dining room.

"*Mes amies,*" I say grandly. "I have a plan."

PJ, Zack, Olivia, Charles, Albert, and Emeline all look up at me in unison.

"Well?" Zack asks. "What is it?"

I give a slight shake of my head and look at the children meaningfully. "Best not to outline the details here. I'm just going to pop out for a bit, and when I'm back, I trust that our dear matriarch will be well on her way." I giggle. "My plan is just *wunderbar*, though, let me tell you. *Ciao*, babies."

Once back out on the rue de Fleurus, I pant for a minute, clutching my BlackBerry. I look around to make sure none of those brats or my fellow babysitters followed me. I'm alone here on this empty Easter morning, but I have to act fast.

It'll just be this one time, I promise myself. I'll get Denny to help me and then be done with him. For good, before anyone knows how close I was to actually kind of falling for him. Tossing back my ponytail with a flick of my head, I dial the numbers I have for Denny.

It goes straight to voice mail.

"Feel like rescuing an American damsel?" I say flirtatiously, knowing he'll eat it up. "I need someone who can *sprechen Deutsch* to play a little trick on a friend of mine. It's important. Call me back. Oh, and . . . I'm sorry for running out the other night. I'll explain when you call."

I'm so caught up in the sheer brilliance of the joke I am about to play on Mme Sanxay that I almost run headfirst into a flower delivery truck barreling down the rue de Fleurus toward the Jardin des Tuileries.

Maybe, just maybe, I plot—about to head home and wash those children's funk right off of me while I have the chance—I can get Mme Sanxay back to Paris and figure out a way to keep the Marquets away from PJ, once and for all.

22. PJ

It All Ends Now

Mme Sanxay's apartment in the Sixth is a shining example of Left Bank living. Nestled in a quiet corner of an austere building, it's what the French call a *six-pieces*—four bedrooms, a decent living room, and even what city dwellers rarely seem to have unless they've inherited a small fortune—a dining room.

Some Parisian women, such as Mme Rouille, might try to shove too many antiques and curiosities into too few rooms. Others, such as the Marquets, turn their homes into museums scattered with things no one really needs to decorate with: old portraits in heavy frames and *objets d'arts* that are expensive but ugly.

But Mme Sanxay's apartment isn't like that. Everything is dirty and stained. There are stacks of bills, magazines, mail, Emeline's coloring books everywhere. The furniture is modern and uncomfortable, and besides, it's covered with toys and books and random bottles of nail polish or talcum powder. Stray diapers dot the floor and the tabletops. The carpets and rugs are loaded with dust bunnies and small bits of cereal and baguette.

It's achingly cold in here this morning, too. Someone left the kitchen and living room windows open at the party last night, and the cold air has penetrated the furniture and even my wool coat, buttoned up to my chin. I look down and see blood on the lapel.

The kitchen sink houses a stack of dishes balancing precariously on one another like a house of cards. Zack has put me in charge of the baby. Charles is hitched up on my hip, his face nestled into my coat. Gingerly, I try to find a glass that I could wash to get some water. I feel like I can't think until I get rid of this awful thirst. I reach my hand into the sink, and my hand grazes a broken glass near the bottom of the soupy pool of dishwater. When it cuts me, it stings first from the slice into my skin, and then from the dish water seeping under the wound.

"Ouch," I curse, popping the bleeding finger into my mouth and tasting first soap and grease, then that metallic blood flavor that reminds me of having mosquito bites summers in Vermont.

"Now, be very good children and take every diaper and put it into this bag," I hear Zack instructing the older Sanxay children in the living room. "And stack all the magazines and papers just like this. And be sure and put all your toys in your room. I'm going to work on the kitchen."

Zack's voice is forced and overly chipper, ringing out with upbeat false certainty that everything is going to be okay. As if the crisis is temporary. As if we can just clean up after the wild party, after what looks like weeks of household neglect, and all of us will be fine.

"I'm not sure if I can go back to Southern California," Olivia says, staring out at another rainy spring morning. It's as if we've been having a conversation this whole time, but we've been silent. "It's just all sunshine, all the time. Sometimes life isn't sunny. Sometimes it sucks."

"Can you hold Charles?" I say in response. "I have to go find a Band-Aid." In the bathroom I clean the cut and wash the blood down the sink's drain in small pink waves.

"That's probably Sara-Louise!" Zack calls a while later when the door buzzer sounds. He's still using that voice, that cheerleader-style determination. "That hot mess was so wasted last night that she left her purse and her keys here."

I don't answer him from the bathroom, nor does Olivia from the kitchen. I hold my breath, wondering if Lycée kids will take over the apartment for the rest of the afternoon, and I'll have to stay in here, waiting until they leave to come out.

"Well, would you get a load of these?" Zack hollers in the foyer. Albert and Emeline are squealing, and I hear Olivia bring Charles out to see what it is.

I come out of the bathroom to see Zack holding two dozen creamy pink roses that smell so delicious that I feel almost woozy standing so close to them. My heart leaps. Somewhere out there, Jay's decided to give me another chance. He's sending me a message that he'll help me, no matter what.

"And *damn*, ladies, would you look at that?" Zack says. "These are for Alex!"

"Alex?" Olivia asks him in disbelief. She looks severely disappointed. Maybe she thought they were from Thomas, apologizing for not standing up to his mom for her last night. "Does Alex have a boyfriend we don't know about?"

"Roses this beautiful have got to be from C.A.B.," Zack says. "I mean, come on. Who else could afford Easter Sunday delivery?" He pulls the card out of the envelope and reads it. Shaking his head in a quick flinch of recognition, Zack immediately stuffs the card back in the envelope. "Whoops. They're not from C.A.B. They're from some guy." He sucks in his cheeks and raises his eyebrows for the benefit of the kids. Emeline and Albert snicker with delight. "*Alex a un petit ami qui s'appelle Dennis, apparemment!* Why didn't you guys tell me?" He puts his hands on his hips. "Even if we weren't speaking. These are things I need to know!" Zack leans down so Emeline can smell the pink roses. She's entranced.

"Dennis?" I watch, as if from across the room, and take the card from Zack's hand and try to open it. It takes a painstakingly long time, since my hands don't seem to work right. The bandaged finger is awkward, but mostly I can't seem to make my fingers bend, make the information come to light. "Are you sure it said Dennis?"

"PJ," Zack laughs quietly. "You nosy thing!"

Finally, the card is released from the envelope.

Happy Easter to a beautiful girl.

My dearest Alex,

My deepest regret is that I did not get to take you to the Dordogne this weekend. Have a wonderful holiday! (You weren't home when I came by with these. It took quite a bit of reconnaissance to discover this address, but as I said, I have a way of finding people.)

Love,

Dennis Marquet

01 55 55 22 22

"These aren't for Alex," I say in shock. "These are for me."

"Uh, PJ, doll," Zack says. His nostrils are flared skeptically. "I think that when a card says Alex on it, it means it's meant for a girl named Alex. I know you and she have had a bit of a rivalry, sweets, but let's let her win this round, don't you think?" He tries to take the card from me, obviously thinking I'm insane.

"To Alex," I say.

"Yes, PJ," Zack says as if I were Emeline. "To *Alex*."

"Read this," I say, thrusting it in front of his face. "Do you see that?"

Zack blinks twice and reads the card. "Yup, to Alex."

"No, Zack, that's not what I mean. Look at the signature!"

Zack looks back down at the card and reads the bottom, where Dennis Marquet's name is carefully scripted.

"Alex is dating someone named Dennis Marquet?" Zack asks.

"What?" Olivia asks, straining forward so she can see it. "What are you saying?"

"Look, Livvy," Zack says, pointing to the name. "The flowers are from someone with the same last name as PJ's host parents."

Olivia gives me a perplexed look. "Do you know him, PJ? This Dennis Marquet person?"

I lean against the doorframe, nodding but not able to explain more. Finally, I choke out, "Those flowers are for me. They're a message." Each rose petal feels like a finger pointing at me, telling the world who and where I am. "How did he know I was here?" My mind is swirling, and I'm dizzy with the simultaneous realization that he's not dead—and he knows where I am.

"Alex isn't dating anyone," Olivia says. "I don't think. I mean, I haven't really talked to her lately about that kind of stuff . . . but she wouldn't keep it a secret. Boys are usually all she can talk about. Why would she not tell us about a new guy?"

"She kept it a secret because Dennis is the Marquets' nephew. He works for them . . . he does whatever they tell him to."

"PJ," Zack says. "What does Dennis Marquet have against you?"

"He wants . . ." I remember him lying on the floor of the apartment in Rouen. Suddenly, I feel a strange pang of relief, like right when you wake up from a bad dream. *He's not dead.* Not if he's here, sending flowers to Alex. I haven't killed anyone. "He's very loyal to his uncle, and his uncle's reputation."

"Then Alex must not understand who he is," Olivia says. "I mean, she's the one who found out for sure that the Lycée knows Monsieur Marquet is a creep. She wouldn't want anything to do with that family!"

"With Alex, all things are possible," I tell her. "Don't you guys get it?"

All my relief at the fact that Dennis is alive is washed away by a scarier realization: He still wants to make me pay for what I did. And now the Marquets have even more that they can use against me . . . attempted homicide. Assisted flight of a known drug dealer—Annabel.

Things are finally coming together. Last night, why Alex stowed me away, why she didn't have any excuse for not telling me that Mme Cuchon knew about the Marquets and didn't do anything to stop them.

Dennis has Alex on his side. Who knows why she wanted in. Maybe she still hasn't let go of her old dislike for me. She could have told him any number of other things that would get me found out by the police and sent home immediately. Sent right to jail with my sister. It has all been a trap, and I've walked right into it!

At that moment, I miss Jay so much I want to crumble to the ground and just give in to this nightmare.

"Seriously, PJ, you can't be right. Alex is not as bad as you think," Zack protests. "She wouldn't betray you."

"Why wouldn't she?" I ask them, waving the card around the apartment we are in, stuck watching three kids we don't even know. "Hasn't she done it before?"

"PJ, no," Olivia says.

"She has! She's betrayed everyone in this room, and then some. Even these kids!"

Charles must sense the tension in the apartment. He starts to cry, his eyes squeezed together. Olivia bounces him a bit, obviously unsure of what to do. I grab the baby from her arms and pull him close to me.

"You're not doing it right!" I scream at her, surprising even myself with how angry I am. "You can't just expect a baby to take care of itself!" I rock Charles in my arms. He's still crying. "You can't just silence him and hope he will go away!"

Zack steps forward and grips my elbows in his hands. "PJ! Stop this! Just relax."

"You don't understand!" I yell, not giving up Charles. "None of you understand! I didn't have a choice! He was following us, and I had to make him go away!"

Zack and Olivia's eyes are enormous, darting from my face to the crying baby in my arms. "PJ, what are you talking about?" Zack asks me.

I pull Charles off my chest and hand him back to Olivia. "Never mind. I have to go. I have to get out of here."

I run all the way to the Pont d'Austerlitz, desperate to get as far out of

Paris as I can. The air burns my lungs as I run, but it feels good—better than standing still. All the way down there in the Thirteenth, I find myself entranced by the trains going over the bridge to the other side of Paris. What if I climbed up there, walked along the tracks? Jumped into the Seine the minute I couldn't take the train whistles anymore? Just like everyone thinks I did in Rouen.

What would it be like, as I fell? Would I be scared, or would it be a relief to finally, finally know that this Parisian nightmare was at last coming to an end?

I buy a ticket to go up into the métro, racing up the stairs as a train comes into the station. As it pulls away, I look down the track and over the bridge to the Right Bank. I could just jump onto the tracks, right here, and play chicken with the Paris Métro. And then tomorrow, all the papers would pronounce me FOUND. But this time I'd be dead for real.

My thoughts are urgent and ridiculous, full of outlandish flights of fancy that for the first time I think I might do for real. Why shouldn't I just end it? What else is there out here for me?

"PJ!" The voice isn't loud, but it's insistent. Across the tracks, only ten feet away from me, is Jay, standing on the platform. "What are you doing here? Zack just called me—I've come to look for you."

I open my mouth, but it seems crazy to say what I was doing here, what I was thinking. Suddenly, all I can think is how much I want to touch him and how I have to get to him as soon as possible. His broad shoulders, the dark cropped hair, the penetrating black eyes . . . every bit of him is where I want to be.

"Just stay there," I say hoarsely. "I'll be right over."

He can't wait either, though. We meet on the lower level, under the tracks, at exactly the same time. When he kisses me, it's the first time I've ever felt like I might die when it's over. That's how much I need him to love me and take care of me.

"Zack said you went crazy. . . ." Jay whispers, smoothing my hair. A train must have just let out going in either direction. People push around us, as though we're an island in the middle of the ocean. We don't move. Locking his arms around my waist, Jay looks me straight in the eye. "What happened?"

In a torrent, it all comes out. "Monsieur Marquet . . . he tried to . . . and his wife . . . they hate me . . . and Dennis Marquet is going out with Alex, and Alex is in on it. . . ."

"Monsieur Marquet tried to what?" Jay's dark eyes are liquid. He doesn't move, not even a small motion, until his suspicion is confirmed.

"You know," I hiccup, starting to cry.

"Oh, God, PJ, no. And Alex knows about this?" Jay takes my hand in his and hustles me back up the stairs to the métro.

"No . . . well, yes," I say, feeling the whoosh of another train approaching. Jay hustles us onto it and steadies me against him and the door. "I just don't understand what I ever did to make Alex hate me so much. . . ."

"We'll deal with Alex later," Jay says and stares intently out the window of the train at the passing neon lights of Paris.

"What do you mean?" I'm terrified, not sure of where we're going.

"I've had enough of this, PJ," Jay says. "This ends tonight. You've been tortured by something, someone in Paris for too long. Now that I know who it is, I'm not letting him get away with it anymore."

"No, Jay," I beg quietly. "I just wanted to be a good daughter. It wasn't even them that was so bad, not really. . . ."

"It's not fair, PJ," Jay snaps. "They did this to you!" He brushes tears off my cheeks. "They did *this* to you!"

Jay won't listen to me as the métro roars through Paris all the way up to Ternes, my old métro stop. We blast through the station, bright and white and sterile under the florescent lights. When we surge onto the street, I know I can't stop him. He thinks he can reason with M. Marquet. "We'll tell him he's got to get out of town," Jay says. "That he has to leave you alone or you'll sue. You'll tell everyone, and he'll lose his office. It'll work. Then you can stop hiding, and we can finally just be together the way we were always supposed to be."

On the Place des Ternes, I feel asphyxiated by the familiar and haunting sights and smells of my old neighborhood. It was here that I spent hours alone, waiting for Sonia, the maid, to come by and exchange a few words with me. I wanted company, comfort, so badly. The Marquets wouldn't give it. There was only malice in what they had to offer.

As soon as we get to the Marquets' apartment, my stomach flipping with dread, Jay pounds on the door loud enough to send ghosts down from the rafters. A moment later, the latch gives way on the heavy oak doors, and M. Marquet is in the doorway.

The flirtatious, gallant man I remember is not here. This man is drunk, cradling a bottle of Bourbon in his arm. He swigs from it wildly, spilling some onto the Oriental rug beneath his shoeless feet. "You!" he shrieks when he sees me. "You were never dead!"

"Don't talk to her!" Jay yells at him, all attempts at reason thrown immediately aside. "Don't say another word to her!"

In a heavy, hard motion, Jay lunges forward and tackles the older man, easily pulling him to the ground. I hear a crack as Jay hits him in the face, and I smell the stench of Bourbon as the bottle tips over and spills all over the floor around them.

"No, Jay!" I cry, stepping forward onto the soft rug to reach my hands out to stop him. I pull at his jacket, not able to get a hold on him and pull him off M. Marquet. "Please, Jay, not like this."

"Say you won't threaten my girlfriend," Jay says, leaning over the middle-aged man menacingly. "Say you'll get out of town and leave her alone. Forever."

"Or you'll do what?" M. Marquet laughs sloppily in Jay's face. "You'll kill me? You wouldn't."

"I will," Jay whispers. "Don't underestimate what I am capable of doing to scum like you."

I'm pulling and pulling at him with all my might when suddenly something gives way, and Jay isn't straddling M. Marquet anymore.

Similarly, I'm being pulled across the room, away from the two of them, screaming and crying.

"Hey, PJ, it's okay." The voice is soft, familiar.

Blurrily, I realize that it's Alex, and she's holding me back from Jay.

Jay's been pinned by someone on the other side of the room.

"No!" I shout. "Alex, please don't help them! Please!"

It's Dennis Marquet. Back from the dead. He has Jay against a wall. Jay's struggling hard, but Dennis is more sturdily built than he is—he'll never be able to get out from behind him.

"The *flics* are on their way," Dennis says, regarding me calmly, holding Jay back.

I listen. I do hear the sirens getting louder. They must be right outside.

All the fight goes out of my body. I hang limp in Alex's arms, almost relieved. It's over. It's finally over. Soon I'll be arrested and put on a plane heading for jail with Annabel and my parents.

"Fine, Alex," I say. "You win."

In a daze, I watch the cops come into the apartment, lift M. Marquet's sloppy, exhausted body off the floor and prop him up to attention so that they can cuff him. I assume there's been a mistake, and I am waiting for them to cuff me, too. They leave, pushing M. Marquet in front of them. One cop nods slightly at me, and then they exit the apartment.

I look from Alex to Jay and Dennis huddled in the corner, completely stunned.

"Alex?" I say. "What's happening?"

Alex comes over and puts her arms around me.

"Denny told the cops some stuff that will keep you safe, PJ," she says. "I know you must think he's a bad guy, but he didn't know how gross and screwed up his uncle was. I told him when I came over today that he has to protect you, or I'll blow the lid on the whole thing with the Lycee. Denny?"

Dennis walks toward me, his sandy-colored head bowed. "Penelope," he says, his voice cracking. "There's so much I need to explain."

Jay folds his arms across his chest, staring hard at Dennis. "Start explaining, then."

"I thought you were dead," I whisper. "I thought I killed you."

"No," he says. "Just gave me a bit of a headache, that's all."

"You followed me. You made us miserable!" I say. "Tell me why!"

"My uncle told me you were using him," he says. "He told me that you were blackmailing him with a scandal. He told me you came on to him, and when he refused you, you got mad and told him you'd get even. So then he sent me to find you, to appease you, to give you and your sister whatever you wanted."

Jay shakes his head, looking like he might be sick.

"Why didn't you tell me that's why you were following us?"

"I was trying to blackmail a blackmailer," he says with a sheepish grin. "I couldn't give everything away until I knew I had you where I wanted you."

Alex rolls her eyes. "You screwed up."

"I know. I'm sorry," Dennis says. "I want to fix it. Everything. My uncle's going to jail, and they're going to dig stuff up on him that no one even knows about yet. It's a mess. The more I learn about my own uncle, the more I come to despise him. I can no longer be loyal to him."

"Be loyal to this," Jay says calmly. He then hits Dennis squarely, right on the jaw. Dennis's lip splits and bleeds, but he doesn't hit back.

"Okay," Jay says. "We're done. This is over."

"Jay," Alex says, putting her hand on his arm. "What do you mean?"

"Whatever you want with this guy," he says to her, in a tone more complicated than I can understand, "keep PJ and me out of it, okay?"

Alex nods, her curvy body very still and poised. There's a tension here that I don't quite recognize, but then again, nothing has been normal for a long time. Why would tonight be any different?

"And Alex?" Jay says softly as he leaves.

"Yeah?" she asks, not looking at any of us.

"Be careful."

She finally meets our eyes and gives us a tight smile. "Good night, you two."

23. OLIVIA

Good Secrets, Bad Secrets

onday morning Mme Cuchon calls me into her office.

I take a seat on the big green leather couch, my hands laced together in my lap. She's on the phone with someone, and the lights on her little switchboard are all blinking. The publicity about PJ and the Marquets is insane.

"The press conference will take place at two this afternoon," she says into her extension. "I will answer all inquiries about the Fletcher-Marquet situation at that time." Mme Cuchon hangs up and puts her head in her hands.

"What a year," she moans, and then composes herself. "You're failing," she says bluntly, looking back up at me with cloudless gray eyes. "You promised me you'd pull your grades up. You haven't."

"Mme Cuchon, I'm sorry," I say. "I've only just started to feel more like myself over spring break. There's still time for me to get all my work done. Just give me another chance—"

Mme Cuchon cuts right into me, no longer as sympathetic as she once was. "Olivia, I understand you've been through a lot. But we took a chance on you, letting you dance with that Underground troupe, and you are not proving yourself to be able to handle it. There is not enough time to make up work that you have not completed already."

"No, I still could," I say. "I know I could!"

"It's not just about you, Olivia. It's also about the school's reputation. As you Americans say, we've 'taken a beating.' We can't afford to have good students failing like this. I'm sorry, but I am not going to be able to let you pass this semester. You will have to repeat a semester's worth of classes on your own time. Now, if you'll excuse me, I have a press conference to prepare for." She looks at the door.

I put my palms facedown on her oak desk in a plain gesture of desperation. "No, Madame Cuchon, please. Don't do this. My parents will kill me. They didn't want me to do the Underground in the first place."

"Their instincts were right," she says. "Good-bye, Olivia." She stands up and holds the door open for me to pass in front of her on her way out.

★ ★ ★

Every student at the Lycée gathers outside in front of the school for the press conference. It seems like every media outlet in Europe is here, along with CNN World and all the national news organizations from the States. Everyone is dying to get the official scoop on what this blonde beauty from the woods had to do to escape her evil host father.

"There have been allegations of misconduct on the part of Monsieur and Madame Marquet," Mme Cuchon reads from her notes into the microphone in front of the crowd. PJ stands next to her, and Mme Sanxay next to her. "These have not proven to be substantial in the case of Penelope Fletcher. In our investigations into the matter, the Lycée de Monceau was also not responsible for what happened to Penelope. Penelope was just confused about family issues at home in the United States and chose to leave her host family. She pretended to commit suicide because she was under the false impression that she would be somehow punished for the actions of her parents and the crimes of her sister Annabel Fletcher in the United States, which she played no part in whatsoever. With the help of the Lycée's guidance counselor, we are working to help Penelope heal from the emotional trauma of her life before she came to France as a student."

Standing next to Alex and Zack in the crowd, I hear confused murmurs all around us. No one is buying the story. Mme Cuchon holds firm. "Penelope is a very special young lady, and like everyone else at the Lycée, I am very glad to have her back with us. We have extended a full-year scholarship for Penelope for the following scholastic year so that she can continue to study with us during this difficult time for her American family. Please respect her privacy as she readjusts to life at our school. We also have no comment on the matters of Magistrate Marquet and his personal legal affairs that have come to light in recent days. We won't be taking any questions this afternoon. Thank you very much."

One of the reporters, an American from a cable newsmagazine, fires a question at Mme Cuchon despite her saying she wouldn't answer any. "Madame Cuchon, what of the allegations that Magistrate Marquet attacked Penelope Fletcher in the living room of his Ternes apartment building last weekend, causing his nephew to call the police and have him arrested for assault? Is there a history of abuse between M. and Mme Marquet and the American Lycée de Monceau students they have hosted over the years?"

Penelope mumbles something to Mme Cuchon. I wonder if PJ is going to expose M. Marquet for the creep that he really is. Mme Cuchon raises her eyebrows doubtfully, but she steps away from the microphone so that PJ can speak into it.

"The Marquets were very loving host parents," she tells the reporter. "Monsieur Marquet was never untoward with me in anyway. I was not aware of the misdoings he's now been accused of by the French government. Unfortunately, the misunderstanding in the Marquets' apartment caused the French police to scrutinize some other of the Marquets' dealings and has now found them to be suspects in a large money laundering scheme that I am, of course, not a part of. I feel badly for them but, I just want to move forward with my life in Paris. No further questions." I've never seen her like this—she sounds like a robot, and I can see she's only saying what she's been told to say. It's all a hoax. It's all lies. But it's these lies that are going to make everything okay for PJ now. I'm stunned.

With that, PJ and Mme Cuchon glide back through the front entrance of the Lycée.

"Penelope! Penelope! Why did you run away in the first place? Why did you pretend to commit suicide?" the reporters shout at their backs. I guess the tabloids will never be able to tell the real truth about PJ's year in Paris, but then again, tabloids never are very good at keeping their facts straight. The story, now that it is resolved, will die soon enough. And PJ will finally get a chance to be really happy.

Alex grins at me. "Crafty girl, that one. I think she gets it from me," she whispers.

I squeeze her hand, brushing a thin gold bangle on her wrist.

"Pretty bracelet," I say. "Did your mom send it to you?"

Alex laughs. "Nope. Denny came over last night and gave it to me in hopes that I'd let him take me on another date."

"Are you going to?" I ask. "That's a very nice gift, after all." Alex's version of events painted Denny to be some sort of mixture between a villain and a hero—a dark prince of sorts. And very uncharacteristically, she seems to be keeping her own counsel about whatever is going on with them.

"Ach, Livvy, you sound like me," Alex giggles. "I told him, that yes, I would go out with him—not because of the bracelet but because of how he saved the day with PJ and Jay. And you should have heard him pretending to be the German police looking for an AWOL Alsatian-French single mother holing up in Baden Baden and refusing to come home to her children. It was priceless!"

"Oh, Alex," I say, wiping a sudden tear out of my eye. "That's so sweet. He seems like a really great guy." I'm so proud of Alex for thinking so carefully about her new guy. She's not getting as swept up in him as quickly as she did with George, and because of that, she's finding out that appearances aren't what they seem: this time, in a good way. Denny was able to get the police to come to the Marquets' apartment, and because of that, they could make sure that PJ was safe. That's all that really matters.

"Denny's different," Alex says, shifting her weight from one high-heeled oxford shoe to the other. For the press conference, she's dressed very conservatively but with great style, of course. I suppose, she thought she might get interviewed by one of the dozens of reporters here. In her black shirt dress and trendy shoes, she looks like a very credible source.

But none of the reporters try to interview Alex. We watch everyone disperse, and the scene feels almost like a funeral. Everyone's finally going to lay this whole thing to rest.

I follow Alex and Zack into the Courcelles métro stop so that we can all go back to Cambronne after school on Friday afternoon; Alex's host parents have agreed to take me on since they have an alcove in their front office where I can sleep. Mme Rouille and I have not spoken, but she signed off on this permanent move. Thomas and I have not spoken either. After everything that's happened to me this year, I think this is what shocks me the most.

Mme Sanxay, maybe feeling sympathy for PJ—or perhaps because of a nice sum donated by the Lycée—has agreed to let PJ live with her. She's even going to let PJ take over Alex's nannying job and pay her over the summer until PJ starts her senior year at the Lycée.

Down on the platform in the white-tiled station, we find Sara-Louise, Mary, and Anouk talking to Elena. Elena spent all last week with her family in Morocco on spring break. Her olive skin is tanned from the trip. Alex walks up to her and tells her she likes the new bright blue scarf holding back her shiny brown hair.

"Very boho," Alex says. "And did you get those bangles there, too?"

"Aren't they cute?" Elena says. "Morocco was amazing. You guys have to go there someday. It was by far my favorite place I've ever been."

"Girl, you might have gone on one of the best spring breaks of anyone in the Programme, " Zack says enviously. "Though I did hear that Sammy went to Santorini. I bet that was to die for. I love me some feta cheese, don't you know. And that olive oil? I could bathe in a vat of that. Mmm mmm!"

Sara-Louise and Mary giggle.

"There's nowhere better than Paris," Alex defends the city. "Except maybe New York. I'm glad I stayed here for the break."

"Like you had a choice!" Zack teases.

I put my arms around Alex's waist and give her another squeeze to show her how proud I am of her.

"Thank goodness you didn't leave Paris for the break," I say. "We have you and Denny to thank for everything!"

The three girls and Zack pat Alex on the back appreciatively. "That's right, Alex," Mary says. "That rocked! Way to go! PJ's safe, she gets to start all over again at the Lycée, and the Marquets and their drama are gone from Paris for good!"

"And she got a new boyfriend out of the deal," Zack reminds everyone. He pinches Alex's rouged cheek. "Only you, *ma belle.*"

Alex just tosses her head nonchalantly, but I know she's on top of the world.

"So, are you guys studying for the SAT tonight or what?" Alex asks the girls. "We're getting together at my house if you want to come over. We could all quiz each other and stuff."

Alex, the perfectly prepared student! Miracles never cease. Of all of us, Alex has been scoring the highest on our SAT practice tests.

"Actually, we're going to the picnic right now. You guys should come."

I look at Alex and Zack. "No, thanks," I say on all of our behalves.

The train comes, and we all get on it and find a block of empty seats.

Chatting awkwardly about the SAT test tomorrow, we have a hard time even filling the time until we've gone two stops, where the three of us are going to change trains.

"See you guys later," Zack says. "Have fun at the party."

"Y'all have a good night," Sara-Louise calls.

"*Au revoir*, guys!" Elena adds.

We shuffle to our connecting train, a little disappointed.

"Do you guys ever think that we really missed out, not becoming friends with French kids?" I ask them.

"We have French friends," Alex says. "You have your dancer friends and Thomas."

"I most definitely do not have Thomas," I say, laughing. "But, yeah. I guess."

"I don't have any French friends," Zack says. "The only friends I've made this year are you guys and a couple of failed romances—if you can call those friends. They might say we're enemies."

Alex chews on that for a minute, and then she says, "Well, *I* have French friends. Their names are Charles, Emeline, Albert . . ." She counts them off on her fingers. "What do you guys say to stopping by and saying hi to them this afternoon instead of getting off at Cambronne?"

"Oh, Alex," Zack moans. "I thought your mongrel-sitting job was over. Now you're actually volunteering to do it?"

"Come on," Alex says. "It's so gorgeous out. Let's take them to the Jardin du Luxembourg. We can still make the puppet show!"

"That sounds fun," I say. I feel my phone vibrate then. "Hold on a sec." I pull it out of my pocket and drop my jaw when I see who it is.

Thomas.

FEEL LIKE COMING OVER? is all it says. My heart leaps into my throat, and suddenly the train feels hot and sweaty.

"Actually," I tell them, "you guys go. I'll meet you there."

Alex and Zack narrow their eyes at me. "Who was that?" Alex demands.

"I just have to go work something out," is all I will say.

Just past the Jardin du Luxembourg, I get off at the Sorbonne and head for Thomas's dorm. When he answers the door, he doesn't say anything, just pulls me into his lanky arms and strokes my hair.

I push him gently away. "What's this all about, Thomas?"

Thomas steps aside and lets me in. His bed is unmade and covered with opened books. "Sorry," he says, knocking them to floor so that I can sit down. "I've been studying."

"That's good!" I laugh, feeling like I'm outside my body, watching this scene from above. "I wish I'd been doing more of that lately."

Thomas gives me a confused look. I just shake my head. "It's a long story."

"Olivia," Thomas says, dropping to the floor and crouching at my feet. "I text you because I have to apologize for my mother's behavior. She doesn't thinking. She doesn't know how much we love each other!"

I swallow hard. "Love each other? I thought you fell out of love with me . . . because I wasn't wearing flowered shirts anymore."

Thomas shakes his head violently, and then leans over to rest it in my lap. "That night," he says, the words muffled into my lap. "I realized then how much I missed you. Please take me back, Olivia!"

I push him off my lap. "Thomas, you've got to be kidding me!" I'm shocked to hear the words I wanted so badly only a month ago.

"Why?" he asks me. "You could stay here at the dorm room, we could start it all over again. Wouldn't that be nice? It is just what I want. Please take me, Olivia." Sitting on the floor like that, all his limbs pointing in every direction, with his shame written all over his face, he feels like someone I knew a long time ago. Familiar, but nothing else. No passion. No urgency. Thomas is trying to figure his life out, not even sure what he really wants. I don't believe that he wants *this*, either—me, the relationship he's begging to have back.

I take one giant breath.

"Thomas, I think we had a great thing," I say. "I will always cherish our time together. But we both know that we aren't right for each other. It took me a while to see it as clearly as you did, but I get it now."

"It was a mistake, Olivia! One that I will always regret," Thomas says. "Please let's give it another chance."

"It wasn't a mistake," I say. "I didn't know who I was. I was trying on a new me. I mean, I'm still not exactly sure who I am, but I know that I'm on my way to finding out."

Thomas looks *really* confused now, and I wonder if it is the language barrier or just the fact that I'm saying no to him. His eyebrows are raised in confusion, almost right up to the curls on his forehead. His green eyes look hopeful.

"I'm sorry, Thomas," I say, wriggling off the bed and back to the door. "I've got to go. *Bon après-midi*, okay?"

Thomas looks destroyed as I let myself out, but somehow I have a feeling that he's going to be just fine.

I gulp in the fresh spring air and hurry over to the puppet show at the Jardin du Luxembourg to meet Alex, Zack, and the kids. As I walk, my spine tingles and I feel taller, like I'm shedding a weight off my shoulders.

I look around me at the buildings of Paris and take in the smell of the city. My city.

★ ★ ★

Saturday morning, Alex and I meet Zack in front of the métro stop and head up together to the SAT testing center in the Ninth. All the Programme Americain kids are there.

Tackling the math section in the second half of the test, I find myself stumped by only the third problem. I read it over several times and look around the room as if by osmosis I can catch up on my trigonometry. The proctor gives me a severe look. I look back down at my desk, blushing.

During the SAT break, PJ floats over to me. I hadn't even seen her come in to the testing center earlier.

"Hey!" I say, giving her a hug. She still feels too skinny. Stiff, too. I wonder if she's been getting enough to eat and if she's been feeling okay. "Every time I see you, I get so happy. Thank God you're okay."

"Livvy," PJ chokes out. "I wanted to tell you that I'm so sorry for everything I've put you through this year. I know I've kept a lot of secrets from you. I'm . . . I'm not a very good friend. I've done so much damage around here."

I stroke her arm, trying to comfort her. She sounds so distressed. "PJ, you don't have to say that. Everyone has secrets. We were just worried about you. We're elated that things are finally better. Okay?"

I wait until she nods.

"Good. So, how's your test going?"

"Oh, it's okay," PJ says, playing idly with the ends of her translucent blonde hair. All the other students from the Lycée are watching her, still not used to her being back in our midst. "What about you?"

I sigh and roll my eyes. "I think I've really blown it with school this year. I don't deserve to do well on this test. It kind of serves me right."

"Why do you say that?"

"I've just been such a mess," I say. "I didn't even start studying for the SAT until, like, last weekend."

"Livvy, you are not a mess. Trust me," PJ lets out a small rueful chuckle. It's the first time I think I've seen her smile since long before she disappeared. "I know one when I see one. Remember what a mess I was when you came to that beauty salon and had to help me convince the girl not to cut off all my hair?"

I laugh. "Hair like yours is a crime to get rid of."

"Well, you saw me at a crazy moment, and you not only fixed everything, but didn't demand anything from me, either. You're a rare find, Livvy."

I'm taken aback. This is a side of PJ I've never seen before: talkative, circumspect, desperate to connect.

"Thanks, PJ," I say. We head back into our respective testing *salles* to finish the SAT. While I'm muddling through the reading section, it occurs to me that PJ's still keeping secrets so that the Lycée can save face and she can finally get what she wants: Paris.

If she can, I think, then what's to stop me from doing the same thing? I can get the Lycée to keep a few face-saving secrets, and then I can stay in Paris, too.

Back at Alex's homestay, I type an e-mail to my mom, eager to get rid of a few secrets of my own.

Hey Mommy,

There're a couple things I was hoping we could talk about soon. I have to tell you about something that happened with a boy in the program . . . and I also need to tell you that I'm going to stay in France and dance full time.

I love you and Daddy so much.

Call me when you can!

Livvy

"I'd like to do an extra-credit project," I tell Mme Cuchon the first chance I have to get her alone. "I'd like to write a paper about the underground arts movement in Paris. I can do interviews with Henri, the choreographer, and Kiki, our accompanist. I have first-person experience; the paper will be a really unique project."

"Olivia, I already told you it's too late to make up the work you didn't complete for this semester," Mme Cuchon responds, not even looking up from the pile of papers on her desk. "You need to make arrangements to enroll in summer school when you get back to San Diego. Otherwise you will not be starting your senior year as scheduled."

"Um," I say. "I think I should be able to start my senior year whenever I want to." I say *whenever* because I am not quite sure what I want to do with my future, but I no longer think it is any of the Lycée's business to decide. "Please just let me do the project." My palms are sweating, but I try not to let her know how scared I am right now. "I know that you were aware of Monsieur Marquet's inappropriate behavior with young women. I know how the board makes you keep quiet so as not to upset wealthy donors."

Mme Cuchon finally looks up from her desk. "What?"

"You heard me," I say. Inside my body is an earthquake, but my exterior is cool. I know if I blow this, I'll lose all my power again. And I can't let that happen. "You'd have to recant that whole press conference. The allegations about Monsieur Marquet would be proven correct."

Mme Cuchon stands and walks around her desk. Perching on it, she takes a long look at me. "Who told you this?"

"I just know, okay?" I say. "But no one else does. Just let me do my project and pass the year. I won't say anything. Believe me, I don't want to. I love this school." It's true; I have had wonderful times here. And made the best friends of my life because of its American study-abroad program. I don't want to have to take Mme Cuchon down.

Mme Cuchon lets out a long, low breath. She looks at me, and then closes her eyes. "All right, Olivia. Do as you wish."

"Really?" I squeak. "And I'll turn it in by the last day of school?"

"Just make sure it's really, really good," Mme Cuchon says and opens the door for me. "And I mean *parfait.*"

"It will be the best paper you've ever read!" I say. I feel like springing into a pirouette, but I keep both feet on the ground. "You're making the right decision. Thank you!"

It's so strange, I think as I go back to class: what turns out to be a good secret and what secrets are *so* bad you really shouldn't try to keep them to yourself.

24. ZACK

Wish You Were Here

*P*aris in the springtime is as good as they say. The outdoor café tables start to fill up with people, bright flowers sprout up in every available patch of earth, and the spirit of the city is as light and romantic as a glass of *vin blanc*.

One Saturday afternoon at the end of April, I meet Alex in the gardens behind the Musée Rodin. It's the first time we've hung out by ourselves since we started talking again. Neither of us really feels like going inside to see the sculptures, but it's so balmy outside, you might mistake the season for summer. We spread my old pashmina out on the grass and share some takeaway couscous I bought on the rue Cler. I only got one plastic fork, so Alex and I take turns.

This is a picnic like a million I've had with Alex last semester—sharing baguettes, croissants, sandwiches, cartons of soup, chocolate bars. But I still feel a little unsure of her friendship after our time away from one another.

Alex stretches out, half on the grass and half on the pashmina, and lays her head down on her tote bag. She pats the ground next to her. "Come on. Let's take a nap."

I follow her lead, but I am not as immediately comfortable as I once would have been. I find myself feeling so distanced from her still.

Alex's eyes close behind her sunglasses.

"When did you get so Zen, Alex?"

"Hmmm," she answers. "Probably around the time I found myself washing Albert's urine out of my favorite dress—by hand, mind you," Alex tells me.

"Maybe it's your newfound love," I say.

"Love?" Alex asks. "I don't know anything about love. I just take each day as it comes. With Denny and everything else."

"So you're not as eager to couple anymore?" I ask her.

"I'm thinking that being independent is super-hot for spring," Alex says. "Besides, college is only a year or so away. And after that, everyone is going to be trying to get married and have kids. I think I'm going to try to enjoy my youth while I can."

"But you like him, huh?" I ask.

Alex dissolves into very hyper, un-Zen-like giggles. "Yeah. I really do! Even though he's French. He's a sweet French! Did I show you the bracelet he gave me?" She holds up her arm. The gold glints in the sunlight.

"Only about a thousand times."

I should have known that Alex Nguyen would never let herself give up on a pact. She's definitely got a boyfriend, just as she said she was going to so many months ago, when we first became friends—even if she can't admit it to herself yet.

★ ★ ★

When I get home, Romy tells me someone called for me while I was out. "André?" I ask her.

"No, the boy who came to visit you," she says, wiping her hands on a towel and digging out the piece of paper she wrote the number down on. "I gave him your mobile number, too. Did he call you?"

"It's okay," I say, already going into my room. "I have his number. He already has my cell phone number, too."

I stop to gather my wits before scrolling down to Bobby's number and pushing send on my cell phone. Here goes. Bobby answers, and hearing his voice again floods me with warm feelings about how easy he is to talk to.

"Hi, Bobby!" I say, my voice almost girlishly high. I'm suddenly really hot, as if I have a fever. I open my window and lean out against the waist-high railing.

"Zack," Bobby says. "Are you okay?"

"Yes, I'm fine," I say, trying not to breathe too hard into the phone. Heavy breathing is so gross. "What's up?"

"I'm in Paris." Out the window, I watch two men come out of the bakery down the street. They must be feeding a crowd because they each have about five baguettes under their arms. One of them leans closer to a window to check the price on a window display as they pass. The other pats the other one's back while he waits. It's not a gesture friends make, it's a gesture boyfriends make.

"You're *where*?"

"I'm here with my parents," Bobby says. "They're here for some convention, and they flew me down to meet them for a visit."

"Oh, wow," I say. "How long are you here for?"

"Just till tomorrow morning," he says. "I wasn't going to call you, but I just couldn't leave without talking to you. Do you want to go grab a bite to eat?"

"Definitely," I say. "What hotel are you staying in?"

He tells me, and before I hang up, I ask him, "How come you called me at my homestay, and not on my cell?"

"I just wanted to make sure I didn't call you in the middle of something," Bobby says. "I wasn't sure what you'd be up to."

In the middle of something like hanging out with André, that is.

I go back into the kitchen and grab a chunk of bread from the cutting board. Romy's cutting up garlic and putting the pieces into a pan full of lemon juice and white wine. The whole room smells like summer. "Did you call Bobby back?" she asks me.

"Yes," I say, giving her a funny look. She doesn't usually check up on me.

"He's your boyfriend?" she asks. "*N'est-ce pas?*"

I raise my eyebrows, immediately so embarrassed I could die. I chew on my bread and blush furiously. Romy smiles at me, then turns back to the stove to add cream to her sauce.

I stare at her back for a while in wonder. *She knows I'm gay*, I think. *And she could not care less. She's probably thought that this whole year!*

I smile at her back, even though she can't see me. Those few words, that straightforward question, made me more eager to come out of the closet than anything anyone has ever said to me before. I get on the first bus that passes me and take it to the Sixteenth, where all the embassies are. I find Bobby's hotel easily. Before I have the front desk ring his room to tell him I am here, I find a mirror so that I can fix my hair and make sure I'm not sweaty or flushed or anything. I don't want to be a mess when I greet Bobby.

My stomach does cartwheels even after waiting several minutes. I'm really that nervous to see him again.

Finally, I ring for Bobby, and he comes down the main staircase, wearing a dark button-down shirt and a trim motorcycle jacket over jeans. That shock of blond hair catches me off guard, the way it always does, but the real kicker is that smile. He waves at the front desk, and the girl and the guy behind the counter both look smitten. It stings to see how much other people notice that when it took me so long to see what a prize he is. He could have been mine, but I threw him away. Like a total fool.

"You hungry?" he asks me.

This is too bizarre for me to be hungry. "Are you?" I ask.

"Eh," Bobby says. "You want to go walk around until we see something that looks good?"

The Sixteenth Arrondissement is a very genteel, very official-looking area of Paris. We don't say hardly anything as we stroll. I look around for something, anything of note to mention and get a conversation started but my tongue feels absolutely bloated and incompetent inside my mouth. I hope it will get better once we sit down to eat. We walk past a ton of gorgeous nineteenth century buildings, lit up to display flags from around the world, but we see few restaurants that are appropriate for young people like us.

"Let's just go sit at the Trocadero and get a crepe," Bobby suggests.

"That sound okay?"

"It sounds perfect," I say, grateful for his suggestion. The plaza is mobbed by people taking photos of the lit-up Eiffel Tower across the Seine, but once we get hot crepes stuffed with mushrooms and cheese, we find a quiet spot to lean against the railing and have relative privacy.

I take a bite into my crepe, which is still way too hot to eat. I immediately drop the bite right out of my mouth before I can stop myself. At the same time, I let out a guttural, wounded animal noise. I sound like my dog back in Tennessee when someone steps on her toe.

"Bobby, yikes," I say, realizing how terrible my manners are. "I don't know what the heck is wrong with me! Sorry—my crepe was just real hot."

Bobby laughs. "Looks like it. That's okay."

"I feel like an ass," I say. "Look at me! Spittin' up my food. I'm a mess."

"You doing all right?" Bobby asks, taking a bite of his crepe now that it's cooled. "You seem preoccupied."

I chew on my crepe just to have something to do. I can't taste it; my tongue is too burnt.

Bobby turns and leans against the granite ledge, facing me. His jacket opens, and I see he's wearing an old vest, like that one André has. Even with Bobby right in front of me, all the way on the other side of Paris from Oberkampf and André's apartment, I'm still always having little moments of remembering how much fun I had with André. The good times were amazing, but the bad times . . . they weren't just bad, they were knock-you-under-the-table horrible.

Bobby laughs. "Dude, you're a heartbreaker. When you're out of the closet, I hope you'll give me a call. But until then, I think we better stay away from each other. I like you too much. I'm in love with your potential!"

I smile, flattered. "Don't say that you want to stay away from each other. That's mean!"

"Oh, like you ain't done nothing mean to me since I've known you, dude. I remember taking quite the cold bath in a river canal at your insistence. Which I still haven't gotten you back for!"

I laugh. "Hey, you want to meet someone you might love?"

"Sure," Bobby agrees. A few minutes later, Alex teeters over to us across the Trocadero plaza in skintight black jeans and high heels. Now that she's not babysitting anymore, she's been dressing more outrageously than ever.

"I didn't expect to see you again so soon, my love," Alex says, bending forward to kiss me on either cheek. "Twice in one day is a rare treat lately." She turns to Bobby and holds out both hands to him. Her nails are painted green. "Who are you, handsome?"

I clear my throat. "This is Bobby. Bobby, this is my friend Alex Nguyen."

"Hi, Alex," Bobby says with a big smile. "I've heard a lot about you. Glad to see Zack's speaking to you again!"

"Moody, isn't he?" she says. I half expect her to light up a cigarette so that she'll have something to gesture with while she talks. When Bobby looks away, she looks over at me and gives me a huge thumbs-up and a grin. "Anybody feel like ice cream?"

We wander over to Berthillon, the place I took Bobby before that he liked so much. "My treat!" Alex announces, and buys us each a double-scoop cone.

"This is so weird," Bobby says. "My ice cream totally smells like bananas."

"I thought you got vanilla and chocolate," I say, licking my mandarin flavored scoop.

"Seriously, dude," Bobby says. "Do you smell that?" He puts his ice cream in front of me so that I can smell it. I lean my nose really close to it. It doesn't smell anything like bananas.

Before I raise my nose back up, Bobby smashes the vanilla ice cream into my face. He and Alex shriek with laughter as I register the shock of the cold ice cream up my nostrils. "Hey!" I yell. "That's not funny."

"Oh, I'd say it's about as funny as falling into a canal in January," Bobby says. "Now, I've got you back."

Alex looks at me quizzically.

"I'll tell you later," I tell her. Alex hands me a silk scarf so that I can wipe my face off. Sticky vanilla ice cream is streaked all over the blue fabric. Alex doesn't seem to mind in the slightest.

She can't stop laughing. "Bobby, you are my hero. That was classic!"

We walk her back to her homestay after that, pretty much having made a giant loop around Paris. Alex is enamored with Bobby by the end of our walk. She's laced her arms into his and kisses him several times on his cheeks before going up into her apartment.

When we get to Bobby's hotel, it's pretty late. There aren't usually a lot of people on the street in the Sixteenth, but at night, it's practically desolate.

"So, we're finally even," Bobby says. "Not bad, if I do say so myself."

"No we're not," I say. "Not yet." I gather up every last bit of nerve and lean forward. Then I kiss him, pressing my lips very softly onto his.

Like you'd expect, Bobby's an *amazing* kisser.

"Hmm," he says when we pull apart. "You taste like vanilla."

"Oh, not banana?"

"Nope, not at all, actually. Funny how that works."

"Keep in touch, Bobby," I say.

"I will," Bobby answers me. "And hey, Zack?"

"Yeah?"

"I'm glad you and Alex got back together."

"Oh, Alex." I shrug. "How could I resist?"

Bobby nods. "See you later, dude." He goes back into his hotel, and I almost call for him not to go yet. Almost.

★ ★ ★

I stay up late that night writing draft after draft of a letter to my parents. I don't know how much to tell them. Do I start from the moment I first noticed that I felt weird when they made me play football at recess? How far back do I go?

Finally, I take a fresh sheet of notebook paper and write *I'm gay. I love you. I hope you still love me. See you at the end of May.*

I fold it up and put it into one of my prepaid international envelopes that I got in the grocery store checkout aisle before I realized that I don't really write letters very often.

★ ★ ★

The next morning, Bobby calls and asks if I have time for brunch before he goes. His flight is in a couple of hours.

"I'm sorry, I can't," I tell him. "I have other plans. Maybe next time?"

"That's cool, dude," Bobby says. "See you, Zack."

It's cooler today than yesterday. I grab a jacket and slip the letter I wrote last night into the pocket.

I take a train up to Oberkampf and stand in front of André's favorite vintage clothing store, waiting for my date to arrive.

She's late but comes bearing gifts. "Chocolates," Alex says, holding them out to me. "They're from Denny. Have as many as you want."

"Hey Alex," I say. "When we finish shopping, you feel like coming to the post office with me?"

"Sure, for what?" she asks.

"Oh, I just have to mail this letter to my parents," I say, pulling it out of my jacket pocket. "It's just a little note to tell them I love them, and that I am gay."

"Holy shit!" Alex cries. "I'll be there. Good thing I brought my camera. I want to snap a photo while you drop it in the slot!" Alex may be a tad ridiculous, I think, as I watch her do a funny little booty-shaking dance of joy right there on the sidewalk. She has put me through a lot this year. But then again, she's always loved me for who I am, even when I didn't. In my book, that's pretty much the definition of a good friend.

25. ALEX

Absolutely Glowing

*M*aton opens our math class by handing out our evaluation summaries—basically report cards for the entire year at the Lycée. As my name comes halfway through the alphabet, I have to wait way too long for him to hand me mine. When I get it, I tear into the envelope, nearly ripping the packet of evaluations and classwork scores in half.

I scream out loud when I read through them all. Every single one is absolutely glowing!

After school I go to a call center and fax the report summary to my mom's office in New York, even though the Lycée is sending our parents these documents, too. I don't want to have to wait to hear how proud she is of me.

Just a few minutes later, my BlackBerry rings and it's my mom.

"Oh, Alex," she says, laughing. "You are indeed a phoenix, aren't you?"

"What do you mean?"

"This is the kind of comeback people pay big commissions for in Hollywood, my darling. I've never had a more startling reminder of how good you are when you want to be," she says. "Well done, Alexandra."

"Thanks, Mommy." I beam. "And I paid Madame Sanxay back, too. *And* helped my friend. Just like I'd been trying to do all along," I add pointedly.

"So, I've just had my assistant book me in Paris for next week," my mom says. "And then she's got us at the Coup de Grace spa in the Loire Valley for five days when you finish school. You're not too busy, right?"

"We're going to a spa?" I croak. "Together?" I can't even recall the last time we had a spa day together. I think it was after Jeremy broke up with me back in Brooklyn.

"Get yourself nice and ready to be pampered, darling. See you next week!"

★ ★ ★

I go over to the Sanxays so that I can say good-bye to Albert, Emeline, and Charles before school ends and I go away with my mom. Mme Sanxay answers the door. She wraps her arms around me, and then shows me around the apartment. "I'd say we're in better shape than we were, wouldn't you say?"

The apartment is spotless, for once. Toys and other household articles are no longer spread out all over the floor, and the place smells fresher than it ever did when I was babysitting. Mme Sanxay looks really proud. "I think I'm finally getting it together."

"Men are assholes," I tell her bluntly. "You're better off without that ex-husband of yours."

Mme Sanxay laughs and goes into the nursery to wake Charles. "Oh, my dear Alex, this family certainly has learned a lot from you." She hands me the baby. He's all mushy and soft from being asleep.

Emeline and Albert get home shortly after that, and they burst into excited squeals when they see me. Emeline grabs the one hand that's not hanging on to Charles, and Albert shows off all the new things he's learned to say in English since the last time he saw me.

"How about a trip to the Jardin du Luxembourg on the house?" I offer. "We can let your mom have some 'me' time."

Mme Sanxay makes a sour face. "You don't have to do that, Alex. You're not their nanny anymore. That's PJ's job now."

"Where is PJ, anyway?" I ask. "Did you give her the afternoon off?"

"She's out with her friend Jay," Mme Sanxay says. "Do you know him? He seems like a nice boy. One of the good ones."

"He is," I say, feeling almost sad at how true that is. "Anyway, it would be my absolute *pleasure* to take the little ones to the park. Shall we, *mes petits amis?*"

At the playground, I cuddle Charles and look on happily as Albert and Emeline terrorize the playground, as they tend to do. It's so nice to be their friend and not their disciplinarian. I'm going to miss them, I realize. Especially Charles, with his big blue eyes and that sweet baby powder smell.

"Ah, isn't this a familiar scene?"

I turn around and see Denny standing there. He's got a small bouquet of daisies in his hands. "For you," he says.

I look at him in amusement. "You don't quit, chocolates, flowers, dresses . . . you must really thin! who can be bought, huh?"

"When I see beautiful things, I think of you," Denny answers. simple. And, no, I won't quit. I seem to remember you saying that you o go on another date with me. I mean, if getting my uncle arrested wasn't the way to your heart, I don't know what is! And if I understand correctly, you don't have much time left here in Paris."

"Nope," I say. "I'm actually leaving in a couple days."

"So, no chance of a date tonight then?" Denny asks.

"Sorry, buddy," I say. "Your timing's terrible!"

Denny sighs with a smile. "Well, I'm sorry I didn't seek you out earlier. I've been taking care of some things with my family. I'll just have to try and woo you from afar."

"Does that mean I have to give you the bracelet back?" I ask, slipping it off my wrist and handing it over. "Because that date never happened?"

"Please keep it," Denny says. "That way, I can always track you down under the guise of getting it back." I can't help grinning a little.

"And we do know you are very good at tracking people down."

Dennis takes my wrist and puts the bracelet back on. Before he lets go, he kisses my hand sweetly. Charles looks on, perfectly placid.

★ ★ ★

The last day of school at the Lycée is surreal. We have to take another test, similar to the Final Comp, but no one is as freaked out this time. As long as our grades before the test were okay, we should be fine. After all, we can't come back anyway, right? So they can't kick us out.

Olivia studies hard for the test and spends the entire three-hour testing iod slaving away in a blue book. When she comes out and joins Zack and me on the front steps of the Lycée, she looks spent.

"You'll be okay," Zack says. "I think they'd be cruel to fail you after all that's happened."

"They won't fail me," Olivia says, looking back at the door she just walked out of. "It'll be fine. Did you guys clean out your lockers and stuff already?"

"Yup," Zack and I say together, standing up and brushing ourselves off.

"*Est-ce que vous voulez aller à l'Hôtel de Crillon avec moi?*" I ask them. My mom's flight landed this morning, and we're meeting her at our favorite hotel in Paris for lunch and then maybe some shopping. I'm really hoping she'll swing me right into Chloé and buy me a dress to wear tonight, because my mom and I are hosting a cocktail party at the top of the Tour Montparnasse for all the Programme Americain students and our host families. And it won't be just any party—it will be the best party anyone in this program has ever been to. I need to look *perfect*.

My mom's assistant called me and asked me to tell her everything I wanted for the party so that she could set it up from their office in New York. I told her that we definitely had to have lots of champagne and cocktails, smooth, modern furniture and lighting, a fantastic view of Paris, amazing weather, and twinkling lights all over the party space. Besides the weather, my mom's assistant promised she'd see to everything and make sure it was perfect.

"Hold on one second," Zack says and dashes ahead to catch up with George, who's walking out of the test with Robbie. Olivia and I watch from the steps, wondering what on earth Zack has to say to George.

Zack hands him a crumpled pink piece of paper. "I think you

dropped this," he says.

George looks at it but doesn't take it. "That's not mine."

"I know it's yours, George," Zack says. "You want to explain why you left this in my mail slot?"

"I don't know what you're talking about." Typical, cocky George has a disgusting smirk on his face. I look at Olivia, but she's as clueless as I am.

"I'll tell you what," Zack says to George, grabbing his palm and pressing the pink paper into it. "You stay away from the party tonight, and I won't give the Lycée the handwriting test I had done on this piece of paper as compared to your most recent French homework assignment. You show up and try to party with us, and I'll hand deliver those results to Madame Cuchon right in front of you. In fact, I'll bring them with me tonight just in case you try to come."

George narrows his eyes. "Are you for real?"

"Real as it gets, George," Zack says. I cover my mouth because I might laugh, despite myself. "Real as it gets."

George takes off with Robbie following.

"Too bad they can't make it tonight," Zack says sadly when he comes back over to us. "They have other plans."

"What was that about?" I ask. "What was that paper you had?"

"Oh, just a love letter I found of his. He wrote it to Drew, after Drew got kicked out," Zack says. "Feel free to spread that around, Alex."

Olivia chuckles. "Come on, you guys, we're going to be late."

"And C.A.B. waits for no one!" Zack cries. We rush down into the métro, my arms linked inside one of each of theirs.

★ ★ ★

My mom, of course, adores Zack and Olivia when she meets them in the restaurant at the Hôtel de Crillon, the luxury hotel where she always stays in Paris. She asks them a million questions about themselves, compliments them on their French, and coos over how stylish they are, with their hipster haircuts. After lunch, she kisses them both and sends them back to Cambronne while she and I hit up the rue de Faubourg Saint-Honoré.

"Ah, Alex," my mom says, squeezing me tight to her. "I've missed you so much."

"You have not," I scoff.

"I have! The house is so quiet and clean without you. I almost got a puppy to make up for the lack of energy," my mom tells me. She reaches out and holds my face in her hand, the metal of her rings cool on my skin. "But in the end, I went to the shelter and got a big fat tabby cat."

"Mom," I say, stopping right in the middle of the sidewalk, Italian tourists pushing around me. "You. Got a cat. From a shelter. I don't believe you."

"Yes!" she giggles. "His name is Oscar. I adore him. We're besties!"

"*Don't* say 'besties,' Mom." I grab the handle of the door to Comme des Garçons. "Let's go in here."

My mom picks out at least a dozen short, vampy cocktail dresses for me to try on, but each one feels too formal, too stylized. Finally, I chuck the last one over the top of the dressing room door and tell her I'm through.

"I have dresses back at my homestay," I tell her, exhausted. "I'll just wear one of those."

"Are you sure?" she says. "I really wanted to treat you."

"Let's go get our hair done," I say, gathering all my black tresses at the nape of my neck. "What I could *desperately* use is a blowout."

We head back to de Crillon. In my mom's suite, a stylist combs, tugs, and teases my hair into a half-up bouffant. When she's done, my mom brings some dresses for me to try on from what she's brought with her.

"Why don't you wear this one?" she says. "It's too young for me, anyway. You can have it."

The dress she has selected is a black cap-sleeve vintage sheath with a ruffle around the hem. The length just grazes the top of my knee. In it, I look classy, responsible, and totally hot.

"It's perfect!" I say.

My mom puts a silk blazer on with a chiffon skirt. We both wear dainty black heels, mine with flower appliqués on the straps.

"Shall we?" my mom says, and we descend into the lobby to greet our waiting town car.

★ ★ ★

From the moment the elevator doors open at the top of the Tour Montparnasse, I know that this party is going be spectacular.

My mom's assistant did an excellent job with the details, but the vision was all mine. Just as I had wanted, tiny sparkling lights cover the entire ceiling. The room is perfectly dimmed so that the view of Paris on all sides is like a bright painting that goes on forever. The furniture that the Tour usually sets out for tourists to sit on when they come to the top of the tower has been stored somewhere and replaced with plush black leather lounges and benches. Ice buckets hold bottles of expensive champagne, and waiters are making sure everyone has something to drink and lots of little appetizers so no one will starve.

All the Programme Americain students (besides George, Robby, and

Patty, that is) are in attendance. Their host families are having a ball. Even Mme Cuchon seems to have cut loose a little bit. My mom and I glide around, greeting everyone, accepting tons of compliments on the beautiful party.

Though privately my mom, however, still seems skeptical about my choice of venue.

"Alex," she says, as we take a moment to share a glass of white wine, looking out toward the north-facing window. "I have to say, I can't understand what you see in this place."

"*La Tour Montparnasse*?" I ask. "What's wrong with it?" I'm being mischievous, because I know *exactly* what's wrong with it. The Montparnasse tower is a hideous black skyscraper that totally does not jive with the low-slung skyline of Paris buildings around it. A sort of poor-man's Eiffel Tower, it has a viewing room at the top of the commercial spaces for tourists. Even better, it has a rooftop open-air viewing area that is windy and loud and feels a tiny bit dangerous. Every time I came to Paris with my mom, I always wanted to go inside the tower, but she always turned up her nose at it.

I made Zack come with me one wintry December day last year. We paid the student rate and took the elevators to the top. The viewing room has tacky blue carpet and cheesy signs telling you what all the buildings are. When my mom asked me where I wanted to have the cocktail party, it was the only place I asked for. For some reason, I just can't get enough of being on such a tall rooftop, looking over Paris.

"It smells like sausage, even after the event planners came through and fixed it up," my mom says. "And don't you think the windows look dirty?"

"Mom," I say. "It's gorgeous. Thank you so much."

"So, Alex," she says, tipping the last of her wine into her mouth. "I'd expect that you'd have a date at this soirée. Where's the lucky guy?"

I turn and face the Eiffel Tower, which looks positively diminutive from this height. "Mom," I say. "I like to think of myself as a free agent. Always up for an adventure, never tied down!"

"That's a good girl, Alex," my mom says, putting her arm around my shoulders.

"All right, everybody!" Sara-Louise calls over the party in that familiar twang. "My host dad is gonna take a picture of us upstairs on the viewing platform. Get on up there!"

The wind is blowing hard up here, making our short skirts flutter dangerously. All the host families and Lycée students and teachers gather together for a big group picture.

Zack folds his arms around Olivia and me, and we all smile broadly. My mom holds my hand and looks at me so proudly I almost cry.

Then the group's pose crumbles around us, everyone wandering away to take more pictures in smaller groups. Olivia and Zack and I still have our arms tightly around each other, all still grinning. My mom takes my camera from me and snaps several pictures of us.

"You three are just gorgeous," she says. "I should put you in my magazine."

We giggle.

"You did a good job taking care of each other this year, didn't you? Look at you all, surviving a whole year on your own in Paris. And none of you worse for the wear."

We look at each other knowingly. Yes, it's true. We may not have ken the best care of our*selves* this year, but we did end up taking very good care of each other, and PJ, too, wherever she is tonight.

"*Je vous aime, mes amis,*" I say before I let my friends go. "*Toujours!*"

Mme Cuchon comes over to say something to my mom, and all of us are pulled away by different classmates to say good-bye. Finally, a little brain-dead from so much small talk, I escape to the bathroom and pull my BlackBerry out of my clutch.

"Always ready for an adventure," I say to myself as I find Denny's number and begin to text him.

CAN I CHANGE MY MIND ABOUT THAT DATE? I punch in. WOULD BE LOVELY TO CELEBRATE MY LAST NIGHT IN PARIS W/ AN ACTUAL PARISIAN, AND NOT A ROOM FULL OF AMERICANS. . . . Before anyone can see me, I'm in the elevator, clamoring to get back out on the streets of my favorite city for one last night on the town.

26. PJ

We Could Be Happy

"Are you sure you don't mind missing the party?" I ask Jay when he picks me up from the Sanxays house Friday evening.

Walking along the rapidly darkening streets of Paris as the arrondissements change from swanky and austere to bright and lively, he takes my hand. His is a little damp but pleasantly warm. I'm chilly, even though it's getting warmer and warmer in Paris every day. I can't quite figure out how to walk hand in hand with Jay. It's still awkward, after everything that's happened. We're not quite a couple. I'm not sure what we are.

All I know is that I want to be with him. I'm at my happiest, my safest, when he's around. I tell myself that this is okay. It's normal. I can finally be like everyone else.

"I mean, *I* don't want to go," I stammer. "But that doesn't mean I would be mad if you did. You can still change your mind. . . ."

"No, man," Jay says. I love how he can say that he loves me, but then still call me "man." Everything is so easy with him.

Even though he's not going to Alex's party, Jay is dressed up in a nice blue shirt and dark gray slacks. He's freshly shaven and his hair is even shorter than it was the last time I saw him. As usual, my stomach flips when I look at him. He is really an amazing creature: sensitive and beautiful and radiant with kindness and good humor. "I'll see Cory tomorrow before he flies back to Denver. I don't need to say good-bye to any of those other fools."

"What about Zack and Alex? And Olivia?" I laugh. "Don't you want to say good-bye to them?"

Jay shrugs. "Alex is nothing but trouble." There's a twinkle in his brown eyes.

"Jay!" I chide him. "Alex saved us both. From almost certain ruin. You should be grateful. And what about the other two?"

"We'll keep in touch," Jay says. "And since when do you stick up for Alex? She's the reason you became a live-in nanny!"

"We like to call ourselves *au pairs*, Jay," I correct him.

"So, you feel like Chinese for dinner?" Jay asks, grinning. "I'm starved."

I haven't eaten since I made *croque monsieurs* for Albert and Emeline's lunch this afternoon. "Uh, sure," I say. "Chinese sounds good."

"Don't tell me you're not hungry."

"No!" I say quickly. "I am. I definitely want to go to dinner."

We walk along avenue des Gobelins toward the far southeastern corner of Paris. Jay's an aficionado of Asian food. He knows all the best places in the Quartier Chinois.

This part of Paris is full of big government housing, huge apartment buildings with hole-in-the-wall Asian restaurants and grocery stores lining the street. Every few feet is a bright neon sign in Chinese or Japanese lettering. The names of the businesses are either beautiful or cute in their French translations: "La Belle Rose Café" or "Le Marché au Poulet Joyeux."

After a long stroll down into the Thirteenth, Jay brings me to a small, unmarked restaurant hung with red lanterns. The room is dimly lit, the threadbare antique wooden chairs hiding in the darkness. Everything is hushed and loaded with a romantic mood. Our table is covered with a dragon-patterned cloth and is very dark save for one votive candle. We order soup, rice, and seasoned duck with chilies. I eat without saying much, obviously too hungry to concentrate.

"What's on your mind, PJ?" Jay asks me.

I shake my head. Blissfully, I'm not worried about anything in this moment.

"Nothing?" he asks, not buying it.

"Seriously, nothing," I laugh.

"I have a feeling you'd be a mystery no matter what was happening in your life," Jay says. "A beautiful mystery."

"No, Jay," I shake my head. "No more secrets. Now that you know everything, I'm an open book."

"I don't know everything," Jay says, looking at me steadily from across the table. "Do I?"

I laugh and sigh at the same time. "Well, there's one thing I haven't told you."

"What is it?"

"I beat up Dennis Marquet, that guy Alex is seeing," I say. "Or was seeing, or whatever. When he came to try and get my sister and me to come back to the Marquets, I pushed him so hard he lost consciousness."

"What a thug!" Jay says.

"He is and he isn't," I say. "I mean, he did help us to get Monsieur Marquet to just leave me alone. And you could have done something you'd really regret if Dennis hadn't stepped in when he did."

"No, I meant *you. You're* the thug. My gorgeous thug. If you got to beat someone up, then I should have gotten to as well," Jay laughs. "Don't you think? It's only fair."

My face cracks into a smile. It feels so strange to laugh about this with him. Strange, but such a relief. Slowly but surely, I'm coming around to thinking that this nightmare might really be over.

And not for the first time, my heart aches to think of Jay going back to the U.S. tomorrow.

Jay seems to be reading my thoughts. "You sad about tomorrow?"

"Really sad," I say. "It's not fair. I feel like we only just got to know each other."

"Well, I've been thinking that I could, I don't know . . . if I take summer school in Minneapolis this summer, I actually have enough credits to graduate already. I was just going to take electives next year. But if I get my diploma, I found out about this college here in Paris. They focus on international law. I was thinking the program looked kinda cool."

"You're kidding! You might come back?" My heart jumps into my chest. I can feel my hope growing, the hope that we might really get more time together.

"I'm serious," Jay says. "I want to be with you."

"For real," I whisper. "Finally be together for real." I can't even imagine it.

Jay reaches into his back pocket for his wallet and pays for our dinner. We get up to leave as quietly as we came in. Back on the street, the sun has gone down. In the distance, you can see the lights on at the top of the Tour Montparnasse. We look at each other and smile.

Jay puts his arm around me, and we walk back north so I can go back to the Sanxays'. At a crosswalk, waiting for the light to change, he kisses me very gently.

"We'll get a chance to start over, together," he whispers.

I nod.

"Starting over would be good," I say. "Let's start right now." I attempt to smile charmingly, the way I might have if I'd met Jay last year, before Annabel's wedding day.

I put my hand out and pretend to introduce myself. "Hi, you look nice. I'm PJ and I'm from Vermont. My parents are going to jail for drug trafficking, and it turns out my sister was trying to skim off their profits so she's going to jail, too. I like painting, going to museums, and traveling. Want to be friends?"

"That's much better than the original version of events," Jay says, tapping me on the tip of my nose. "And, yes, I'd *love* to be friends."

He kisses me again, and I swear it feels like the last year was just a dream I had of Paris.

ACKNOWLEDGMENTS

Writing this trilogy has been the most fun thing I have ever done in my life, not just because I got to go to Paris and dream up wild adventures, but also because I got to work with amazing people. Molly Friedrich, Lexa Hillyer, and Ben Schrank gave me the opportunity to write exactly the kind of books I wanted to write, and then helped me make them better than I ever thought they could be.

Additionally, Lucy Carson is probably the most organized person on the planet, and when I call her, she always makes things happen, like magic. One day I will think up the perfect thing to knit for her to adequately show my gratitude. Right now, a beret just doesn't quite cover it.

Thank you also to Alex Genis and Allison Verost at Penguin Young Readers for helping me to find an audience for these books. You guys rock!

Having worked in publishing for a while, I know that there are lots of other people that work on a book that the author never knows about, or only trades a couple of emails with to make sure a very specific and important thing gets done. For example, William Prince has been humoring me by letting me make all kinds of last minute changes to this book even though he probably doesn't have to do that. Thank you to him and everyone else who's helped me at Razorbill and Penguin—the books are gorgeous, my name is spelled right, and best of all, they are actually available for me to cheesily point out to people when I go into book stores from Boulder to Iowa City to Austin.

Leah Kahn helped me with my Spanish in this particular volume of the series, and Natalie Hall was the expert I consulted for Britishisms. I am so lucky to be surrounded by people with such worldly talents. I wrote this book in a gorgeously situated apartment in Oberkampf owned by Eva Lange, who is the best foreign landlord ever. Just like with *Wanderlust*, I did the revisions upstairs at my parents' house in Des Moines, and they fueled me with Diet Coke and reality TV breaks, for which I am also quite grateful. But most of all I owe thanks to Doug Wagner, who has read every book in this trilogy before it has gone to press, and always makes me feel like I can finally let go of all the drafts and stop worrying and go have fun again. He is a great unofficial copy editor and I love him to pieces.